Royal Merry-Go-Round

Royal
Merry-Go-Round

F. W. Kenyon

THOMAS Y. CROWELL COMPANY

NEW YORK

77257

I

THE gathering at the Tuileries Palace was the most brilliant since the death of the old King, but much of this splendor was lost on the new King, Louis the Fifteenth. He stood there naked and shivering on the dais. He was so cold that goose-pimples covered his arms and legs, and he wanted desperately to hide himself from the staring eyes of the lords and ladies of the court. He had been King of France for two years, and today, his seventh birthday, was a most important day in his life.

The solemn-faced court physicians continued their scrupulous examination of the royal body while Louis himself, trying with a pitiful dignity to keep his teeth from chattering, looked nervously about him. Seeking an encouraging smile, his eyes rested first on the Duc d'Orleans, regent till he came of age, but all he saw was a watchful sternness. He looked next at Madame de Ventadour, his guardian since the death of his parents, and grew alarmed when he saw that she, his own "Mamma" Ventadour, had been crying. Finally, refusing entirely to meet the gaze of the sharp-eyed Marshal de Villeroi, his eyes sought those of the sixty-three-year-old Fleury, Bishop of Fréjus. The tall and stately Bishop gave him a surprisingly mischievous look and dropped his right eyelid in an unexpected wink.

Happier now, the child looked slowly and haughtily at the sea of faces which surrounded the dais. He straightened his smooth shoulders and began to feel impatient with the lengthiness of this traditional and therefore inescapable ceremony. He thought of his kittens and wished he could have brought them with him; he thought of his glow-worms and decided that the air of Versailles, where he would live permanently when he came of age, was healthier for them than that of Paris; and finally he thought of his great-grandfather, the late King, remembering with a little chuckle of pleasure how the old gentleman had once scolded him for sticking out his tongue at the ugly old Bishop of Metz.

Meanwhile the examination, the Ceremony of Identification, was nearing its conclusion. The chief physician bowed low, stepped down from the dais and stood before the Regent. Heads were craned and a little murmur of interest passed from mouth to mouth. The elegant Marquise de Prie, mistress of the Duc de Bourbon, whispered racily to another lady that his Majesty was well-made and showed great promise. Both ladies looked with appreciation at the boy's large black eyes, his small, full mouth and his long dark hair. They made active calculations in their scheming minds and came regretfully to the conclusion that when the King was old enough to take an interest in women they themselves might be too old to share or stimulate it.

The Regent, more serious than Louis had ever known him, addressed the chief physician.

"You have completed your examination?"

"I have, your Highness."

"How, then, do you find his most Christian Majesty?"

"Having examined him limb by limb I find his most Christian Majesty healthy, well-nourished and entirely sound in all his members."

(The Marquise de Prie nudged her companion and giggled. "Most sound," she whispered.)

"There is no disfigurement?" the Regent asked.

"There is no disfigurement, your Highness."

"You certify that his most Christian Majesty is of the male sex?"

"I certify, upon my honor, that his most Christian Majesty is of the male sex."

Louis, who had recently discovered the interesting physical difference between male and female, smiled broadly and wanted to say: "Really, my lords and ladies, what a stupid question!" but the discouraging gaze of the Regent kept him silent.

A valet stepped forward with a cloak. The Regent himself took it and placed it about the boy's shoulders. Then, with a curt gesture he summoned Madame de Ventadour, whose eyes were now red and swollen.

"Madame," the Regent said, "you have heard the words of the chief physician. Are you satisfied with his report?"

Making silent assent Madame de Ventadour forced back her tears.

"And you are now prepared to place his Majesty's person in my hands?"

Again she made silent assent.

Louis looked suspiciously from the Regent to his guardian.

"Mamma Ventadour," he whispered urgently, "what does this mean?"

"Be brave, Sire," she whispered back, "be brave and sensible."

Whenever Mamma Ventadour told him to be brave and sensible Louis knew that something unpleasant was about to happen. He wanted to seize her hands and cling to them, but aware of the searching eyes of the court he remained immovable, hiding his suspicion and fear with a proud tilt of the head.

With another curt gesture the Regent brought Marshal de Villeroi forward and addressed him harshly.

"Monsieur de Villeroi, I give into your hands his most Christian Majesty, King Louis the Fifteenth. Your responsibility is great and terrible. Continue the work already begun by Madame de Ventadour, discharge your sacred duty with integrity and faithfulness, and God, in whose name I demand it, will reward you."

The Marshal bowed and stepped towards Louis. The boy looked at him coldly and with a neutral hatred. Nobody had

3

warned him of this. The traditional ceremony, yes, but not *this*. He had always believed that Mamma Ventadour would remain at his side, helping him and teaching him and mothering him, until he was old enough to reign alone. He had never for one moment dreamed—

"Be brave, Sire," Madame de Ventadour was whispering. "The Marshal is a good man. He will teach you the true meaning of kingship. It is a man's business, Sire, not a woman's."

Louis flung his arms round her neck.

"I am King," he sobbed. "I may please myself. I want you —*you*, Mamma Ventadour, not the Marshal. He's not as ugly as the Bishop of Metz, but I hate him!" And out came the royal tongue, pink, rigid and pointing.

Madame Ventadour tried to soothe him. "Remember, Sire, the words of the late King. Remember how he commanded you to be greater and better than he, how he warned you to face with courage the difficult choice between right and wrong."

"Enough, Madame!" the Regent said impatiently, and thrust her aside. "Come, your Majesty, Monsieur de Villeroi is waiting. Would you have it said that the King of France wants to shelter forever behind the skirts of a woman?"

The boy felt the hard fingers of the Regent's hand pressing through the thin stuff of the cloak.

"Come!" the Regent repeated.

Louis twisted suddenly, wriggled free of the fingers and left the cloak in the Regent's hand. A moment later, threading his way swiftly in and out of the lords and ladies, he was lost from sight.

There was a light but insistent scratching at the door. Louis looked up but made no attempt to control his weeping.

"Go away!" he cried brokenly. "It is not my wish to see anyone. I am the King. This is a royal command."

The door swung slowly open and there stood the Bishop of Fréjus, holding the discarded cloak. He looked taller than

4

closed the door and came forward with the cloak.

Louis remembered the way the Bishop had winked at him; here at all events was a friend.

"Go away," he said, but with very little conviction.

He was still naked and his teeth were chattering. Fleury placed the cloak about his shoulders, bowed and led him to a chair.

"I am, I admit," he remarked smoothly, "but a poor substitute for Mamma Ventadour, but in this life even a king must make the best of things, until he grows up, that is, and may please himself."

"What do you mean?" Louis demanded sulkily.

Fleury looked down his nose. "The Marshal, poor fool, is nominally in charge of your Majesty, is in fact your Majesty's new guardian, but I, by the will of the late King, am to be your tutor."

Louis smiled bleakly. He liked the words, *The Marshal, poor fool*. He looked for a long moment at Fleury, so dignified in his bishop's clothes and yet so kindly, and began to feel happier. Fleury was an old, old man, yet when he talked to you and smiled at you, you had the feeling that he was just a boy like yourself.

Fleury drew up a chair. "With your Majesty's permission . . . ?"

Louis inclined his head. "Sit if you must."

Fleury seated himself. For a few moments, and in silence, he gazed contemplatively at the boy King. Though growing old, Fleury was a man of great ambition. The son of a collector of taxes, he had chosen a career in the church, not because he had any strong religious feelings, but because he knew that through the church he had every chance of gaining worldly advancement. As a young man he was softly spoken and exceedingly tactful. Through a prominent cardinal, whom he flattered shamelessly but with subtlety, he was appointed one of the Queen's almoners, and on her Majesty's death he was transferred to the King's household. Louis the Fourteenth, liking his ready wit, made him a

5

bishop, but the See of Fréjus being small and unimportant, Fleury soon presented himself at court again. Later, just before his death, the King named him tutor to the future King, once Louis reached his seventh birthday. This was all Fleury needed to convince himself that in the course of time he would, providing he were shrewd enough, become as powerful in the future as Cardinal Richelieu had been in the past.

"When your Majesty is thirteen," Fleury murmured, "you will, by the law of France, be absolute ruler, and the services of the Marshal, or even those of the Regent himself, may be dispensed with."

"Six years is a long time to wait," Louis grumbled.

"Ah, but if you choose, Sire, they can be happy years. There will be lessons, yes, but lessons need not be as tedious as you might think." He brushed an imaginary speck of dust from his sleeve. "Take history, for example. To know that this king won an important battle and that king lost one is necessary, even to the exact date, but to learn also that one of them tired of a certain mistress at the same time and took another should, by the association of an amusing idea, stimulate the memory and lighten the task beyond all expectation."

Louis chuckled.

Fleury, his head on one side, his eyes wide and alert, his whole attitude resembling that of a bird listening for a worm in the ground, chuckled too. He thought how fortunate it was that death had swept away two generations, leaving this great-grandson, this boy King, to mount the throne of France.

"Your Majesty," he said, still chuckling, "has no real wish, I hope, to thrust out your tongue at me, even though I am a bishop too."

Louis rocked with laughter. An amusing person, this Fleury.

"We are to be friends, Sire?"

Louis leaped from his chair and flung his arms round Fleury's neck. "Oh yes, Fleury, indeed yes!"

6

"And your Majesty, if pleased with me, might some day make me a cardinal?"

"Better than that, Fleury, a pope!"

Fleury sighed and made a face. "A great pity, but even the King of France lacks the power to do that."

But Louis was no longer listening.

"I'm hungry," he said.

Fleury rose. "Then we shall have something sent up from the kitchens."

"No, wait!" Louis cried. "I'd rather go down to the kitchens and make something for myself. I've always wanted to do that but nobody has ever let me."

Fleury hesitated for a moment. He remembered the boy's healthy appetite and his inordinate interest in food. What better way to the royal heart, he thought, than through the royal stomach?

"Come, Sire," he said. "Let us go down together and make an omelette."

". . . and finally," Louis concluded, "myself, King Louis the Fifteenth. There, you see, Fleury! I know them all. Every king there ever was in France."

"A prodigious memory," Fleury admitted gravely.

The boy's eyes narrowed. "How many popes have there been, Fleury, and what were their names?" Fleury made a face, the corners of his mouth turning sharply down. "Come, my lord Bishop, how many!"

"Bless my soul," Fleury wailed, "I have no idea whatever."

"There!" Louis chuckled, "I knew it! I'm a great deal cleverer than my tutor."

Fleury shrugged. "Indeed yes, without the slightest doubt."

"But I get so tired of it all," Louis said, and heaved a deep sigh. "History and Latin and mathematics and astronomy and—oh, and all the rest."

"But out of the love your Majesty bears me," Fleury murmured, "you will persevere, I know."

7

"We-ell . . ." Louis said, half-scowling.

One by one Fleury began to remove the curling papers which the boy had twined about his long gray locks. Louis was almost eleven now. He had lost much of his earlier prettiness but was growing slim and handsome. It was good to think, Fleury reflected, that though he still spoke with affection of "Mamma" Ventadour and undoubtedly loved her, the boy's heart was given almost wholly to his tutor.

"It is not enough for the King of France to be handsome and graceful," Fleury went on, "he must be clever too. Otherwise his good looks would become merely vapid."

Louis gave him a shrewd look. "Mamma Ventadour says that if you continue to flatter me you will ruin me, and ruin France too."

" 'Pon my soul," Fleury expostulated, "I have never flattered you in my life. When I say that your Majesty is handsome and graceful I speak the bare truth."

Louis nodded wisely. "I know you do, Fleury, even if the Regent says the same as Mamma Ventadour."

Fleury's eyes narrowed. "His Royal Highness the Regent waited on you this morning, I believe."

"Yes!" Louis chortled, "and can you guess what I made him do?"

Fleury smiled. "You refused to listen to his complaints and made him crack nuts for you."

"Yes, and how he hated it. I made Bourbon crack nuts too."

"Ah, so Monsieur le duc de Bourbon was here also."

The boy nodded. "The Marquise de Prie was with him. Just *what* is a mistress, Fleury?"

Fleury lifted his shoulders eloquently. "A mistress is an amusement and a diversion. She is less than a wife, yet more than a wife. All men of fashion have mistresses. I have told your Majesty before."

"Yes, Fleury, but the Marquise de Prie is so bossy."

"Ah, that bossiness," Fleury laughed. "When your Majesty is old enough to take a mistress you must guard against bossiness. A royal personage makes a grave mistake when he permits his mistress to be too ambitious. The Regent is wiser

8

than the Duc de Bourbon. He never permits his mistress to
meddle in state affairs."

"Why do the Regent and Bourbon hate each other?" Louis
asked.

Fleury smiled faintly. "Tell me just who they are, Sire,
and the answer will surely occur to you."

Louis said promptly, "My cousin the Regent is the son of
my great-grandfather's younger brother. He married Mademoiselle de Blois, one of my great-grandfather's legitimized
daughters. My cousin the Duc de Bourbon is a prince of the
House of Condé but prefers to be known as Monsieur le
Duc de Bourbon. His mother is another of my great-grandfather's legitimized daughters." He paused, losing interest.
"Yes, Fleury?"

"Both are ambitious men," Fleury concluded for him, "and
think of the day when a regent will be no longer necessary.
They ask each other the same question: Who will then be
chief minister?"

"I'd rather *you* became my chief minister," Louis said.

"Your Majesty was going to make me first a cardinal, then
a pope," Fleury teased, "but all I ask is to be your humble
servant and dearest friend. For the rest I care nothing."

But to himself he said "Liar!" His ambition was as strong
as ever, yet he was a man of infinite patience, content to
watch and wait, meanwhile consolidating his position by flattery. Let the Regent and the Duc de Bourbon plot and
scheme, he was more convinced than ever that in due course
his own time would come.

"What did the Duc de Bourbon want?" he asked.

Louis made a face. "He came to tell me about my marriage."

Fleury chuckled to himself. He had heard what was afoot.
If Louis died without issue the Regent, next in the line of
succession, would mount the throne. Bourbon hated the
thought of such a possibility—it would prevent him from
attaining any sort of lasting power at court—and alarmed by
a recent illness of the King's had urged the Regent to make
immediate marriage plans. Much to his surprise the Regent
had agreed, Spain had been consulted and a union had been

9

agreed upon between Louis and the Infanta. Fleury chuckled again. Too late, Bourbon realized that he had set a possible trap for himself. He wanted a marriage that could be consummated in four or five years; all he had achieved was one that could not be consummated before the passing of at least ten years, for the little Infanta was only four years old.

"When am I to marry the Infanta?" Louis asked.

Fleury, looking at the boyish face, felt a pang of tenderness. Eleven years old and asking so serious a question.

"Not for some years yet," he said gently.

Louis was silent for a few moments. At last, his eyes dreamy, he said: "I can hardly wait."

"For your marriage, Sire?"

"Oh, *that!*" Louis scoffed. "Bourbon said she is being brought to France to be educated and trained, but I shall only marry her if I like the look of her."

"Then your Majesty can hardly wait for . . . what?"

"My coming of age, of course, and my coronation."

"Just two more years," Fleury said. And softly he added, "I can hardly wait myself."

The Coronation ceremony, which had taken place in the Cathedral of Rheims, was over, and now, in strict accordance with tradition, Louis was going to hear mass at the little Church of St. Rémi. Absolute monarch at the age of thirteen he might be, but his back was beginning to ache, he was tired and bored, and the sticky feel of the oil with which he had been consecrated was making him feel irritable. He told himself petulantly that he would rather be a cook's son than a king, and he began to think with longing of the little corner of the royal kitchens that had been set aside for his especial use. "The best chef in France, that's what I am!" he boasted.

A swelling shout of "Long live the King!" brought him back to reality. He bowed from his horse and smiled politely, first to the left, then to the right. The shouting, rising like thunder from the crowds behind the long lines of Swiss Guards, made him think of the flattering words uttered recently by the Duc de Bourbon: "The people belong to the King." Then he thought of Fleury gently correcting Bourbon, "No, no, the King belongs to the people." But Fleury had spoken with an indulgent smile, bent merely, Louis was sure, on contradicting Bourbon, otherwise pupil and tutor might well have had their first serious quarrel. Nevertheless, Louis began to feel that the King did indeed belong to the people, otherwise he would not be here now, enduring all this tiresome pomp and ceremony.

He stared wrathfully ahead at the Black and White Musketeers who were leading the procession. He was dressed in deep red velvet; the cloak thrown negligently over his graceful shoulders was of cloth of gold, held in place with a diamond clip. "Your Majesty has never looked more handsome," Fleury had said, as he pinned to his chest the Order of the Holy Spirit. Louis smiled slightly now and remembered the sight of himself in the long mirror. But still, "The King belongs to the people!" He was the people's plaything; he could please himself in nothing, still less now that he was crowned and consecrated and able to preside over council meetings. "But wait," he said aloud, "only wait! I shall change it all one of these days, by the Holy Virgin I shall!"

When the procession was over and he was seated in the stillness of the church he fidgeted continually. "One of these days," he muttered, "I shall let everybody know that if I do belong to the people I don't belong to the Church. Mass, I hate every minute of it!" This made him feel guilty, but willfully he repeated, "Every minute of it!" He thought of the Regent, whose office would now be dispensed with. He found mass boring, too, and often took with him the stories of Rabelais bound in the manner of a prayer-book. "Yes," he told himself, "and I shall do the same."

Later he found himself alone for a moment with Fleury.

"Fleury," he whispered, "I'm hungry."

Fleury made a face. "So for the matter of that am I."

"Then do something about it, for both our sakes!"

"Impossible, your Majesty. The second procession is about to begin."

Louis scowled and stamped his foot. He had quite forgotten the second procession. After a king was crowned he heard mass, then went, again in ceremonial procession, to touch for the King's Evil.

"How can I touch for the King's Evil on am empty stomach?" he demanded.

Fleury winked. "On an empty stomach one is more likely to be in a state of grace than at any other time."

Louis giggled. Fleury was an old dog and should never have been a priest.

"Do I really have the power to heal sick people?" he asked.

Fleury looked down his nose. "Undoubtedly, Sire."

The Lord High Almoner approached and bowed. Fleury fumbled in a pocket concealed beneath his robe, found what he was seeking and slipped it neatly into the boy's hand. He winked as he did so and Louis, knowing by the feel of it that it was a small packet of sweetmeats, winked back.

"His Majesty," Fleury announced solemnly, "is ready to proceed."

A throng of two thousand people was waiting for the King. All were suffering from scrofula and had come in the fervent hope of gaining a miraculous cure, many from as far away as Gascony and Provence. They had been lined up in rows and had the look of a ragged, ill-disciplined army. Louis, munching one of Fleury's sweetmeats, was led to the beginning of the first row. On either side of him stood an Usher of the Chamber, dressed in white satin. The Lord High Almoner stood immediately behind him. There was a sudden hush. All eyes were on the King. He repressed a giggle and hoped that everybody would take the movement of his jaws for silent prayer.

"Your Majesty will touch each person on the cheek with the back of your hand," the Lord High Almoner whispered, "and your Majesty will say, 'It is the King who touches you; he prays that God will heal you.'"

"Two thousand times!" Louis shuddered.

The Lord High Almoner gave a signal. The Swiss Guards, wrists raised elegantly, began to beat their drums, and the drum roll, rising and falling impressively, continued as Louis moved along the rows of sufferers. Twice he slipped a sweetmeat into his mouth and by keeping it between teeth and cheek managed to articulate with reasonable clarity: "It is the King who touches you; he prays that God will heal you."

When all was over, when the echo of the last drum roll had faded away, Louis tugged sharply at Fleury's sleeve.

"A large omelette," he said, "a great large omelette, and fat with oysters, Fleury!"

II

IT WAS Sunday, the day of the *grand couvert,* the meal which once a week Louis took in public. With the palace thrown open to all who wished to enter, the great dining-hall was crammed with spectators—aristocrats, middle-class "ladies" and "gentlemen" and a sprinkling of peasants and the poorer citizens of Paris. These latter had come out to Versailles in *pots-de-chambre,* those large, cage-like vehicles drawn by eight stout horses. It cost ten sous to sit in them, having your bones shaken to pieces and your nostrils filled with dust. It was expensive and uncomfortable, but the King belonged to you, and even if you managed on less bread during the next week it was necessary that you should visit Versailles at least once in your life to watch his Majesty consuming a meal in public.

At first Louis had found the *grand couvert* as great an ordeal as the Ceremony of Identification, but now, through a happy accident, he was well used to it and regarded it as a game, just as he regarded the *lever* and the *coucher,* the dressing and undressing which he was obliged to make each morning and evening in public. Once, in a fit of anger and nervousness, he had struck viciously with his fork at the top of a boiled egg. To his amazement the top had bounced neatly off and all the spectators had laughed and applauded.

The Duc de Bourbon, sitting at his side, had said, "You must do it again, the people like it." And so now, after much practice, he could always be relied upon to slice off the top of an egg with equal neatness and gain the same laughter and applause. He sometimes felt like a caged animal, and he ate more boiled eggs than anybody else in the kingdom, but the fear of the *grand couvert* was gone forever.

A servant placed a boiled egg before him. He took up his fork and fixed the top of the egg with a steady eye. Somebody cried for silence; everybody held his breath. Louis struck sharply. There was laughter, hand-clapping and a cry of "Long live the King!"

Bourbon, seated next to Fleury, laughed mockingly.

"They come to see the King perform," he jeered, "not to admire his good looks, as you are always telling him."

Fleury smiled amiably. He took up his own fork and fixed the boiled egg which had been placed before him with a stern eye. Suddenly he struck, and the top of the egg flew neatly off. There was more laughter and applause, and a cry of "Bravo, Fleury!" from the King, while one of the watchers shouted "Long live the Bishop!"

Fleury gave Bourbon a sidelong glance. "Ah yes, the Bishop, still merely the Bishop."

"These things take time," Bourbon said stiffly.

Fleury pretended not to hear and fell to studying the Duc de Bourbon. "What an unlovely sight!" he thought. Bourbon, handsome and dashing in his youth, was now a queer-looking, birdlike creature, tall and thin, with an abnormal stoop, and blind in one eye, which had been injured while hunting. Staring reflectively at this opaque, red-rimmed eye, Fleury remembered how, immediately after the coronation, Monsieur le duc had urged him to join forces with those in opposition to the Regent. A nod of his old head, Bourbon had urged, would dispense with the Duc d'Orleans, but Fleury, still cautiously biding his time, had held his hand and remained undisturbed while Orleans, relinquishing the regency, had become chief minister. "And how wise of me!" Fleury thought, for in less than a year Orleans had died and, indeed at the nod of his head, Fleury had given Bourbon his

15

wish. "And why?" Fleury asked himself. "Out of vanity, sheer vanity!" For Bourbon, claiming influence at Rome, had promised him the much desired cardinal's hat.

"I know it is over a year ago," Bourbon said, and repeated, "These things take time."

"Of which, of course, there is plenty," Fleury murmured, "and chief ministers, as I must have remarked before, have a way of coming and going. They are, at best, the stiff-limbed puppets of fate."

Something close to fear was reflected for a moment in Bourbon's good eye. He made to speak, then thought better of it.

"A profound observation," Fleury chuckled, "and a neat phrase, that . . . *the stiff-limbed puppets of fate.*" And to himself he added, savoring the words, "The master pulls the strings; dance, little minister, and, for that matter, dance, little King."

Bourbon changed the subject hurriedly, remarking that the King looked pale. "If he should become ill again . . ." he said.

Fleury shrugged. "He rose at five this morning and rode to Rambouillet at a frantic pace. He hunted all day and took little to eat. Now he is making a royal pig of himself and will soon turn green. An imminent bilious attack, that and nothing more."

"Nevertheless . . ."

Fleury hid a smile. He knew what was in Bourbon's mind. He felt—as indeed Fleury himself felt—that the Infanta of Spain, lonely and neglected at the French court, should be sent back home. The former Regent might be dead, but his son, the new Duc d'Orleans, was the King's heir. If Louis died suddenly that would be the end of Bourbon, and the end, quite likely, of the Bishop who wanted to be a cardinal.

"The King is fifteen," Bourbon said, "and old enough for —hum—"

"The purposes of propagation?" Fleury added smoothly.

Bourbon's good eye glinted. "Yes."

"I quite agree," Fleury smiled, "that the little Infanta can be sent home. A few presents and many expressions of regret

16

and apology . . . Such a blessing no actual marriage has taken place."

"But can I," Bourbon urged, "rely on you to persuade the King that an immediate marriage with an older princess is necessary?"

"Ah, that is the question, my friend."

They exchanged a long glance. There was hostility in it, but hostility held in check by the pressure of mutual interests.

Louis smiled sheepishly.

"Fleury," he said, "I want to apologize for losing my temper last night."

Fleury bowed ironically. "You are the King; I, at best, am nothing more than a humble servant."

"But a wise and considerate one!" Louis said warmly.

"If I remember rightly," Fleury sighed, "I took you to task for neglecting your studies. You told me to mind my own business and suggested that for a king who had been crowned lessons were no longer necessary."

Louis laughed impishly. "No more they are, but what really made me lose my temper was your suggestion that the Infanta should be sent home."

"Your Majesty has never taken any real interest in her."

Louis frowned. "She's no more than a pretty little doll and I've long since passed the age for playing with dolls, but wouldn't it be cruel to disappoint the child? And besides, Spain would feel insulted. A promise, Fleury, is a promise."

"Well said, Sire, but the promise was made by the late Regent, not by you yourself. But in any case, are you not the king of the greatest country in the world? Are you not therefore the greatest king in the world? Surely your Majesty may make a change of policy without considering too much the feelings of Spain."

But Louis was barely listening.

"It would be fun to be married," he said.

"Indeed it would!"

Fleury reflected that though the boy was well-developed

17

for his age he still regarded marriage, not as a physical act, but as an amusing boyish game. And yet he was by no means ignorant of the real meaning of marriage. No boy living at the Court of Versailles could be, and the full significance of the manifestations of puberty had long since been explained to him.

"May I marry any girl I like?" Louis asked.

"There are certain limitations," Fleury said. "Your Majesty must, for instance, choose a young lady of royal blood."

"That," Louis commented haughtily, "is naturally understood."

"There are, however, so many eligible young princesses," Fleury went on, "that the choice is likely to prove difficult. I have had a complete list compiled. There are, in all, ninety-one to choose from."

Louis made a face. "Ninety-one! It might take me *years* to decide."

Fleury smiled. "I have taken the liberty of striking eighty-two from the list, so why not pass on to me the tedious task of eliminating eight from the remaining nine?"

Louis gave a few moments' serious thought to this. One girl, he supposed, was much the same as another, providing she was of royal blood and not actually ugly.

"You may rely on me," Fleury purred, "to make a good choice."

"I know I can," Louis said warmly. "When I want a new dog or a horse you always choose the best for me, so why not a princess. You're the best friend I have in the world, Fleury."

And just as he had done countless times as a child he flung his arms round Fleury's neck; and then, remembering his position and his new manhood—was he not about to take a wife?—he drew back and blushed.

"Ah, we grow up, Sire, we grow up," Fleury remarked, shaking his head sadly.

Louis, his blush deepening, apologized swiftly.

"Make the marriage for me as quickly as you can," he commanded, "otherwise I might find it necessary to take a mistress."

"I find it surprising that your Majesty has not done so already," Fleury chuckled.

Louis smiled sheepishly. "Bourbon thinks I ought to, in order to—well, to prepare me for—for the other thing."

Fleury's eyes narrowed. The mention of Bourbon reminded him of a resolve he had made during the night.

"One important matter," he said negligently; "that is, if your Majesty is in a mood to discuss state affairs."

"Discuss them if you must, but be brief," Louis assented.

"I have a feeling that we chose badly," Fleury went on thoughtfully, "when we made the Duc de Bourbon chief minister."

Louis shrugged. "Dismiss him if you wish."

Fleury hid a smile. A pity Bourbon was not present to hear the boy's words and note his easy unquestioning compliance.

"No, no," Fleury said, satisfied for the present to remain completely behind the scene, "all I suggest is that we limit his authority and see to it that he is never permitted to confer with you alone, but only in my presence."

"Granted," said the boy, grandly.

When Fleury discussed the marriage question with Bourbon he was amused to note that Monsieur le duc was finding it hard to keep his temper. He had now been informed, casually by letter, that he was excluded from the royal confidence and would know, Fleury reflected, just who was responsible for that decision. Indeed, he had said only last night—and his words had naturally reached Fleury's ears—"That vain old devil and his cardinal's hat!"

"Nine names remain on the list," Fleury said. "Shall we consider each young lady on her merit?"

Bourbon glanced at Fleury's list.

"It amazes me," he growled, "that you should have placed my two young sisters at the head of it."

"One endeavors at all times to be polite, Monsieur," Fleury said amiably, "but his Majesty's marriage with a sister of yours would promote the interests of your family a little too much for my liking."

"The choice is the King's, not yours!"

Fleury shrugged. The King's choice was his choice. Or did he mean that his choice was the King's? An interesting point, that, and Bourbon, seeing the shrug, was quick to understand its meaning.

"Three names stand out," Fleury went on. "Elizabeth of Russia, Anne of England, granddaughter of George, and Marie of Poland. Elizabeth of Russia comes of bad stock. Her father is a drunkard and it is suspected that the girl herself is mentally deficient. I admire the English in many things. I myself am as pig-headed as an Englishman. But we are not in need of England's friendship and Anne of England is a Protestant. We are therefore left with Marie of Poland."

"The daughter of an ex-king," Bourbon said contemptuously. "She lives in exile with her father at Weissemburg. She is the least worthy of them all."

"She is poverty-stricken, I admit," Fleury said, "but eminently suitable. She would bring me—I beg your pardon—she would bring France less complications than any of the others."

"Your meaning is clear, by heaven it is!" Bourbon cried heatedly. "You expect to influence her just as greatly as you influence the King!"

Fleury looked shocked. "That is beside the point. She is reputed to have grace and charm, if not actual beauty. She has been well brought up. Exile and adversity have made her humble, docile and submissive. His Majesty's choice, I assure you, will be Marie of Poland. And, let me hasten to add modestly, mine also."

Bourbon's face broke into a slow smile. It was time, he thought, that his capable mistress, the Marquise de Prie, made a discreet entry in the domestic-cum-political arena, but naturally he kept this promising thought to himself.

Stanislas Leszczynski, ex-King of Poland, shifted uneasily from one foot to the other as he looked at his daughter Marie. She was gazing in silence at the newly arrived portrait of the boy-King of France. The offer of marriage, com-

20

ing so suddenly and unexpectedly, had delighted Stanislas, but Marie, always grave and thoughtful, and older by far than her twenty-two years, had shown no real enthusiasm. If only she would smile, he thought. There was a calm clear beauty in her wide-set eyes when she smiled.

"He looks more than fifteen," she said at last.

"Very advanced for his years," Stanislas told her eagerly.

He began to prowl about the room, treading remarkably softly for so heavily built a man. He thought nervously that the decision was his to make, not Marie's. Whether or not she wanted to marry the King of France (and he suspected that she was insane enough not to appreciate fully the high honor of the offer) she was a dutiful daughter.

"We must give an answer soon," he said, his large, full face framed by the heavy, powdered wig revealing his anxiety.

Marie looked at him unsmilingly and nodded.

"It is a very great honor indeed," he pressed.

"Yes, Father, I do realize that."

"An almost unbelievable honor, Marie."

She nodded again, thinking of the Duc d'Antin who, bringing the offer, had made such a stir in Weissemburg with his retinue of a hundred-and-fifty French soldiers and his eight resplendent coaches. Certainly it was a magnificent offer, and certainly an answer must be given soon, if only because of the expense of entertaining the visitors, an expense which her father could ill-afford. His poverty, she knew, was a continual source of embarrassment, and only recently, to his lasting shame, he had been obliged to pledge the family jewels with a moneylender in Frankfurt.

"When one considers my many unsuccessful attempts to get you married . . ." Stanislas said.

He saw, too late, that he had hurt her feelings, but the truth had to be faced. Nobody wanted the daughter of an exile, a king without a country, a king moreover who was living on the bounty of his less unfortunate "cousins," the Kings of Europe. Nobody except, amazingly enough, the King of France!

"My dear," he blundered on, "this honor should do much

to restore our pride. It should make you very happy and very proud."

"It is the greatness of the honor that frightens me," Marie said.

"Frightens you?" Stanislas pooh-poohed the idea. "But how silly of you, Marie!"

She felt that perhaps he was right and tried to understand her fear. It was something she found impossible to explain, something instinctive. It was like waking up suddenly from a nightmare to forget the horror of the dream but retain its fear.

"Think, child, what it will mean!" Stanislas cried. "The Queen of the greatest country in the world!"

She smiled at last, gently. She felt very maternal towards him; she wanted to comfort and please him, to give him what she knew he regarded as the greatest opportunity of his life.

"How greatly your heart is set on my going to France," she said.

"So greatly," he told her pathetically, "that it might break if you refuse." He prowled about the room again. "Here in Weissemburg we are poor. We live in exile; we hide our faces in shame. In France we would be rich; life would have a new and splendid meaning; the greatest people in the land would bow before us, and some day . . ." He broke off and went to take her hands in his. "You know what is in my mind, child?"

"Yes, Father," she said, "you think that it might be possible to persuade the King of France, your son-in-law, to help you recover your throne."

"Yes, Marie, yes! A dream, of course, but through you it could become a reality. You will go to France, child?"

"Did you think I might refuse, even if I had the right to do so?"

"Force," Stanislas argued uneasily, "is something I would never employ. The choice is yours."

And the responsibility of making it, she thought sadly.

"You have nothing to fear," he pressed. "Nothing at all. You will be Queen; you will play the chief part."

To escape his wavering glance and the weakness betrayed

by his eyes, and the hope as well, she embraced him quickly.

"Tell the Duc d'Antin," she said quietly, "that we appreciate the high honor done to us and that we are as eager as the
King of France to begin negotiations."

Followed by Fleury and the Duc de Bourbon, Louis
stepped lightly onto the balcony and gazed down at the
great gathering of his people waiting below. When the
tumultuous cries of "Long live the King!" had died away he
took another step forward, tossing back his dark curls as he
did so and negligently adjusting his cloak. Gravely, his voice
cracking just a little, he made the well-rehearsed announcement.

"It has been decided that I shall marry the Princess of
Poland. Her name is Marie Leszczynski. She was born on
the 23rd of June, 1703. She is the only daughter of Stanislas
Leszczynski, one-time Starost of Adelnau, later Palatine of
Posnania, and then, by election, King of Poland."

He stepped back as the cries of "Long live the King!" rose
again and, eyes twinkling like great black stars, he whispered
to Fleury:

"What impossible names! I don't know how the devil I got
my tongue round them."

Louis was not in the best of humors and though he had
agreed to receive the Duc de Bourbon and Madame la Marquise de Prie he scowled up at them as they approached. He
was lying on the carpet on his stomach, his chin cupped in
his hands, his two favorite cats, Pasca and Charlotte, close by.
He reached out and fondled Charlotte gently. She was off
her food today and the fear that she might die was more than
he could endure.

"I expect you're here," he said sulkily, "to ask some favor."

"On the contrary," Bourbon smiled, "I am here to present
Madame la Marquise who has a wish to offer your Majesty
her services."

"Or more correctly, Sire," the Marquise interposed in her

23

low, rather husky and altogether intimate voice, "I have a wish to offer the Princess Marie my services."

Louis glanced at her insolently. She was slender and tall with flashing, almond-shaped eyes. Without quite understanding the meaning of the words, Louis had heard the English ambassador speak of her as a jade of the most corrupt and ambitious order. He remembered that Fleury despised her and giggled to himself. He was a little vexed with Fleury, who had reproved him last night for gambling at cards and for slapping the face of one of his young companions. He was a little ashamed of having lost his temper—he had sent the young fellow a present only this morning—but to be reproved at his age, he being a man now and about to take a wife, still rankled. Because of this he had consented to receive Bourbon without Fleury being present. Not that he would listen if Bourbon attempted to speak of state affairs, but it was necessary, surely, to teach Fleury a lesson.

"But first," the Marquise was saying, "I bring a little present for the royal cats."

Louis' face brightened. "How very kind of you!"

Bourbon smiled and relaxed. The Marquise was without doubt a clever woman. Already she had written to ex-King Stanislas, informing him in devious but unmistakable language that she and she alone had been responsible for the offer of marriage. Such a move, she had said, would bring her the ex-King's gratitude and induce the Princess Marie to turn to her as a friend. "Two," she had said, "can play Fleury's game."

"Am I permitted to approach?" the Marquise was asking Louis.

"But of course," he said graciously.

The scheme had been carefully planned. The two cats were fastidious animals. It had always been understood that they would eat nothing but raw fish and raw meat, but by a fortunate accident Bourbon had come across them a few days ago ravenously consuming a piece of rabbit. And rabbit, he had discovered, was never included in their diet.

"Is the present something to eat?" Louis asked.

"It is, Sire," the Marquise told him.

"Charlotte is off her food," Louis wailed. "Persuade her to eat and I shall be your friend for life."

The Marquise, knowing quite well that the wretched cat was off her food, sated no doubt with the best fish and the best meat procurable, went down on her knees at the boy's side. Concealed in each palm was a tasty piece of rabbit. Pasca, his nostrils twitching, rubbed himself sensuously against her while Charlotte began to nose and pat at her closed hands.

Louis was delighted. "But don't aggravate her!" he warned.

The Marquise dropped a piece of rabbit in front of each cat and as they fell upon it Louis jumped to his feet, clapped his hands and danced about the room, his slender figure reflected again and again in the tall, gilt-framed wall-mirrors.

"Ask anything, Madame, anything!" he cried.

The Marquise murmured that all she asked was the privilege and honor of becoming lady-in-waiting to the new Queen.

"Granted!" Louis said.

At that moment there was a light scratching on the door and Fleury, as was his habit these days, entered the royal sitting-room without waiting for permission to do so. Dignified as ever, he came forward carrying an unframed canvas. If he was taken aback at the sight of the King's visitors he showed no sign of it.

"A portrait of the Princess Marie," he announced.

Louis scowled. He thought it just as well to let Fleury know that he was still vexed with him.

"Take it away, Fleury. I don't want to see it. Give it to the Marquise. Better still, throw it out of the window."

Fleury bowed. He went to one of the windows, opened it and threw the canvas into the courtyard below. Louis felt like giggling but he decided to scowl all the more.

"The Princess," Fleury said, "will soon be ready to leave for France."

"I understand," Bourbon put in smoothly, "that the marriage by proxy is to take place at Strasbourg."

25

Fleury nodded briefly. "Upon which the new Queen will travel to Fontainebleau for the second ceremony."

"Am I expected to meet her en route?" Louis demanded.

Fleury looked down his nose. "It would be a handsome gesture, but since your Majesty is in no mood to think of making handsome gestures . . ."

"You may withdraw, Fleury!" Louis said haughtily.

Bourbon and the Marquise exchanged a swift look of satisfaction.

"I beg your Majesty's pardon," Fleury said amiably, "but old age is making me a little deaf."

Louis chuckled suddenly.

"You old rogue, Fleury!"

Bourbon and the Marquise exchanged another swift look, this time a gloomy one.

"There is," said Fleury, "the question of selecting the Princess's ladies-in-waiting."

Louis avoided Fleury's eyes. "I have already appointed Madame la Marquise to be chief lady-in-waiting. Select the others yourself."

Fleury glanced casually at the Marquise; she dropped her eyes demurely. He glanced just as casually at Bourbon; *he* grinned openly. Fleury's eyes glinted but he made no comment, no protest. It was a move he should have anticipated and taken steps to counter, and this realization made him angry with himself.

"A wise appointment, let us hope," he murmured. "Madame la Marquise is a woman of wide experience. Your Majesty, I take it, has no wish to meet the Princess en route."

Louis pouted. "How can I possibly say? When I see her, at Fontainebleau or possibly en route, I may even decide against marrying her."

"By then, Sire, you will be married to her—by proxy."

Louis grinned wickedly. "Even so I could always send her home."

Bourbon and the Marquise looked at him in horror; Fleury alone remained unperturbed. Louis pointed a finger at the Marquise, then at Bourbon. He roared with laughter.

"Your faces, oh your faces!"

III

THE royal coach, followed by a long line of equally resplendent coaches, was approaching Moret, and it was expected that soon the advance riders of Marie Leszczynski's party would come into sight. Seated at the King's side was Fleury, apparently lost in thought and nodding sleepily. Seated opposite them was the Duc de Bourbon, busy with his own thoughts and wondering what progress the Marquise de Prie had made at Strasbourg where she had gone to join the new Queen.

"I shall be ill if the coach rocks much more," Louis complained.

"Your Majesty ate too many sweetmeats at the beginning of the journey," Bourbon remarked.

Louis frowned. "Have the goodness, cousin," he said coldly, "not to address me as if I were a child."

"A thousand pardons," Bourbon said humbly.

"Please remember," Louis went on, "that though I am only fifteen I am tall for my age and quite well developed."

"Also," Fleury murmured, "you happen to be King of France and may eat as many sweetmeats as you like."

Louis giggled, coughed quickly and tried to recover his kingly dignity.

"I find," he said loftily, "that my wife is not very pretty."

"Ah, so your Majesty examined the portrait after all."

"The Queen is handsome, not merely pretty," Bourbon put in.

"Handsome? That is what one says of a man. That, as a matter of fact, is what people say of me."

"When you were young," Bourbon made the clumsy mistake of saying, "we all thought you pretty too."

Louis snorted. "Are you suggesting that I used to look girlish?"

"Pretty," Bourbon amended hurriedly, "is a vapid description at the best of times. The Queen may not possess remarkable looks but her features are regular and reflect both refinement and good breeding."

The sound of racing hoofbeats prevented further conversation. The Queen's advance riders passed in a cloud of dust and returned a moment later, the horses pawing the ground.

"Stop the coach!" Louis ordered.

Fleury gave the order and smiled at Louis who, suddenly nervous, was squirming in his seat.

"Your Majesty is beginning to feel excited?" Bourbon suggested.

"Oh yes, I—!" Louis began, then pulled himself up sharply. With supreme dignity he said: "Excited? Nonsense! I am neither a child nor a sentimental woman. I am a man and a king. We can," he concluded, using the royal plural, "meet the present situation with dignity and restraint."

Fleury climbed stiffly down from the coach and began to stretch his cramped limbs. They were close to the crossroads and there the Queen's coach was being brought to a halt. Louis leaped down and tried to strike a nonchalant pose. Liveried servants, sweating and panting, were hurriedly laying carpets between Louis' coach and the Queen's. A few moments later Marie, followed by her father, was handed down, and behind them, Bourbon saw, was the Marquise de Prie. Louis clutched suddenly at Fleury's arm.

"Fleury, I never felt so nervous in my life!"

Fleury chuckled softly. "You, a man and a King?"

Louis drew himself up to his full height. Smiling faintly he said, "Curse you, Fleury!" and strode forward alone to

28

meet his wife. The distance seemed intolerably long; he felt that at any moment he might turn and run back to Fleury. Marie, at a whisper from the Marquise, had fallen to her knees. Reaching her side at last Louis was conscious of all the staring eyes of his court, for the ladies and gentlemen had left their coaches and formed a half-circle behind him. He tried to utter a few polite words of greeting, failed miserably and bit his lip. *A man and a King!* he jeered at himself. Feeling the warm blood mounting his cheeks, he steeled himself to look down at his wife. For a moment their eyes met, and the steady, gentle look Marie gave him helped a little to restore his self-confidence. Awkwardly he reached down and raised her to her feet. Under the heavy velvet travelling cloak she wore a dress of silver brocade, the elbow-length sleeves frothy with silver lace. Their eyes met again and Marie smiled encouragingly.

"Welcome to France," Louis mumbled.

Marie inclined her head. "Your Majesty is most gracious."

He wondered how best to maintain the conversation.

"The journey must have been tiresome," he said.

"Yes, at least it was at first."

He saw in surprise that in spite of her apparent calmness she was trembling.

"There was much rain," she went on, in a low voice which he thought pleasant, "and at times the roads were almost impassable. On one occasion my coach actually floated."

He clapped his hands in delight. "Then one would need to be a good sailor!"

Marie nodded and laughed. He clapped his hands again and smiled and laughed with her. The watching members of the court, too far away to hear what was being said, laughed also in spontaneous obedience. The King was pleased; the King had undoubtedly made a joke. The laughter rose to a restrained roar. Louis, with a little pecking movement, kissed Marie on the brow and then, taking her by the arm, led her towards his own coach. The tension, for both of them, was passing.

"I propose," he said, a man and a king once more, "that you pass the night at the nearby Chateau de Rohan. Tomorrow, when you are rested, you shall join me at Fontaine-bleau."

"Your Majesty is most considerate."

"I shall, of course, accompany you to the Chateau."

Somebody shouted "Long live the King!" The cry was heartily taken up. Somebody else shouted "Long live the Queen!" and this too was taken up.

"The Queen . . ." Louis mused. "The Queen, and my wife. I—I think I like the thought of it, Marie."

Meanwhile Bourbon had joined the Marquise de Prie and withdrawing with her from the other watchers was questioning her eagerly.

"Up to now," she told him, "it has not been possible for me to have a moment alone with her Majesty."

"Pah!" Bourbon exploded.

"Nevertheless, I know she likes me, and her father and I have become very good friends. You see, I gave him my sympathy, and yours too, when he received word from Fleury that no attempt must be made to involve France in a war for the purpose of restoring his lost throne."

"You seem to have made a little progress," Bourbon admitted grudgingly.

"We must move cautiously, Henri. I do admit that Fleury's influence is great, but now, with a new influence entering the King's life, a *feminine* influence—"

"An influence that will count for little," Bourbon broke in, "unless he falls in love with his wife."

"I expect him to do that," the Marquise said confidently. "Remember his youth, his total lack of experience. Far better that you were not allowed to have your way and provide him with a mistress first. A wife will be more of a novelty, and, I hope, an engrossing one. Schooled by me, the Queen will manage the King as he has never been managed before. If you were a boy of fifteen, who would have the greater influence, a young and attractive woman, or an old man of seventy?"

Bourbon chuckled. "When *I* was fifteen—nay, when I was no more than fourteen—!"

30

"Precisely."

He looked at her lewdly. His tall thin frame shook with silent laughter. "Schooled by you—yes, that will be excellent. No woman better than you could teach a virgin wife how best to please her husband."

"Ah, look!" the Marquise cried.

The royal coach was turning. Seated in it was the King of fifteen and at his side the Queen of twenty-two, while Fleury, obviously having been ordered to follow in another coach, was waving and crying "Long live their Majesties!"

"You must try one of my sweetmeats," Louis was saying eagerly to Marie. "I had them made from a special recipe of my own."

Marie, over-tired after the excitement and the long journey, had been escorted to her temporary apartments at the Chateau de Rohan. She was in a fainting condition and the Marquise, firmly closing the door on everybody, had taken complete control of the situation. Busying herself now, she stripped the Queen to her shift, placed a warming pan in the bed and made considerable use of lavender water. She thought there was something appealing about the young woman, though with her broad shoulders, her too-thick neck and waist, she was anything but beautiful. Her skin, of course, was good, her hair soft and sleek, and she had the look—yes, that was it!—she had the look of healthy virginity.

"You are much too kind, Madame," Marie said, and burst into tears.

"My *dear!*" the Marquise cried, aghast.

Marie made an effort to control herself. "This is weak and silly of me, I know, but—"

"Oh, nonsense! I know just how you feel. The strain of the tiresome journey, the excitement of your meeting with the King, the staring, curious eyes of the court, the sudden loneliness that only a stranger in a strange land can feel . . ."

Her voice trailed into silence and she waited for the younger woman to take the cue so subtly given her.

31

"What an understanding person you are," Marie said.

"I am older and more experienced, that is all. Your Majesty begins to feel a little better now?"

"Oh yes, Madame, thanks to you."

The Marquise laughed lightly. "As if I deserved your gratitude!"

"Oh, but you do, all the gratitude I can give you. You see, you make me feel less lonely. I know now that I shall have at least one true friend at court."

The Marquise, amply satisfied, all but purred.

"If I can help your Majesty at any time," she said, "pray call on me. I know the many pitfalls of life at court, the insincerity of almost all the people who will surround you, the secret intrigues of the place-seekers—" She broke off with a little laugh. "But enough for the present, your Majesty. Try to rest now, and remember, when I am needed I shall be waiting for your summons."

"Thank you," Marie said humbly, "thank you from the bottom of my heart."

Louis, attended by his chief valet, Bachelier, and numerous gentlemen of the royal household, was dressing for the wedding ceremony. Fleury, lounging in a corner, glanced from time to time at his young master and his heart was filled with tenderness. On rising that morning the boy, pale and troubled, had confided in him that he had dreamed of his wife, the Queen. "Delightful," Fleury had murmured, "delightful." Louis had looked more troubled than ever. "But Fleury, the dream was loathsome. If that is what marriage is I think I shall hate it." Fleury had understood instantly. "Your Majesty has had such dreams before. They are the natural—hum—manifestations of—hum—manhood." With this Louis had scowled and thrown up his hands in despair. "There have been dreams like that, yes, but vague, with no real person concerned in them. It was horrible to dream of Marie like that, more horrible still when never in my life have I had a woman." Fleury had done his best to soothe the boy, to assure him that imagination, stimulated

32

by his meeting with the Queen and the gossip he had heard about such things, was alone responsible. "And after to-night, Sire, the repetition of such a dream is most unlikely." In the end Louis had flung his arms round Fleury's neck in the old way, kissed him on both cheeks and declared that he felt better about it all. Nodding and smiling to himself now Fleury reflected that he had nothing to fear from the plots and schemes of Bourbon and his mistress. He alone had the King's trust; if they ruined anybody by their meddling it would not be he but they themselves.

"Bachelier," Louis complained, "the coat is tight under the arms."

"Merciful heavens," one of the gentlemen cried, "his Majesty's coat is tight under the arms!"

"Send for the tailor," another wailed. "Throw the wretch in prison!"

Fleury swept Bachelier aside. He took the coat by the collar and pulled it up; he took it by the lapels and pulled it forward; he took it by the hem and pulled it down.

"There!" he said.

"The fit is perfect," Louis pronounced.

"Now the hat," Fleury commanded.

Bachelier placed the hat with its high feathers on his Majesty's head. Louis muttered querulously that the feathers, handsome as they might be, were much *too* high.

"Nonsense," Fleury declared. "If they were any shorter they would be lacking in dignity." He chuckled and whispered into the boy's ear: "Dignity and restraint, Sire; remember your own words."

Louis smiled and strutted in front of the long mirror.

Fleury turned to the anxious Bachelier. "Gold brocade and white feathers, an excellent combination. Permit me, my dear Bachelier, to compliment you. I have never seen his Majesty look more handsome. Without a doubt his will be the most commanding figure in the chapel this morning."

Louis continued to strut. He bowed to his reflection and clapped his hands in delight.

"You flattering old rogue, Fleury," he cried, "but how I love you."

33

Marie, who had reached Fontainebleau early that morning, had completed her preparations for the ceremony and was alone for the moment with the Marquise de Prie. Her gown, tight at the waist and full in the skirt, was edged with ermine and covered with golden *fleur-de-lis*. She felt over-dressed and because of the rouge which the Marquise had insisted on painting on her cheeks ("This is France, your Majesty, not Weissemburg!") she also felt uncomfortable and a little unclean.

"Will it be long before the procession begins?" she asked.

She was trying to remain calm but her voice shook and she was obliged to clench her hands to still their trembling.

"We may expect the word at any moment," the Marquise told her. She looked at Marie critically. "I think a little more rouge is needed, your Majesty. The court would never forgive me if I permitted you to go to your wedding with a pale face."

"I look like a tavern wench already," Marie protested.

The Marquise laughed tinklingly. "I doubt if you have ever seen such a creature in your life."

Marie smiled and began to feel more at ease. During the early part of last night she had been restless, but finally, after telling herself over and over again that she was a grown woman, not an hysterical girl, she had fallen into a tranquil sleep. On waking vague groundless fears had assailed her again, but now the presence of Madame la Marquise was having a steadying effect.

"Will the ceremony be a long one?" she asked.

The Marquise nodded sympathetically. "I fear it will."

"And the chapel will be full of staring people!"

"Pooh, what of it? A queen must get used to being stared at, and the spectators will be there to admire as well as stare."

"The honor, I know, is great."

"And the power it will bring, also," the Marquise said, seizing another opportunity to further her own and Bourbon's cause. "As the wife of a boy-king you will have even more than the usual power of a queen. Your influence with his Majesty will be exceptional."

"If it really is," Marie said fervently, "I hope I shall always have the strength to use it wisely."

"Ah, and that will be the most difficult part of your Majesty's life at court. Your power could be so easily misdirected. Great care and great judgment will be necessary all the time. Many people will come to you with secret aims and desires. In your innocence your Majesty could so easily make wrong decisions."

"Yes, I do see that," Marie said gravely, and then she smiled and spoke the words the Marquise was waiting for. "But I shall have you to guide me, Madame."

The Marquise bowed her head. "Your Majesty is most gracious."

The King was leading the procession from his apartments to the chapel. The pace was slow and Louis, hiding his nervousness beneath a haughty look, sauntered forward gracefully. With the exception of the Duc de Bourbon and the young Duc d'Orleans, all the princes of the blood-royal followed immediately behind him. A continual fanfare of trumpets and an exciting rattle of drums accompanied the royal progress along the Gallery of Francis the First and down the Stairway of Honor. Still sauntering, Louis passed between the ranks of the stiff, unsmiling Swiss Guards, and though ceremonial practices bored him he admitted to himself that it was a magnificent, glittering spectacle.

Close behind Louis and his retinue came Marie, attended by the Duc de Bourbon and the Duc d'Orleans. She glanced as she walked at the rich hangings decorated with *fleur-de-lis,* the dazzling jewelry worn by the lords and ladies, the haughty, impersonal guard of honor and thought "All this because of me!" She thought, too, of the starving poor she had seen in the villages she had passed through and remembered how the Czar of Russia had remarked, after visiting France some years ago, that the wanton luxury of the French court would some day destroy that court.

As the procession entered the chapel the trumpets and

the drums fell silent and the Lord High Almoner came forward to greet the King and Queen. Feeling like a puppet on strings Marie passed up the aisle and took her place at the side of the boy to whom she had already been married by proxy. In something of a daze she listened attentively to the words of the Lord High Almoner and, when the time came, made her responses in a voice which, though clear and firm, she scarcely recognized as her own. Several times, suspecting that Louis was just as nervous as she was, she glanced at him encouragingly, and as at their first meeting he gained confidence from her eyes. She felt that she loved him already, but more as a mother than a wife. She felt this again when the Lord High Almoner, closing the ceremony, spoke grandly of the King's illustrious ancestors and, a trifle condescendingly, of the virtuous and prudent woman God had given him for his queen.

The procession back to the Grand Chamber of the King was made with much less solemnity. There was excited laughter and resounding cheering, while the liveried servants ran in and out of the crowd distributing the special medals which had been struck to commemorate the important occasion.

Later, as course followed course in the elaborate state dinner, Marie felt that a timeless age had passed since she had come to Fontainebleau that morning. She tried to think back to the main events of the day and failing looked helplessly round the crowded dining hall. Presently a hand was placed timidly in hers and she turned to smile at her husband.

"Are you bored, Marie?" Louis asked.

"No, Sire," she answered, "just a little confused."

He giggled on a high note. "Well, *I* am bored, so don't be afraid to admit it if you really are."

"Well, then, I am, a little," she smiled.

He looked at her shyly. "I like you, Marie. I like you very much."

Quick tears came to her eyes. "I like you too, Sire."

Louis blushed and looked away. He said: "You aren't

36

eating much. Do try a little of this special *ragout*, I invented it myself."

He offered her a little on his fork.

"Delicious," she said, "but you aren't eating much yourself."

"No," he admitted, frowning, "and usually I have a splendid appetite. Fleury would say I was sickening for something, and Bourbon," he added knowingly, but blushing as he spoke, "would say that it was only love."

Marie felt more maternal than ever and pressed warmly the hand that lay in hers.

"The real trouble," he said, with a quick dignity, "is the sight of all this food, and so many people, eating, every single one of them, as if they'd been fasting for a month. I never fast if I can help it. Do you?"

"Only on the proper fast days," she told him.

Louis looked at her gravely. "I hope you're not *too* religious. Do you know what I like best? Oysters."

"Oysters are my favorite too," she said.

He felt suddenly very pleased. Fleury had indeed found him a wife after his own heart.

"I can eat twenty-five dozen at a sitting," he boasted. "I like them in omelettes too. Tomorrow I shall make you the best oyster omelette you ever tasted."

There was a discreet little cough behind them. It came from Bachelier who was waiting for permission to whisper in the King's ear.

"Well?" Louis asked eagerly.

"All is in readiness, your Majesty. Your Majesty's wishes have been carried out in every detail."

Louis placed a finger to his lips and rose cautiously from the table.

"Quickly, Marie," he whispered, "we'll slip away before they miss us."

Outside the dining hall Louis laughed boyishly.

"Bachelier will stay here and cover our retreat."

Grasping Marie's hand, and half-running, he hurried her up several stairways and along numerous passages. Presently he threw open a door and ushered her into a small tapestried room where two places had been laid at a small table.

"Supper for two!" he cried, "and we shall have a little competition." He looked questioningly at Marie, for she had grown suddenly very quiet. "Is something the matter?"

"No," she said softly, "nothing."

"Thirty dozen oysters each!" he cried gaily, and then he pouted. "You think I'm behaving like a silly child, is that the trouble?"

Marie shook her head. "No, Louis, of course not."

"Why, there are tears in your eyes!"

"I love you," she said simply.

"I love you too," he affirmed, and kissed her, awkwardly, on the brow. "And now, our competition!"

Meanwhile there was considerable consternation in the dining hall. Bourbon was sure that the King and Queen, attempting to escape the traditional ceremony, had slipped away to bed, and that was unthinkable. Bachelier was found and questioned, and persuaded after many threats to give his explanation.

"Leave them in peace," Fleury ordered. "The traditional ceremony will certainly take place when the time comes."

Marie, surrounded by her ladies-in-waiting, was seated in her boudoir. Other ladies of the court were present and many gentlemen too. The room was crammed with people and at the open door Marie caught a glimpse of others pushing and shoving to gain a clearer view of her. The hot blood mounted her cheeks; she felt her limbs quiver in horror.

"Is all this really necessary?" she asked of the Marquise de Prie.

"It is the custom, your Majesty."

"But to undress in public . . . !"

"The public undressing of a new queen on her first night is an important ceremony."

"But with all these gentlemen present!"

"The gentlemen will withdraw before the removal of the shift."

38

The Marquise, having suspected it before, concluded that the Queen was a prude. Nevertheless she thought it wise to pretend an understanding sympathy and murmured that she herself would see to it that the inevitable ordeal was as short as possible.

The undressing began.

Marie, after one swift glance about the room—a glance which revealed two gentlemen climbing on a single chair—closed her eyes and struggled to keep back the tears of shame. She felt her ladies remove the wedding gown, she heard one of them exclaim in delight that her Majesty's skin was the creamiest and most flawless she had ever seen, and then, after they had fussed over her for a few moments, she heard the Duc de Bourbon's voice in her ear. She opened her eyes. She was in her shift. Bourbon, bowing low before her, was holding her nightgown in extended hands. With his inflamed and sightless eye, his long thin body, she thought him the most repulsive sight she had ever seen.

"Madame," he said, "on behalf of the court I wish you all happiness."

She stammered her thanks. She tried to remember that the Marquise, and her father also, had assured her that Bourbon, the chief minister, was a true, good friend. A moment later, to her intense relief, he and the other gentlemen withdrew.

"If your Majesty wishes it," the Marquise whispered, "you may retain the shift. It is autumn, after all, and the weather is chilly."

Marie gave her a grateful look. The shift was retained—not without shrugs and suppressed giggles from some of the ladies—the nightgown was placed over her shoulders and a handsome nightcap, trimmed with *fleur-de-lis,* was adjusted on her head. She rose, placing a hand on the Marquise's shoulder to steady herself, and tried to smile.

"It appears that I am ready," she faltered.

The voice of Bachelier was heard in the passage. His announcement was taken up by several ladies and the Marquise repeated it.

"His Majesty the King awaits your pleasure, Madame."

39

They led her to the state bedchamber and there, standing at the door, was Louis. He looked childish and cherubic in his nightshirt and his freshly brushed curls glinted richly in the flickering candlelight. The room behind him was a sea of bobbing faces. The young Duc d'Orleans stepped forward and escorted him to the bedside. The curtains were drawn back and more like a child than ever the King leaped into bed. The Marquise de Prie touched Marie lightly on the arm. Understanding, Marie moved forward to the left side of the bed and assisted by two of her ladies she climbed up and slid beneath the covers. "If only they would go!" she thought, but suddenly the vast state bed was completely surrounded and eager hands were tearing the curtains fully open. "Long live their Majesties!" everybody shouted. With a tremendous effort Marie inclined her head and smiled, while Louis giggled and clapped his hands. Madame la Marquise began to put out the candles until only one remained alight. The ladies and gentlemen, shouting and laughing and glancing back over their shoulders, moved reluctantly to the door. Finally the Marquise alone remained. She bowed deeply, first to Louis, then to Marie, and going softly from the room closed the door behind her.

There was a long silence.

"Marie . . ." Louis said tentatively.

Marie looked at him quickly. The inclination to giggle had passed and a rich blush was mounting his cheeks. His eyes looked bigger and blacker than ever in the light of the single candle. His curls, crowning his head like a dark halo, gave him the pure ageless look of an angel.

"Marie . . ." he said again.

He knew what he was expected to do. Bourbon had told him many times and had explained the act, in detail and in mime, while assisting him to undress. There had been something unpleasant, Louis thought now, in Bourbon's manner, something unhealthy, and without quite knowing why, he was glad that Fleury had said no to the suggestion that he should first take a mistress.

"Yes, Louis?" Marie whispered.

He gave her a boyish, puzzled look. One should be

naked, Bourbon had stressed; it was better that way. With a quick movement he stripped off his nightshirt and sitting up posed before her with an easy grace, slim and smooth-limbed. The beauty of his young body smote her heart with a sharp stab of pain.

"Please . . . ?" he questioned, and tugged lightly at the neck of her nightgown.

Marie looked at him dumbly. Her heart was torn between the maternal love she had first felt and a new and demanding desire. He glanced over his shoulder at the flickering candle flame, then back at her. She answered his unspoken question with a little shake of the head. Modesty struggled with pride; she was his wife and she knew that her body was desirable; she knew it now though before she had always guarded herself carefully against such a thought. To be ashamed of his seeing her as she now saw him would surely be an obscenity. With trembling hands she removed the nightgown and he, his hands trembling too, helped her with the ugly shift. Just as he would have stroked his favorite cat, he began to stroke her shoulders and arms.

"Nice," he lisped, "nice . . ."

Suddenly he buried his burning face in her breast and sobbed quietly.

"My darling," she murmured.

"I feel so shy," he said.

She touched his curls lightly. "So do I, Louis."

After a moment he looked up at her quickly.

"I never saw a more lovely sight than you, Marie, and I feel so proud. I—" his voice broke—"I'll be different from an ordinary king. I'm so glad they didn't get me a mistress first. I swear, Marie, that I'll be faithful to you till the day I die."

IV

"How much longer," the Duc de Bourbon asked, "do we have to wait before moving against Fleury through the Queen?"

"Be patient, Henri," the Marquise de Prie counselled. Her Majesty has been in France only three months."

"Pah!" Bourbon snapped. "I expected better things of you."

The Marquise shot him an angry glance. The Queen, since her marriage night, had grown much too sure of herself. It was plain that she adored her boy husband and that he in his turn adored her. She had time for no one else and though she spoke occasionally of the Marquise as her one true friend at court she was aloof even from her and lost entirely in a little world of love.

"I had thought of a petition," Bourbon said, "a petition asking for Fleury's dismissal. Since I cannot see the King without Fleury being present it would have to be presented to his Majesty by the Queen."

"Too bold," the Marquise said thoughtfully. "It would be better to undermine him gradually."

"That would take too long," Bourbon answered impatiently.

The Marquise frowned, then smiled suddenly. "Flattery,"

she cried. "Fleury has established himself by flattering the King, so why not dispose of him by the same means? The Archbishop of Rheims is about to retire. Suggest to the King at the next council meeting that Fleury will fill the post in a most distinguished manner. He would then be forced to live at Rheims."

"Worth trying," Bourbon grunted, "but if it fails the petition is our only recourse."

And fail it did, for Fleury told his Majesty that his one ambition was to remain at court, serving the King he loved so dearly. "And stay you shall!" Louis cried, and in a counter move against the Bourbon intrigue Fleury bribed Bachelier, the greedy royal valet, to give him immediate warning of any unusual activity on the part of Madame de Prie.

Having failed in this first move, Bourbon insisted on Fleury being attacked without further waste of time through the Queen and the petition. Accordingly, Fleury's enemies met in secret and a petition was drawn up listing various complaints and "praying" for Fleury's dismissal. Reluctantly the Marquise approached the Queen.

Marie at this time was happier than she could ever have thought possible. She grew even to like the vastness of the Palace of Versailles, though she still got lost in the countless corridors and galleries. She loved her own apartments, the traditional Queen's rooms, which Louis was going to have redecorated to suit her own special taste, and she felt a little thrill of anticipation each night when her ladies announced that his Majesty, having made the formal *coucher* in his state bedroom, was on his way to join her. Louis was almost always in a good humor. He chattered like a boy and made love like a man, for he had been quick to learn. True, he was wilful at times, a little too haughty and distressingly self-indulgent, but she was sure that because of her love for him she would soon make of him a fine man and a good king.

In spite of her happiness, however, the problem of her father was always with her. Stanislas Leszczynski was now installed at the Chateau de Chambord, which had been redecorated for him. He was a frequent visitor at Fontainebleau, where the court was still in residence, but though he was happy to see Marie happy, he betrayed an occasional fretfulness. Marie knew the reason for this and constantly assured him that in spite of the royal decree against it she would one day persuade Louis to give him all assistance in a bid to regain the throne of Poland. She had already mentioned the subject to Fleury, discreetly of course, but Fleury had refused to understand her delicate hints. She was not surprised, for the Marquise de Prie had told her that the responsibility for the decree was Fleury's, and though she thought the bishop a nice old man in many ways she now came close to disliking him. It was odd, she thought, that Fleury, holding no more important position at court than that of King's tutor, should have greater influence than the chief minister.

She was therefore ready to listen with considerable sympathy when the Marquise approached the subject of the petition by suggesting that the King's faith in Fleury was misplaced. There were many at court, she stressed, who regarded Fleury's influence, which he had gained by flattery, with absolute horror.

"An excellent old man in many ways," she said, "he has developed in the King two regrettable traits, wilfulness and conceit."

Wilfulness and conceit were certainly there, Marie admitted to herself.

"The King is still young," the Marquise continued. "If during the next few formative years of his life Fleury is permitted to remain so close to him, dominating him— But the thought is most disturbing."

Marie began to feel distressed. She saw at once that the Marquise was right. Further, she saw that Fleury, remaining at court, would bring to nothing her ardent desire to make of Louis a fine man and a splendid king.

"Do you think I ought to speak to the King?" she faltered.

"Dear me no!" the Marquise protested. "To say to his Majesty, 'You are conceited and wilful, Fleury is responsible and must be dismissed . . .' No, no, your Majesty, that would antagonize him."

"Then—?"

44

"I have here a petition, your Majesty, expressing concern at the way Fleury is seizing power. The Duc de Bourbon wishes me to present it to your Majesty so that you in turn may present it to the King. All petitions, except those presented through you, must first go to Fleury, so you see . . ." And the Marquise shrugged.

Marie was suddenly afraid. "It was never my wish to meddle in state affairs."

"It is for the good of the King and the country. And remember, your Majesty, Fleury is the only one who stands between your father and the throne that is rightfully his."

Marie made up her mind at once. "Let me have the petition," she said resolutely.

Fleury was making his *petit-coucher*. His enemies, he knew, sneered at him and said that in preparing for bed in public he was aping royalty, but since the King himself approved of this little vanity, which after all was a spectacular way of keeping himself in the public eye, he could afford to laugh at the sneers. In addition it let the people know that he lived frugally, for his apartments were plainly and sparsely furnished.

This evening, as he was brushing his thinning hair, he noticed Bachelier, the King's valet, coming forward from the back of the crowd. Reading the message in Bachelier's eyes Fleury gave a signal. His own valet dismissed the spectators, went out himself and closed the door.

"Well, my dear Bachelier?" Fleury asked.

"Monsieur," said Bachelier, dropping his voice to a conspiratorial whisper, "the King is closeted with the Queen in her Majesty's apartments. A document has changed hands. Your lordship's name was mentioned. Then his Majesty sent for the Duc de Bourbon and the Marquise de Prie."

"And for me also?" Fleury demanded sharply.

"No, Monsieur. That was why I thought . . ."

"Thank you," Fleury said thoughtfully. Then he sighed. He had been looking forward to a quiet hour of reading and cursed Bourbon and his mistress beneath his breath.

45

"Help me dress," he said briskly.

The moment he was dressed he went quickly to the Queen's apartments, but at the door of the sitting-room he found his way barred by the Marquise de Prie.

"Ah," he wheezed, "how delightful you look, Madame. A trifle flushed, perhaps, but still . . . charming."

She looked at him sharply, half in triumph, and told him that her Majesty was occupied and could receive no one.

"Is that you, Fleury?" the King's voice called from within the room. "Come in, please."

The Marquise uttered an unpleasant word beneath her breath and Fleury, brushing past her, entered the sitting-room. It was large and spacious, with fawn-colored carpets on the parquet floor, elaborate candelabra set in the walls and enamelled furniture embellished with chased silver. He bowed low to the Queen, who was looking distressed, ignored Bourbon and spoke to Louis as if he were a naughty child.

"It is evident that your Majesty has ridden too hard today at Rambouillet and overtired yourself."

Louis frowned. "Fleury, I have a petition here." He picked up a crumpled document from a table. "It was drawn up by Bourbon and some of his friends and presented to me by the Queen. Read it."

Fleury noticed that Louis had spoken arrogantly. He was the King and a man, not a boy just back from a hard day's hunting.

"I guess the contents and scorn to touch it," Fleury said. "My conscience is clear. In serving God, my King and my country I have always endeavored to do my duty. I have nothing to conceal, Sire."

"But Fleury . . ." Louis began weakly.

Fleury backed to the door. "I beg to be excused, your Majesty. I shall prepare for a journey to my estate at Issy. There I will find peace and quiet. I am an old man, too old to battle against younger men when it comes to court intrigue. With your Majesty's permission . . ." He bowed and withdrew.

"You see, Sire!" the Marquise cried excitedly. "He condemns himself by running away."

Louis flung himself into a chair. He felt weary. During the day one horse had dropped beneath him and a second had been brought close to exhaustion. His only desire had been to return quickly from Rambouillet and, taking supper quietly with Marie, boast a little of his day's activities. Instead there had been this wretched petition and now Fleury had taken offense. He looked resentfully at Marie. It was all her fault.

"Sire," she ventured, "Madame la Marquise speaks the obvious truth. The Bishop of Fréjus does condemn himself by refusing to answer the charges."

"Oh hold your silly tongue!" Louis cried pettishly. He drew himself up, scowling at Bourbon and the Marquise. "Please withdraw," he said haughtily, "both of you."

They hesitated, looking at each other. Louis scowled at them again. The Marquise shrugged slightly, bowed to Louis, then to Marie, and backed gracefully from the King's presence. Bourbon did likewise. For some moments after they had gone Louis stared broodingly at the door.

"Why do you hate Fleury?" he demanded of Marie. "I love him as much as if he were my father. He has been that to me, more than that, ever since I was seven."

"I understand how you feel," Marie said gently, "but if the Bishop has done things that are bad for France—"

"Things that are bad for France!" he took her up. "That is ridiculous! Fleury holds no office. You talk as if he were chief minister and had brought in an unjust law."

"It was his influence I was thinking of," she was unwise enough to say.

"His influence with *me*?"

"Well, yes." Marie folded her hands in her lap and tried to speak calmly. "You consult him in all things. Often you allow him to make a decision entirely on his own account. He has power if not actual office."

"Ah, so you're jealous of him!" Louis cried. "Like Bourbon and his wretched mistress. And you prefer them to him.

47

You actually make friends of the enemies of the best friend I ever had!"

"Only for the country's sake, Louis."

He laughed shrewdly. "You think he spoils me, don't you! Well, I like being spoiled." With a sudden change of mood he dropped to his knees at Marie's side. He took her hands in his and thrust his head deep in her lap. "Oh, *Marie!*" he said.

"Are you very displeased with me?" she asked.

"Yes," he said resentfully. "I was so happy, too, and now you want to make me hate you."

Marie freed her hands and ran her fingers through his thick tangled curls. He raised his head and looked at her petulantly.

"If only I knew what to do for the best," he complained. "I wish I were older. Oh Marie, I wish I were really a man!"

She kissed him gently, without passion. He was not yet sixteen. He was her husband, but he was also her baby.

The next morning, just as Fleury was preparing to go down to the coach that was to take him to Issy, Bachelier was ushered into his presence. He beamed on the royal valet. Without a doubt the King wished to see him. The summons he had been waiting for had come. The King was about to beg him to remain at court and offer to dispense with Bourbon.

"Madame de Ventadour," Bachelier announced, "has been sent for by the Duc de Bourbon. She is with him now and Madame la Marquise is also present."

"You bring no message from the King?"

"None, Monsieur."

Fleury was puzzled, even slightly alarmed. Then his active mind dwelt solely on this new move of Bourbon's. The King's former guardian, an elderly lady now, was still at court. Louis was still deeply attached to her and still addressed her as "Mamma" Ventadour. In his own absence, Fleury saw, she was the one person the boy-king might be expected to turn to for love and help.

"There's one other thing," Bachelier said. "The King is most displeased with the Queen."

Fleury's eyebrows shot up. "But he spent the night with her."

The valet sniggered. "There was an argument this morning. Being a woman of small experience her Majesty made the mistake of speaking after the act instead of before it. I myself heard her urge the King to let you go to Issy."

"And then . . . ?"

"His Majesty accused her of meddling in state affairs and left her in anger."

Fleury smiled happily, but his happiness soon faded. Angry the King might be, but he, Fleury, and entirely at his own choosing, was still to go to Issy. He wondered if he had been a little too hasty, if he had not made enough allowance for the boy's belief that he, a husband of three or four months' standing, was now a full grown man. He came to a quick decision and instructed Bachelier to bring Madame de Ventadour to him the moment she left Bourbon's apartments. A few moments later the valet was back with her; and Fleury, fussing over her, made her sit in a comfortable chair.

"Madame," he said, looking at her with his head on one side, "I need your help."

"So I imagined," she said dryly.

Fleury beamed on her. "We have always had one all-engrossing interest in common, the welfare of his Majesty the King."

"What has this to do with your needing my help, Monsieur?"

"What I really mean, Madame, is that the King needs your help. By helping me you will be helping him."

Madame de Ventadour permitted herself a faint smile. "How odd. The Duc de Bourbon used a similar phrase." She rose and added warmly, "This is the first time I have been drawn into court intrigue and I have no liking for it."

"Ah, but when you have been at court as long as I," Fleury said gaily, "you will regard court intrigue as I now regard my morning chocolate, an everyday necessity."

"I think not, Monsieur."

He sighed gently. She was devoid of a sense of humor; people like that were always devilish difficult to deal with.

"Madame," he said, giving up the struggle, "on whose side do you stand, mine—or Monsieur le Duc's?"

"If I were forced to make a choice," she said, "I would unwillingly say yours."

"Unwillingly?"

"Your influence on state affairs is better than Monsieur le Duc's, but I find it impossible to close my eyes to the fact that you have gained your unique position by flattering and spoiling the King beyond all reason." She turned and went quickly to the door. "I remain aloof, entirely aloof, Monsieur."

At this point the door was flung open in her face and Bachelier all but tumbled into the room. He seized her by the arm and half-dragging her down the passage told her that the King was asking for her.

"The Queen has been taken ill," he panted. "His Majesty wants you to go to her at once."

Fleury, his stiff legs making greater pace than usual, followed Bachelier and Madame de Ventadour to the Queen's apartments. In the outer room Louis, biting his fingernails, was surrounded by a twittering group of ladies-in-waiting. "Thank God!" he cried, when his eyes fell on Madame de Ventadour. He took her by the arm and hurried her into the Queen's bedroom. When he came back he addressed the watchful Fleury in broken sentences.

"All my fault, Fleury— Unkind to her— Treated her coldly, shouted at her— And now she faints. First she is sick, then she faints—"

A few moments later Madame de Ventadour came back to the outer room, followed by the Queen's personal physician.

"How is she?" Louis demanded. "Oh, I blame myself!"

The physician smiled broadly. "We all blame you, Sire."

"And you smile! You actually smile!"

"Sire," Madame de Ventadour said, with a happy little

chuckle, "the King who is not yet sixteen is going to be a father."

Louis stared at her in amazement. All eyes were on him, and conscious of this he remembered that he was a King and a man as well as a husband and prospective father.

"Goodness," he said nonchalantly, "is *that* all!"

But later, when all but Madame de Ventadour had been sent away, he admitted that he was really frightened. Laughing gently she told him that with the whole of his kingdom ready to rejoice he had nothing to be frightened of.

"But there are decisions to be made," he said.

"You may leave everything to me," she assured him. "Her Majesty shall be my especial responsibility."

"I mean decisions about other things."

"I know, Sire. You are worried about this quarrel between the Duc de Bourbon and the Bishop of Fréjus."

"You actually know about it?"

"I have been approached by both parties, Sire."

"You—? But why *you*, Madame?"

Madame de Ventadour took from the folds of her voluminous gown a jewelled snuff-box, a present from the late King. She snapped it open and delicately inserted a pinch of snuff in each nostril. Louis watched her in fascination. All fashionable ladies carried snuff-boxes, but only the older ones still maintained the earlier habit of snuff-taking.

"Each," she said, "wants me to use my influence with you."

"*Each?* Fleury as well as Bourbon?"

Louis began to feel distressed. Fleury, his closest friend! The man who had his full confidence! To seek out Mamma Ventadour, just as Bourbon had done—that was stupid. Unless, of course, Bourbon's accusations were true and Fleury was afraid.

"Mamma Ventadour, what am I to do?"

"Let them fight it out between themselves, and when each has revealed his hand, dismiss the one you can no longer trust."

Louis' face cleared. "How wise you are, for a woman!"

51

Louis acted at once by sending for both Bourbon and Fleury. When they came he faced them with folded arms and a stern countenance. He ordered them to forget their quarrel and work together in friendliness for the country's sake. Fleury demanded an apology from Bourbon, but Bourbon said heatedly, "Never!"

Fleury shrugged. "Then what else can I do but go to Issy?"

Louis' heart missed a beat. He tried to steady himself, to make his voice deep and manly.

"As you wish, Fleury. You may withdraw."

Fleury waited for a moment, hid his disappointment as Louis remained silent and went quickly from the room. Louis turned to Bourbon.

"Well, cousin?"

"Sire," Bourbon said, "there are many urgent matters that should be discussed at once."

"Discuss them, then."

Bourbon, with growing confidence, spoke of the financial situation which, to say the least, was depressing. He pointed out that previously when he had wanted to take certain measures to refill the royal purse Fleury had prevented him from speaking his mind.

"Speak it now," Louis said curtly.

He felt that he had complete control of the situation, and though his heart was empty at the thought of Fleury's withdrawal to Issy he told himself that he was behaving in a very kingly manner.

Bourbon, warming to his subject, suggested new taxation measures, a tariff on certain commodities, forced salary reductions and a temporary debasement of the coinage.

"Fleury," Louis said, "would advise against debasement."

"He would also reduce your Majesty's private revenues and that, with your Majesty now married and about to become a father, must be avoided."

Louis laughed boyishly. "I do like spending money, don't I! And there never seems to be enough for all the things I need. Very well, you shall have your way."

Bourbon bowed himself to the door, which he found slightly ajar. Flinging it fully open he almost fell over Fleury,

52

who was straightening himself up from an attitude of listening.

"You were eavesdropping," he sneered.

"Indeed I was."

Bourbon closed the door carefully and moved along the passage with Fleury.

"Perhaps you have decided to remain at court?" he said.

"Dear me no! I leave almost immediately for Issy. And knowing your plans—yes, yes, I heard every word!—I go with a light heart. When you are an old man, Monsieur, you will realize how easy it is to wait, to bide one's time. The coming months, I feel sure, will reveal many things."

V

MORE *pots-de-chambre* than ever before were on the road, as well as carriages of every description, gentlemen on horseback and farm carts crowded with shouting, gesticulating peasants, for word had got about that her Majesty the Queen had been brought to bed with child.

"The Queen is in labor!" everybody was crying.

At the Palace of Versailles itself the excitement was intense. Marie's apartments were crammed to overflowing and physicians by the dozen were constantly in and out of her bedroom, the door of which was guarded by a grim-faced Madame de Ventadour. She knew that presently she would be obliged to open the door to as many members of the court as could crowd into the room, but for the sake of the Queen, who shrank from the ordeal of gaping faces, she was prepared to resist this traditional necessity till the last possible moment.

Meanwhile Louis, now sixteen ("In my seventeenth year," he insisted) and a king of eleven years' standing, had summoned his ministers to the council chamber. This had surprised everybody, for usually it was the Duc de Bourbon who called the ministers together while Louis, declaring himself bored, gave only a pretended interest to state affairs. Sitting in his place now, with the cat Charlotte on his knees, he glanced fretfully at his ministers.

"Monsieur le Duc," he said, his eyes centering on the chief minister, "I have a complaint to make. Are you aware that there are riots at Rouen and Rennes and Caen, that there is unrest in many other parts and that the people are crying 'Down with Bourbon!' even 'Down with the King!'?"

Bourbon paled in anger, while his friends on the council looked at him uneasily and his enemies gleefully.

"It is impossible to please all the people all the time," he shrugged.

Louis opened a folded sheet of paper and began to read from it.

" 'Without doubt,' " he read, " 'your Majesty is unaware of what is happening in the provinces, for Monsieur le Duc would be afraid to tell you. His policy has debased the coinage and increased the cost of living. It has lowered wages and imposed crippling taxes. The risings at Rouen, Rennes and Caen, with theirs cries against not only Monsieur le Duc but against your Majesty, are only the beginning. Unless this ruinous policy is reversed France will be torn from end to end with unrest and risings, possibly with revolution.' "

Bourbon was on his feet. "I demand to know the name of the writer of that infamous letter!"

For answer Louis said: "Fleury shall be brought back from Issy. You, personally, will send him a letter begging him to return. You will send it at once, Monsieur."

He dismissed his ministers and stood alone in the council chamber, absently caressing Charlotte. "I should never have let Fleury go," he said aloud. Then he went quickly to the Queen's apartments. The chattering courtiers fell silent as he entered the anteroom. Madame de Ventadour opened the bedroom door for him, admitted him and closed it again. He thrust the cat into her arms and fell on his knees at the bedside.

"Marie!"

Marie's face was pale and drawn, and she was struggling

to control her labored breathing. One hand strayed to Louis' curls and lingered there caressingly. Louis glanced up at the physician who stood at the other side of the bed.

"Will it be long?"

"The worst is to come, Sire."

Louis seized Marie's hand. He kissed it wildly, yet he had the sensation of standing aside from himself, looking on at what he believed to be the correct behavior of an anxious husband and father-to-be.

"If only I could suffer for you!" he cried, approving warmly of the words as he uttered them. He looked at the physician again. "Do we expect a boy or a girl?"

The physician smiled. "Madame de Ventadour, who presumes to know more of these things than a doctor, expects a girl, but there is no way of knowing."

Louis considered this. "A girl would disappoint the court, but I wouldn't mind." He giggled boyishly. "I hope it *is* a girl, just to upset my ministers. It makes me sick the way they talk. Anyone would think I married the Queen just to provide France with a dauphin."

The physician shrugged, his manner saying plainly, *Well, what other reason could there have been?*

"Marie," Louis begged, "do you still love me?"

"More than ever, Louis."

"Then nothing else matters; nothing else will ever matter!"

Marie, writhing suddenly, bit back an involuntary cry. The physician bent over her and made a quick examination.

"Let the other physicians be summoned," he said importantly.

Louis flew to the door and flung it open. Madame de Ventadour, reading the message of his eyes, sent a lady-in-waiting to call the other court physicians. She had intended closing the door again but the young Duc d'Orleans was too quick for her. She was swept roughly aside and several prominent members of the court, led by d'Orleans, surged into the bedroom. Others, pushing at each other, fighting madly for a vantage point, crowded after them.

"Mamma Ventadour!" Louis cried pathetically.

"If the Queen can suffer their staring eyes," Madame de Ventadour said, "so must you."

"Call me when you have news," he said, and fled to his own apartments.

Marie, aware only of the gaping, fantastic faces of the people crowding about her bed, closed her eyes and prayed for strength. She remembered the humiliation of the wedding night and knew that now, even as then, ladies and gentlemen would be climbing on chairs in order to gain a better view. She told herself that the child would belong to the people, that tradition was tradition and must be suffered, that she, the Queen, must submit with fortitude and dignity. Dignity! she thought; dear heaven, dignity at a time like this!

Presently she was aware of the physicians above her, reaching down to her, doing their utmost with their practiced hands to help her. She heard one of them complain about the stuffiness of the atmosphere, the lack of air, and she said foolishly, "Really, Monsieur, *you* should be having this baby, then you would know all about that!" She heard another of them call out for hot water, and though, after what seemed an age, it was brought, the unyielding push of people so hampered the servants that it was tipped on the carpet. Steam billowed up in clouds. Marie laughed wildly. "What a pity," she said, "they won't be able to see me so clearly now!" The steam took on amazing shapes, like figures in a nightmare. One in particular had the look of an old witch. "You are very welcome, Madame," she said, "but please leave your broomstick in the anteroom." The apparition bobbed its head and in doing so became the Bishop of Fréjus, who really ought to be at.Issy. He said, "A girl!" only it was one of the physicians who had spoken the words.

"A girl," he repeated, "a dauphine!"

The cry was taken up.

"But wait!" another physican shouted. "Great heavens, I would never have thought it—twins!"

"Ah, but there may be more," Marie heard herself giggle.

"A whole litter, perhaps. Just think of the sensation, the Queen of France gives birth to a litter, and all girls!"

And then she lost consciousness.

She was still unconscious when Louis came to her side, and by then the second child, another girl, had been safely delivered. Louis stood over her, staring down at her in horror.

"Is she dead?" he asked in a whisper.

He was assured that the Queen, a strong and healthy woman, was merely exhausted. One of the physicians bent over her and swiftly lanced her left foot. A few moments later, when the blood was flowing freely, Marie opened her eyes and smiled faintly at the blurred face which she knew to be her husband's. Louis laughed hysterically.

"Oh, you wretch, Marie! Twins! And both of them girls!"

When Fleury returned from Issy, Louis was inspecting the fine new coach which he had bought in honor of the birth of his twin daughters. The old man came hobbling forward on his stick. Quick tears sprang to Louis' eyes as he embraced him. Presently Fleury freed himself and pointed his stick at Louis.

"Twins!" he cackled.

"Yes," Louis acknowledged seriously. "What other husband in France can boast, at the age of sixteen, of being the father of twins?" He began to strut a little. "I am well content, Fleury."

"You must never say that, Sire, until the Queen has borne you a son."

"We shall have a son next time, Fleury."

After a little silence, while Louis continued his examination of the coach, Fleury uttered the one word, "Bourbon?"

Louis smiled. He had that morning issued a *lettre de cachet,* that much-feared royal order of either imprisonment or dismissal, or both.

"He has gone," he said, "and the Marquise de Prie also."

"Into exile, Sire?"

"Yes. Do you like my new coach, Fleury?"

58

"Most handsome, your Majesty."

Louis chuckled. "Fit for a cardinal, do you think? You shall have it in a few months when you become one."

Fleury kissed the boy's hands. "Who is to replace Bourbon?"

Louis roared with laughter. "You would never guess!"

"Then tell me, Sire," Fleury whispered.

Louis struck a magnificent pose. "Who else but his Majesty the King! I intend to be my own chief minister, just as my great-grandfather was."

Fleury smiled. He was well satisfied. To be a cardinal and at the same time the undisputed power behind the throne was all he wanted. The power but not the office, that would be excellent. The power without the responsibility, *that* was better by far.

"How much do you think the coach is worth?" Louis asked.

"Now let me see . . ." Fleury pondered. I, being still a mere bishop, would expect to pay six thousand livres for it; you, being King must have paid eight thousand."

"They charged me thirty thousand," Louis cried.

"Then they must be made to refund the difference, Sire. And that, never paying more for a thing than it is worth, must be our future policy in all things. Otherwise France will never recover from the stupid blundering of the Duc de Bourbon."

But Louis was barely listening.

"Twins," he laughed, "and do you know why? Because I always eat such a lot of oysters, Fleury!"

VI

A BALL was in progress at Versailles.

Marie, surrounded by her ladies, thought it the gayest sight she had yet seen at this fabulous Palace of Versailles, the countless chandeliers and candelabra glittering like a thousand stars, the parquet floor crammed with magnificent lords and ladies and the great tall mirrors reflecting and enlarging the whole resplendent scene. Her searching eyes came to rest on Louis, tall and gracious as he stood in the midst of it all, smiling happily. How quickly the years were slipping away! Louis was now twenty; she was twenty-eight. Soon she would be thirty and that, for a woman at the court of his most Christian Majesty, was middle-aged. Twenty-eight and the mother of three daughters, for, disappointing the court, another girl had been born last year, a sickly child who was not expected to survive. The twins, one of the physicians had said, had placed too great a strain on her Majesty's constitution.

Presently she was joined by Louis and her father, who had arrived earlier from Chambord. She thought that Louis, though still slender, had lost his boyish looks. He was indeed a man now, virile, energetic and restless. She felt sad at the thought that a king of twenty, with a wife and three children, should be so easily bored. Once, when he had complained of boredom, she had suggested that an active interest in state affairs might fill his days with personal satisfaction, but he had laughed scornfully and said that he had Fleury and a score of ministers to look after things as dull as that. Fleury was in complete control and though eighty now, stiffer in his limbs and slower of speech, he was as mentally alert as ever. People were calling him Cardinal Eternity, and certainly it looked as if he might live forever.

Louis invited her to dance again, but she excused herself, saying she felt tired. This brought a frown to his face. He looked at her critically. She was pale and obviously tired, but worse than that she had a homely, almost commonplace look which the elaborate court dress and the diamonds in her hair failed entirely to disguise. He told her brusquely that she ought to use more rouge.

"Paleness is out of place at Versailles," he said.

Hurt, she tried to make light of his words. "I always forget that in France one must face the world with bravely painted cheeks."

"France," her father mocked, "is such a civilized country."

"The English," Marie laughed, "would take you up on that."

"As if *their* opinion matters!" Louis scoffed. "A dull race, surely, and how they condemn my hunting parties, my wicked gambling and my drinking. Why, it is even whispered in Londin that having taken to drink at the age of sixteen I am now a hopeless drunkard." He turned on his heels. "Well, I shall find somebody else to dance with."

Presently, Marie knew, he would grow tired of dancing and retire to his inner apartments where he would play basset or faro till three or four in the morning. In all probability he would rise at six and spend the best part of the following day hunting, straining every nerve to exceed his recent record of two hundred head of game in one day.

"Marie," her father said, "I have news from Poland."

She smiled at him affectionately but her heart grew sad. It was coming again, yet another plea for French aid in a wild bid to regain his lost throne.

61

"The country is torn with unrest," he went on. "If I were to appear there with a French army behind me . . ."

In spite of her desire to help him if she could she felt a little stab of resentment. After all, he was not an hereditary king and had less reason than any other king for involving himself and others in the troubled question of the Polish succession. Fourteen years ago he had been a happy and unambitious Polish nobleman, but his eventual election to the throne had changed all that. In Poland the nobles elected their own king, and had it not been for her father's friendship with the King of Sweden he would never have been nominated, let alone elected. Later, with Sweden suffering reverses at the hands of Russia, the Russians had set up Augustus the Second against Stanislas and exile had followed.

Her father went on to say that he had approached Louis, who, while showing a certain sympathy, had referred him to Cardinal Fleury.

"I quite understand," Marie said gently. "You want me to plead your cause with Fleury."

"And you will, my dear, I know you will!" he said eagerly.

She sighed. "You know that the Cardinal dislikes me, but if I can help you at all I will."

Fleury stood with his back to a cheerful fire, warming his dry old hands behind him and peering short-sightedly at the physician Pérard. Pérard found the room airless and stuffy, but the Cardinal, winter and summer alike, always had a fire in his apartments these days.

"I understand," Fleury remarked, "that her Majesty the Queen left the ball last night in a fainting condition. Is she better or worse this morning?"

"Her Majesty is better but she needs rest and quiet. She has a brave spirit and a strong will, but—"

"Granted, granted," Fleury interrupted, "but what I am anxious to ascertain is whether or not the Queen's condition indicates what such a condition so often does in a virtuous married woman."

"Fortunately, no," Pérard replied warmly.

Fleury's eyebrows shot up. "You say *fortunately?*"

"Your eminence, I take little pleasure in discussing such a matter with you, but in my opinion her Majesty's health prohibits the bearing of another child for at least a year. I would even go so far as to say that another child, now or later, might cost the Queen her life."

Fleury closed his eyes and swayed on his feet. He clicked his tongue, but hardly in sympathy for her Majesty, Pérard decided.

"Is the Queen aware of your opinion?" Fleury asked.

"Yes."

"And the King?"

"No."

"Her Majesty has forbidden his being told?"

"No, but she is afraid to tell him, and so am I."

"Yet he must be told," Fleury murmured. "But dear me, what an unhappy situation for a King so ardent and young. And in addition France must surely have a dauphin. I wonder, Pérard, if your opinion is not a little too pessimistic?"

"My knowledge of the case is profound," Pérard said with dignity, "and I would remind you that my qualifications—"

"Of course, of course," Fleury said soothingly. He turned and bent over the glowing embers. He sighed deeply and appeared to come to an unwilling decision. "Since the truth must be faced," he wheezed, "I myself will undertake the unpleasant duty of telling his Majesty."

When the physician had withdrawn Fleury threw back his head and laughed. It was an old man's laugh which, beginning on a high thin note and ending in a fit of coughing, all but shook him off his feet.

Five minutes later, on entering the Queen's apartments, he made a great to-do of settling in the chair which one of the ladies brought forward. He wheezed and he sighed; he lowered himself gingerly; he stretched out his thin legs cautiously.

63

"Dear me," he cackled, "there are times when my eighty years make themselves unpleasantly felt. Nevertheless, I shall reach a hundred. Cardinal Eternity, that is my name."

He looked hopefully at Marie, expecting some reassuring compliment. She merely smiled faintly, as if he were some comic object, confound her! and nodded to her ladies to withdraw.

"Your Majesty expressed a wish to see me," he said, somewhat snappishly. "Of what service can I be?"

Marie came to the point at once. "Cardinal Fleury, I want to discuss the Polish situation with you."

"Ah, so."

He looked at her blandly and smiled. He said that the weather was most chilly, that he found it surprising that her Majesty, who was in poor health, had no fire in the room.

Marie steeled herself to press her point, but Fleury interrupted her at her first few words.

"Madame," he said, "I will be frank with you. Your father's rightful place is undoubtedly on the throne of Poland. I applaud his long-deferred hope and sympathize with his distress, but I consider it foolish for France to squander precious money in a foreign war."

Marie felt her cheeks grow warm with anger and helplessness. Taxation and other revenues yielded the crown a matter of a hundred and eighty million livres a year. Even a fraction of the amount spent each year on royal pleasure-making would be sufficient to equip and support the army her father required. His cause might be a vain one, but better, she thought, to squander money on vain causes than on pleasure-making.

"Your Majesty," Fleury went on, "may I beg leave to ask an intimate question? Pérard, you see, has given me a complete report on your state of health."

Marie was horrified. "A *complete* report?"

Fleury looked at her curiously. "It embarrasses you?"

"How dare he!" she cried. "He had no right!"

"He had every right. The bearing of children by a queen is a public, not a private, matter. A delicate one, I admit, but

I am an old man and a priest. Surely it is better to discuss it with me than to have it debated at a council meeting."

"A council meeting!" she exclaimed. "That would be detestable."

He looked at her blandly. "Madame, we demand a dauphin. Your duty to King and State is clear."

Marie felt her anger mounting again. He should have said: If the King dies without male issue the present Duc d'Orleans will mount the throne and I will be sent into exile.

"Are you insisting on my risking my life?" she asked.

Fleury shrugged. "I am thinking, Madame, of your sacred duty."

"If the King were to hear you—!"

"He would applaud my words. Only yesterday he said, 'A boy next time, or I must find myself another wife.'"

"He was joking!"

"Jokes often become reality."

"If he were told," Marie said, "he would show himself more considerate than you suggest. I know he would."

Fleury looked down his nose. "Deny himself the pleasure of your Majesty's bed, you mean?"

A deep blush mounted from her neck to her cheeks.

"I have a suggestion to make," Fleury said. "Ignore Pérard's questionable report, keep the whole matter from the King and I will agree to involve France in a needless war for your father's sake."

Marie was horrified, not at what Fleury was asking of her —she was, she hoped, a dutiful wife and queen and she loved her husband—but at his attitude in trying thus to bribe her.

"There is another interesting aspect to this most interesting situation," Fleury went on dreamily. "Your Majesty, I feel sure, understands fully the significance of obeying Pérard's ruling. The King's devotion to you and his utter, not to say remarkable, faithfulness might be seriously shaken."

Marie rose swiftly and went to the window, hiding her shame and fear, but the cracked old voice still reached her.

"The King is young, high-spirited and ardent."

Marie turned but avoided the searching eyes.

65

"You shall have your way," she said.

But later she realized that from the first she should have suspected trickery. Within three months she was pregnant again, yet no move was made to gather together the promised army. Fleury merely shrugged when she reproached him and murmured that such things took time. In desperation she brought up the matter with Louis but the moment the word Poland passed her lips he frowned and said, "Speak to Fleury." She told him she had already done so, that Fleury had made a promise. "He keeps his promises," Louis assured her. "Give him time but please don't talk to me about it. I am not, I assure you, the sort of king who finds romance in war."

In the end, with her nerves frayed and Louis more than usually bored with life at court, they quarrelled. He remarked acidly that she seemed always to be out of temper these days. He supposed that a woman found the months of pregnancy somewhat tiresome, but after all, this was only the third month, and pregnancy in any case was a normal function, not an illness.

"You take too much notice of Pérard," he raged. "The man is bad for you. As Fleury says, he pampers you."

"Fleury said *that*?"

"Oh come, Marie, when you frown you look a great deal older than you really are."

Hot tears pricked her eyes. "The fault is naturally mine if the difference in our ages is beginning to annoy you."

"Please don't speak to me as if I were still a child. It emphasizes the difference even more."

"*Louis!*"

"And now," he complained, "I suppose you'll begin to cry."

He looked and felt ashamed of himself, but he was the King, he was bored, and his wife, not only out of temper, was bent on flinging her pregnancy in his face.

"I assure you," he cried, "I'm not a child any more. I doubt if I ever was one. I've been a king so long and a husband so long I feel like an old man."

Marie felt infinitely sorry for him, and for that reason

66

rather than any other the tears came unbidden and flowed beyond her control.

"There!" he shouted. "I knew it!"

There was a scratching at the door.

"Enter!" Louis thundered.

Madame de Mailly, a young and newly appointed lady-in-waiting, came into the room. She announced in a clear boyish voice that the carriage was waiting.

"I ordered no carriage," Marie said.

Madame de Mailly apologized. "Madame de Ventadour suggested that since the weather is mild and sunny your Majesty might like to take a drive. I naturally assumed that a carriage would be required."

"Later," Louis said shortly. "Please withdraw."

The young woman curtsied and went out. Louis stared after her broodingly.

"A new face," he said, glad to speak of other things.

"Julie de Mailly," Marie explained. "She has just taken up her duties."

"Alexandre de Mailly's wife?"

"Yes."

Louis grunted. "I never saw an uglier face, nor, for that matter, a more attractive one."

"Her face might be plain but hardly ugly," Marie argued.

"I beg to differ, but please remember I said it was attractive too. Are you pleased with her?"

"Her conversation is intelligent and her manners incomparable."

"Intelligent!" Louis laughed. "No doubt you read religious books together." He turned on his heels. "Be ready in an hour. I shall accompany you on your drive."

Passing through the anteroom he came face to face with Julie de Mailly. He stopped for a moment and engaged her in conversation. She looked down demurely, almost in confusion, but there was no tremor in her voice when she answered his questions.

"Are you happy with the Queen?" he asked politely.

"Indeed yes, your Majesty."

"Splendid. We—er—must see more of you."

She met his eyes then, giving him a delightfully puzzled look. *"We,* Sire?"

"I speak in the royal plural. I naturally mean I myself."

He began to blush. He had never dallied with a woman before and here, all unconsciously—perhaps because he had quarrelled with Marie—he was on the point of doing so now. He smiled uncertainly and went hastily from the room. Two days later he engaged her in conversation again. He spoke abruptly of a ball, a quiet affair, mind you, which was to be held in his private apartments.

"You will please attend it," he commanded.

She gave him a shy smile. "A ball in your Majesty's apartments is always very select."

He wondered if she was laughing at him and found himself staring fixedly at her face. The shy smile made her lips turn up at the corners and removed from her face the ugliness he had first seen there. She had large eyes which were twinkling now, and a brow which he knew Marie would call intelligent. Her skin was flawless. The dark red gown she wore was low-cut and revealed the pearl-like quality of her full round breasts. Another glance at her still-twinkling eyes made him lose his nerve.

"Her Majesty will naturally be present," he said quickly. All I ask is that you should attend her."

"The honor is nonetheless great, Sire," she said.

"Excuse me," he stammered, and left her.

On learning that Louis had commanded Madame de Mailly to attend her, Marie went to the ball with some misgiving. She was made all the more unhappy when he opened it by dancing with the girl, and she spoke sharply to him when, later, he reproached her for sitting in a corner and refusing to take a real part in the dancing.

"There is such a thing as etiquette," she said. "Until the King dances with the Queen no other gentleman has the right to approach her. Would you have *me* approach *them?"*

"This is anything but a formal gathering," he complained. "Surely in my own apartments I may enjoy a little freedom from court etiquette!"

The next day the gossip started. The King had opened the

68

ball with Madame de Mailly. He had ignored the Queen and danced with Madame de Mailly. He had danced with her several times and not even once with the Queen. Without a doubt the King was going to prove himself a real man and a real King at last.

And this gossip, of course, was quick to reach Cardinal Fleury.

When Julie de Mailly entered Fleury's apartments he was standing as usual with his back to the fire.

"Brrrh!" he greeted her, "how cold it is for this time of the year. Come, my dear, take a chair by the fire."

Julie complied demurely and staring thoughtfully into the fire sat waiting. She knew why she had been sent for. The King had looked at her, danced with her, singled her out for his especial attention, and now the formidable cardinal was either going to scold her or dismiss her, or both.

"Young lady," he said affably, "I feel that in your capacity of lady-in-waiting to the Queen you can be of some small service to me."

This was a surprising opening. She still stared into the fire and waited.

"You could, for example, tell me if the lamentable strain which exists between their Majesties is as serious as I fear."

Julie looked at him with an expression on her face which people, not really knowing her, were apt to call mouse-like. Frowning delicately she murmured that the King visited the Queen once a day, spoke of her health, talked about the children and then, never having been alone with her, withdrew.

"Hastily?" Fleury chirped.

"Yes."

He half-closed his eyes. "What progress are you making with his Majesty?"

Julie contrived to give him a shocked look. "Really, your Eminence!"

"Come, come, Madame, the King's interest in you is well known to all of us."

69

"But his faithfulness to the Queen is beyond question."

"But for how long?" Fleury wheezed. "His Majesty is not the man to live like a monk."

Julie tried not to show the distaste she felt. She thought him unnecessarily suggestive. To her mind there was nothing more revolting in an old man, more especially when he was a priest, than lewdness. The thought made her feel unclean.

"Since there is a law against seduction," Fleury went on with a chuckle, "a law which applies equally to men and women, I have no wish to see you endanger your life by seducing a faithful husband who is also extremely shy, therefore I ask you—"

"To spy on the Queen?"

"What an unfortunate choice of words!"

"On the King, then?"

"Ah, I see that I must be completely frank with you. The King's faithfulness is beyond question, *at present,* but the time is coming when a change will inevitably take place, as you no doubt hope."

Julie laughed dryly. It was of course a shrewd observation. She had admired the King from the first—he was the most handsome man in the world—and she coveted his god-like beauty, but he *was* extremely shy, and there *was* a law against seduction.

"All I ask," Fleury said, "is that I am informed of the change when it takes place."

"I may have no knowledge of it."

"I think you will, my dear."

"Has the King spoken about me?" she asked eagerly.

"Several times," Fleury lied.

Their eyes met. She knew his real purpose now. The Queen, who disliked him, was losing favor; a mistress might replace her; Fleury, greedily guarding the power he possessed, wanted to be in a position to use that mistress.

"I wonder," Fleury murmured, "if our thoughts coincide."

"That is possible, your Eminence."

He came and stood over her. "Then remember this, young lady: I am the most powerful man in France; if I wished I could have you sent from Versailles immediately, before the thing you dream of has a chance of taking place."

A stab of fear gripped Julie's heart. Necessity had married her to a man who was a fool and a fop, a man who preferred the slim figure of a boy to the rounded entirely feminine figure of his wife. Ambition had brought her to court and she was determined to remain here. Not that she had contemplated, until she had seen the spark of nervous interest in the King's eyes, the possibility of becoming a royal mistress, but since it *was* a possibility, and she was young and ardent and unloved by her husband, the last thing she wanted was to be sent away.

"I hope I make myself clear?" Fleury said.

Julie rose. "I—I'll do whatever your Eminence asks of me," she stammered.

VII

PARIS, Louis was told, had gone wild with joy. There were bonfires everywhere, the mayor had ordered the greatest fireworks display in the history of the city and the aldermen, showing a generosity they would afterwards regret, had set up great casks of wine in the streets. In the Queen's room Louis held the child in his arms and looked down on his crumpled face. Foolishly and a little theatrically he said: "My son!"

Marie lay back on the pillows, white, exhausted but conscious. She had now borne her husband (or the state, she told herself bitterly) four children, even though the sickly third daughter had died some little time ago. Louis gave the Dauphin to Madame de Ventadour.

"Is he healthy?" he asked. "Will he live?"

He was assured that the child would live. Marie, hearing this answer to the question she had lacked the courage to ask, breathed more freely. Louis bent quickly, kissed her dutifully on the brow and hurried away. He had, she knew, postponed a hunting trip on her account and was anxious now to reach Rambouillet.

The crowd in the room began to dwindle. One of the last to go was Cardinal Fleury, and with him the physician

Pérard. Fleury murmured that apparently Pérard's earlier fear on the Queen's account had been quite misplaced.

"By the grace of God, yes," Pérard replied.

"There is no doubt that the child will survive?"

"None whatever."

"And the Queen?"

"Recovery will be slow. My earlier warning must be repeated, this time with greater emphasis. This time his Majesty must be told."

"He shall be, I promise you that," Fleury said.

A plan had already formed in his mind. It had come to him while standing in the Queen's room. He thought of it again and laughed, and decided that he had better send for Madame de Mailly. She came promptly and, teasing her a little, he remarked that in the past few months she had made little or no progress with the King.

"His Majesty is as shy as ever," she said. "And in any case you warned me not to act until you gave the word."

"True, true, and for a very good reason. Her Majesty will have full confidence in you now, and believe me, when she recovers her strength she will need a sympathetic friend."

"What do you want me to do, Monsieur?"

"Her Majesty has a grave decision to make and a delicate piece of information to convey to the King. Being so close to you she may well confide in you, and once she has done that you will be able to suggest a way of breaking the news to his Majesty."

Julie de Mailly was interested but puzzled. Fleury, in sudden playfulness, tweaked her nose, then caught her ear in a bony grip, tugged it towards his lips and whispered into it. When he had finished he chuckled and wheezed, and Julie, though she felt a little conscience-stricken at what she knew she would do, smiled her satisfaction.

As they waited, Fleury and Julie de Mailly, Marie slowly recovered her strength. Louis himself, seeking pleasure feverishly, spent his days hunting and his nights at the card table, but with scrupulous care he visited his wife for an hour each day. For the most part he was gentle and kindly and spoke to her affectionately, but there was impatience in his voice when he urged her for his sake to get well quickly.

"I am not the man," he said on one occasion, uttering the words Fleury often whispered in his ear, "to live like a monk forever."

This, with Pérard's solemn warning still echoing in her ears, was an opportunity for Marie to speak, but she let it go. What right, she excused herself, had she to deny him? Pérard had been wrong once; he could be wrong again. She was in such a mood when Julie de Mailly, giving her a cue, spoke of a friend who had lost a child at birth and was unable, without imperilling her life, to bear another.

"Heaven be praised it is not the same with your Majesty," Julie said piously.

With that Marie, weeping a little, told Julie of Pérard's warning.

"Oh, but the tragedy of it!" Julie cried, and made a show of tears herself. "And what courage it will need to tell the King."

"I would rather die than tell him!" Marie said passionately.

"But he must be told, your Majesty. He would *want* to be told. Think what would happen if you should die. His Majesty would blame himself for the rest of his life."

Marie admitted that this was right. "But I could never tell him myself, never!"

"An unenviable task for any wife," Julie said sympathetically. "I wonder if I may suggest, your Majesty, that I—"

"*You?*"

This, as Cardinal Fleury had warned, was the danger point of the whole scheme and might well wreck it. Not being able to blush at will, Julie looked down in well-simulated confusion.

"Please forgive me," she murmured. "It was wrong and presumptuous of me even to hint at such a course."

"No," Marie said kindly. "His Majesty likes you, and you

are a married woman. If you feel that you can speak of the matter delicately . . ."

"I think I could, your Majesty," Julie said earnestly. (But what an innocent, what a fool, this queen was!) "Your Majesty's uncertain health, the reason for it, the danger of bearing another child . . . those are the things I would stress and leave the rest to the King's understanding and sympathy."

"Very well," Marie agreed, and then: "No! I—I must think about it first, really I must."

Soon after this, when it was assumed that Marie was fully recovered, Louis announced one morning that he was going to Rambouillet for the day. He complimented Marie on her appearance. He told her playfully that she looked almost young again, and sweeping her into a passionate embrace muttered a trifle thickly that he would join her in her room that night. It was late evening when he returned, and while having eaten little during the day he had drunk heartily. As a result he was in a jolly mood and intoxicated enough for his speech to be slurred. He went straight to Marie's apartments. In the anteroom he came face to face with Julie de Mailly, who had been waiting and listening for him. She placed a finger to her lips.

"Quietly, I beg of you, Sire. Her Majesty has retired."

"As early as this?" Louis laughed. "Well, well, she must be as eager as I am, but get her up. We shall have supper together first."

Julie shook her head sadly. "Her Majesty, I regret, is indisposed."

"Indisposed?" Anger flared up in him suddenly. "She was in excellent spirits and the best of health this morning."

"Nevertheless, Sire—"

He tried to push past her but she stood her ground. Swaying on his feet he glared at her wildly.

"Your attitude suggests that I, the King, am not to be admitted."

"Well, Sire—"

"Is this by her Majesty's orders?"

Julie nodded. She wanted to laugh aloud. The King was

giving her her lines as skilfully as if they were both acting in a court play. Nothing could have been better rehearsed.

"Come, Madame," he thundered, "stand aside!"

"The Queen's door is locked."

"Locked!"

It was a tense moment. Julie, trembling with excitement, waited for Louis to test the lie, for with Marie still undecided, she had taken matters into her own hands. She said quickly.

"Her Majesty locked it when I left her a few minutes ago."

Louis stared at the door. A vein throbbed in his temple.

"She knew my intention," he said harshly. "She deliberately planned this insult."

Julie, fearing that perhaps she had gone too far, touched him lightly on the arm. "If only I could tell you how sorry I am, Sire."

"Sorry?" He laughed loudly. "So the plainest face in France masks the kindest heart."

"If it pleases your Majesty to mock at my poor looks . . ."

"God!" Louis cried, and swept her into a swift embrace. "Mock at them? Heaven forbid! Your plainness is something in which I have always found beauty." He giggled suddenly. "Wine makes me bold. Sober, I would tremble before you like a callow boy and remain silent." He felt himself growing in stature. He remembered the blood that flowed in his veins. He remembered that he was the King. The people belonged to him, not he to the people. At all events one of them did and he would claim her now while his need was so great.

"I want a little gaiety," he said, "and you shall share it with me. Rambouillet again. A midnight party in the forest. A party for two. A rejected husband, when he is also the King of France, is not the helpless fool his wife might think him!"

It was late afternoon. Bachelier, rousing the old Cardinal from the doze he had fallen into over the fire, informed him that the King and Madame de Mailly had just returned from Rambouillet, and that the Queen, visiting the King's apartments, had been refused admission. Wasting no time, Fleury sent his own valet to fetch Madame de Mailly. The man returned in a few moments to report that the door was locked and no answer had been received to his scratching. Fleury sent him again an hour later. This time he returned to say that Madame de Mailly had yawned in his face and said that she was much too tired to leave her room. Furious, Fleury hobbled to the room himself. The door was locked. He scratched on it so violently that he hurt his fingernails. His anger increased and he fell on the door with clenched fists. Scratching might be the polite fashion of requesting an entry but it was anything but effective in a case like this. Finally, chuckling deep in her throat, Julie opened the door.

She was wearing a negligée which had been thrown carelessly over her shoulders. Her eyes were bright and her face was flushed. She looked almost pretty and her body, barely concealed by the ridiculous wisp of a negligée, was undoubtedly beautiful. She carried herself, Fleury reflected, with an impudent attractiveness which the Queen, virtuous woman that she was, could never achieve. Panting with the exertion of his unaccustomed activity he entered the room. The russet-colored riding costume, as well as a shift and other pieces of underclothing, was lying on the floor. Julie invited him sweetly to be seated.

"I prefer to stand!" he snarled.

"At your time of life, and having come without your stick?" she chided him. "Come, your Eminence, take this comfortable chair and let me send for a footstool."

Fleury made an effort to control his anger. "Give me your report at once, Madame."

Julie affected surprise. "My . . . report?"

"This procrastination is deliberate, by all the saints in heaven it is. Tell me at once what occurred last night between the King and you."

"Oh, Monsieur!" she giggled.

Fleury tottered to the chair she had offered him and all but fell into it.

"The events of last night," he sneered, "seem to have gone to your head. Must I remind you of my warning? And must I add that if you continue this foolishness you will live to regret it?"

Julie yawned. "How tired I feel."

"Bah!" he shouted. "You think that having won the King, if indeed you *have* won him, you can snap your fingers at me!"

"Presumptuous of me, but . . . yes."

"I still possess the power to ruin you," Fleury said, more quietly now.

She laughed tinklingly. "You make me tremble with fear."

"You seem to have forgotten one important factor, a gentleman by the name of Monsieur le Comte de Mailly."

"My husband!" Julie exclaimed.

"Monsieur le Comte could be soothed and sent away, or he could be retained to create a scandal, a scandal which his Majesty would dislike intensely."

There was a slight rustle of curtains at the door which opened onto the gallery.

"Most intensely," said Louis, stepping into the room.

"Your Majesty!" Fleury cried, and rose shakily.

Louis yawned and stretched like a lazy, well-fed cat. His eyes were just as bright, his face just as flushed, as Julie's; he was fully dressed but his clothing was in considerable disarray. Fleury, smiling faintly, concluded that the orgy begun in the forest and continued at the nearby chateau was still in progress.

"Forgive me, Sire," Fleury murmured, "for bursting in on your privacy, but Madame de Mailly did admit me and this, I always understood, is her own room." Louis, not entirely bereft of shame, fingered his crumpled ruffle uneasily. "Your Majesty heard everything I said?"

"I did."

"I rather thought," Julie chuckled, "that the King might find it interesting and enlightening."

Fleury bobbed his head. "I bow to your superior cleverness, Madame." He turned to Louis. "I apologize, Sire. It

78

was never my intention to interfere, merely to watch and—hum—guard your interests."

"To watch and guard your own, you mean!" Louis said hotly.

"But, Sire—"

"Madame de Mailly has told me everything."

"*Everything,* your Majesty?"

Louis scowled. Fleury was beginning to bore him. What an idiot the old man was not to see that all he wanted just now was to be left undisturbed with Julie.

He said: "Obviously you feared your power might be slipping from you and were taking steps to strengthen it by an understanding with a young woman you thought might win my—" He was about to say "love" but shyness of the word checked him. "My interest," he concluded lamely.

Fleury sighed elaborately. "Your Majesty, as usual, is clever enough to see through my little schemes."

"I admire your strategy but deplore your methods," Louis said, trying to look severe. "I am most displeased with you. Please withdraw."

Fleury bobbed his head and making a great display of his stiff-limbed old age tottered from the room. Julie waited till he had closed the door behind him, then she laughed merrily.

"*Very* amusing," Louis said dryly.

She became instantly contrite. "Your Majesty is really angry with me?"

Her negligée, apparently of its own accord, had fallen open. Louis' eyes fastened on the triangle formed by her large nipples and deep navel. He took her roughly in his arms and kissed her.

"If not with me, then with Cardinal Fleury?"

"A little," Louis admitted, "but it was all so unnecessary. I love him like a father. He gives me everything and asks nothing for himself. His life is frugal. All he craves is power. He has no wish for me to govern the country, even though I do call myself chief minister, and nor, thank heaven, have I! He has improved the financial position. I have all the money I want, and more. He has economized, he has eliminated graft, or most of it. He has avoided war and placed the currency on a stable basis."

"The cardinal is truly a great man," Julie said humbly.

"Yes," Louis agreed warmly, "and because of that and the love I have for him I want no feminine influence in state affairs."

"I have no interest in such things," Julie said quickly, and nor had she.

"Then not a word against Fleury, now or ever. I may be a little displeased with him, but his position is in no way shaken."

"And what of my position?" Julie asked softly.

"*Your* position?"

"Last night your Majesty led me to believe—"

"Last night," Louis broke in roughly, "I was angry with the Queen, and I was also a little drunk."

She sighed and turned from him. "I understand, and for a time I gave you a little distraction, but now . . ." She sighed again. "Ah well, I am happy to have served my King, if only for a fleeting moment, and after all—" she smiled brightly—"every woman at court will envy me." She bent and picked up the discarded shift. "Torn," she remarked absently. "I wonder when it happened. Last night, or just now, before Fleury came . . ."

Louis took her in his arms again. "You smell delightful. You distracted me last night, you distract me all over again now."

"And yet I am to be dismissed."

"What utter nonsense!"

He felt that he had never known her, that he had always known her, that she was the only woman in the world and a complete mystery. He knew that he must renew himself with her again and again and keep her with him always. It was a new and dizzy love, beside which the love he had felt for Marie was as dull and tepid as unfermented wine. He was no longer in awe of her and nervous, and he reflected that had he not been drunk last night the courage which he had needed to turn him from Marie would never have been his.

Julie smiled up at him. "So I am not to be dismissed."

"Tell me what position you want and you shall have it."

Her eyes twinkled. "It is customary for a woman who has been selected by the King to be granted private apartments. It is also customary for her to be openly recognized."

"I know all about historical precedent," he chuckled.

"Paradoxically it gives her respectability."

Louis roared with laughter. "How I love your sense of humor!"

"Open recognition shall be mine?"

"Anything you wish, but keep your nose out of state affairs."

"I have only one desire," Julie said gravely, her hot face against his breast. "It is my sole aim to give you rest when you feel weary, to distract you when you are harassed, to make you laugh when you feel bored."

"And to love me, sweetheart?"

"With all my heart and soul and body."

"And to be faithful?"

"Till the day I die."

"No, not that!" he cried. He remembered what he had said to Marie on their wedding night, and what she had said to him. "Anything but that!"

"If the thought of my faithfulness offends you . . ." she began.

"No, no, it pleases me."

"If you doubt my ability to be faithful," she said, still puzzled by his attitude, "the future will prove you wrong."

"Oh, to the devil with the future!" he cried. "The present is all that matters."

Fleury, still uncertain of the King's attitude, said unctuously: "What I did was foolish, Sire, but my motive had little connection with personal ambition. I merely wanted to keep a close watch on Madame de Mailly in order to ascertain that she was not being used by a political clique with aims contrary to the best interests of France."

"Liar!" Louis laughed.

Fleury smiled happily. "You propose to establish her, of course?"

"Of course, but as you know—" Louis was blushing faintly—"I have never done this sort of thing before."

"There is always a first time, Sire."

"Precisely, and for that reason I need your help. The wretched husband, for instance."

Fleury bobbed his head. "I sent for him. He is waiting in the anteroom now, but naturally I shall interview him alone. It would not be fitting for your Majesty to take a part in the —hum—negotiations."

"You dog!" Louis cried. "You think of everything."

Monsieur le Comte de Mailly minced forward as Fleury entered the anteroom. He was a man of middle height, handsome in a weak fashion, fussy, exquisitely dressed and, at the moment, somewhat plaintive.

"I am overwhelmed," he simpered.

"So for that matter am I," said Fleury.

Monsieur le Comte struck a dramatic pose. "'Pon my oath, I fail to see why so eminent an Eminence should wish to see *me*. 'He is much too old,' I tried to tell myself, and then I remembered an incident when I was sixteen. At Rouen, it was, and pon my soul *he* was well over eighty."

"Monsieur le Comte—" Fleury began.

But the fantastic creature was running on again. "At first I thought the lackey—your own valet, I believe, and a most handsome lad—said Tourney, and that I naturally understood. The dear fellow designs the most fascinating, the most *cunning* cravats. But of course your Eminence has no interest in cravats, only in *hats*, which is the one thing I utterly envy in a cardinal. Such a devastating shade of red."

"Monsieur," Fleury said wearily, "I have something more important to discuss than cravats."

"My dear Cardinal, to me there is *nothing* more important, except perhaps a smart, gaily painted carriage with a liveried postilion. Ah me, what it is to be poor and possess nothing better than an old broken down fiacre!"

"Monsieur," Fleury all but shouted, "I want to discuss your wife."

Monsieur le Comte raised his hands in fluttering horror. "Dear me, the girl is making a nuisance of herself at court? You propose to dismiss her and that will ruin me—but utterly! My income is barely enough for myself and—"

"Enough, for pity's sake!" Fleury said, and thrust his stick sharply into Monsieur le Comte's stomach. "Now listen to me, Monsieur, please!"

Speaking rapidly, and emphasizing his words with a continual poking of his stick, Fleury told the Comte that his wife was making anything but a nuisance of herself at court, that she had, in fact, become indispensable to the King. The man became instantly brisk and business-like and a look of cunning intelligence came to his eyes.

"How much?" he demanded.

Fleury blinked. "I beg your pardon?"

"A neglected husband naturally expects some small monetary compensation."

Fleury fixed the "neglected husband" with his rheumy old eyes. "You shall have a sum sufficiently large for you to acquire a new carriage and a liveried postilion as well as a whole wardrobe of devastating cravats."

Monsieur le Comte gave a little squeal of delight and flying at Fleury kissed him on both cheeks.

"Who am I," he declaimed, "to say 'no' to his Majesty the King!"

Marie, having dismissed her ladies and refused to receive her father, who had come she knew to commiserate with her, sat alone in her apartments at Versailles. A week had passed since the establishment of Julie de Mailly and the court was still twittering about it. The general opinion was that the King's action had been inevitable and that, after

83

unnecessary delay, he had proved himself not only a real man at last, but a real king in the grand tradition of his great-grandfather. She knew that Louis was pleased with this comment and ready to strut a little and thrust out his chest, but she suspected that he was also ashamed of what he had done, for he had steadily refused to meet her privately. As for the newly established mistress, Marie had neither seen her nor had speech with her since the night Louis had taken her to Rambouillet.

She felt utterly miserable. She had been like this for days and yesterday, overcome with grief and hardly knowing what she was doing, she had broken down in Madame de Ventadour's presence and confided in her fully. Restlessly she tried to read, and finding concentration impossible went to the nursery to play for a while with the children. The twins, Louise-Elizabeth and Anne-Henriette, were lively and pretty, and the baby Louis was showing excellent promise. Fearing that she might weep in front of them, she went back to her apartments and there, to her delight and horror, she found Louis waiting for her. After one swift, nervous glance at her he picked up the book she had dropped and pretended to look at it.

"If I intrude," he mumbled, "please forgive me."

"You are the King," she said simply.

He flung down the book and came to her side. He looked more handsome than ever in a new gold-embroidered coat. He fell on his knees and took her hands in his. Her heart missed a beat and her eyes softened.

"Poor Louis," she said, involuntarily.

He rose abruptly. "Bah! You still think I'm a child!"

He picked up the book again and turned his back on her. She waited, wondering what he would do or say next. Without moving he said:

"I want to talk to you. I have just come from Mamma Ventadour."

"You—? Oh, I see!"

"The old lady presumed, as usual, on the fact that she was once my guardian."

"I swear I begged her to say nothing!" Marie cried.

84

"She told me that. You confided in her extensively, it seems."

"I had to talk to somebody, Louis."

"Yes . . ." He was nervous and embarrassed and he felt wretched. He wished he had ignored the impulse to come straight from Mamma Ventadour to Marie. "My dear," he said, "Mamma Ventadour told me something I never knew."

"Yes?"

"The warning given by Pérard after the birth of Louis. Had I known, my attitude would have been less harsh."

"I thought Madame de Mailly had told you."

"Julie? In heaven's name why Julie?"

"I confided in her, Louis. I was afraid to tell you myself. Madame de Mailly offered to tell you. I demurred, but I felt sure she had told you that night you took her to Rambouillet."

Louis laughed shortly. "Apparently she played a trick on you, and on me too. She merely told me you preferred not to receive me, that your door was locked against me."

Marie looked at him in speechless horror. Louis laughed again, the pleasant laugh of an amused man. He turned, still laughing.

"It was clever of her," he said.

"You actually admire her for what she did?"

Louis shrugged. "She was in love with me. It was an opportunity and she took it."

Marie buried her head in her hands. She began to sob painfully, uncontrollably. Louis shuffled his feet and made an impatient gesture.

"I understand," he said, "that Pérard issued the same warning before you were carrying Louis."

"Yes."

Marie had told Madame de Ventadour about this too, but she had refrained from mentioning Fleury's offer. She might be submissive and docile, she might lack real spirit, but she was determined to deal with Fleury in her own way when the time came.

"You should have told me," Louis said indignantly.

"Should I?"

"You might think me selfish and heartless but I would have heeded the warning."

No longer weeping she said: "You have a kind heart. I shall always love you for that."

"Not so kind as you think," he laughed. "I intend to keep Julie at court. She—well, she is necessary. You see that, surely!"

"Do I . . ."

"I'm young, Marie, *young!*"

"Men are beasts," she said.

"Only a chaste woman would say a thing like that. The others have a better understanding. In any case, out of consideration for you . . . And I, as you say, being a beast . . ." He made an impatient gesture; he was, Marie saw, hotly confused and defiant. "Oh, do I have to put it into even plainer language?" he cried. He came to her again and knelt. "Forgive me," he said simply.

She touched his hair. It was crisp and curly. She remembered their wedding night. She saw him again as a boy of fifteen, graceful, slim, smooth-limbed, so shy and eager and so beautiful to look upon. She could feel him stroking her bare shoulder, whispering "Nice, nice . . ." Was that what he said to Julie de Mailly, or had he become that hateful thing, sophisticated?

"Louis," she said in a trembling voice, "Pérard made a mistake."

"He—? What do you mean, Marie?"

"He admitted it this morning," she went on, elaborating the lie, "He said he was pleased with my health. He feels sure, now, that I could bear a dozen children more easily than most women."

Louis rose. "God, what a farce!"

She reached up and put her arms round his neck.

"Surely it pleases you, Louis?"

"Why not? My ministers are always telling me that one son is not enough."

She leaned heavily against him. A chaste woman! she thought. As if any woman was chaste in the presence of the man she loved and desired. She felt the beating of his heart

86

quicken, but this failed to deceive her. Since Julie de Mailly had brought to life the lustful man that Louis really was, any woman, if she were young and ready, could quicken the beating of his heart. He kissed her forcefully, without a sign of his former boyish gentleness. Too ashamed of herself to respond with equal vigor, she submitted passively and he barely seemed to notice.

Afterwards, while he was dressing, he talked excitedly about the money he had lost to Richelieu and others at the card table. She asked him nervously if Julie de Mailly need remain at court, now. He looked at her for a brief moment and grinned impishly.

"She's just as necessary. A little more so, even."

He kissed her absently and humming a little tune went quickly from the room.

VIII

A FEW well-favored guests were assembling for one of the King's intimate and informal supper parties and Bachelier, list in hand, was striking out the names as the guests entered. The anteroom was crammed with hopeful courtiers and from these, when the last name was called out, arose little cries of disappointment. Presently Cardinal Fleury came hobbling into the room. *His* name was never on the list; *he* had entrée at all times. In the private dining hall, with its great tapestries depicting numerous royal hunts of the past, he went straight to the King's table, bobbing his head from side to side to the people at the smaller tables. He had been seated on Louis' left for several moments before he noticed that the Queen was present. He smiled at her, thought how dowdy she looked and uttered the hope that she was in good health.

Marie replied politely that she had never felt better. Three years had passed since the establishment of Julie de Mailly and Marie had recently recovered from her sixth pregnancy. Pérard, it seemed, had been wrong after all, or at all events, as he claimed warmly, the treatment he had prescribed was proving a lasting cure. A second son had been born, then two girls, Adelaide and Victoire. Louis in this respect, and despite the continued presence of Julie de Mailly, was an attentive husband--attentive, at least, until he knew that Marie was pregnant again, upon which he shunned her bed. "I have done my duty," he would say punctiliously.

Marie, hating his attitude, had long since learned the virtue of complete submission, and though she had once prayed for death she admitted readily now that she was greedy for life, greedy for more and more children, for in the nursery, as in her own apartments, she reigned supreme. She lived a secluded life and found ample satisfaction (or so she told herself) in domestic duties, religious observances and the reading of serious literature. She cared little, or so she told herself, what Louis did or how many mistresses he might establish. She had made this almost unprecedented appearance at the royal supper table because of the news which had come that day from Poland. Her father's usurper was dead and she was determined to interest Louis in the election of a new King of Poland.

"Your Majesty," Fleury was saying, not to her but to Louis, "should take life a little more quietly."

"At *my* age?" Louis laughed. "Oh nonsense!"

Marie was inclined to agree with Fleury, but Louis was his own master and might please himself. It was no concern of hers if he taxed his strength beyond normal endurance at nightlong parties and hunts at which he wore out both horses and dogs.

"Your Majesty," Fleury continued, "is becoming a constant source of anxiety to the physicians."

"Pooh! A set of old women!"

"The physicians fear a serious breakdown," Fleury persisted. "They—"

Louis' fists crashed on the table. "Enough, Fleury, enough!"

"Let us talk of something else," Marie interposed.

"Gladly," Louis said. "Fleury, for instance, and *his* health. He is eighty-five. Surely, at that age, state affairs would weigh heavily on any man. Long before that age I shall abdicate in favor of my son." His eyes twinkled but his manner grew serious. "Why not think about retirement, Fleury? You have a beautiful estate at Issy. You could spend the last years of your life in comfort there. You could even write your memoirs."

Fleury laughed uneasily. "Your Majesty is joking."

"Indeed no," Louis said warmly. "I love you too well to want to see you collapse under the weight of state affairs."

"I wish for nothing else, Sire!"

"I warn you, you old rogue, that unless you retire voluntarily I shall be forced, one of these days, to show you who is master here."

Fleury tried to steady the shaking of his hands. He was quivering all over and the hand that held his fork was white at the knuckles. "Julie de Mailly," he thought; "she's responsible for this." Marie remarked gently that Cardinal Eternity was in good health, with faculties unimpaired, and should be left in peace to do as he wished. Fleury gave her a baleful look and thought: "She wants something, otherwise she would never indulge in flattery." And then he remembered that he wanted something of her and a final more cheering thought slipped into his mind. "We shall make a bargain, she and I."

A sudden silence had fallen on the supper table. Louis cleared his throat quickly and Marie, following the direction of his gaze, gave a little start of surprise. Julie de Mailly, escorted by a solemn-faced Bachelier, was approaching the royal table. She, like Fleury, had undisputed entrée, but Louis, having warned her that Marie would be present tonight, was a little taken aback by her appearance. Marie rose quickly.

"With your Majesty's permission . . ." she said formally.

"Wait!" Louis cried. "I—my dear, I want you to remain. There's a new dish, another little invention of mine, I want you to try."

"I prefer to withdraw," Marie said.

He shrugged easily. "But good lord, my dear, you should have got over this fastidiousness by now!"

Marie turned on her heels and went to the door. Fleury, watching her, found himself admiring her quiet dignity. He had already made up his mind and presently, excusing himself on account of the lateness of the hour, he withdrew. He went straight to the Queen's apartments and Marie, thinking of Poland and her father, agreed at once to receive him.

Fleury began by expressing his sorrow at the needlessness of the embarrassment to which she had just been exposed and added, with a sly smile, that the time had come for them to make their peace, one with the other.

"At my age," he said unctuously, "a man sees the futility of enmity and seeks of people nothing but friendship."

Marie laughed dryly. "What do you want with me, a neglected wife? What real use can I be to you?" She laughed again. "You should approach Madame de Mailly, not me."

"I happen to think otherwise, your Majesty."

Marie smiled faintly. Julie de Mailly, obviously in league with him at first, had shunned him ever since her establishment. Undoubtedly his vanity had been hurt, was still hurt, and now Louis, urged no doubt by Julie, was suggesting retirement.

"Well?" she questioned, still smiling.

Fleury returned the smile. "Permit me to say in all kindness that your Majesty is allowing yourself to grow old and dowdy, chiefly because you have surrounded yourself with ladies-in-waiting who are elderly and dull. As the King himself has remarked, your Majesty's retinue somewhat mars the splendor of his court."

Marie held back her indignation and waited for him to continue.

"I suggest," he said softly, "the appointment of at least one young lady who is gay and vivacious. Oh, not for the King's sake, but for your own."

"You have such a person in mind?"

"Yes." Fleury looked down his nose. "Pauline de Nesle, a younger sister of—hum—Madame de Mailly."

Marie was puzzled. "But—"

"Naturally you would expect the suggestion to come from Madame de Mailly herself, but the little Pauline is pretty, and there are times when his Majesty grows bored with his —hum—present mistress. Indeed, Pauline, who is still in a convent, is eager to come to court and Madame de Mailly has forbidden it."

Marie rose angrily. "Are you suggesting that I, the Queen, should try to dispose of one royal mistress by bringing forward a new candidate?" Fleury nodded and then Marie, in spite of her anger, laughed loudly. "This is the craziest intrigue I ever heard of!"

"I am determined," Fleury chirped, "to remain at court until the day I die."

Marie saw clearly what was in his scheming mind. Pauline de Nesle would be brought to court by him, would be pushed forward by him, and being suitably grateful would see to it that he remained in power. She saw too, that Louis, being the sort of man he was, Julie de Mailly would certainly be followed some day by other favorites.

"Cardinal Fleury—" she began.

"Ah yes, Poland!" he interrupted her.

"Yes," she smiled. "Poland."

He shook his head. "I still want to keep France from the complications of a foreign war."

"But the situation has changed," Marie said eagerly. "Augustus is dead and a new king must be appointed. All I ask for my father is money, not an army."

"Money?" he said sharply. He knew what she meant. The Polish nobles were corrupt and open to bribery. A discreet distribution of money might well assure the re-election of Stanislas. "I have a reputation for meanness where money is concerned," he cackled.

Marie's voice hardened. "Would you rather I went to the King and told him how you forced me to bear another child when Pérard advised against it? How you made a promise then and broke it? How you made it *intending* to break it?"

Fleury rose shakily. Old age was slowing him down. His wits were losing their keenness. There were times, like the present moment, when he felt his courage failing him, and when it came to an argument he was not half so self-confident as in former years.

He bowed stiffly. "It seems we make a bargain, Madame."

Julie de Mailly, sitting in the coach with Louis, tried to smile with a brightness she by no means felt. An hour ago, at five o'clock, Louis had dragged her from her bed shouting boisterously that they were to leave at once for Rambouillet. She shuddered at the memory, for only two hours earlier, after having sat up all night at cards with him, she had fallen exhausted into bed.

"Your sister," Louis remarked, "is a pretty little thing."

Julie forced herself to keep on smiling. "One never thinks one's own sister pretty."

Pauline had been at court for a week and Louis, who rarely visited the Queen's apartments, had seen her yesterday for the first time. Julie was furious with Fleury and furious with the Queen, but there was nothing, she saw clearly, that she could do about it. She tried to change the subject by asking when the Queen's father would leave for Poland.

"Tomorrow," Louis said indifferently.

Fleury had brought up the matter at a council meeting, a meeting which Louis, chief minister in name only, had attended with his usual reluctance. It had been decided that Stanislas should leave in disguise for Poland, taking with him eleven million livres and a chest of jewelry for distribution among the wives of the Polish nobles.

"Her Majesty must be very pleased," Julie suggested.

Louis nodded. He was delighted that Marie, poor soul, should be pleased, but his interest was slight. He supposed that Fleury knew what he was doing—he must, since he was actually spending money on the venture—and that was that. He yawned and stretched.

"God! How tired I am!"

"No more tired than I," Julie complained.

"How plaintive we sound!" He slapped her knee and chuckled. "Do I set too swift a pace for you, sweetheart?"

"For me, and for yourself too, Louis."

"Oh nonsense!"

"But Louis—"

"Not another word! I see the warning in your eyes. 'Take things more quietly, the physicians are most anxious.' Pah!

If I listened to them they would have me on a couch all day and bleed and bleed me till I resembled a wilted lily. If I relax I shall grow fat and lose my good looks."

"Better that than an early grave."

He looked at her sourly. "I dislike you intensely this morning, Julie. I should have left you at Versailles."

She made no reply. Louis, as he was this morning, was a very different person from the romantic young king with whom she had fallen so deeply in love. Dissipation was leaving its mark. Beneath the curled and powdered wig, for he had now submitted to the prevailing fashion, his face was heavy, his skin discolored, his eyes weary. Almost always he was bored and she could do little to amuse him. He was, she feared, a man old long before his time.

"Yes," he said, giving her a brooding look, "your sister, whatever you might say to the contrary, is very pretty."

Bachelier stood before Cardinal Fleury and waited for permission to speak. He thought for a moment that the old man crouching over the fire, a blanket wrapped about his knees, was asleep, but a second glance showed him that the bleary eyes were surveying him with a placid interest.

"Well, you rogue?"

Bachelier made his report. The King had returned last night from Rambouillet in a bad temper. He had apparently quarrelled with Madame de Mailly. He told her to go to bed for a week and went to the Queen's apartments, where he insisted on taking supper. The new lady-in-waiting was present. He retired early and in good spirits. Pauline de Nesle, he said, was a delightful creature.

"And now, this morning," Bachelier rounded off, "his Majesty issues a formal invitation to Madame de Mailly. She is to take supper with him tonight, accompanied by the young sister. There will be no other guests. I was about to deliver the invitation when your Eminence sent for me."

Fleury's head shot up. He laughed his old man's laugh. When the fit of coughing had subsided and he had spat expertly into the fire he rose and reached for his stick.

"Bachelier, I have business myself with Madame de Mailly. You may safely leave me to deliver the invitation."

When Bachelier had withdrawn Fleury sent for his own valet.

"Barjac," he said, "take a message to the new lady-in-waiting, Mademoiselle de Nesle. Inform the young lady that she is to take supper with the King tonight in his private apartments. Swear her to secrecy. No one else must know, not even her sister, Madame de Mailly."

So great was Fleury's excitement that he grew alarmingly agitated as the day progressed, and he was trembling in every limb when, at supper time, he stood in the gloom of the King's anteroom, waiting for Pauline de Nesle to make her appearance. Promptly at the stated time she passed through the anteroom and with a pleasing self-assurance scratched at the inner door. She stood there waiting, slim and straight and young, until Bachelier opened the door and ushered her up the private stairway. Fleury, for all his years and the painful stiffness of his limbs, managed a little skip of delight. The comedy, he felt sure, was just beginning.

Louis was a little startled at the sight of Pauline de Nesle entering the room alone, but in a moment he was smiling at the easy grace of her curtsy. He murmured that her sister was no doubt delayed and would join them later.

"If that is her intention," Pauline said, in her high clear voice, "I knew nothing of it."

Louis frowned. "I invited both of you, my dear."

Pauline gave him a pert look. "Unless a mistake has been made the invitation was for me alone, Sire."

Louis scowled at Bachelier, who was hovering near the door. The fellow had blundered, though of course no very great harm had been done. He glanced swiftly at Pauline, so fresh and young in a white, gold-embroidered gown. Certainly no very great harm had been done!

"Where is Madame de Mailly?" Louis demanded of his valet.

"I assumed she was already here, your Majesty."

95

"Dolt!" Louis cried. "Bring her at once."

He turned to Pauline again and stared at her for a long moment. To have thought her pretty was wrong, but happily she had none of her sister's plainness. She appeared to have a slim, boyish figure, though one could never be certain of such a thing when a woman wore a hooped skirt. At all events she had a neat arrogant little head and all the self-confidence in the world. Her voice was certainly boyish and her eyes, holding his now, were disconcerting in the frankness of their scrutiny. How different, how delightfully different, she was from the rather mouse-like Julie!

"Would your Majesty prefer me to withdraw?" she asked.

"Not unless you want to!"

She smiled, and the sight of her white, even teeth, and the pinkness of the top gum, entranced him.

"His Majesty the King," she pronounced, "is an honorable gentleman. I am quite content to remain."

Despite the fact that where women were concerned Louis now considered himself a nonchalant, glibly spoken man of the world, he felt rather at a loss. He laughed nervously, checked the laugh and invited the girl to be seated. She arranged herself gracefully on a high-backed chair and waited. Still struggling with his irritating nervousness he told her he had ordered a magnificent supper, three kinds of soup, a whole lamb stuffed with tiny German sausages and a well-hung hare stewed in wine according to a recipe favored by his great-grandfather.

"And oysters too?" she asked.

"But of course!" he cried. "Ah, only remain at court and I shall teach you what it means to be discriminating in the choice of food and wine." He looked at her tenderly. "Life at court must seem a little strange to you after a convent."

"I am growing accustomed to the difference," she said complacently.

Bachelier came hurrying back to the room. Catching the look in Louis' eyes as he entered his own twinkled and he announced merrily that Madame de Mailly was not to be found. Louis saw the twinkle—*you dog, Bachelier!*—cleared his throat and affected an indignation he by no means felt.

"Then find her, idiot!"

He regretted the words soon after uttering them, but Bachelier was already hurrying away.

"This," he growled, "is rapidly becoming farcical."

Pauline rose. "Perhaps it really would be better if I withdrew, Sire."

Louis strode to her side. "Do I give the impression that I want you to withdraw?"

She pouted bewitchingly. "You give me the impression that for the sake of my honor—or could it be for the sake of your own?—you think we ought to be chaperoned."

Louis roared with laughter. Bored for days, he was no longer bored. He wondered if he was falling in love again and decided that if such were not the actual case it very soon would be.

"Your youth and high spirits are most refreshing," he said gallantly.

She made him a pretty little curtsy. "I have no intention of permitting myself to grow old and tired, like Julie."

Reminded of Julie, he frowned. Certainly she was permitting herself to grow old and tired. Not that she didn't try to be bright, poor creature; it was just that she was losing the zest for living that had so attracted him.

"Do you ride?" he asked boyishly. "Do you follow the hunt?" He laughed quickly before she could reply. "But as if that would be possible, hidden behind convent walls!"

"I never found the walls insurmountable," Pauline said gaily.

"Yet your sister thinks you amenable to direction and utterly demure."

"Poor, poor Julie!"

Bachelier entered the room once more, but slowly, with a sorrowful look in his eyes.

"Madame de Mailly has been found," he announced. "She will join your Majesty in a few moments."

"Damnation!" Louis exploded.

Bachelier made a wry face. "What a great idiot I am, Sire."

Louis chuckled. He glanced questioningly at Pauline. She smiled guilelessly, her lips slightly apart, the pinkness of the

97

top gum disturbingly visible. She looked far too knowledg-able to be what she undoubtedly was, a virgin. He felt the blood leap in veins, and told himself lyrically that he was like a young tree in the spring with the sap rising. He was in love again, of that he was sure. No, no, not *again*. For the first time in his life, dizzily, intoxicatingly. He fixed his valet with a stern eye.

"His Majesty," Bachelier murmured, "has changed his mind. His Majesty now intends to retire early."

"As early as possible, you dog!" Louis shouted. "Now be off with you. Station yourself at the bottom door. See that no one enters."

Bachelier bowed and withdrew. Down in the anteroom he found Cardinal Fleury hobbling forward from the shadows.

"Things are progressing well?" Fleury asked.

"Excellently, your Eminence."

"The King is reconciled, then, to the absence of Madame de Mailly?"

A burst of laughter from above reached their ears.

"There is your answer," Bachelier smirked.

IX

WITH a little whoop of sheer joy Pauline de Nesle flung herself into her room at Versailles. Gathering her riding habit up to her knees she danced round the room. Finally she tossed her hat into a corner, her riding whip into another and threw herself face down on the bed. She pretended not to have seen her sister Julie who, grim of countenance, was sitting waiting in a chair. Julie rose from the chair and stood over the bed. She was quivering with anger.

"Well?" she demanded.

"Well . . . what?" Pauline said cheekily.

"Where have you been all this time? Come, answer me!"

Pauline turned and sat up. She made an attractive, tomboyish picture in her crumpled, russet-colored riding habit.

"To Rambouillet with the King," she said gaily.

"When did you leave Versailles?"

"Six this morning, if it's any concern of yours."

"You were with the King from supper time last night till then?"

"Possibly, possibly."

Julie shook the girl by the shoulders. "Answer me, you wretched child, answer me!"

Pauline freed herself and sprang from the bed. Julie was

at liberty to think what she pleased. The actual truth was that the King had indeed retired early but, to his intense disappointment, alone. A kiss, yes; a hasty, fumbling embrace, but no more. Pauline was much too wise for that, and not being in love with him the refusal had been easy.

"I left his Majesty at eleven," she said.

"Liar! I was in the anteroom till twelve."

"I left by the other entrance."

Julie looked at her sister tragically. "Oh Pauline, what in the world has come over you? This defiant attitude, your evident delight in my despair . . . You used to be so gentle, so demure."

"Much chance I had of being anything else."

"I ought never to have let you come to court. The best thing I can do is send you back to the convent."

"Pooh! The King would never permit it."

"His Majesty will do whatever I say."

"You really believe that—*now?*"

Julie flew at her sister and shook her again. Pauline reached out for her hair. In the struggle that followed both fell to the floor, Julie screaming, Pauline roaring with laughter.

"Ladies! Ladies!" an old voice reproved.

Julie sprang to her feet and faced Cardinal Fleury.

"*You!*" she spat, and panting ran from the room.

Pauline got to her feet and chuckled. "My sister is a little distraught."

"And small wonder," Fleury murmured, "after last night."

Pauline looked at him coolly. "What do *you* know of last night?"

"A little, but not everything. However, if I were a gambling man I would wager a thousand livres that you are no longer the chaste young woman who left the convent so short a time ago."

"You would lose your money."

He looked at her in admiration. "My dear, I compliment you on your tactics." He went to a chair and eased himself gently into it. "You know, of course, that it was I who brought you to court."

"Yes, and I thank you for it."

"You also know that it was I who made your supper with the King possible?"

"How could I?"

Fleury told her briefly what he had done. Pauline laughed merrily and remarked that it was the first time she had heard of a priest playing the role of a pimp. He laughed too and reminded her that as far as state affairs were concerned he was also a man of the world. He went on to tell her that the King was beginning to insist on his retirement and that her sister was partly, if not wholly, responsible.

"And so you want her replaced," Pauline said, "by someone who will make it her business to change the King's mind."

"Precisely."

Grandly Pauline said: "Cardinal Fleury, I give you my word that if I ever have the power to influence the King you shall remain at court for the rest of your life." She threw back her head and laughed. "Poor Julie, and poor King Louis. If I were a gambling woman I would wager a thousand livres that she is with him now, storming and weeping!"

But Julie was neither storming nor weeping. She had intended doing the former and had feared that the latter would be inevitable, but on her way to the King's apartments a possible solution to her problem had occurred to her and she was now in a calmer frame of mind.

She found Louis a little shame-faced.

"Whatever it is you want," he said hastily, "pray be brief. I have—er—ah yes! A council meeting in a few minutes."

She found it impossible not to smile. "I want to talk about my sister."

Louis jumped. "Er—Pauline?"

"Or rather, I want to discuss her marriage."

Louis jumped again, in a quite different manner. He stared at Julie.

"Her—*what*?" he gasped.

"Surely," she said calmly, "you agree that it is time she married."

Louis sighed gently and felt vastly relieved. So there was not to be a scene, after all. It almost seemed that Julie knew nothing of last night and the agreeable little jaunt to Rambouillet this morning. Nevertheless, marriage was the last thing he wanted for Pauline until he had possessed her himself.

"It is a royal precedent," Julie continued, "that a lady-in-waiting should be a married woman."

"Precedents! Must we always be ruled by precedents!" he raged.

"I merely thought," Julie went on, still calmly, "that you might give me some help in the matter. I naturally want Pauline to make a good match. Of course, if you prefer not to be troubled by this domestic matter I could always apply to the Queen."

"That," Louis said hastily, "will not be necessary. I shall give the matter my personal attention—er—later."

"Later might mean never."

"Really," he exploded, "this haste has an almost indecent flavor!" Suddenly he remembered Julie's husband and the ease with which he had been "bought off". This made him feel happier. "Oh well, since your heart appears to be set on it . . ."

"Thank you," she said.

Julie was thinking of her husband too. It made her fear that there was a certain weakness in her scheme. A husband was hardly an obstacle when a king desired a woman.

"Have you anyone in mind?" Louis asked.

"Yes. The son of the Marquis de Fontenelle. Our families have been friendly for generations."

Louis frowned. "Their estates are in Provence. They rarely come to court."

"True," she admitted innocently, "but a good match."

He saw what was in her mind and gave her a smile of grudging admiration. Dismissing her abruptly he went in search of Fleury. He told the Cardinal what Julie had said and what he suspected her of planning. Smiling boyishly he added that since Fleury always knew everything that went on at court he must now be aware of his more than casual interest in the entrancing Mademoiselle de Nesle. Fleury bobbed his head and smiled.

"But Julie," Louis said sternly, "must be prevented from going to the Queen. I have no wish—no wish *yet*, that is—to see Pauline married."

Fleury, hugely amused, recollected that her Majesty was a party to the setting up of Pauline de Nesle, but thought it better to keep this fact from the King. An immediate marriage, he murmured, would be most convenient from every point of view.

"What the devil do you mean by that?" Louis demanded.

"It would give the young lady respectability. The lords and ladies of the court are rarely kind to a young woman of—hum—loose morals who remains here unmarried."

"Hypocrites!" Louis thundered.

"In addition, Sire, marriage would make the husband entirely responsible in the event, the quite likely event, of your growing tired of her."

Louis looked troubled. "You think I might tire of her? You really think that, Fleury?" Fleury smiled impassively. "But I—damn it all, I'm in love with her! Dizzily, intoxicatingly!"

"In that case, Sire, I predict an early appearance of the reactionary boredom."

Louis scowled like a child, but in the end he was obliged to laugh and agree. He was young, vigorous, ardent: no woman living could satisfy him forever.

"The man," Fleury suggested, "could be selected carefully. He could be brought from a great distance, married to the young lady and sent away again—alone."

"You old fox!" Louis chortled, and mentioned the son of the Marquis de Fontenelle.

Fleury shook his head. "No, no, a strong-minded race, the Fontenelles. We must choose a man who will give us no trouble."

"Not *we*, Fleury, but *you*. I leave the whole thing in your most capable hands."

Fleury bowed. "I shall attend to the matter at once."

Julie and Pauline, each summoned to the King's apartments, met in the anteroom and were alone together for a few moments before Bachelier announced them. As they waited Fleury passed through the room with a strange young man, plainly dressed and grave of countenance. Julie, playing with the fan that Louis had given her for her last birthday, repressed a chuckle as she watched the young man pass up the private stairway with Fleury.

Over a week had passed since Pauline's supper tete-a-tete with the King. During this time he had treated Julie coolly, almost completely ignoring her, and had taken Pauline to Rambouillet three times. The whole court was gossiping and sniggering and everybody, sure that Pauline de Nesle was already the King's mistress, was waiting impatiently for the announcement of her official establishment. Thinking of this now Pauline smiled lazily. Having played her hand skilfully she was still, as Fleury would put it, a chaste young lady.

Bachelier appeared, nodded significantly, and led Julie and Pauline up the stairs. They found a smiling Louis lounging against a table. Fleury was seated impassively in an easy chair and the strange young man was standing respectfully at his side.

"My dear," said Louis, addressing himself to Julie, "your wishes have been respected. A husband has been found for the little Pauline."

Julie smiled happily while Pauline, utterly horrified, mouthed the word "Husband!"

Louis' eyes twinkled. "Surely, Mademoiselle, you find nothing surprising in that. After all, young ladies of your age and station—"

"But your Majesty gave me to understand—" Pauline cried, "led me to imagine—!"

"Hold your tongue, Pauline!" Julie said curtly.

Louis turned courteously to the strange young man who, prodded by Fleury's stick, stepped solemnly forward.

"Monsieur le Comte," Louis said, "permit me to present your future wife, Mademoiselle Pauline de Nesle." He beamed on Pauline. "My dear, permit me to present your future husband, Monsieur le Comte de Vintimille."

Pauline, now watchfully on her guard, pouted delight-fully.

"Your Majesty might have found me at least a marquis."

"He comes from La Vendée," Louis continued. "An ob-scure family, I admit, but an excellent one and very loyal."

"But La Vendée is miles from Versailles!" Pauline said. She was losing control again; there was an edge to her boyish voice and her lips were trembling. "La Vendée is the other side of the world!"

"The climate is quite good and the scenery exquisite," Julie murmured.

Pauline turned on her with a little cry of rage. "Oh hold your silly tongue! I hate you, I hate you!" She shot Fleury a venomous glance. "And you, too, Cardinal Fleury. I won't marry this person! I refuse, I refuse!"

Louis looked at her with pleasure. She was delightful when she was in a temper. "This," he said mildly, "is a royal command. We have selected you a husband. You will submit to our wishes and marry him. You should feel honored at our interest and express a suitable gratitude."

"Gratitude!" she spat.

Louis chuckled. "Complete arrangements have been made. The ceremony, a simple one, will take place quietly in the royal chapel."

"Within the hour," Fleury remarked.

Louis indicated that the interview was at an end. Bache-lier was called, and he and Julie led a white-faced, wild-eyed Pauline from the royal presence. Louis turned with a smile to the Comte de Vintimille and asked him what he thought of the wife that had been chosen for him.

"She seems most charming," the young man said politely.

Louis agreed. "Cardinal Fleury has acquainted you with all the details of the marriage?"

The young man bowed.

"He has a thorough grasp of all that is expected of him," Fleury supplemented.

"But I must say," Louis smiled, "that by the look of his face he finds the arrangement a little unusual."

The young man bowed again.

105

"My family," he said, placing a hand on his sword, "is renowned for its loyalty. I recognize my duty and am eager to perform it meticulously."

"If I were in your position, Monsieur," Louis laughed, "I should be prepared to do anything but my duty. However, things being as they are I can only thank heaven that I am not, and be suitably grateful that there are still such families in France as yours." He extended his hand with an easy gesture. "You may kiss our hand, Monsieur."

The marriage ceremony had been performed. The young husband had retired mysteriously with Fleury, Pauline, silent and angry, had been sent to her room to pack her trunks and for the moment Julie, a quietly triumphant Julie, was alone with Louis.

"What a handsome couple they make," she remarked.

Louis smothered a yawn. "Very, my dear, very."

"Pauline should consider herself fortunate," she went on happily. "For the young man's sake as well as her own let us hope she will soon grow reconciled."

"To what?" Louis demanded.

"To living so far away as La Vendée."

"Oh, *that!*" Louis said, and found it impossible to suppress the laughter that welled up in him.

Julie felt a stab of uneasiness. "Is anything the matter, Louis?"

He looked at her broodingly. "This marriage, you know, was merely expedient. It was necessary for Mademoiselle de Nesle to become Madame de Vintimille before my plans for her could be brought to a satisfactory conclusion."

"Your *plans* for her?" Julie said faintly.

"My poor Julie, in urging me to arrange a marriage for her you have failed, as surely you must now suspect, to achieve your intended object."

Quick tears pricked Julie's eyes. "Are you dismissing me?"

Louis avoided her eyes. "Obviously."

"But what am I to do? Where am I to go?"

"You have a husband, my dear, but if you wish you may remain quietly—*quietly,* mind you—at Versailles."

"That would be humiliating," she cried hotly. "I would prefer to go to Choisy."

"Why Choisy?"

"Your Majesty was giving me a house there. Only yesterday the decorators reported that it was ready."

Louis smiled pleasantly. "I intend the house at Choisy to be a wedding present for Pauline. But enough," he added briskly. "Let us say goodbye and be done with it. To linger over this parting would only make it painful for both of us."

"So your Majesty might find it painful! That is excellent!"

He took her hands quickly in his.

"My dear," he said contritely, "be sensible and try to forget me. King I might be, but I often suspect, when I have the courage to think of it, that as a man I am a most unworthy person." Tears were flowing down her cheeks now and her nose, making her an altogether unlovely sight, was pinched and red. Louis began to feel angry with her and with himself. "That is an admission I never made before," he concluded roughly, "and will try never to make again. Forget me, Julie, and find a little pity in your heart for your sister."

Pauline was bending over a still-empty trunk when Louis entered her room. She ignored him as he strode jauntily to the window. For a moment he looked casually round the room and chuckled at the thought that, too concerned before with other matters, he had failed to notice its flowered velvet decorations and the gay abandonment of the nymphs and satyrs on the frieze. He glanced out of the window, smiled at something he saw and moved to Pauline's side. He bowed elaborately.

"Madame la Comtesse de Vintimille."

Pauline rose and stared at him defiantly.

"What," he cried, "no tears?"

She tossed her head. "I may be hurt and disappointed, but never in my life have I had use for tears."

"Ah, splendid, splendid! When the day comes for your own dismissal the parting will be easy."

Pauline looked puzzled. "Surely that day has come now."

Louis took her by the arm and dragged her to the window. He told her to look down into the courtyard. There she saw a coach. Cardinal Fleury and her husband were standing near it. As she watched the Comte de Vintimille leaped into the coach and the horses were whipped into motion.

"But—he's leaving, and alone!" she cried.

"So he is."

"For—for La Vendée?"

"Where else, sweetheart?"

"But *alone!*"

"Most certainly alone. You need never see him again unless you wish it. Assuredly this is your wedding day but the man in your bed tonight will not be your husband."

Mastering her excitement Pauline evaded him neatly as he made to embrace her.

"You spoke just now of my dismissal," she said.

"Pooh! A matter for the future. For all we know you may remain at court for the rest of your life."

"That is what I intend, or not at all."

And then, evading him again, she stated her terms. She was ambitious. She would never be content, like her sister Julie, to remain in the background, a mere plaything. She wanted a hand in state affairs.

"Fleury would never permit it," Louis scowled.

"Then the cardinal must retire."

"Pah!" Louis cried, and accepted her terms without further argument.

She smiled happily and offered no resistance when, for a third time, he made to embrace her. As he kissed her she thought: "The reign of Cardinal Fleury is at an end; the King has danced to a man's tune far too long and shall now dance to a woman's." Louis kissed her again and complained boyishly that tonight was several hours away. Pauline laughed and indicated that as far as she was concerned it was quite unnecessary to wait.

"You are the King," she said. "Your will is law."

X

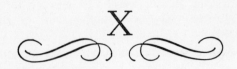

LOUIS, waiting for Richelieu to present himself, was studying his face in a silver-mounted hand-mirror. He shuddered in mock horror at what he saw. "A rake, a dissipated rake," he told himself gaily. Not yet thirty, he was the father of eight living children, for of the ten that Marie had given birth to another, the second boy, had died. Seven girls, he thought, and only one boy, but little Louis, he was glad to say, was a healthy child. Six months ago, after the birth of the last girl, he had told Marie that if she was as tired of carrying children as he was of seeing her grow big and ugly while doing so, he would be glad to tell his ministers that he and the Queen had done their duty for the last time.

A light scratching at the door brought a smile of pleasure to his face. Richelieu at last! Richelieu, the most amiable, the most amusing, of his many boon companions. "Enter!" he cried, but it was Marie, not Richelieu, who opened the door.

"Oh, you, my dear," he said. "Well, providing you neither try to save my soul nor talk about your father you may as well remain till Richelieu comes."

Marie smiled calmly and took the chair he offered her.

"I long ago gave up any hope I had," she said, "of trying to save your soul."

"Thank heaven for that!" Louis laughed.

"Nevertheless," she said seriously, "your refusal to take the sacraments is giving many people grave concern."

"I am much too great a sinner," he said airily, "but I still give my confessor occasional employment, so be content with that."

Marie shrugged and refrained from embarking on an argument. She was living a more secluded life than ever these days. Her mornings were generally given to prayer and serious reading, her afternoons to sedate music and her evenings to embroidery and a discussion of the morning's reading with her ladies. She went to mass daily, made a simple *toilette* at midday and dined quietly with a few members of her own household. Occasionally Louis took a punctilious supper with her, from which, she knew, he was always glad to escape. Occasionally, too, he asked her if she was happy, to which she always replied that happiness being a state of mind, a compromise with life as one was forced by circumstances to live it, she believed that she was.

Louis was looking at her absently. She wore a gray silk dress, very neat, very precise, and a black lace cap which covered her faded hair. Her only jewelry was an enamel broach set in gold. He thought she looked more like an old maid than the mother of many children.

"What shall we talk about?" he asked fretfully.

"You forbade it, but I want to talk about my father."

"You need have no further anxiety on his behalf," he told her. "We shall make peace with Austria and your father shall be the nominal ruler of Lorraine."

"Thank you, Louis," she said simply.

"Thank Fleury, not me."

"Fleury?" she said, in surprise.

"The old rogue may still be in retirement, but he sends occasional advice from Issy."

"Ah, I understand."

She wondered if her father would be content with Lorraine and concluded that he, too, must compromise with life as one was forced by circumstances to live it. Almost from the first things had gone wrong in Poland. The Polish nobles had re-elected him, certainly, but a Russian army, advancing on Warsaw, had forced him to escape to Danzig. Later he had been obliged to flee into Prussia, where he had been given shelter, and then, with a new usurper on the Polish throne, France had become involved in a war with Austria. As a result of this France had annexed Lorraine.

There was a scratching at the door. Louis, vastly relieved, shouted a hearty "Enter!" Marie remained long enough to exchange civilities with the elegant Richelieu who, she knew, was eager to make himself as powerful as his great-uncle, the legendary Cardinal Richelieu. Great soldier that he was, his moral looseness horrified her, but she liked him a little, if only because he was bold enough on occasion to speak scathingly of Pauline de Vintimille's interference in state affairs.

Withdrawing from Louis' apartments she smiled at a passing thought. How much longer, she asked herself, would Madame la Comtesse retain her position?

Pauline and Louis were driving along the Rambouillet road in an open carriage and Louis, glad to escape from Versailles, was in the best of spirits. Presently he began to sing a popular song the words of which, composed by a court wit, were both daring and suggestive. They told a racy story of the fall of Julie de Mailly, the sudden elevation of Pauline and the reluctant retirement of Cardinal Eternity. Pauline thought of her sister with pity. Julie was still at court, haunting the passages of Versailles like a gray unhappy ghost, her life brightened only on the rare occasions that Louis (out of pity, he assured Pauline) took supper with her and permitted her (an act of kindness merely) to spend the night with him. Louis finished the song with a roar.

"How fortunate that I have a sense of humor!" he laughed.

"You seem to be in the best of moods today," Pauline remarked.

"Today, sweetheart, I love the whole world."

She smiled her satisfaction. Though from time to time the inevitable fits of boredom overtook him they were less pronounced since her establishment than ever before, and he still insisted that he was in love for the first and only time in his life. She had every intention of keeping him like that, not by bowing to his smallest whim and exhibiting a dog-like devotion, but by remaining a complete individual.

There was only one way, she had decided at the beginning, to hold the interest of a man as lusty and demanding as Louis, and that was to remain tantalizingly aloof on every possible occasion, thus making the eventual strategic surrender seem like the beginning of an exciting new *affaire*. As a result he was her willing slave and called her "the woman of a thousand charms." As for being in love herself, she doubted if she ever would be with any man. She was quite heartwhole. The most she felt for Louis was a maternal affection, but she was determined to be wiser than the Queen and give not the slightest hint of it.

From the first she had felt her way cautiously. True, Louis had promised her a hand in state affairs, had agreed that Cardinal Fleury was too old to remain at court, but she had judged it safer to consolidate her position before pressing her ambition too far.

"How serious you look," Louis remarked.

"Forgive me," she smiled. "Seriousness, at the court of his Most Christian Majesty, is of course an unforgivable sin."

He laughed and kissed her lightly on the cheek. Seriousness, providing it were not taken too far, became her admirably. She had grown up in the last few months, matured delightfully. No longer a tomboy, but capable still of a fetching liveliness, she had become an elegant, graceful woman, queenly, almost, in a way that Marie, poor woman, would never be. She was indeed a credit to him and he swelled with pride at the thought of what his love had done for her.

"Come," he said indulgently, "tell me about these deep, deep thoughts of yours. I do admit that a little seriousness in a woman is as necessary as salt in a rabbit pie."

"I was thinking about France," she said. "I want to see her great again, and her people happy and respected. Before I came to Versailles, while I was still in the convent, I used to dream of the day when I might be in a position to do something for my country."

"A second Joan of Arc!" he teased.

Smiling disarmingly she said: "The King is a lazy, pleasure-seeking fellow. Therefore the greatest instrument of his pleasure who, in spite of being a woman, is a patriot at heart, must play the part of his deputy."

She saw the well-known look of desire darken his eyes.

"You should be content to remain just that," he said thickly, "the greatest instrument of his pleasure."

She placed a hand lightly on his knee. "Why else are we going to Rambouillet?"

"God, you drive me crazy!" he cried. "Must we wait, Pauline? Why not a quiet hour in the forest first?"

"There was rain last night. The grass is sure to be quite damp."

"As if I cared about that!"

"You might catch a fever."

"Sweetheart, I am devoured by one as it is!"

She slipped from his reaching arms. "Be serious for one moment more, Louis."

"The devil is in you today, I quite see that!"

"What I want," she went on, "is an official position. Richelieu and others complain of my interference. Richelieu is in league with Cardinal Fleury; he visits him often at Issy. An official position would silence my enemies."

"What do you mean by an official position?" Louis demanded.

"I—well—I would suggest—"

"Wait!" Louis interrupted. "I believe you have a sincere love for your country, but *how* sincere? If I asked you to choose between me, the man and the King, and these rather masculine ambitions of yours, how would you choose?"

"That," she replied promptly, "would be setting up a struggle between my heart and my head, between the woman who loves you and the patriot who loves France. Have pity on me, Sire. Please refrain from asking me to make so difficult a choice."

Louis was deeply moved. "What a strange creature you are. I never knew a woman like you. Most women would try to gain their way by feminine wiles. By flattery or love-making or, when all else failed, a storm of tears. *You* have a different method; *you* follow a bolder course."

"Does it displease you?"

"'Pon my oath, no! It endears you to me all the more. And yet, it appears that if I insisted on your making a choice, you would reject me and choose France."

"No, Sire, no!" Pauline cried, a suitable note of passion in her voice. "If I were forced to make a choice I would be as weak as any woman."

"In that case," he cried gaily, "a compromise is indicated. You shall have me and my country too."

"Then grant me a seat on your Majesty's privy council," she said promptly.

Louis slapped his thighs and roared with laughter. "Imagine the consternation among my ministers if I did that."

"And think of the amusement it would give you!"

"Yes!" he cried, but he had a sobering thought. "You might grow bossy, like the Duc de Bourbon's mistress. You shall have all the power you desire, but no official appointment."

Pauline masked her disappointment. "How foolish of people to claim that the King is weak."

"Weak, perhaps, in the hands of a woman," Louis smiled.

"Ah, but in her arms," she said softly, "strong, always strong."

"By heaven, yes!" They were passing through a forest glade. He half-rose in his seat and ordered the carriage to be stopped. "Who cares if the grass *is* damp? We'll never feel it, I vow!"

He leaped from the carriage and waited to help her down. She held back for a moment, a reflective smile on her face.

"I should dearly love to see your ministers' faces," she laughed, "if I took my seat at the council table."

"And so you shall, confound you!" Louis cried.

Whether or not the grass had been damp, Louis complained next day of cold shivers down his back. Later in the day Richelieu, returning from a visit to Cardinal Fleury, found the palace in an uproar. The King, he was told, had been taken suddenly ill. He hastened to the royal apartments and pushing roughly through the crowd in the anteroom came face to face with Pauline and the Secretary of State, Phélippeaux de Maurepas.

"The King has driven himself too hard for years," Maurepas was complaining. "He has little reserve, almost no resistance. Even a slight fever might kill him."

Richelieu moved away. He learned that the surgeon and some of the physicians were with the King, that no one, not even Pauline de Vintimille, had been permitted to see him. Presently, as Richelieu waited, Peyronie came solemnly into the anteroom. A silence fell. All eyes were centered on Peyronie.

"His Majesty has been bled," he announced, "but—"

A little cry of horror interrupted him. It was well known that the King, always unreasonable in such matters, hated to be bled and invariably fought against it. Therefore his Majesty's condition, everybody felt sure, was very grave indeed. Silence fell again.

"The King," Peyronie continued, "is suffering a high fever and it is my solemn duty to warn the court that his Majesty's condition is extremely serious."

Louis was terrified.

With his elbows thrust deep in the pillow he was half-sitting, half-lying on the royal bed. The room was in darkness. Peyronie, he knew, was sitting close at hand, for he

116

could hear the man's steady breathing. The only other sound came from the anteroom where a low murmur of voices rose and fell and rose again. They were waiting for him to die. Yes, that was it, waiting for him to die!

A cold and clammy perspiration covered his whole body. Groaning, he pulled the blankets up to his ears. He turned on his side, drew up his knees and tried to master the terror that possessed him. He was much too young to die, and much too sinful. "Only let me live," he prayed, "and I swear I shall be a better king."

Quite suddenly he remembered being led, at the age of five, to the death bed of his great-grandfather, the Sun King. The memory was so vivid that the words of the dying king echoed in his ears. *You must think of your people always and endeavor to promote their interests before your own. Your own must be placed last, not first, as so often happens where a king is concerned.* Louis shuddered. "Where *I* have been concerned, heaven pity me!" He had treated his wife shamefully; he had been selfish and vain; he had thought of a woman only in relation to the pleasure her body might give him. Oh yes, he was much too sinful to die! And above and beyond all this he had never really considered his people. He had left state affairs to others, asking only one thing, that money should be found for his pleasure, his selfish pleasure.

"Only let me live," he prayed again, "and I swear I'll be a better king, a *real* king!"

XI

"AN AMAZING recovery," Peyronie commented.

"A miracle, a blessed miracle!" Louis cried devoutly.

The night, the horror-ridden night, had passed. A flat ray of yellow sunshine streamed through the window and touched the foot of the bed. Louis sat up and felt that he must pinch himself to make absolutely sure that he was really alive.

"If I may say so," Peyronie joked, "your Majesty has the constitution of an ox. However, unless greater care is taken in future, I—"

"In future," Louis cried, "I shall live the frugal life of a hermit." Peyronie's brows shot up in amusement. "At least," Louis amended, "I shall try my best. I shall eat less, drink less. I shall even endeavor to invent some new dishes that are health-giving as well as merely tasty. I shall go to bed earlier. I—" He remembered his resolve to be a better king, a real king. "I shall take my duties as chief minister with complete seriousness." A murmur from the anteroom caught his ears. "The court is still in attendance, Peyronie?"

"An all-night vigil has been kept, your Majesty."

"Even by the Queen?"

"Well—no, your Majesty."

Louis was disappointed. "Ah well, one can scarcely blame her, poor soul. By Madame la Comtesse, of course?"

"Madame de Vintimille retired at midnight, but one of her maids remained."

Louis was more than disappointed.

"I have done nothing to hurt *her*," he said indignantly. A sudden and most exciting idea occurred to him. "Peyronie, I want you to do something for me!"

Peyronie bowed. "Anything I can, Sire, gladly."

"Go to the anteroom. Tell the court that my condition is extremely serious, that you can hold out no hope for my recovery."

"If you insist, Sire, but I fail to understand—"

"I want to make an experiment," Louis chuckled. "Since Fleury retired there has been nothing but intrigue at court. I want to see what will happen if the various factions believe that I am about to die. Oblige me, please, by keeping your counsel and co-operating with me in this. It might prove most amusing, Peyronie."

"But possibly dangerous to your Majesty's peace of mind," Peyronie said gravely. "Such an experiment might put human nature to too great a test."

"It might, but I shall at least discover who are my enemies and who my true friends. Make the announcement at once, Peyronie. Come, come, man, at once!"

"We must be brave, Madame," Maurepas said.

Pauline looked at him impatiently. His manner suggested that the only consideration was the approaching death of the King, whereas—

"But we must also keep our heads," he added.

She smiled her relief. She had almost made a mistake. Maurepas was not the figure of fun she had often believed, in spite of his mincing attitude and the impression he gave of femininity. All that, she began to see now, was sheer affectation. Underneath he was hard and ruthless and no more sentimental than she was. Not that she would not be grieved by the death of Louis, but the loss of her power would grieve her a great deal more. And it was obviously the same with Maurepas who, a Secretary of State since the age of fifteen, had been at court over twenty years, during which time not even Cardinal Fleury, who disliked him, had been able to dislodge him.

"Even if his Majesty lives," Maurepas went on thoughtfully, "the illness will be a long one. Certain important decisions will have to be made and nobody, *at present*, holds sufficient authority. Of course, if Cardinal Fleury were here—"

"But he's not, thank heaven!"

"He might have been sent for, Madame."

"By the King?"

"No, by Richelieu, who has sent a messenger to Issy. It is only a question of time, I feel sure, before Fleury pays us a visit."

"Then we must act quickly!" Pauline cried, deeply alarmed.

"We need either a deputy chief minister or a regent, Madame."

"A regent?"

"When a king is desperately ill a regency is often proclaimed, and if his Majesty dies, the Dauphin being too young to rule, a Regent will certainly be necessary."

Pauline frowned. The Duc d'Orleans, son of the former Regent, would be the obvious choice, and Orleans, the sort of young man to take such an office seriously, had never been sympathetic towards her. Orleans if the King died; quite possibly Fleury if he lived. It was anything but a pleasant prospect, whichever way you looked at it. And then, as hopelessness was getting the better of her, a daring yet possible solution flashed through her mind and took complete control of her imagination.

Maurepas smiled at the change of her expression. "You have an idea, Madame?"

Pauline nodded vigorously, turned on her heels and left him without a word.

Having sent word with one of her ladies that she had no wish to receive anyone, still less Madame de Vintimille, Marie looked up with a start of surprise and indignation when Pauline came swiftly into the room, curtsied and without waiting for permission to speak said quickly:

"Forgive this unwarranted intrusion, your Majesty, but my business is urgent."

"Unwarranted intrusion is certainly the way to describe your entry," Marie said quietly. "As for your business being urgent, what possible business can I have with you, however urgent you might consider it?"

Pauline bit her lip. She had been prepared for a rebuff but not one so cold and shattering as this. Dowdy as the Queen looked in her plain gray dress, her natural dignity was certainly undeniable. Ignoring Pauline she bent industriously over the tapestry on which she had been working. Pauline gave her an angry look, but compromising with her pride she spoke in a low, beseeching voice.

"In all humility I beg your Majesty to hear me."

Marie continued to ignore her. Pauline tried again.

"Cardinal Fleury is about to return to Versailles."

Marie looked up quickly. "The King has sent for him?"

"No, but Richelieu has."

Marie shrugged. "I have no interest in state affairs."

"A queen who says that," Pauline stated boldly, "is sadly lacking in her duty."

Marie rose quickly. "How dare you, Madame!"

"I would dare even more for the sake of France, your Majesty," Pauline said warmly.

Marie considered this for a moment. "What do you want of me?"

"I suggest that your Majesty should take steps to prevent the Cardinal from resuming his old position," Pauline said, and after something of a struggle with herself fell on her knees at Marie's feet. "Your Majesty has every right to feel bitter about my association with the King, but please believe me when I say that my dearest wish has always been to use my influence for the good of France."

121

"You *sound* sincere," Marie admitted.

"Your Majesty *must* believe me, for only through mutual trust and understanding can we do the right thing."

Marie remembered that she had always liked Pauline and that she had allowed the girl to be brought to court for the purpose of replacing her sister. Since Louis would always find a mistress necessary, there could be many worse than this earnest young woman who knelt before her pleading on behalf of France.

"What do you mean by the *right thing?*" she asked.

"The setting up of a regency, your Majesty."

"Under the Duc d'Orleans, you mean?"

Pauline smiled engagingly. "No, your Majesty, under a woman. The King has grown to see that a woman might have a greater grasp, a more human grasp, of state affairs than a man."

Marie laughed drily. "If you aspire to the regency yourself, Madame—"

"How could I do that? A regent must be a person of royal blood, but not necessarily a man. There are precedents . . ."

"Is it possible," Marie gasped, "that you think *I* should become Regent?"

"It is indeed," Pauline said warmly.

"And you yourself—?"

"I think I could fill the position of chief minister adequately."

Marie began to laugh, and the more she tried to control her laughter the more it got the better of her.

"I, the neglected wife," she gasped, "you, the mistress! Both of us working together, *ruling* together—!"

Pauline began to laugh, too. Marie touched her lightly on the shoulder.

"Do get up, Madame. It makes me uncomfortable to see you kneeling all the time."

Pauline rose and at a gesture from Marie seated herself. She began to feel that she was making real progress at last.

"A new rule," Marie pondered, "a rule of women . . ."

Women, she was sure, if given the chance, could do a great deal more for their country than men. And once a rule of women was established Louis, being easy-going, would allow it to continue. Not for one moment did she fear that he would die. He was much too wicked for that.

"If I agree," she said briskly, "how do you suggest that we should proceed with the plan?"

Pauline was prepared for this. "Maurepas shall call a council meeting. He himself will suggest that your Majesty should become Regent. In the absence of Cardinal Fleury he carries sufficient weight to influence the majority of the ministers."

"But what of the King?"

Pauline had already forgotten Louis. "The King is much too ill to be troubled."

But Marie baulked at this. "He must be consulted," she insisted. "And being so ill he will probably agree to what I ask." She smiled engagingly. "After all, when Louis is ill, even just a little ill, he has trouble with his conscience where I am concerned."

"But his Majesty has refused to see anybody."

"I am the Queen," Marie said, with a quiet dignity. "The physicians will admit me if I demand it."

When Marie presented herself at the royal sickroom she was told that Louis was sleeping. It was late afternoon and so, urged by Pauline that delay was dangerous, she presented herself again in the early evening. Peyronie respectfully asked her business. She uttered three words: "Urgent state affairs." He went to Louis with this information. Louis smiled. Urgent state affairs! In all conscience Marie was growing bold. "Somebody is behind her in this," he said. "I wonder who it is." He considered the problem for a few moments. Finally he said, "Let her Majesty prepare a memorandum."

With that Marie, too timid after all to insist on talking to Louis, withdrew to her own apartments, and with Pauline, who was fuming at the delay, composed a brief summary of what she "humbly" considered the best course to be taken in "this present distressing crisis."

It was late evening when the memorandum was delivered

to Peyronie who in his turn delivered it to a highly curious Louis. "With her Majesty's compliments," the surgeon said gravely. Louis went swiftly through the memorandum and with a roar of laughter tossed it aside. It was priceless, utterly priceless! Then he took it up and read it again, slowly, and the full significance of the suggestion that Pauline should be appointed chief minister under Marie sank into his mind. Without a doubt Pauline was responsible for the infamous memorandum; Marie herself was a mere pawn. Anger and indignation overwhelmed him.

"Send for the Queen and Madame la Comtesse," he commanded. "Admit them both together."

While waiting for them to come he ordered all the candles except one to be extinguished. It would be much easier to look like a dying man in the light of one candle than a dozen. He even practiced speaking in a low, broken voice and concluded, just as Marie and Pauline were announced, that he would make a very good actor indeed. Peyronie placed two chairs at a little distance from the bed; gravely Marie and Pauline seated themselves.

"Most touching," Louis gasped, when the surgeon had withdrawn. "And your tears, they break my heart."

Neither woman was weeping but each, after a swift glance at the other, made little snuffling noises.

"This nonsense about a regency . . ." he added brokenly.

"But expedient at the moment," Marie managed to say.

"*Most* expedient," Pauline stressed.

Before more could be said there was the sound of a disturbance in the anteroom. Peyronie's voice was raised in protest, but another voice, old and quavering, could be heard.

"Rubbish!" it croaked. "The King himself would be the last to forbid my entry."

"Fleury!" Louis cried.

A few minutes later the door was flung open and Cardinal Fleury, leaning heavily on his stick, tottered into the room. He bobbed his head to Marie, ignored Pauline and hastened to Louis' side. Stiffly he sank to his knees and stiffly he felt for Louis' hand. Tears were running down his wasted cheeks. A lump rose in Louis' throat, tears came to his own eyes. He found it impossible to speak.

"I set out for Versailles the moment the dreadful news reached me," Fleury said brokenly. "Tell me, Sire, that the physicians are mistaken."

Louis sat up. He cleared his throat and called loudly for more candles. Marie gave a little gasp of surprise; Pauline felt her heart miss a beat. More candles were brought. Louis, looking young and boyish in his nightshirt, jumped out of bed, helped Fleury to his feet and made him comfortable in a chair.

"Well," the "dying" monarch laughed, "what do you think of my condition now, eh?"

"Your Majesty must be delirious," Fleury wheezed.

"I wish I were, in one respect. You may as well know the truth, Fleury. This illness of mine has been partly pretense."

"Pretense!" Pauline exclaimed.

"I wanted to know how you would act, all of you, if you thought I was dying. Well, now I know. My unfortunate curiosity has been satisfied."

"Amazing," Fleury chirped, and was thankful that his tears, his quite genuine tears, had flown so freely. Louis placed the memorandum in his hands. He read it carefully and said "Amazing!" again, but with a very different inflection.

"They put their heads together when they thought I was dying—" Louis began.

"And decided," Fleury finished for him, "that a woman would make a better ruler than a man."

"And think of it, the Queen and the mistress to work together for the country's good!"

"The *country's?*" Fleury questioned slyly.

"Of course not! Their own! At least, Madame la Comtesse's own. The Queen was a mere pawn."

"Your Majesty—" Pauline began.

"Hold your tongue!" Louis said rudely.

Marie, confused and a little disappointed—it had been a lovely dream, the dream of a rule of women—pulled herself together and said fussily:

"Do get back into bed, Louis. You look so foolish trying to strike an attitude of righteous indignation in your night-shirt."

Louis looked down at his bare feet. He drew the folds of his nightshirt about him and felt a little silly.

"Please withdraw, all of you," he said stiffly. "Be kind enough, Fleury, to assist her Majesty to her own apartments."

Fleury rose with difficulty and offered Marie his arm. Pauline, standing back while they left the room, looked sullenly at Louis.

"After all," she said, "you did promise me a seat on the privy council."

"You forced it from me at a price," he snapped, "and what a price!" He pointed a long finger at her. "Look at you! Strong and healthy! Your contact with the damp grass was greater than mine. You must have the constitution of an ox."

Pauline forced from herself a merry laugh, but Louis was not amused. He stood there glowering at her, still pointing his finger.

"You really mean me to go?" she faltered.

"I do, Madame, but you may as well hear my decision first. Fleury was the only one who was not moved by a selfish motive. He thought I was dying and he wept bitter tears. Because of that he shall remain at court. As for you—"

"Yes?" she said defiantly.

"You have hurt me deeply. You thought of yourself. All the time you thought of yourself. 'The King is dying,' you said; 'What can I do to save myself?' Pah! Never in the history of France has a woman's interference gone quite so far!"

"But Louis—"

"I am finished with you, completely, utterly. You shall leave Versailles tomorrow. You may go to Choisy, or you may go to your husband, but you leave tomorrow."

Pauline began to laugh. "How stern you sound and how foolish you look!"

"Bachelier!" Louis shouted. "Bachelier!"

She looked at him coldly. "If you really mean me to go I would prefer to do so without waiting to be thrown out by your valet, but first I want to tell you something."

"And that, Madame?"

Bachelier appeared at the door.

"Presently," Louis said, dismissing him, and to Pauline: "Well?"

"I discovered, just before you were taken ill, that the King of France is to become a father for the eleventh time."

Louis understood her instantly but wondered if she were lying in an attempt to make him change his mind. She hoped, without doubt, that once sufficient time had passed for the lie to be discovered he would laugh at her cleverness and permit her to remain at court. He gave her a charming smile.

"How delightful," he said. "For you, I mean. I myself have had so many children that the thought of another, even out of wedlock, could have little novelty."

"It makes no difference to your attitude?" she gasped.

"None whatever. It merely means that if you are telling the truth there is even more reason for you to retire to Choisy." He took her playfully by the ear and dragged her to the door. "Adequate financial provision will be made for you, my dear." He opened the door and gave her a little push, virtuously resisting as he did so the impulse to pinch her bottom. "How fortunate that in exile you will have a womanly interest to occupy your time and thoughts."

Without a pang he closed the door on her and then, lifting the hem of his nightshirt, he did a solemn little dance round the room.

"A king in fact as well as name," he intoned. "My own master at last!"

It was a solemn and inspiring thought. He had never felt so virtuous in his life.

XII

THE King, fresh from a light-hearted romp in the nursery with the children, was taking supper tete-a-tete with the Queen. Simple pleasures, he thought—only thus could a man hope to find a really lasting joy. A week had passed since the dismissal of Pauline de Vintimille, and yesterday the physicians had declared him completely well again. Looking in his mirror that morning he had been delighted to see a thoroughly healthy young man with pink and white cheeks and not even a trace of dissipation in his face. He felt better than he had ever felt before and was, he told himself, in the highest of spirits. A man should suffer a dose of high fever every now and then, it was good both for his body and his immortal soul.

"How thoughtful you look," Marie remarked.

Louis gave her what he knew to be a sweet smile. "I am planning my future Way of Life. Early nights, continent habits, a serious interest in state affairs." He threw out his arms in an expansive gesture. "Ah, but life is good, good!" He glanced at Marie critically, half-expecting her to laugh or jeer. "You look thoughtful yourself, my dear."

She smiled gently. "Supper tete-a-tete with my husband is something of a novelty. I must make the most of it."

"You have Pauline's dismissal to thank for my new interest in domesticity," he told her gaily.

"That and the fact that she has not yet been replaced," Marie said with gentle irony.

"Replaced?" Louis looked shocked; he almost *felt* shocked. "I have no intention of replacing her." He glanced at Marie questioningly. "My dear, I—" He stopped, overcome with embarrassment, though it was ridiculous, he thought, to feel like this in the presence of the woman who had borne him ten children. "I—hum—I am quite ready," he stammered, "to be a real husband again."

Marie repressed a shudder. To resume the same old round, pregnancy after pregnancy, confinement after confinement . . . What an appalling prospect! All she wanted now was to be left in peace. Her habits had become fixed; she was growing middle-aged and staid; there was no place in her life for a man who, even if he *had* reformed, was as lusty and energetic as ever.

"Ah, I make you blush!" Louis cried. He leaned across the table and pinched her cheek. "Well, my love? Am I to instruct your ladies to place an extra pillow in your bed tonight?"

She felt herself growing hot with alarm. She tried to reason with herself that there was such a thing as wifely duty; she even tried to tell herself that she still loved him that way, yet she was overcome with horror at the thought of his touching her. Still blushing she mumbled an excuse which many a woman had made before, but which, she thought, was entirely original.

"Oh," he said, taken aback, and then, tentatively: "But what of it?"

Marie was really trapped. If she submitted now he would discover that she had lied, and that might easily send him to the arms of the first woman he could find. Not that he would need to look far; Versailles was full of women ready and eager so to be honored by their sovereign lord and king.

"No?" he questioned.

"Oh Louis, I couldn't!"

129

"Oh well," he said jauntily, "no doubt I deserve to be kept waiting a few days."

He rose and strode restlessly about the room. The night was young. He hated the thought of going to bed alone, or going to bed at all for hours and hours. Rambouillet, perhaps? A midnight party with Richelieu and the others? He remembered his new resolutions and the memory engulfed him like a cold dark cloud.

"Damnation!" he exploded, "what a curse it is to be a king!"

A week, a month, two months, and still the strange new virtue controlled his life. He hunted wildly, he shot more game than ever before, he attended one dreary council meeting after another until the deadly boredom which he had hoped would never torment him again swamped him utterly.

"Continence!" he fumed— "how it *stifles* one!"

He was inclined to blame Marie. The extra pillow was placed repeatedly in her bed, but he was finding her apathetic—submissive, yes, as a wife should be, but apathetic. In the end, though he still took an occasional supper with her, he no longer lingered over it, and feeling that it was no more terrible for a man to return to a forgotten mistress than for a dog to return to its vomit, he sought out Julie de Mailly, who after all still loved him.

A third month passed, then a fourth. His restlessness increased. He was shunning the council chamber now, for why should he weary himself with state affairs when Fleury was on hand with his still agile mind? The extra pillow no longer appeared in Marie's bed—he was pleased for her sake that no pregnancy had resulted from his brief spell of husbandly attentions—and Julie, with her excess of devotion, was beginning to sicken him.

He often found himself brooding over Pauline. He knew by this time that she had not been lying, that he was indeed to become a father for the eleventh time; and he wondered as he trembled on the brink of sentimentality whether her child would be a boy or a girl. More than once he toyed with the thought of going to the house at Choisy, but that, inevitably, would result in her reinstatement. In any case Fleury would object and Pauline, after all, had used him shamefully.

"Unless something happens to brighten my life," he raged, "I shall go crazy!"

Gradually he fell into his old habits again, and eight months after Pauline's dismissal—(her time was getting closer, he thought broodingly)—he was sitting late over cards and rising early to lead the chase at Rambouillet or Fontaine-bleau. During one hectic week he excelled himself. On the Monday he hunted all day and returned to Versailles for a late supper, upon which he remembered that there was a masked ball in Paris and called for his coach. He danced till four in the morning and reached Versailles once more at six. He slept till eleven, cursed himself for not waking earlier and spent the rest of the day—Tuesday, he thought it was —hunting again. By Saturday he had spent only twenty hours in bed in six days, so to shake up his liver he rode three horses for an hour each in quick, furious succession. The next day he woke with a slight cold; by evening there was a touch of fever; by midnight, when his body was cov-ered in a cold and clammy sweat, the terror was upon him again. He was about to die, yet he was far too great a sin-ner to face his maker. He sent for Marie and asked her where he had failed, what he should do, always supposing he lived, to make amends. She whispered that the one thing he had shunned might bring him comfort.

"Religion?" he said sulkily.

"Yes, Louis."

He said he would think about it.

Three days later he was allowed to get up. He felt as well as ever again, but the terror still lingered. He was sud-denly determined to be not just a better king but a saintly one. He would go to confession more often; he would ob-serve all the fast days; he would even take the sacraments again. France had already had one king known to history as Saint Louis; she should have another, a greater, a more saintly.

131

He went that night to take supper with Marie. Her apartments had been refurnished once more, special attention having been given to the bedroom, the walls of which were now hung with tapestries representing scenes from the Bible. He looked at her critically as he sat opposite her and suspected that she feared he would ask for an extra pillow in her bed. He wanted to pat her cheek and assure her gently that, motivated by the new religious fervor now warming his heart, he was finished with "all that." He wanted to but the words stuck in his throat. Confound it all, he was young, really *young*, and in all conscience why should the Church do anything but smile on a repentant sinner seeking the blessèd comfort of his wife's bed?

After her first words of greeting Marie remarked, oh so casually, that Pauline de Vintimille had given birth to a son. Louis scowled. He said he already knew of this by no means unusual event; he said that as far as he was concerned Pauline could give birth to a dozen sons. And he added earnestly that not only was he an utterly faithful husband, now and forever, but one whose every action would henceforth be cloaked in religious zeal and piety. He sighed deeply as he said this and looked so long and gloomy of countenance that Marie burst into peals of laughter.

"So I amuse you, Madame!" he complained.

Marie shrugged. She knew well enough that religious zeal and piety would bore him more quickly than anything else, though while this low fever lasted—for fever it was— she was afraid she would have on her hands a husband ready to excuse his physical attentions by a profession of piety well-nigh insupportable.

"I think you should forgive Pauline," Marie said, "and ask her to forgive you."

"Nonsense!" he blustered.

"Unless, of course, you now regret having sent her away," Marie replied.

"What makes you think I regret that?" he asked curiously.

"Why, nothing, Louis, but I can't help thinking you treated her harshly."

"This conversation," he grunted, "is taking a most unusual turn."

Marie hid a smile. She felt that her hastily improvised plan to retain her freedom was going to succeed. It was, of course, a sinful thing to do, and afterwards she would pray for forgiveness, but do it she most certainly would.

"If you find it embarrassing for me to speak of your former mistress—" she went on.

"I do, Madame, I do!"

"What queer creatures men are. But seriously, Louis, Pauline de Vintimille is at least sincere in her professed patriotism. She succeeded in convincing even me of that."

Louis looked at her oddly. "'Pon my oath, you almost sound as if you want me to bring her back!"

"Hardly that," she demurred, "though I admit that the devil one knows is generally more welcome than the devil one has yet to meet."

His brows shot up. "In other words, you would rather see Pauline return than—?"

"Yes, Louis," and Marie looked down modestly.

Louis laughed suddenly, and gaily. Piety! Religious zeal! What utter nonsense! *Saint* Louis indeed! One saint in the long line of French monarchs was quite enough. He felt younger than ever and ten times more ardent. With the blood rising in his veins he remembered that Pauline was the woman of a thousand charms whose anything but modest little tricks of love had woven about him a magic spell. Moreover, she was now the mother of his child, which made her all the more dear to him, all the more desirable.

"Marie," he cried, "I like and adore your sense of humor, and I thank you from the bottom of my heart for giving me a most delightful idea." He kissed her swiftly on the brow. "Pray excuse me!"

"But Louis," Marie said, just as he reached the door, "I had invited the Grand Almoner to join us tonight." It was a lie, but, she thought, an appropriate one. "You see, knowing your wish to take a real interest in religious matters . . ."

Louis slapped his thighs and roared with laughter.

"Tell the Grand Almoner to go to the devil. He has more chance of converting him than me!"

Attended by Bachelier, Louis wasted no time in taking the Choisy road. It was a dark and starless night with low threatening clouds in the sky. Depressing, really, if you permitted it to depress you, but Louis was in the best of spirits. He poked the sleepy Bachelier in the ribs several times and said, "You dog, oh you dog!" He had not made up his mind what he was going to do about Pauline, except forgive her. He would probably permit her to return to Versailles but placate Fleury by forbidding her even the slightest interest in state affairs.

On reaching the house he leaped from the coach and ran lightly to the front door. A grave-faced servant admitted him.

"Tell me where Madame la Comtesse is," he cried, "and I'll announce myself."

The man hesitated, then stood back in relief as a young woman approached from the far end of the hall. At first Louis thought she was Pauline, so striking was the resemblance. She curtsied solemnly and waited for him to speak. He remembered her then; she was another of Pauline's sisters.

"Anne, isn't it, Marquise de la Tournelle?" he said.

The young woman inclined her head.

He recalled that she was a widow, that she had joined Pauline at Choisy just before the confinement. He looked at her curiously. The gravity of her manner was beginning to disturb him.

"Is anything the matter?" he asked.

"There is sickness in the house, Sire."

"Sickness?" Fear gripped his heart. "Pauline?"

"Yes, your Majesty."

"But the birth was easy. There were no complications."

"She was taken ill this afternoon. A physician is with her now!"

134

The Marquise led him up the stairway and when she came to Pauline's room scratched lightly on the door. A man opened it. He was obviously the physician.

"Is there any change, Monsieur?" the Marquise asked.

The physician shook his head, bowed deeply to Louis and stood aside. Louis tip-toed into the room. A single candle was burning by the bedside. At first he thought Pauline was dead, but the almost imperceptible rising and falling of her breast told him that she was either sleeping or unconscious.

"My God," he whispered in horror, "what a dreadful change!"

He scarcely recognized her. Her face was pale and drawn. There were deep shadows beneath her closed eyes. Her nose and cheek-bones stood out with a horrible prominence.

"Fever?" Louis asked the physician.

"I imagine so, your Majesty."

"You *imagine?*"

"There was delirium, which I understand, but also convulsions."

"Convulsions?" Louis withdrew from the room and called Bachelier. "Go back and fetch Peyronie at once," he ordered.

His anxiety was pitiful. He felt that Pauline might die without having spoken to him or recognized him. If that happened he would never be able to forgive himself. He went back to Pauline's room. He dismissed the physician and told the Marquise, whose dark watchful eyes disturbed him, that he wanted to be alone with her sister. Beside himself, he seized Pauline's hands in his, patting them and caressing them and whispering foolish endearments. Once he felt her shudder, and once he heard her utter his name, but he knew that she spoke it without recognition. When Peyronie arrived he was sure that her hands were colder than ever.

"Do all you can to save her," he pleaded.

"Of course, but I really must insist on your Majesty retiring."

"And so must I," the Marquise said. She had come silently into the room. "Accommodation," she added, "has been prepared for your Majesty. I, personally, will call you if a change takes place."

Louis allowed himself to be led away. He remembered the baby and asked about him. The Marquise replied that he was doing well, that Pauline had decided to have him adopted by a suitable family.

"Adopted?" Louis was indignant. "In the name of heaven, why?"

"Your Majesty had taken no interest. My sister felt that adoption would be best."

Louis' indignation grew. "Royal bastards are always well cared for. My great-grandfather even legitimized a number of them."

Once in the room that had been prepared for him he began to feel angry with Pauline. A woman who even considered adoption was unfit to have a child. One would have thought that she would have been proud of her son: it wasn't every woman who had the privilege of bearing a royal bastard. Obviously she was not a maternal woman; she was too full of masculine ambitions. Thus consoling himself a little, thus casting aside the guilt he felt—and felt, confound it, for no definite reason—he lay down fully dressed and composed himself for sleep.

But his anger soon passed. Twice he got up and went to the door, but each time he returned irresolutely to the bed. The Marquise had promised to call him if necessary. Presently he fell into a fitful dose, and then into a deep and troubled slumber. When he opened his eyes again it was daylight and somebody was shaking him gently by the shoulder. He sat up.

"Ah, Bachelier."

Standing behind Bachelier was Peyronie. He remembered where he was. He took in their unsmiling faces and fear gripped his heart.

"Well?" he whispered.

Peyronie stepped forward. "My courage fails me, Sire."

"Pauline is—dead?"

Peyronie nodded gravely. Louis leaped from the bed. To steady himself he took Bachelier's arm.

"When?" he demanded. "Why wasn't I called?"

"Death came suddenly, your Majesty. There was no time. There were severe convulsions then, without warning, the end."

Quick tears came to Louis' eyes.

"Take me to her," he begged brokenly.

Bachelier led him out to the passage and along it to the stairs. Louis, weeping shamelessly, pointed out that they were going the wrong way.

"The body has been removed," Bachelier told him.

"Removed? Why?"

"Your Majesty forgets," said Peyronie, "that death is never permitted to remain beneath the same roof as his Majesty the King."

"So once again I am the victim of custom and superstition!" Louis raged.

They led him down the stairs and out to a courtyard at the side of the house. There a little hostile crowd had gathered. Louis was appalled at the hissing and booing that rose from it and barely ceased when it was seen that the King was present.

"Dear heaven," he whispered, "a demonstration against a dead woman!"

"Against what she represented, rather," Peyronie told him, and urged him to return to the house.

"A pretty sight," Louis said, "a king fleeing from a handful of peasants!"

Nevertheless he withdrew from the courtyard but instead of returning indoors he called for his coach.

"Let the body be given a christian burial," he ordered.

Peyronie bowed. "But there will be an inquiry, your Majesty?"

"An inquiry?"

"It was not a natural death, Sire. Madame la Comtesse died of poison."

The inquiry, even though Fleury advised against it, was held before a meeting of his Majesty's Privy Council. Anne, Marquise de la Tournelle, was brought to Versailles as the chief witness. With a sad-faced Louis asking most of the questions, she gave her evidence, such as it was, in a steady monotone. When asked if Pauline had had any visitors before being taken ill she spoke of Maurepas and Richelieu, both of whom were present at the inquiry and both of whom looked sheepish and a little afraid.

"Monsieur le Comte de Maurepas called in the early evening," the Marquise said. "After he had gone Monsieur le Duc de Richelieu arrived. That was the day before my sister was taken ill."

"Why did you call on her?" Louis asked Maurepas.

Maurepas shrugged. "I merely wished to pay my respects and offer my sympathy."

"Sympathy?"

"She considered that she had been treated harshly."

Louis flushed. She had, of course, been treated harshly. He would never be able to forgive himself, never! He turned wearily to Richelieu.

"And what took you to Choisy?"

"Your Majesty—" Fleury interposed.

"Let Richelieu speak for himself," Louis insisted.

"But since he went to Choisy at my suggestion—"

"*Your* suggestion, Fleury?"

Fleury looked down his nose. "He had spoken against her many times. I wanted him to make his peace with her."

"I think you lie," Louis said heatedly. "Both you and Maurepas. You felt, both of you, that sooner or later I would bring her back to court. Maurepas, her friend, would have liked that, of course, but you and Richelieu would have hated it."

"I brought her to court in the first place," Fleury pointed out. "Surely your Majesty is not suggesting that I sent Richelieu to Choisy to poison Madame la Comtesse?"

Louis held Fleury's eyes for a moment, then looked away. Perhaps he had gone too far, yet *somebody* had poisoned Pauline.

138

"My sister spoke of both interviews," the Marquise intervened. "Each of the gentlemen offered to influence her return to court. The price, in each case, was a division of power."

Louis considered this. "If suspicion still falls on anyone it falls on Richelieu."

He looked broodingly at Richelieu, his friend, his boon companion at many an all-night party, and tried to set aside such an accusation. He thought of all he knew of this elegant courtier, this daring soldier, this man of great resource and inordinate ambition. He could indeed have poisoned Pauline. Louis shuddered at the thought. It was too horrible to contemplate, the more so since it would implicate Fleury.

"Permit me to speak boldly, Sire," Fleury said. "I myself can see no evidence of murder, only—" the words came with a gentle little sigh—"only of suicide."

Louis gave a start of horror. "Suicide?"

Fleury glanced slowly and deliberately at the people in the room and suggested that it would be better if they all withdrew. They hesitated, looking at Louis. Here was a pretty piece of scandal to relate to their mistresses and perhaps to their wives. To withdraw now was unthinkable.

"I must insist," Fleury said.

Louis nodded a general dismissal and a few moments later he found himself alone with Fleury and the Marquise. He buried his head in his hands. It was a fine, melodramatic gesture and part of himself, as if standing watchfully aside, enjoyed and applauded it.

"Maurepas and Richelieu were at Choisy the night before Madame la Comtesse was taken ill. She was taken ill in the late afternoon. Poison acts quickly, Sire."

Louis lifted his head wearily. "Why should she want to kill herself?" He knew the answer and flung up his arms. "Suicide, because of me!" He felt more wretched than ever; he wondered if he ought to beat his breast. "Because of *me!*" he stressed.

"Not in the sense you mean it," Fleury said testily. "She never loved you, Sire; she only loved power. If she committed suicide she did so out of disappointment, in thwarted anger, one might almost say."

"You say *if* she committed suicide?" Louis demanded eagerly.

"We have no evidence either of murder or suicide. All I want to stress is that an inquiry can do no good at all."

Louis rose. "The inquiry is closed. Please leave me, Fleury."

Fleury bobbed his head and hobbled from the room. Louis stared in horror at the Marquise who still remained.

"Suicide!" he whispered.

"It was wrong of the Cardinal to make such a suggestion," she said hotly.

Louis felt his heart warm to her. He wanted to seize her hands and cling to her like the lost child he was.

"If you wish me to go, Sire . . ." she said gently.

"No, stay for a moment! I—" He broke off and looked at her beseechingly. "Tell me, Madame, as Pauline's sister, as the woman so close to her at Choisy, do *you* think it was suicide?"

"Until Cardinal Fleury spoke the word I had never for one moment thought of it."

"You hadn't?" They were the kindest words he had ever heard spoken. "She was not unhappy, then, at Choisy?"

"She was not *too* unhappy," she lied.

It was not until Pauline's death that Anne, Marquise de la Tournelle, had seen and fully recognized her opportunity. As capable of devotion as her other sister, Julie, she was just as ambitious as Pauline. She was neither as plain as Julie nor as attractive as Pauline had once been, though she resembled Pauline strongly. And she was, or so she had been told, a great deal cleverer than Pauline.

"She was never despondent," she went on (Pauline had raved like a mad woman and said often that life was no longer worth living), "and still loving you—" (she had said repeatedly that she hated him)—"she was sure, even when you preferred not to see her and the child, that in the end you would forgive her and recall her."

"Then it could never have been suicide!"

"That is what we must try to believe. More, Sire, it is what she would want us to believe."

"Yes! I do see that! I—" Louis broke off suddenly and shouted: "Stop, woman! In heaven's name stop! I can't bear the sight of it! Stop, I say!"

The Marquise felt puzzled. "Your Majesty—"

"You made a gesture, a gesture so typical of your sister. Dear heaven, how deep the resemblance is! Your every movement, your incomparable gracefulness, your eyes, your smile! Everything about you except, thank heaven, your voice!"

"We were sisters, your Majesty, and even as children—"

"Silence!" Louis sobbed. "You must go. You must leave Versailles." His voice rose to a scream. "Go, Madame, for pity's sake go!"

When Richelieu found him, Fleury was standing at the rail of one of the inner galleries of the palace. Gazing down into the courtyard he thought what a pity it was that of all his senses the sense of smell alone had been left unimpaired by the ravages of old age. Even as he stood there a footman brushed past him and flung the contents of a pail into the courtyard below. And a moment later a chambermaid, not even troubling to cry a warning, did likewise from the gallery above.

"There are times," he remarked to Richelieu, "when the stench which surrounds the splendor of Versailles is more than I can bear."

Richelieu, always a fastidious man, agreed with a shrug. It had always been like this and always would be, and at the Louvre and the Tuileries it was a great deal worse.

"Is the King any better today?" he asked.

"If anything he is worse."

A week had passed since the unfortunate inquiry into the death of Pauline de Vintimille, and after sending her sister away Louis had shut himself in his apartments, refusing to see anybody but Bachelier and Peyronie.

"According to Bachelier," Richelieu went on, "his Majesty still blames himself for Pauline de Vintimille's death.

He is quite inconsolable. He beats his breast, he cries continually that he and he alone was responsible."

"What a waste of emotion!" Fleury laughed.

"I agree, your Eminence, but he might lose his reason, and that would mean a regency, and a regency—"

"Would mean the end of Richelieu and Fleury," Fleury concluded. "Something must be done, I agree, but what?"

Richelieu smiled. "Pauline de Vintimille's confessor died last night." His smile broadened. "He knew too much. He knew the name of the person who poisoned Pauline. That was why he was poisoned himself."

"Whereas, in actual fact he knew nothing and died a perfectly normal death, eh?"

"Precisely, but we must convince the King that the wretched woman did not die by her own hand."

"You make an apt pupil, Richelieu," Fleury chuckled. "Nevertheless, the King might ask for proof of what you suggest."

"I think not, not in his present state of mind."

Fleury nodded his agreement. "You will make a worthy successor, my friend, providing you live long enough. Cardinal Eternity is most reluctant to die. Er—Pauline de Vintimille did die by her own hand, of course?"

"No one will ever know, poor soul."

"Poor soul," Fleury echoed, and crossed himself absently.

XIII

"Another glass of wine?" Louis suggested.

Fleury shook his old head. "Thank you, no, Sire."

Louis and Fleury were taking supper together. Several weeks had passed since Fleury had broken the news of the "poisoning" of Pauline de Vintimille's confessor, and Louis, though still in low spirits, was making what he called a valiant attempt to resume his normal course of life.

"Try a little of this tart," Louis invited. "I prepared it myself from an old recipe favored by my great-grandfather. Let me see, now . . . Ah yes, a boiled potato mashed up with several quinces and simmered in red wine. After which, at the *right* moment, I added finely chopped dates, six egg yolks, a little butter and a dash of rosewater."

"Delicious, no doubt," Fleury said, "but cautious eating and cautious drinking, that is the secret of my long life."

"Then I," said Louis gloomily, "shall undoubtedly die at an early age."

Death of late had been much in his thoughts. The mystery of it held for him a morbid fascination, a fascination which, he told himself, was almost romantic and certainly fitting in a man as miserable as he. He even felt that it might be interesting to die soon, just for the sake of solving the mystery.

He was reasonably sure that he would go to hell, but hell would have certain compensations. Heaven, he had told Marie only yesterday, would surely bore him.

"Good food and good wine, but both in moderation," Fleury murmured, and added, in the manner of an afterthought, "I have called a council meeting for tomorrow at eleven."

"Excellent," Louis pronounced, "but I have no intention of being present."

"I fear that you must, Sire. It is necessary to discuss the question of the Dauphin's marriage."

Louis was greatly taken aback. He had quite forgotten that his son was growing up. He smiled somberly at the thought of his becoming a grandfather one of these days—if he lived long enough.

"The boy is barely thirteen," he objected. "Still, I was married at fifteen myself. A political necessity, of course, like all royal marriages. Have you chosen a bride for my son?"

Fleury said that subject to his Majesty's approval he had and spoke at length of the suitability of an Austrian alliance. He mentioned that the Austrian question, a question of increasing importance since the termination of the Polish trouble, had been debated so heatedly of late that it would be a relief to bring it to a happy conclusion. Louis, trying to take an intelligent interest, remarked that an Austrian marriage might range Prussia and England against them.

"Surely your Majesty is not in favor of a Prussian or English marriage," said Fleury, growing irritated.

"Perhaps," Louis said, beginning to enjoy himself.

"If your Majesty leans to Prussia or England because Madame de Vintimille suggested it—and I remember that she did—you are permitting sentiment to get the better of sound judgment."

"And you, in leaning to Austria," Louis said cunningly, "are doing the same, though *your* sentiment has a religious flavor."

They began to argue, a thing that had never happened before. In the end Louis, no longer enjoying himself, said crushingly that he would be swayed by one thing only, that which was best for France. With this he refilled his glass and, draining it, noticed that Fleury was trembling like a leaf.

"Forgive me, old friend," he cried impulsively. "It was not my intention to upset you." He flung his glass to the floor. "God! I've never been so bored in my life. That was why I argued."

"Your Majesty," Fleury suggested, "is in need of a little feminine society."

Louis gave a theatrical groan. In need of Pauline's, hers and hers alone! Liking the sound of it, he repeated the groan. His heart, he told himself, was torn by an emotion composed of loneliness as well as boredom. He thought of Pauline's sister, Julie. He had sent her away—she was talking, so gossip had it, of becoming a nun—and wondered whether he should bring her back. The thought of Julie reminded him of Pauline's other sister, Anne.

"Fleury," he said broodingly, "do you remember the Marquise de la Tournelle?"

"Perfectly, Sire."

"Her resemblance to Pauline was more than I could bear. To send her away as I did was the action of a coward. Where is she now, Fleury?"

"She is still at Choisy." Fleury gave the information unwillingly, feeling that he had been unwise to speak of feminine society. "She asked permission to remain there while straightening out her sister's affairs."

"Ah!" said Louis. He rose and laid an affectionate hand on Fleury's shoulder. "You look pale, Fleury. Let me prepare some broth for you. I know just the right recipe. Most strengthening, they say. Blanched almonds, pounded, of course, with the brains of a capon and plenty of cream."

Fleury shuddered delicately. "No, no, I beg of you, Sire."

"Still at Choisy, you say?" Louis pondered.

Fleury coughed. "Your Majesty will remember tomorrow's council meeting, I trust."

"It *was* cowardly, the way I treated the Marquise."

"At eleven in the morning," Fleury stressed.

"I ought to apologize, really I ought."

"Your Majesty—!"

"And by heaven, apologize I shall!"

If Anne, Marquise de la Tournelle, felt any surprise at Louis' late visit she gave no sign of it. He apologized for its unexpectedness and the lateness of the hour, and while doing so stood first on one foot, then on the other, like a tongue-tied schoolboy. Anne, in her turn, apologized for having remained so long at Choisy and assured him that she would be leaving in the very near future.

"Remain as long as you choose," he cried. "Consider this house your own."

"Your Majesty is much too kind."

There was an uncomfortable pause. Anne was wearing a thin silk negligée, pale blue in color, which veiled rather than hid the figure beneath it. He noted absently that it was a better figure than Pauline's, the high firm breasts larger, the legs longer. He recalled, still absently, that Pauline's legs, once the hooped skirt had been set aside, had faintly disappointed him.

"Madame," he said hurriedly, "I have come here for two reasons. In the first place I want to apologize for my rudeness in screaming at you and sending you away."

"Your Majesty *was* rather rude," Anne acknowledged coolly.

"I raved like a madman."

"Indeed you did."

Her attitude took him aback and reminded him afresh of Pauline. He smiled grimly. To face the Marquise now, reviving so many memories—in short, to torture himself—what could be more excellent in the way of a penance!

"I trust you bear me no resentment," he said.

"None whatever."

He glanced about the intimate little *salon*, remembering that it had been redecorated for Julie but had been taken over by Pauline before Julie could enjoy it. He reflected that the delicate pink of the walls and the little groups of cupids on the panels made a fitting background for the provocative Marquise.

"You are sweet and kind," he said. "I thank you from the bottom of my heart."

Anne inclined her head. "Your Majesty spoke of *two* reasons for coming to Choisy."

"Yes." He gulped and began to trace patterns on the carpet with his toe. "The second is your resemblance to Pauline. It has been too strong for me. It draws me as a candle flame draws a moth. A hundred times since I sent you away I have wanted to see you. It has become an obsession. I must continue to see you. I must have you near me."

Supremely sure of herself Anne said: "Would that be wise?"

"Wise?" He flung up his arms. "What do I care for wisdom?"

"To be constantly reminded of Pauline would pain you."

"I deserve to be pained. I want to punish myself."

"Your Majesty has an uncomfortable conscience."

"I have indeed." He sighed elaborately. "I was born with it, I fear. Only come to Versailles and everything I can give will be yours, everything I planned for Pauline." He paused, and added hastily: "I ask it for her sake, not my own."

"Not for your own at all?" Anne's eyes were twinkling.

"For my own a little, perhaps."

"So that you may constantly see in me a woman who is dead?"

"Yes!"

"I would be treated honorably? Platonically, one might say?"

"Yes, yes, platonically!" he agreed, though a new exciting desire was beginning to struggle with the idea of a perpetual penance.

Anne chuckled softly, then gracefully, without undue haste, she came to him. A moment later, as if it were something she had done of long habit, she slipped her arms lightly round his neck and turned up her face to his. The tip of her tongue, moist and tempting, was just visible between her slightly parted lips.

"I am flesh and blood," she murmured, "warm flesh and warm blood."

Louis kissed her. He recollected his penance and apologized. He kissed her again. They were short kisses, yet the second left him breathless and shaken.

"No woman," Anne said, "takes pleasure in having herself compared with a hairshirt. Except, of course, that hairshirts are meant to be worn."

"Dear heaven!" Louis wailed, and kissed her again.

Sighing gently she gave her mind to the kiss. She enjoyed it thoroughly. Though she never lost her head over men she liked them. They were necessary to her and Louis was a splendid specimen of a man. Nevertheless, as her blood warmed and she came close to losing herself in his embrace, her ultimate object remained strong and clear in her mind. Presently she freed herself.

"Pauline would be so pleased," she said. "The prospect of living again, and so very thoroughly, through me, would delight her."

"Pauline?" Louis said roughly. "Who the devil is Pauline?"

Without seeming to hear, Anne went on: "Just as she was taken ill, and knowing, as I see now, that she was going to die, she asked me to carry on her work for France if the opportunity ever presented itself."

"It presents itself now!" Louis cried.

"Your Majesty is willing to grant me the same power that Pauline enjoyed?"

"Gladly, gladly!" He took her in his arms again. "But remember how the rabble hissed and booed when she lay dead."

Anne laughed scornfully. "You think I fear the rabble? What nonsense! Besides, they only knew her as a parasite, not as she really was, a patriot."

Louis was entranced. "I see that you resemble her, even in courage." Had she been a courageous woman? He scarcely remembered, but the words rang splendidly in his ears. "Why, in time to come you and she will be one and the same person."

Anne pressed herself warmly against him. "I prefer simply to be myself, Sire, a complete individual. And I ask the same question you asked a moment ago. Who the devil is Pauline?"

Louis remained at Choisy for three days.

Fleury, knowing full well what had happened, sent an ironical message asking if his Majesty, who appeared to have urgent business at Choisy, would like the council to assemble there. "The old rogue!" Louis laughed, and scribbled a hasty note which he instructed Fleury to read to the court.

"I wish it to be known," the note read, "that I strongly disapprove of the gloomy atmosphere that hung over Versailles when I left. The death of the Comtesse de Vintimille is a thing of the past and must remain in the past. On my return there must be merrymaking and gaiety again. I, the King, command it."

His first decision on returning to Versailles was that Anne, Marquise de la Tournelle, should have a title of her own, not merely one conferred by courtesy of a husband now dead. She was to be known henceforth, he announced, as Anne, Duchesse de Chateauroux, and enjoy the newly created official position of Declared Mistress, which carried the income of fifty thousand livres a year. A few days later Anne arrived at Versailles and took possession of the apartments prepared for her by Louis. As the Duchesse de Chateauroux she was received by the Queen, and Marie, with a shrug, accepted her with a cold but nonetheless unquestioning graciousness, remarking without a smile that the position of Declared Mistress was obviously one of great honor.

Then, and only then, did Louis permit a discussion of the Dauphin's marriage. He listened quietly while argument followed argument, rose when bitter recriminations were being flung across the council table and called sternly for silence.

"In actual fact the matter has been settled already," he said. "My son will marry the Infanta Marie-Therese of Spain."

Somebody suggested weakly that it was a happy compromise.

"And one put forward by Madame la Duchesse?" Fleury murmured.

Louis shrugged, but smiled a trifle sheepishly.

Maurepas, speaking up boldly, said that such a marriage might have unhappy repercussions. Spain openly coveted territory in Italy that fell under the jurisdiction of Austria.

"What of it?" Louis replied, and uttered the words given to him by Anne herself. "In the event of war with Austria we will have a strong ally in Spain, and in the event of war with England our southern border will benefit by the additional protection of a Spanish army. The decision has been made, gentlemen. There is nothing more to be said."

And to himself he murmured: "Louis the Strong, that is what future generations will call me."

Fleury, his knees swathed in a blanket, was seated before the fire. He was fascinated by the pictures forming in the burning coals, so fascinated that he forgot the presence of Richelieu, whom he had sent for urgently. One picture, or so he fancied, showed him the King as a boy of seven, standing naked before the court at the ceremony of identification. Another showed him Louis, still only a boy, with his arms round the neck of an ambitious churchman who was still only a bishop. A sudden stab of pain gripped him and presently he glanced up in surprise at Richelieu as he stood there delicately taking snuff.

"And who, Monsieur, may you be?" he asked haughtily.

"Why, Richelieu, your Eminence," Richelieu said in surprise. "You wanted to see me."

"Richelieu, and I sent for him!" Fleury sounded deeply amazed. "I, the lowly Fleury, sent for the great Cardinal Richelieu! And miracle of miracles, he came! I trust that your Eminence is happy in hell."

Richelieu tried not to smile. "You speak to the great-nephew, not the long-dead Cardinal."

Fleury shook himself gingerly. "Fool! I know that without being told."

Richelieu looked at the old man with less alarm. "I see you are feeling better."

"Better? Have I been ill?"

"You complained of a severe pain in the chest and you fainted. His Majesty sent Peyronie himself to look after you."

Snatches of memory began to return, but only snatches. The old cardinal looked at Richelieu pathetically.

"What day is it?"

"Wednesday, your Eminence."

"And the month?"

"November."

"And the—year?"

"Seventeen hundred and forty-two."

Fleury began to weep, silently, horribly, the big sluggish tears rolling down the coarse and withered cheeks.

"I remember so little," he sobbed. "The establishment of the new favorite, yes; the betrothal of the Dauphin, yes; but nothing else, nothing at all. Take pity on me, Richelieu. Tell me what is happening at court."

Richelieu told him, among other things, that France was now at war again.

"But why?" Fleury demanded.

"To decide the question of the Austrian succession. On the death of Emperor Charles the Austrian court was eager to recognize his daughter, Maria-Theresa, and France, as you yourself advised, promised to observe all previous understandings with that court."

Fleury nodded. "Ah, I begin to remember. But events were too much for me. The Bavarian claimant caused himself to be crowned and war became inevitable. But we opposed Maria-Theresa, did we not?"

"Yes, your Eminence."

"Actually going back on our word!"

"Yes," Richelieu said. "It is feared that if she were ever to reign unopposed too much power might fall into the hands

151

of her husband, once Duke of Lorraine, and France has no wish to lose Lorraine."

But Fleury was barely listening now.

"The new favorite—" his old eyes snapped angrily—"the King granted her fifty thousand livres a year."

"More has been added. She now enjoys eighty thousand, with an additional thirty for her household. If she ever retires she will receive a pension of twenty-five thousand."

Suddenly, as he shook his head over this, Fleury thought of something else. "Maurepas, is he hand in glove with the new strumpet?"

"Oddly enough, no." Richelieu smiled, a smile that became a well-bred sneer. "Maurepas is a conscientious man. He believes that Madame la Duchesse is too ambitious. He feels that her influence is bad. He will oppose her whenever he can."

Fleury began to laugh gently. "Now I know why I sent for you. Have you opposed her yet yourself?"

"No, your Eminence, but I intend to. She grows too arrogant. Her position, which after all is only that of a glorified whore, has gone to her head. All she seeks is power and more power for herself."

Fleury chuckled. "A disease suffered by many of us, eh, Richelieu?" He reached out and seized Richelieu's hand in a clawlike grip. "My own place will soon be vacant, and a woman already covets it. To oppose her openly would bring about your ruin. Pay her lip service, Richelieu. Flatter her, make a friend of her—" He broke off and groaned, clutching at his breast. "Peyronie! Call Peyronie!"

Though at times it seemed that the old Cardinal might die at any moment he rallied again and again and tightened, rather than relaxed, his grip on state affairs. He became obsessed with the need for economy, an obsession which affected even the King's family. The royal daughters, he stressed, were expensive luxuries, and should be sent away to convents where their education would be less costly. Louis, ready to grant him anything, quickly agreed, but neither he nor Fleury had taken into account the strong will of Adelaide, the favorite daughter. Now fifteen and pretty and appealing in the light, feathery dresses she wore, she was also shrewd and cunning beyond her years. Biding her time she waited until Louis made one of his infrequent attendances at mass, then flung herself into his arms the moment he returned. The sight of her pleading look, as well as her whispered declaration that to be parted from him would break her heart, affected him deeply. He tweaked her nose, he kissed and fondled her, he called her his little sweetheart, he even wept a little.

"The others shall go, but Adelaide remains," he told Fleury.

Fleury, unequal to the struggle, shrugged. "A minx, and a clever one, Sire. She caught you in a moment of weakness, at a time when she assumed you to be in a state of grace. Watch her, for she will rule you and the country if she gets the chance."

Meanwhile Richelieu stood by, making no attempt to participate in state affairs and concerning himself chiefly with military matters. Knowing that Madame la Duchesse was suspicious of him and jealous of his friendship with the King, he made no direct move to win her friendship but contented himself with being pleasant to her whenever he met her.

Maurepas, on the other hand, opposed her openly and protested to Louis himself about her interference. He pointed out that the rise in the price of bread was causing hostile demonstrations and he claimed that the abandoned gaiety of life at court, in contrast with the dire poverty of the people, was causing widespread resentment. The people, he said, blamed the Duchesse de Chateauroux.

"And so do I, your Majesty," he added warmly.

Louis only laughed. "You are one of the few men at court not afraid to say what you think. I admire you for it, Maurepas, otherwise—" And he shrugged significantly.

Still determined to speak his mind, Maurepas went on: "Since she came to court Madame la Duchesse has grown increasingly reckless and extravagant. She has been heard to say publicly that she wants to see your Majesty become the greatest King in the world, *at any cost.*"

"An ambition not shared by you, apparently," Louis said mildly.

"I would like to see your Majesty become the greatest King in the world, but not at any cost."

"Enough, enough!" Louis said, in sudden anger.

He was angry with himself as well as Maurepas, for he remembered the time when he had resolved to be a better king, a *real* king. Setting this aside he argued with himself that a king, really, was nothing but a figurehead. As for becoming the greatest king in the world, he was, he told himself, a simple soul at heart: the hunt, an occasional ball, a few merry companions at the card table, a bottle of good wine and, of course, a capable mistress—those were the only things he asked of life.

He forgot all this when it became evident that Fleury could linger only a few days more. He went constantly to his old friend's apartments and only rarely did he leave his side for more than a few moments at a time. Once, when Louis was temporarily absent, the dying cardinal summoned Richelieu and uttered a few broken sentences about the Duchesse de Chateauroux.

"And when she falls—as fall she will—friendship with the new favorite. Always a favorite, Richelieu. The King—ruled by women till he dies. But remember this, any power you gain —use it for the good of France. Human nature is frail, but try—"

Fleury was scarcely conscious when, Richelieu dismissed, he spoke his last words to Louis.

"Your Majesty will miss Cardinal Eternity?"

"Your passing will leave an emptiness that no one will ever fill," Louis said brokenly.

"Ah, but many will rejoice. And rightly. My influence has not always been good. Strange how a man must reach the point of death to see his mistakes. Is it fear, or the prickings of conscience?"

Louis clutched at the old dry hands. Would it be the same with him, he wondered, when his own time came? Was life so stupid that only in death did one see, or imagine one saw, where one's faults had lain? He put his lips close to Fleury's ear.

"I have no complaints, you old rogue," he whispered.

But Fleury seemed not to hear. "Flattery, I reached for power through flattery. Now, in the presence of my maker, I ask forgiveness. And I pray—that you, my son—and France also—will not pay too heavy a price—" his lips were moving painfully—"for an old man's vanity."

Later Louis took a gloomy supper alone with Anne in the intimacy of her boudoir, which had been recently redecorated with gold-embroidered white satin. He broke silence once only.

"Fleury is dead," he pronounced. "This is the end of an era."

Anne hid a smile.

"It is certainly the beginning of a new one," she said softly.

XIV

"A FINE array of men," Louis remarked.

Temporarily in residence at the Tuileries, he was reviewing a new detachment of volunteers. Madame la Duchesse
stood on his right, Richelieu on his left, and behind him
Maurepas, now Minister of Defence. Anne wore yet another
new gown, square of neckline, the waist tightly laced and
the hooped skirt more pronounced than ever. Instead of
carrying one of the fashionable parasols she wore a new imitation peasant hat under which bobbed the ringlets that
were still all the rage. She remarked that the sight of so many
brave and loyal soldiers made her proud to be a French-
woman, and Richelieu, stifling a yawn, mocked her with his
eyes.

During the year that had passed since Cardinal Fleury's
death Anne had waited patiently for Richelieu to declare
himself either for or against her. He had delayed, she
thought, in the hope that the King might tire of her and turn
elsewhere, but that was hardly likely. She had become a
physical habit, and taking from Louis as she did the
"burden" of state affairs, she had also become a political necessity. And so, in the last month, Richelieu had approached
her, suggesting what he called a pact of mutual friendship
and protection.

Before accepting this she had pointed out that he, along with his by no means lamented friend, Fleury, had been her sister Pauline's enemy, upon which he had replied that circumstances altered cases, that he was the most adaptable of men. He had further suggested that, being the King's closest friend where merrymaking was concerned, he would be able to protect her interests not a little. Asked in what way, he had replied that he alone had the power to turn the King from those distressing fits of depression which assailed him, fits during which he often declared himself the most sinful man in the world. "At such times," Richelieu had said, "his Majesty is ready and eager to dismiss the royal favorite."

Anne repressed a little shudder now as she thought of the King's moods. She knew all about those fits of depression and the maudlin feeling which accompanied them that his most Christian Majesty should seek comfort in religion. She shuddered again. Louis had in his nature an incipient urge that might well make him a fanatic, and Louis, in that guise, would be insupportable. And so the pact had been made, though she had little trust in Richelieu, knowing that his help was hers only so long as she was of use to him.

"Yes, a fine array of men," Louis repeated.

"A truly amazing sight," Maurepas remarked.

"Amazing?" Louis took him up. "What makes you say it in that tone of voice?"

"I hardly expected so many volunteers, Sire," Maurepas said.

"My people are very loyal," Louis said with dignity, "and pon my soul I see nothing amazing in loyalty."

"Loyalty?" Maurepas grunted. "Call it empty stomachs, Sire. Enlistment is preferable to starvation."

The parade over, Louis led the way indoors. He was faintly alarmed at what Maurepas had said. He wondered why he kept the man at court, especially since he made no attempt to hide his dislike of Anne, but as he wondered he chuckled a little and forgot his alarm. The conflict which existed between the two amused him vastly, and Maurepas, despite what Anne said to the contrary, was an excellent fellow with a shrewd and clever brain.

"I never felt more exhilarated in my life," Anne said.

"You women!" Louis laughed. "The thought of war, the sight of a handsome uniform, the smell of blood . . . !"

"You wrong me there," she pouted. "The thought of war appalls me, though in this case I can think of nothing but the glorification it will bring my King and country."

Louis beamed his delight.

"Is it your Majesty's intention to lead the army in Flanders yourself?" Maurepas asked.

Louis hesitated. "You think I ought?"

Maurepas said gravely: "It would give your Majesty prestige with the people. It might even recall the glorious days of Louis the Fourteenth."

Louis began to feel uncomfortable. He hoped he was not a coward but he had never had any love of militarism.

"My great-grandfather was something of a warrior," he laughed. "He loved war for its own sake."

"But even so, Sire—"

"Yes, yes, quite. Prestige, and that sort of thing." He smiled broadly. "The people would say, 'Why, he can do more than drink and gamble and fornicate, he can *fight*'." He made up his mind, but not too happily. "Very well, I shall go to Flanders."

Anne said quickly, "May I accompany you, Sire?"

"Dear me, do you want to?" It was of course a happy thought.

"Your great-grandfather always took his ladies of the court when he went to war."

"A remarkable man, the last Louis," Richelieu joked. "Not only the Queen accompanied him, but two or three favorites as well. And generally they all travelled happily together in the same coach. That, of course, was before he reformed."

Louis was both amused and appalled. "Great heavens, you dog, do you suggest that I should take Madame la Duchesse and the Queen as well?"

"Women at army headquarters," Maurepas frowned, "would prove an embarrassment."

Louis smiled. He knew quite well what was in the wily Maurepas' mind. Anne, alone at Versailles in the King's absence, would be shorn of much of her power; Anne, at army headquarters in Flanders would have a say in every decision that was made.

"I merely feel," Maurepas added quickly, "that your Majesty might win greater favor with the people if women are forbidden."

Anne glared at Maurepas. "Why should the King be asked to sacrifice all his pleasures because of the people?"

Maurepas wanted to say, "Pleasures will be there; there will be the usual camp followers." But he said simply, "This, Madame, is war."

"Yes," Louis sighed, "this is war." He sighed again. "No women at army headquarters, I see I must insist on that. Why, if I took a handful of women they would begin to call me a petticoat soldier."

Anne was furious. With the King in Flanders, Maurepas would hamper her at every turn. And then, remembering that he was Minister of Defence, she conceived what she considered a brilliant idea for getting rid of him.

"Would it not be wise," she murmured, "if our Minister of Defence were to make a tour of the coastal defences?"

Louis laughed. He saw her game. He saw it even before the look of annoyance crossed Maurepas' face. He slapped his thighs, he tweaked Anne's nose, he winked broadly at Richelieu.

"The coastal defences await you, Maurepas," he cried.

Maurepas bowed. "If your Majesty wishes me to make a tour that any general could make, I will naturally obey the royal command."

Louis roared with laughter. "Never cross a woman, my dear fellow. I doubt if it is ever worthwhile."

And so Maurepas went grimly on his tour of inspection, Louis and Richelieu went bravely to war, taking between them over a hundred pack horses to bear their personal baggage, and Anne, determined to join Louis later, remained at court in full command of state affairs.

News soon began to reach Versailles from Flanders. Louis had "stormed" Coutrai, Louis had "taken" Menin, Louis had "forced" the enemy into flight at Ypres: he was an "inspiration" to his men, who "adored" him and were now speaking of him not only as Louis the Brave but Louis the Well-Beloved. Anne, in exaggerating these reports from Flanders, did much to bring about a similar enthusiasm in Paris itself, upon which she decided that it was time to join Louis at Metz, where he was now stationed. Richelieu supported her in this decision, saying in a letter that Louis was growing bored and would welcome her gladly. Planning her journey, she thought that it should be made with as much ceremony as possible, and though Richelieu had warned her that too much ostentation might bring the rabble hissing at her heels, she ordered her coach to be re-painted in the gayest possible colors. And then, before the paint was scarcely dry, grave and disturbing news came from Metz.

"The King is seriously ill," said the brief note brought to Anne by Richelieu's special courier. "Peyronie fears that he might die."

Anne, ready within an hour, set forth on her journey in a fever of excitement. It was essential, she told herself, if the King were really dying, to reach Metz before Maurepas did. The Minister of Defence was probably in the region of Dunkirk, but having his spies everywhere, he could have been informed almost as quickly as she of Louis' illness and might even now be speeding to Metz.

At the end of her journey, a journey made at breakneck pace, she was met by Richelieu, and together they went to Louis' quarters. There they found Peyronie, surrounded by the King's staff and such members of the court who had been allowed to follow his Majesty to Metz. All wore gloomy faces and spoke in anxious whispers.

Anne demanded immediate admittance to the King's presence, but Peyronie barred her way. Smiling a superior little smile he said that the King was in no condition to be disturbed. Anne was furious and sprang at him, seized him by the coat and shook him. Richelieu, silent and watchful, and a little contemptuous of the vulgarity of her rage, made no attempt to interfere. He remembered that when the King

160

was ill an over-tender and quite ridiculous conscience reminded him that he had a wife whom he had neglected shockingly. It would be wise, Richelieu reflected, to hold one's hand and wait until her Majesty, with whom one had always been on good terms, was sent for. Peyronie freed himself and Anne flew at the King's door. She found it locked.

"Is Maurepas here yet?" she asked Richelieu.

"Not as far as I know."

"Has he been sent for?"

"Possibly."

Anne frowned. "On one occasion the King pretended a serious illness. Is it possible, this time, that—"

"The King's condition is really desperate," Richelieu assured her. "I saw him for a few minutes myself. There is no pretense this time."

"His Majesty's condition could not be worse," Peyronie added. "Ten physicians besides myself have seen him. We all agree that the King has but a few days to live."

"I pray you are all mistaken," Richelieu said emotionally.

"Amen to that," Anne recollected herself sufficiently to cry, and changing her tactics she took Peyronie's hands in hers, wept pitifully and begged him, from the bottom of her heart, to admit her. "I love the King," she sobbed. "Can you blame me for wanting to see him?"

Peyronie weakened. "For a few moments only, then, but no politics, no state affairs, Madame."

"Oh thank you, thank you!" she cried.

Richelieu gave her his arm and led her to the King's door.

"Has his Majesty been confessed?" she asked.

"No, Madame," Peyronie replied. "He refuses to recognize the seriousness of his condition." He took a key from his pocket and unlocked the door. "One moment, I must see his Majesty before I admit you," he said, and slipping into the room locked the door again behind him.

But while the door had been open Anne had heard voices, and one, she was sure, was Maurepas'. Richelieu was sure, too, but he made light of it.

"Peyronie is in the pay of Maurepas!" she cried.

A few moments later the door was unlocked again and Maurepas, smiling broadly at the sight of Anne's face, stepped into the anteroom. She heard the key turn in the lock behind him.

"How the devil did you get here?" Richelieu asked mildly.

Maurepas laughed gaily. "My dear Richelieu, I always carry a broomstick."

"Pah! I could kill you!" Anne shouted.

"So could many people, but not his Majesty the King, who has been most gracious. He has now been made to realize, let me add, that he is close to death. A priest has been sent for and presently the Bishop of Soissons will administer the last sacraments. You know what this will mean to you, Madame."

"This is a plot!" she raged. "A plot to bring about my dismissal!"

"The King's illness is no plot, Madame. And take my advice, hurry from Metz before the people in the town rise against you. The Queen is well-loved in Metz and once it is known that the King has dismissed you—"

"You seem to have made good use of your time with his Majesty!"

"Indeed yes. Her Majesty has been sent for, also the Dauphin and all the princes of the blood royal. Be wise, Madame, and go quickly from Metz."

Anne pushed past Maurepas and flung herself at the locked door. She began to hammer on it with her clenched fists.

"Let me in!" she cried. "Order them to let me in!"

The key was heard to turn in the lock. The door was opened a few inches and Peyronie's shocked face peered out.

"Quietly, Madame, I beseech you!" he whispered.

"Let her in, Peyronie," Louis' voice was heard to say.

"With your leave, Monsieur," Anne said haughtily, and stepped into the room.

She ran to the bed and flung herself on Louis. Peyronie, quickly behind her, tried to restrain her. She shook him off.

"Why was I kept out?" she cried. "Am I a stranger? Have we grown so far apart that I must be treated like a leper?"

Louis groaned. His head, which seemed much too heavy for him, lolled on the pillow. Anne saw how strained and frightened his eyes were, how hectic his color.

"Oh Sire," she wept, "to see you like this!"

"You come too close," Louis moaned. "The fever is infectious."

"As if I cared about that! Have you ever known me play the coward?"

"Peyronie . . ." Louis begged helplessly.

Peyronie took Anne by the shoulders and dragged her back from the bed. He warned her that unless she restrained herself he would be forced to ask her to withdraw.

"You should never have come," Louis said.

"You sound ill-pleased to see me," she reproached him.

"Quietly, Madame," he said. "You weary me."

Anne flung up her arms. "I see it all! That wretched Maurepas! He came to you with lies! Lies, lies and more lies!"

Louis sighed. "He said nothing against you."

"Then why this change? Why, why, *why?*"

"Would you have me die an unrepentant sinner?"

"There are many greater sinners in the world than you, Louis."

"Ah, but I am the King," he said apathetically. "My responsibility has been greater than any other man's. Would you have me face a greater king than I with my sins heavy on my soul?" The drama of it all began to please him. He stirred himself, spoke in a louder voice. "I must put you out of my mind. I must never see you again."

"But Louis—"

Anne checked herself and glanced at Peyronie. It would be stupid in the presence of a third person—a third person who, moreover, would run and warn Maurepas—to utter the things that must be uttered if she was to save herself.

"Grant me a few moments alone with you," she begged.

Louis shook his head. Nothing, he knew, could be more unsafe than that. It was only by keeping his eyes firmly averted from Anne's that he was able to steel himself against the urge to grant her anything she asked. She went down

163

on her knees at the bedside and, her eyes watchfully on Peyronie, began to whisper urgently in Louis' ear.

"France needs me, Sire. I am indispensable to your government. One small line in your will and my position is assured. One small line, Louis!"

He affected not to hear her, and a resentment he had not previously felt rose in his breast. Anne was the same as Pauline; all she cared for was herself.

"I shall pray for you," he said, turning up his eyes, "and believe me, I am very sorry for you."

There being nothing else to do, Anne began to weep again.

"No tears," Louis begged, "unless they are tears of repentance."

"Repentance!" she moaned. "What a hypocrite I'd be if I repented one moment, one smallest action!"

It was an admirable retort, or would have been if Louis had been in good health.

"When death comes to you, Anne," he said sorrowfully, "it will be different. We are cowards and weaklings when death beckons, every single one of us." He called Peyronie. "Tell Maurepas, the Queen. I can scarcely wait. I have only one wish now, the Queen, my wife . . ."

When Marie reached Metz she was told by Peyronie that Louis was sinking fast. By this time Louis had been confessed, and from the hands of the Bishop of Soissons, forgetting that he had once resolved never to take them, he had received the last sacraments. According to Peyronie, if the King lasted one day more it would be nothing short of a miracle.

Escorted by Richelieu, Marie passed through the now overcrowded anteroom. Tired and travel-stained as she was, she felt amazingly composed and reproached herself for an attitude which, in her own eyes, seemed heartless. The sight of Louis appalled her. Like Anne she had remembered his earlier pretended illness and had suspected trickery, but there was no pretense or trickery here. She had difficulty in recognizing as her husband the gaunt-faced, hollow-eyed man who lay before her. Quick tears came to her eyes as she knelt at his side. In a voice scarcely above a whisper Louis asked if the Dauphin had accompanied her to Metz. She nodded and told him in broken accents that his son was waiting now to be summoned to his father's presence.

"He must be kept away," Louis said. "The infection is great. The life of my heir must not be endangered."

"Whatever you wish, Louis."

A flicker of life came to his eyes. "You are not afraid yourself, my dear?"

Marie shook her head. "The time when I attached importance to life is long gone."

"Poor child, how badly I have treated you."

She smiled sadly. To be called a child by a husband seven years younger than oneself was almost ludicrous.

"The words were clumsy," she said. "It was not my intention to reproach you. Forgive me."

"No," he said, and was gratified to find a lump in his throat, "you were always gentle, always kind. I have treated you shamefully."

"To dwell on such things is foolish, Louis."

"What a difficult creature you are!" His voice, rising a little, had in it a faint note of irritation. "Grant me the right, please, to ask your forgiveness."

"There's little to forgive."

"Rubbish!" The note of irritation rose; it even seemed to lend strength to his quavering voice. "There is much—much! I pushed you to the background; I placed others before you. Worse, I was often rude to you, overbearing. Why, when I left for Flanders I did so without thinking of you, without bidding you goodbye."

"Please say no more, Louis." She was beginning to feel acutely embarrassed. "You will only tire yourself."

"Does that matter now?" he asked dramatically. "I have made my peace with God; permit me, at least, to make my peace with you."

165

Marie felt at a loss for words, and she fought to control the impulse to laugh at his attempt to dramatize the humility forced upon him by approaching death.

"I have never reproached you," she said. "I bear you no resentment."

"Your submissiveness," Louis complained, "is making things harder for me."

She was unaware that she had spoken submissively. She touched his hand gently; she told him he had never been as great a sinner as he seemed determined to believe. With a petulant gesture, the gesture of a spoiled child suddenly crossed, he withdrew his hand.

"I promise you this," he said rashly, "that if Peyronie and the others are wrong, if I live, I shall be a different man, a better, a more godly man."

"A foolish promise," Marie said lightly. "If you live, and with all my heart I pray that you might, I shall never hold such a promise against you."

"I would want you to hold it against me," he said earnestly. "Promise, Marie, promise!"

"Very well, Louis, I promise."

He sighed deeply. "No more gambling, no more drinking, no more favorites." He sighed again, dramatically. "Ah, but like all great sinners, my repentance comes too late, much too late."

Anne, in defiance of Maurepas' advice, had taken a small house on the outskirts of Metz, and to this house, when Louis had lingered not one day more but three, Richelieu made his thoughtful way. As he had expected, for Maurepas was doing his work well, a little group of townspeople was gathered at the gate. They had a furtive, threatening look; some of them carried sticks and one, a woman, held a stone in her hands. Richelieu ordered his coachman to drive past the gate. At the bend in the road he issued another order. The coach turned and entered the lane which ran behind Anne's house. A few moments later he entered the house by the back door. No one stopped him; the temporarily hired servants, he suspected, had deserted the Duchesse. When he found her—her eyes, he saw, were red with angry weeping—she expressed a jeering surprise that he should take the risk of seeking her out.

"There is such a thing as loyalty," he murmured.

"Loyalty?"

"We made a compact, Madame."

"You are actually still my friend?"

"Why not?"

"What a strange man you are! Or are you playing some deep little game?"

Richelieu hid a smile. That, of course, was exactly what he was doing. The King, contrary to all expectation, was still alive, and if he recovered there was nothing more likely than Anne's reinstatement. A gamble, yes, but there was no greater gambler at court than he, except, perhaps, the King himself.

"A man," he said sorrowfully, "risks the displeasure of the Queen, the Dauphin, the entire court, by coming to the outcast and is received with suspicion. Such gratitude, dear lady, such gratitude!"

"Forgive me," Anne said quickly.

"More," Richelieu went on, "I even risk disgrace myself by coming here with an offer of protection."

For a moment her eyes danced merrily. "What manner of protection, Richelieu?"

"Protection more substantial than the King ever offered you, Madame."

"You relieve me! I thought for a moment you coveted his Majesty's leavings."

Richelieu remembered his reputation as a rake and laughed shortly. "If I were not sated by the pleasures provided by certain delightful camp followers—"

He broke off suddenly, his ears arrested by the sound of booing from the front of the house. A stone crashed through one of the windows and the booing rose in volume. Richelieu and Anne were standing at the back of the little hall. Anne took an angry step towards the front door. Richelieu, following her, stopped her from opening it.

167

"If you think I fear the rabble set on me by Maurepas—!" she cried indignantly.

Richelieu pointed out that this was not the time for heroics, that the wisest thing she could do was leave Metz without delay. The booing was continuous now, and louder. Another stone crashed through a window. Anne paled. Sudden terror filled her heart. She tried to hide it with a defiant laugh, a laugh that echoed mockingly in her own ears.

"My coach is in the lane at the back," Richelieu told her. "If you want to escape we must hurry."

"But where can I go?"

"A friend of mine owns a country house a few leagues from Verdun. You will find a welcome there and ample shelter."

She embraced him impulsively. "Thank you, Richelieu. I shall never doubt your sincerity again."

It was dark by the time Richelieu returned from Verdun. The risk he had taken in leaving Metz with Anne was slight, and he felt reasonably sure that they had not been recognized together in the coach. He had decided, in any case, that if his act of kindness did reach the King's ears, his Majesty would feel not anger but gratitude. To dismiss a favorite because the threat of death had reduced one to a state of grace was one thing; to see her attacked by an incensed rabble quite another. And if by any chance he did recover, his gratitude, once time and improved health had dissipated the state of grace, would be heightened beyond all reason.

When his coach turned into the main street of Metz Richelieu was surprised to see a large gathering of people building bonfires and letting off fireworks. He knew instantly what this meant, but he made the coachman stop, and leaning out of the window asked a lounger the reason for the apparent merrymaking.

"The King has taken a turn for the better," he was told.

He went straight to Louis' headquarters and sought an audience with the Queen. Marie told him that she had been approached that morning by a quack doctor who had

168

sworn that he could cure the King. Knowing that Peyronie would never admit the man to the royal presence, she had managed by subterfuge to smuggle him into the room.

"Within an hour of taking the quack's medicine," Marie said, "his Majesty showed a slight improvement. Two hours later there was no doubt that he had taken a turn for the better."

"And now, your Majesty?"

"Peyronie and the others agree that the King will live."

"Thank heaven, then, for the quack and his medicine."

Withdrawing, Richelieu complimented himself on having gone to Anne and convinced her that he was her one true friend, and though later he learned that the King was a changed man, a veritable saint, he was well content to wait with fortitude for the inevitable reinstatement.

"Whether life is good or bad," he told himself, "it is always amusing."

XV

"GENTLEMEN," Louis said breezily, "I propose, henceforth, to take my office of chief minister with the utmost seriousness.

A few brief and knowing smiles were exchanged by his ministers, all of whom had been summoned to Metz. Seeing the smiles, Louis chuckled merrily.

"You rogues! Take my words lightly if you must, but I do mean business this time."

Louis had made a rapid recovery and now, Peyronie having pronounced him well enough, he had called the first council meeting since his illness. He had put on weight again, but not too much; his eyes were bright, his skin was clear and his step had in it the springiness of youth. Watching his diet under Peyronie's supervision, he was eating sparingly, taking hardly any wine and keeping remarkably early hours. Continually he praised God for having spared him, and he told Him that now as never before he was determined to be a real father to his people.

He turned courteously to the Marquis d'Argenson, his Minister of War. "And now, my dear fellow, I shall welcome your report."

Argenson bowed and assured his Majesty that the campaign in Flanders was a complete triumph. For a few moments, holding his bewigged head proudly erect, he spoke of the eastern flank, the only enemy stronghold of which yet to be taken was Fribourg. Peace, he concluded, and peace on France's own terms, was within sight.

"Splendid!" Louis cried.

Richelieu, thinking of Anne, whom he had advised to go to Paris incognito, suggested that the time had now come for Louis to return to Versailles.

"But go by way of Paris," he said, "where the people are eager to see their king again. Your Majesty will be made very welcome. There are two excellent reasons for public rejoicing, victory and your Majesty's miraculous recovery."

"My recovery would have meant little without victory," Louis said humbly. "Still, if the people of Paris want to line the streets and cheer me, by all means let them."

Louis set out for Paris two days later. Marie and the Dauphin had already left Metz with Louis' words ringing in their ears: "Henceforth I shall be a better husband and a better father; henceforth, by the grace of God, my life shall be dedicated to self-denial and good works."

It was a bitterly cold winter's day when he entered Paris and heavy rain was falling, yet the people did line the streets, cheering and crying, "Long live the King!" His heart swelled with pride and tears filled his eyes. He saw that he was indeed, as several poets were declaring in beautiful verse, "Louis the Well-Beloved."

"A most satisfying welcome," Maurepas remarked.

He, along with Richelieu and Argenson, shared the place of honor in the royal coach. Louis nodded happily. There was a lump in his throat, of which he thoroughly approved, but which made speech impossible.

"The people are wild with joy," Argenson remarked.

Richelieu, smiling gently, decided to test the King's mood by mentioning Anne's now forbidden name. "I fear their joy would be less evident if Madame la Duchesse were sharing the coach with us."

Louis looked pained. "Really, Richelieu, I beg of you!"

He could but agree with Richelieu, yet it pleased as well as pained him to hear Anne spoken of, even like that. He wondered where she was, if she was well, and whether or not she felt herself ill-treated.

"Nevertheless," Richelieu added with a grin, "why anyone should cheer a man for preferring a dull life to a merry one is past my comprehension."

Louis frowned and sighed. Again he could but agree with Richelieu. He sighed again. Anne, and *all that*, must be thrust sternly from his mind. He had given his word; he had promised Marie. He was determined, for the sake of his country, his family and his immortal soul to walk in righteousness. Good works, self-denial and . . . more good works. He shuddered involuntarily, but told himself quickly that the icy blast of the wind was the cause of it.

"If I can reform at my age," he said severely, "surely you, Richelieu, so much older than I, can do likewise."

But Richelieu, looking out of the window, pretended not to hear. He gave a little start of surprise and cried: "Why, look! Madame la Duchesse herself!"

Louis pressed his nose against the glass of the window.

"Where? Standing in the crowd, you mean?"

"I suppose I *could* have been mistaken," said Richelieu, modifying his little fib.

"The Duchesse de Chateauroux," Maurepas sneered, "would never dare to show her face in Paris."

"Anne," Louis told him sharply, "was never a coward. I well remember how—" He checked himself and blushed. The others were looking at him intently: Maurepas in faint alarm, Argenson in frank curiosity and Richelieu with a wide grin on his still-handsome face. "Whether she was ever a coward or not," Louis said airily, "whether it was she in the crowd or not, I have no interest in her now, no interest whatever."

"That is understood, Sire," Richelieu said solemnly. "It was wrong of me to speak of her."

"A continent life," Louis said stoutly, "good works, self-denial and . . . more good works."

"Which reminds me," Richelieu murmured innocently,

"that the Queen is counting on your Majesty attending Holy Communion at Christmas."

"I am counting on it myself," Louis cried.

Louis spent a few days in Paris. Every night bonfires were lit, fireworks displays were held and wine was given away in the streets. Professing himself a little shocked at the drunkenness thus caused while he himself remained sober, Louis left the capital for Versailles. For a full week he was most attentive to Marie and declared himself delighted when, on the first Sunday night of his return, she organized a dull little concert for him. "Innocent pleasures," he enthused, "how satisfying they really are." Marie repeated the concert on the second Sunday night, which seemed to suggest that she was going to make a habit of it.

"Think of it," Louis confided in Richelieu, "every Sunday night for the rest of my life! Harp solos, soulful Italian tenors, breathless German sopranos." He repressed a shudder. "Purgatory, sheer purgatory!"

"We could play a little piquet or cavagnolle after the next concert," Richelieu suggested.

Louis sighed. "What a tempting thought! And perhaps a bottle or two of champagne. The last time I played cavagnolle I lost twenty thousand livres—"

"It was an all-night sitting."

"I won, I lost, I won and I lost again."

"From eleven till four."

"Nearer five than four, Richelieu."

"So it was."

Louis squared his shoulders. He thrust temptation aside. Self-denial and good works; there was no escape. He would give twenty thousand livres to the poor and hope that the tenors would be less soulful, the sopranos less breathless.

The approach of Christmas began to fill Louis with a growing uneasiness. He wondered why. Normally he adored Christmas, especially if there was snow, and loved the giving of presents, the general air of goodwill, superficial as it might be. The uneasiness troubled him sorely. It occurred to him that the milk of human kindness might be turning a little sour within him, yet how could that be possible in a man existing on the high, ecstatic plane known as a State of Grace? And then, when he was despairing of an explanation, he remembered Richelieu's words about Marie counting on his attending Holy Communion at Christmas.

"Damnation!" he muttered.

Concentrating on the happier aspect of Christmas, he began to think of the presents he would give his family. It was no easy task, though Marie herself could be disposed of simply with a richly bound book, strong in moral tone, highly religious in flavor. As for the girls . . . But his thoughts began to wander and he remembered the diamonds he had given Anne last Christmas. Christmas, he brooded, was a time when one forgave one's enemies and asked forgiveness of those one had wronged.

"No, no," he said hastily. "I must remember my promise!"

Nevertheless he had an impulse to ask Richelieu a pertinent question. He managed to restrain himself but the impulse remained to nag him for the rest of the week. And then it was Sunday again, early evening, an hour before Marie's infernal concert was due to commence. In the near distance he could hear a soprano voice running up and down the scale. It belonged to Madame Calonne, the one who gave so many encores. "Pah!" he cried, and the impulse got the better of him.

"Richelieu," he said, when that gentleman stood before him, "what news have you of Anne?"

Richelieu smiled. "Madame la Duchesse is living quietly in Paris."

"Ah . . ."

"To be frank, Sire, I had speech with her yesterday."

"You did?"

"She has taken a small house in the Rue du Bac."

"Really? Well, well, *well!*" Louis avoided Richelieu's eyes. "A brave little woman, living in Paris when popular feeling has been so much against her. The courage, the amazing courage!"

"She has what might be called an unconquerable spirit, Sire."

"Yes indeed! And her health? How did she look? Is she well?"

"A little pale, your Majesty, and her manner is not so gay as formerly. But of course, under the circumstances . . ."

"Quite, quite!" Louis said hastily.

The invisible Madame Calonne, having paused for breath, burst forth again. Louis and Richelieu exchanged a glance. Richelieu turned up his eyes, Louis put his hands over his ears.

"The lady is in excellent voice," Richelieu commented.

Louis groaned. "Another Sunday night concert. Pon my oath, Richelieu, I could never face it."

"Nor I, Sire."

Louis hesitated no longer. "Richelieu, as you love me, call for a coach and take me to the Rue du Bac."

Trembling with excitement Louis sat on the edge of his seat in the coach. He felt like a conspirator and certainly like a truant. As the coach drew near Paris he was consumed with anxiety. Anne might not be at home; she might hate him and have nothing but contempt for him; she might even refuse to receive him. He remembered the journey he had made to Choisy after deciding to forgive Pauline, and remembering it his anxiety turned to fear. Pauline had been taken ill, had died without speaking to him. Was it possible that Anne . . . ? He drew his cloak more warmly about him. Could this dreadful thought, slipping unwanted into his mind, be a premonition?

"After tonight," Richelieu remarked, "I shall be the richer by several thousand livres."

Louis looked at him blankly. "Indeed?"

"A little wager, Sire."

"Great heavens," Louis cried, reading Richelieu's grin correctly, "you have been gambling on the possibility of my restoring Anne to favor!"

"Oh, quite modestly, your Majesty."

"You dog, Richelieu, you dog!"

Louis felt much happier. That he desired to see Anne for a few moments only was all he had been prepared to admit to himself; now he acknowledged freely that he intended to restore her. He pictured himself taking her hands warmly in his, then embracing her and whispering endearments in her ear. He would bite the lobe of each ear gently, and later . . .

"The Rue du Bac," Richelieu announced.

The coach came to a halt.

"Wait here," Louis instructed his friend.

He leaped from the coach and trembling with excitement rapped loudly on the door of the house. One of the maids who had served Anne at Versailles admitted him and after keeping him waiting for only a few moments returned to announce that Madame la Duchesse would be honored to receive his Majesty the King.

"So kind of you, my dear!" he cried, as he entered Anne's boudoir.

He saw, as he hurried forward, intending to take her in his arms, that she was a little pale, as Richelieu had said. She stopped him with a cold little gesture. Her voice when she spoke was icy.

"Please be seated, your Majesty."

Louis sighed sadly. "I deserve this, oh yes, I deserve it."

Anne was wearing a negligée he had never seen before. (He was not to know that Richelieu had sent a messenger post haste in advance of the royal coach.) He studied the negligée, which had been designed to conceal only what it was meant with subtlety to reveal. He remembered that night when he had rushed to her at Choisy. His pulses leaped. Never had he known her more desirable. He knew now how a man, crawling on the hot sand of a desert searching for water, must feel. He recalled virtuously that he had not touched a woman since going to Metz, not even Marie herself, in spite of the reconciliation. A State of Grace was all very well for weaklings and failures, but when a man was in his prime and had real blood in his veins . . . ! He took a quick step forward. Again Anne held him back with a cold little gesture and hard, uncompromising eyes. Was it possible that he had crawled through the sterile sands of self-denial, only to find a mirage?

"I trust I find you well," he stammered.

"Very well, thank you."

He tried again. "Life in Paris is pleasant?"

"Pleasant enough."

"You are not in want, I hope?"

"In want? In want of money, you mean?"

He gave her a suggestive yet sheepish look. "That, and other things."

"I am in want of nothing, not even money," Anne said coolly.

"Confound you, Madame," he exploded, "this cold politeness is nothing less than insulting!"

"I stand in the presence of his Majesty the King. I must remember my place and my manners."

"Pah! If I fall on my knees and beg your pardon, will you unbend a little?"

"Is that why you came, to beg my pardon?"

"Yes! A thousand times yes!" A plaintive note came to his voice. "Oh Anne, my dear, if only you knew how bored I've been! If only you knew how tame life is without you. Versailles these days is as chilly and uninspiring as a morgue. For pity's sake, Anne, come back."

"And run the risk of being disgraced all over again?"

"I never meant to disgrace you. I was ill. I—I was dying. Various people took advantage of my condition. I wasn't responsible. Surely you realize that!"

"Various people might take advantage of you again."

"Never!" he said stoutly.

Anne smiled for the first time. "This is winter. In winter people catch cold easily. A slight cold and your Majesty is likely to become a saint again."

"Never! Never, never, *never!*"

"You are much too vehement, Sire."

"Come back," he urged, "and you shall have anything you ask. *Anything!*"

"I ask only one thing, the dismissal of Maurepas."

"Granted!—" Louis tried to bite off the word but it had

escaped his lips. "I spoke too hastily," he said. "Maurepas is an excellent minister. Irreplaceable, one might say."

Anne shrugged. "In that case—"

"No, no, wait! Maurepas shall have less power; he shall be answerable to you in all things."

Anne relaxed a little. This was better than she had expected, for she had been ready to return to court on any terms. Maurepas, answerable to her, could be humiliated in many ways. There would be more satisfaction in that than his actual dismissal.

"Issue an official invitation, in writing," she said, "and I promise to consider it."

"Gladly, gladly!"

"The invitation shall acknowledge that I have been badly treated, that my old position shall be restored in full."

"Gladly—" the negligée was of a weblike lace, and black—"gladly!"

"It shall be delivered to me by Maurepas and read aloud by him."

"Gladly—" the black of the lace against the flawless ivory of the skin was enough to drive you crazy—"gladly!" He took her in his arms. "You'll return with me now? *Now?*"

Anne freed herself haughtily. "Before the letter is written and delivered?"

"Tomorrow, then?"

"If the letter is delivered in the morning, yes."

Louis looked at her in an agony of doubt. "You propose to turn me away now?"

Anne studied his face for a moment. He was flushed and his eyes were dark with desire. An inclination to giggle was checked by the set of his mouth. It was a smaller mouth than she had thought and it had an ugly look now. In a moment he would be scowling. She concluded that she had driven him far enough. A refusal might prove disastrous. She remembered what had happened when her sister Julie had made him believe that the Queen was turning him from her bed. With a little laugh she stepped lightly into his arms and lifted her face to his.

"I am not as heartless as you think," she whispered.

When Louis, breezily and a little pompously, announced that the favorite was to return to court his words were received with a howl of rage from a group of courtiers who, without Marie's consent, were beginning to call themselves the Queen's Party. Taking a leaf from Pauline de Vintimille's book, they had looked forward, while Louis was ill at Metz, to the setting up of a regency; now they feared that their presence at court, which the King tolerated, would be seriously threatened by Madame la Duchesse's return.

As it happened it was some days before Anne was able to leave Paris, for a cold (only a slight one, she sent word to Louis, and not likely to reduce her to a State of Grace) kept her in bed at the house in the Rue du Bac. During this time obscene verses were written at her expense and circulated not only in the streets of Paris but at Versailles itself. Reading some of them, Louis shook with suppressed laughter, but when others were written at *his* expense he uttered a growl of anger.

The day before Anne returned to Versailles, Maurepas, in no way connected with the so-called Queen's Party, approached Louis on the subject of the favorite's reinstatement. A demonstration against her in the Rue du Bac gave him an excuse for speaking, but he stated boldly that with or without an excuse he was determined to speak his mind. Louis scowled, but a little shame-faced at having forced Maurepas to humble himself before Anne, he listened without protest.

"Your Majesty is more popular with the people than ever before," Maurepas said, "but if Madame la Duchesse is restored to power a loss of prestige will immediately follow."

"Did *you* write those shameful verses?" Louis asked.

Maurepas smiled engagingly. "No, your Majesty, but only because I lack the wit."

Louis made a noise that was half a grunt and half a laugh.

"Nobody suggests," Maurepas went on, "that your Majesty should live the life of a monk. Keep a mistress by all means, keep a dozen if need be, but refrain, I beg of you, from setting up a woman as the power behind the throne. It is that that the people object to."

Louis rose. "Please withdraw," he said sternly. "Try me too far and I shall make Madame la Duchesse my chief minister."

Maurepas bowed. "It would be a pity," he said, as he backed from the royal presence, "to sacrifice the title of Louis the Well-Beloved."

Louis pondered on this parting shot, and the more he pondered the more inclined he was to agree. He thought, too, of that other remark made by Maurepas. "Keep a mistress by all means, keep a dozen if need be." What manner of a man did Maurepas think him? Though surely there was good sense in the suggestion. Just think of it, a dozen, each distinguished by some special, individual charm! A most attractive idea, but one, he thought wistfully, that Anne would no more countenance than the setting aside of the power he had promised to restore to her. "I shall never be a match for these masterful women!" he raged.

On the night of Anne's return he ordered a sumptuous supper, sumptuous, yet one that showed a new restraint. "We have fallen into the habit at Versailles of eating too much and eating it vulgarly," he had pronounced only a few days ago. "Let us have more delicate dishes, prepared with the utmost *finesse;* let us concentrate, not on those heavy dishes that make our minds sluggish, but on the *entrée,* the *salmi* and the *entremets.*"

Surveying the table with satisfaction as he and Anne sat opposite each other, he was conscious nonetheless that something was lacking. Anne, he noted, was pale and her eyes held a somber look. This should be a gay little supper, yet Anne was anything but gay, and she seemed disinclined to make any real conversation.

"Are you ill, my dear?" he asked impatiently.

"I think I must be," she said, "I feel wretched."

He touched her brow and the heat of it alarmed him. He sent for Peyronie. The surgeon clicked his teeth wisely and ordered Anne to be bled. Louis was furious. The first night of her return and this had to happen!

The next morning, just as he was about to leave for Rambouillet with Richelieu, he was informed that Madame la Duchesse was suffering from a severe congestion of the lungs. He hunted all day and spent the night at the little chateau. The following morning on his return he was told that Anne's condition was so grave that a priest had been called. Horrified, he rushed to her bedside. She was so weak that she could do little more than whisper his name, and later her struggle for breath was a torture to watch.

When it was all over he shut himself up in his apartments, not the big state rooms, which he was using now on special occasions only, but the smaller, more intimate apartments he had always liked best. He remained here, going only to the state bedroom for the usual ceremonial *lever* and *coucher*, and there, silent and entirely wrapped in his gloomy thoughts, he was the despair of his gentlemen.

Death, he felt, had a way of haunting him. It had brought him to the throne when by rights he should have remained a carefree prince. Not only had it swept away his brother, his father, his grandfather and his great-grandfather, it had taken Pauline and now Anne—Anne whose loss was a double blow. She had reminded him so strongly of Pauline; that was why he had grown to love her. It was almost as if Pauline had died a second death.

"I shall never look at another woman in my life," he told himself. "I might even abdicate in favor of my son and seek the peace and quiet of a monastery."

XVI

"**I** THINK I may say, my dear Argenson," Richelieu remarked conversationally, "that we have always been the best of friends."

Argenson looked thoughtfully at Richelieu and wondered what his game was. In many ways he envied the man his smooth, engaging manner. Richelieu, one might say, was the perfect courtier, and as such filled Argenson, gruff of manner and clumsy where court intrigue was concerned, with a feeling of inferiority.

"Come to the point and save time," Argenson said.

Richelieu hesitated, wondering how best to deal with this man he had decided to make his ally.

"What do you think of the King's continued piety?" he asked at last.

"It won't last much longer."

Christmas had come and gone and Louis, disappointing the Queen, had refused at the last moment to go to Holy Communion. Nevertheless, his general attitude was still one of self-denial, with the result that he was sulky and inactive most of the time, especially where state affairs were concerned.

Richelieu offered Argenson his gold encrusted snuff-box.

"The court," he went on smoothly, "is on the brink of a

considerable struggle for power. On the one hand we have his royal Highness, the Dauphin, still a boy but most disapproving of his father, and Maurepas, who is busy paying court to the Dauphin. On the other we have a king who is full of good resolutions but stands inactively and fretfully alone."

"What are you driving at?" Argenson demanded.

"My dear Argenson, for many years the balance of power has been decided by his Majesty's habit of maintaining a royal favorite. The King will always be ruled by women. Therefore the only sure way of gaining influence at court is through friendship with the current favorite. The King's present restlessness is a sure sign that he will soon be ready to set up another Declared Mistress."

"He may surprise us all by turning to the Queen."

Richelieu shook his head. "The Queen is middle-aged and staid. She is no more interested in seeing an extra pillow placed in her bed than she is in taking a hand in state affairs. The real danger lies with the Dauphin and Maurepas. To counter that I have a plan which might interest you. In short, I suggest that you and I should select a suitable young woman and bring her skilfully to his Majesty's notice."

"Why do you want to drag me into this, Richelieu?"

Richelieu laughed lightly. "You happen to be clever, really clever, while I am merely a man with a penchant for intrigue. You are sincere too, and will never work for anything but the good of France."

Argenson laughed harshly. "A man seeking power talks of the good of his country—amazing!"

Richelieu reddened at the gibe. He said stiffly: "Do you agree to my plan?"

Argenson remained silent for a moment, staring into space. Richelieu, like the rest, was interested only in himself. The state of the country meant nothing to him. He refused to see that the vast squandering of money, bringing additional taxation to an already over-taxed people, might in the end lead to revolution.

"I agree to your plan," he said at last. "If I can use you, in spite of yourself, for the good of France, use you I shall."

In the weeks that followed Richelieu was in close attendance on the King, whose restlessness grew worse, and several times he tempted him to play a discreet little game of cards, not in the great gallery—that would come later—but in the privacy of his Majesty's library. Following the last of these games, when Louis was making his usual public *coucher*, Richelieu referred to the rumor that the Dauphin's wife was with child.

"No truth in it, thank heaven!" Louis grunted.

Richelieu began to help him out of his shirt. "Ah, your Majesty dislikes the thought of becoming a grandfather."

Louis, his voice muffled by the folds of the shirt, said: "Intensely!"

The *coucher* continued, with the other gentlemen of the bedchamber crowding about the King, ears pricked, brows raised expectantly. Richelieu murmured that to become a grandfather at thirty-five would be something of an achievement.

"Thirty-five?" Louis groaned. "I feel at least a hundred."

Richelieu helped him into his dressing-gown. "A man, they say, is as young as he feels."

"Hold your stupid tongue, Richelieu!"

Richelieu winked at the others. "Peyronie, I believe, has concocted a new tonic for a sluggish liver."

Louis made a face. "I tried it last week. Sheer poison."

"It is my belief," Richelieu said solemnly, "that saintliness is just as disturbing to one's liver as excessive drinking."

"More so, by heaven!" Louis snarled.

The next morning, at the public *lever*, he made a pompous announcement. "It is our wish," he said, "that three days from today the court shall attend a hunt at Sénart. The gentlemen taking part will meet at eight in the morning. The ladies and other spectators will assemble in the forest before midday."

Richelieu smiled and exchanged a knowing glance with Argenson. Both were thinking the same thing. First a royal hunt, then a little royal card-playing in the great gallery, and the King, in all but one respect, would be leading a normal life again.

"The sooner we act the better," Richelieu commented.

"Have you any particular woman in mind?" Argenson asked.

"No, but at supper tonight we shall drink a silent toast to the young woman who, for the moment, we shall call the Unknown."

Argenson, standing alone for a moment, surveyed the scene in the forest. A striped pavilion and some small tents had been set up in a clearing, and here the court was enjoying a long-delayed picnic meal. It was the old story. Everybody but the King was tired; everybody but the King, whose laugh rang out constantly, was eager to return to Versailles. Presently Argenson was joined by Richelieu.

"Here she comes again!" Richelieu cried. "Watch!"

A sky-blue phaeton with a negro postilion driving the horses was approaching the clearing at a brisk pace. A sudden hush fell on the gathering; not only Richelieu and Argenson were watching the phaeton but the whole court. It drew closer, passed through the center of the clearing—for a moment it was within a few paces of Louis himself—then disappeared from sight. And at no time did the young woman sitting back on the cushions look to right or to left.

"It looks as if somebody is trying to steal a march on us," Argenson said dryly.

Richelieu nodded. "But think of it, a blue phaeton, a black postilion and an air of complete indifference! What better way of attracting attention than that!"

The silence had been broken by a rising chatter of excited voices, and the King, Richelieu saw, was hurrying towards him through the crowd.

"You saw her, Richelieu?" Louis cried. "You saw the lovely creature in the blue phaeton?"

"Everybody saw her, Sire."

"Three times she did it! The impudence, and yet the dignity! Who is she? Do you know her?"

"Her identity is a complete mystery to me."

"Then solve the mystery! Solve it and let me know her

name." Louis was flushed and excited. "And send her a present. Some venison or some grouse. See to it, Richelieu, see to it!"

"Certainly I shall see to it," Richelieu murmured, as Louis turned on his heels. "And how fortunate his Majesty gave the order to me, instead of Maurepas, for instance!"

"You propose to make her the center of your plan?" Argenson asked.

"I must, my dear fellow. The King is interested."

"She might not be suitable."

"That will depend on how I handle the matter. Our immediate concern is: who is she and where can we find her?"

"Excuse me, Monsieur le Duc," said a voice.

Richelieu and Argenson swung round. Facing them, and so close that he had obviously heard some of their conversation, was a young man known to them as Binet, one of the Dauphin's valets.

"Well, what is it?" Richelieu demanded angrily.

Binet gave him a mild, sly look. "If you wish it, Monsieur le Duc, I can take you to the young lady who passed just now in the blue phaeton."

Richelieu's eyes narrowed; he suspected a trap. "Your master the Dauphin would hardly be pleased at such a suggestion, for obviously you know my reason for wishing to meet her."

"Obviously," Binet said cheekily. "I saw the sensation she created and I heard his Majesty's words. Then I heard your own words. I think it may be safely concluded that his Majesty no longer remembers Madame la Duchesse de Chateauroux."

"What proof have we," Argenson demanded, "that you are not trying to mislead us on behalf of his royal highness the Dauphin?"

Binet laughed softly. "The young lady is my cousin."

Richelieu gave the young man a haughty look. "So you and she planned this little comedy." Binet nodded. Richelieu's haughtiness deepened. "A little over-ambitious of her, surely, she being the cousin of a valet!"

"We aim high, I admit, Monsieur."

"Too high! The King would never take an interest in any but an aristocrat."

Binet smiled guilelessly. "His Majesty might be persuaded to dispense with such a precedent if my cousin were to enlist the help and advice of a gentleman so deeply versed in court intrigue as Monsieur le Duc de Richelieu."

Mollified and flattered Richelieu asked the girl's name.

"Jeanne Antoinette Lenormant d'Etiole."

"Well-to-do middleclass, I presume?"

Binet nodded. "And apart from that, Toinette, as we call her, is beautiful, clever and well-educated."

"She possesses a husband?"

"Naturally. She is *most* respectable."

"Are there any children?"

"One, a girl."

"Would the husband be likely to prove difficult?"

Binet turned up his eyes. "Heavens, no! He is handsome, weak and a fool. Toinette contrived his absence for a few weeks before launching what we call our campaign. He need be considered in no way."

Richelieu reflected that Toinette sounded like a scheming little baggage. He himself would have chosen someone more demure, more amenable to direction, but the choice, unfortunately, was no longer his. The king had seen her and that was that.

"Where does she live?" he asked.

"In Paris, the Rue St. Honoré."

"Tomorrow, at three in the afternoon, then," Richelieu said.

Though in actual fact Louis had caught but a passing glance of Jeanne Antoinette Lenormant d'Etiole he had spoken of her as a lovely creature. Looking at her now from the distance of a few paces, both Richelieu and Argenson echoed the King's words. She had a white, flawless complexion. Her brows, wide and finely arched, lent distinction to a nose which was perfection itself. Her hair, a rich chestnut, was a striking contrast to the whiteness of her skin. Conscious of her eyes as she smiled at him, Richelieu was struck by their size and color: they were the sort of eyes that would take their shade from the dress she wore but which at all times would have in them a deep and fathomless green. For the rest, she was tall, slim and utterly graceful. She was, Richelieu thought, in something like awe, the most elegant creature he had ever seen.

Her lips curled mockingly. "Even though this is not a slave market, gentlemen, I trust you find my person pleasing."

Richelieu bowed. "Infinitely pleasing, Madame."

The valet Binet, watchfully present, invited the visitors to be seated.

"No, no," Toinette laughed. "Let them stand. It is something of a novelty to receive such homage from a pair of aristocrats."

Richelieu smiled. It would be impossible to take offense at anything she said. Her voice, in keeping with her looks and figure, was utterly entrancing.

"The purpose of our visit is of course known to you," he said.

"Of course, Monsieur."

For a moment, as he looked at her, Richelieu forgot her beauty and thought of her antecedents. Since yesterday he had made swift inquiries and discovered all it was necessary to know. She was twenty-four. Her father, a man by the unprepossessing name of Poisson, was once a clerk holding a government position gained through the judicious distribution by his wife of certain favors in high quarters. She, the mother, had also at one time been the mistress of a wealthy gentleman by the name of Lenormant. Such was Lenormant's infatuation that Toinette had been educated at his expense and then married to his nephew, Lenormant d'Étiole.

"I thank you for coming to see me," Toinette was saying. "I naturally understand that without your help the achievement of my ambition would be most difficult."

"I congratulate you on the wisdom of your attitude," Richelieu said.

Toinette smiled pleasantly. "I said 'most difficult,' Monsieur, not 'impossible'." Richelieu cleared his throat as she added, "It is my habit to get what I want, even when a king is involved."

"You opened your campaign in an original manner," Argenson told her admiringly.

"A touch of genius, I admit," she replied.

"It will need more than a touch of genius," Richelieu snapped, "for a middleclass woman, however beautiful and clever she may be, to take the place of the late Duchesse de Chateauroux."

Toinette smiled sweetly. "Thank you for acknowledging my beauty."

"I always acknowledge beauty when I see it."

"And brains also?"

"In a woman I prefer a preponderance of beauty over brains."

"Ah, but for a middleclass woman, aiming to establish herself at Versailles, the very reverse might be necessary. However, I think I disagree with you a little. I think the King, once his interest is aroused, would take a favorite from the gutter itself."

"Never!" Richelieu was deeply shocked. "A temporary mistress, yes, but not a favorite. And that might apply even to a woman of the middleclass."

Toinette took a graceful step towards the door, the silk of her amber-colored gown rustling softly as she did so.

"I see that I must regretfully bid you good afternoon, gentlemen."

"No, wait!" Richelieu protested.

She turned. Her eyes were mocking. "You think I have a chance?"

"We-ell—"

"I assure you, Monsieur, I *know* I have, even unaided and alone."

"You shall have all the help I can give you, providing—"

"Providing," she broke in, "I use the influence I gain on your behalf."

"I see we understand each other perfectly, Madame."

Toinette inclined her head. "Well, what do you want of me?"

Richelieu considered this. "Up to now the King has merely asked your name and sent you a present of venison. An invitation to supper will probably follow, providing I give his Majesty a good report of you. I suggest that you refuse the invitation and remain aloof and unattainable, yet hold yourself ready to act when I give the word."

Toinette laughed gaily. "I could hardly have given myself better advice. And now—" she made a gesture of dismissal— "if you have nothing more to say . . ."

It was not until Richelieu and Argenson had bowed themselves out that Richelieu realized how easily, almost without a thought, he had permitted himself to be dismissed. Middleclass she might be, with a father who possessed the name of Poisson, namely *fish,* but she had all the command and self-possession of a born aristocrat.

Meanwhile Toinette was looking at her cousin, the Dauphin's valet, with laughter in her eyes. Argenson she liked, admittedly because he had admired her openly, but Richelieu she would never trust.

"Richelieu may condescend as much as he likes," she said scornfully, "but some day I shall make him understand that a woman of the middleclass, a class that generally thinks in terms of money, knows how to demand a good return for services rendered to anybody."

"Jeanne Antoinette . . ." Louis mused. "I like the sound of it. But Toinette . . . no, no, that is too babyish." He took a few paces across the room. He was, Richelieu saw, on the point of scowling. "But—*middleclass!*"

Richelieu smiled broadly. "The people, even those of the middleclass, belong to the King."

"No," Louis sighed, "the King belongs to the people."

"Then in that case, Sire . . ."

Louis grinned boyishly, but a moment later a scowl replaced the grin.

"The whole court would laugh at me."

"If your Majesty were to see her at close quarters the laughter of the court would never trouble you."

"Describe her," Louis commanded.

Richelieu did so.

"I have only one criticism," he concluded. "Mind you, I can't be absolutely certain, today's fashion hides that sort of thing, but I think she is a little narrow in the hips."

Louis laughed shortly. "She is not required for the bearing of children." He looked reflectively at Richelieu. "You make her sound exquisite, my dear fellow—unless you exaggerate."

"No painter in France could do her justice," Richelieu said warmly. "I was tempted, Sire, to tell you she had gone abroad and keep her for myself."

"Were you, you dog! Er—what of her voice?"

"Sweet and clear."

"And her nature?"

"How can I say at so short an acquaintance? Your Majesty, however, would find her comfortable to live with."

Louis frowned. *"Comfortable?"*

"She is, remember, of the middleclass."

Louis made up his mind. "Invite her to supper. A discreet and temporary *affaire* is, I think, the most I could risk." He looked hopefully at Richelieu. "Yes?"

"She has different ideas, Sire."

Louis raised his royal brows. "You actually discussed the matter with her?"

"Briefly, your Majesty, on the assumption that you might consider the establishment of a middleclass favorite something of a novelty."

"Never!"

"Nothing less than establishment appeals to her."

"Then she can go to the devil!"

Richelieu smiled and withdrew. He was in no way disturbed. It was necessary only for the King to gain a close glimpse of Toinette, and he had already decided how best to achieve this. Within the week there was a masked ball in Paris, at the Hotel de Ville. Toinette should attend it, dressed as the huntress Diana, for huntress indeed she was, and the costume would show off her figure to perfection.

Argenson, when told, was inclined to demur about taking the matter further. He thought that Toinette was too self-assured and he suspected, now that the spell of her presence was but a memory, that she might give them too much trouble.

"Choose somebody else," he advised, "and make sure she is an aristocrat."

"Toinette *is* an aristocrat," Richelieu said generously. "Nature has made her one. As for giving trouble, I very much doubt it. Once she comes to Versailles the whole court will band together against her. Even the servants, who are much more class-conscious than anyone else, will laugh at her. She will have no friends except you and me. She will be ours to mold as we wish."

Argenson shrugged. "Suit yourself, but remember that I warned you."

There had been considerable speculation at Versailles as to who would design the most original costume for the masked ball. Louis, entering happily into the spirit of the thing, had declared that if a prize were given for this he, the King, would most certainly win it, and unable to keep the secret to himself he had sworn Richelieu to silence and confided in him.

On the great night itself Richelieu, having attended Louis to the Hotel de Ville and helped him into his costume, slipped away to the Rue St. Honoré where Toinette was waiting for him. He surveyed her with pleasure and assured her that the scanty huntress costume of Diana was most becoming.

"I flatter myself that you speak the truth," she said coolly.

"Of all the virtues you might possess," he laughed, "modesty is not among them."

"Not false modesty, certainly. Does my mask completely disguise me?"

"Completely." He made an impulsive attempt to embrace her. "My dear—"

She slipped from his arms quickly. "My favors are for the King or no one, Monsieur."

"You have never met him," Richelieu said angrily. "You might find him loathsome, that way."

"All men are, either that or ridiculous. Shall we go, Monsieur?"

On reaching the Hotel de Ville she remarked that the King's costume was supposed to be a jealously guarded secret, so how, she wanted to know, was she to recognize him. Richelieu invited her to glance about the brilliant gathering and hazard a guess.

"Is he visible from here?" she asked.

"Yes. You see the row of imitation yew trees to the left of the orchestra?"

Toinette nodded. "The man in the Turkish costume standing near them, is he the King?"

"No, the Turk is Maurepas, the man who will be your greatest enemy at court. Maurepas, the Dauphin and possibly the Queen. That will be the order."

"One of the yew trees moved!" Toinette said.

Richelieu laughed. "That is the King, and I think he must have seen our fair Diana. Go forward alone and stand beneath the trees, and remember, when his Majesty shows interest, tempt him with the unattainable."

Conscious of many eyes upon her, Toinette walked slowly and gracefully towards the yew trees. Her movements, Richelieu noticed, were beautiful; she walked, not from the knees as so many women did, but from the hips, swinging her long slim legs with a freedom of movement that was sheer poetry to watch. And when she reached the trees she stood there, not in simpering modesty, but squarely, balancing herself equally on each sandal-covered foot.

Presently, as she hummed a little tune beneath her breath, she heard a hoarse voice say, "Diana!" She looked innocently at the Turk, who was close at hand.

"Did you speak, Monsieur?"

"No, Madame, but—"

"How odd, I could have sworn—"

"Turn round, you idiot!" the hoarse voice continued, "turn round!"

She looked at the Turk again. His eyes were fixed on the tree behind her. She turned and stared at it.

"Delightful," it said, "delightful!"

"Heavens," she cried, "a talking tree! Of all the marvels of the ball this is the greatest."

"*And* the most uncomfortable," Louis gasped. "The top branches lift off. Help me with them, please."

"That would be unmasking, Monsieur, and no one is allowed to do that until the King gives the word."

"I'm wearing the customary mask also," Louis said. "Come, help me before I suffocate. Take the top firmly in your hands, twist it right and left and lift it."

Toinette followed the instructions carefully but not without difficulty. Finally, with a great upward wrench and a grunt from Louis, the top of the tree came away in her hands.

"Oh Monsieur, how red you are!" she laughed.

"Air!" he gasped. "I must have air!"

Together they went out into the night, Louis with shuffling steps, for his trunk hampered him.

"Slowly," he begged, delighted to have an excuse to hold her arm.

"As slowly as you wish, Monsieur Tree."

"What a merry laugh you have!"

"Thank you, Monsieur."

"And your voice! Such lovely music to the ears." Louis was growing quite excited. Who was she? Could it be possible that there was a woman at court as delightful as this who had not yet been drawn to his attention? "My dear Diana," he went on, "as a man of considerable experience, I assure you that I have never heard a voice that appealed to me more. If the face beneath the mask—" Eagerly he reached out to seize the mask. "Permit me, Madame!"

194

Toinette eluded him swiftly. "Pray remember the King's wish."

"To the devil with the King's wish!"

"Wait!" she cautioned, as he snatched again at her mask. "You may be courting disillusionment."

"Never!"

He tore away the mask and shouted to a nearby torch-bearer to come closer with his light. He seized the flaming torch himself while the man stood back goggle-eyed.

"Well?" Toinette asked, as Louis stared at her.

"Madame, in all humility I bow to you. Diana herself could never have pleased me more."

She turned with a laugh. "We ought to go back to the ball."

Louis took her by the shoulders and spun her round. Richelieu's words came back to him. *White flawless skin, wide arched brows, chestnut hair, green eyes.* And again, *No painter in France could do her justice.* He remembered the fleeting glimpse he had caught of the young woman in the blue phaeton. Suspicion became certainty.

"Is it possible that we have met before?" he asked casually.

"Hardly, Monsieur. Your face is masked but your voice is strange to me."

"Do you possess a blue phaeton and a negro postilion?"

"Why, yes," Toinette said, realizing that it would be stupid to lie.

"And your name is Jeanne Antoinette, known familiarly as Toinette?"

"But this is amazing!" she laughed.

"Indeed it is!" Louis agreed, his voice hardening. "Who brought you here, Madame?"

"Does that really matter?" she parried.

"Answer me! Who brought you here?"

"Your tone is hardly that of a gentleman," she said, and made to move away.

His hand was on her shoulder again. "Wait!"

"I came—" again she saw the futility of lying—"at the invitation of the Duc de Richelieu."

"I knew it, by heaven I knew it!"

"But why so angry, Monsieur?"

"Tell me this, Madame, do you know my true identity?"

"I—" Toinette hesitated.

"Come, Madame, answer me!"

She laughed softly. "Only one man in France could speak with such imperiousness. You are without doubt his Majesty the King."

"How clever you are at evading a direct answer." In spite of his anger there was admiration in Louis' voice. "Very well, you may go back to the ballroom. Richelieu will be waiting anxiously. What a pity that such a neat little scheme should fail."

He watched her go. Middleclass, but the most fascinating creature he had ever seen. He followed her slowly, not realizing that he was still holding the flaming torch. The first person he saw on entering the crowded hall was Maurepas in his Turkish costume, Maurepas who, having recognized the Yew Tree's voice had grown unaccountably anxious.

"Take this," Louis growled, and thrust the torch at him.

He left the amazed Maurepas and went through the ballroom, glaring about him. He was determined not to glance in Toinette's direction, yet hoped that by chance, merely by chance, his eyes would alight on her slim, delightful figure. For the next hour, as he moved about the crowded ballroom, his determination and his hope held him in a firm grip, but never once did he catch sight of her. Finally, in a furious temper, he sought out Richelieu.

"Well, where is she?" he demanded of that gentleman.

"To whom does your Majesty refer?" Richelieu asked politely.

"Toinette, you smooth-tongued rogue!"

"Ah, you recognized her, in spite of the mask."

"So you admit you brought her here, hoping to tempt me further!"

"Nothing was further from my mind," said Richelieu, who had already heard Toinette's account of the debacle. "When your Majesty rejected Toinette because of her middleclass birth I felt I was free to act on my own account."

"Indeed?" said Louis, frigidly.

"Not being of royal birth," Richelieu chuckled, "I saw nothing against furthering my own interest in a beautiful young creature of humble birth."

Louis was vastly taken aback.

"Did she respond to your advances?" he asked haughtily.

Richelieu shrugged. "If she did it was out of sheer politeness."

"Ah! You failed with her!"

"I fear I did, Sire."

"And for an obvious reason, you dog!" Louis chuckled. "She naturally prefers the King to the First Gentleman of the Bedchamber."

"I wonder why?" Richelieu said engagingly. "I often flatter myself that as a man I am just as good as my King, and being older, more experienced."

Louis laughed heartily, but he had a sobering thought. Toinette preferred the King because he *was* the King. She sought power and influence, not love. Such a woman was ten times worse than a common prostitute. Sighing deeply he said as much to Richelieu.

"You wrong her," Richelieu assured him. "As a loyal and dutiful subject she loves the King, but as a woman she is prepared to love the man. Set her up at Versailles, and if she finds it impossible to love you for yourself she will go away of her own accord."

"This is another trick, Richelieu!" Louis accused.

"If it is, Sire, you must admit that I present it skilfully."

"You rogue!" Louis exploded. "Well, where is she?"

"She went home. She felt there was nothing else to be done."

Louis almost stamped his foot. "Then my night is ruined!"

"So great a pity, don't you think," Richelieu laughed, "that the aristocracy has nothing to equal our middleclass Toinette?"

"To the devil with the aristocracy!" Louis raged. "I see no point in being a king unless I may please myself now and again. Toinette shall take supper with me tomorrow night at Versailles. See to it, Richelieu, see to it!"

XVII

"THIS room," Richelieu told Toinette, as they waited in the anteroom at the foot of the private stairway, "is now called the Cabinet des Chiens."

"Indeed?" she said, glancing incuriously at the stag hunt pictured on the stucco frieze.

Richelieu looked at her in surprise and admiration. This was her first visit to the private apartments of Versailles, yet the look on her face was one of utter composure. If she felt any excitement, and Richelieu began to doubt that she did, she betrayed it in no way.

"The King," he said, "is still in two minds about your coming here, and tomorrow, when the court raises its brows and sniggers politely his nerve may fail him altogether. Indeed, he might decide against sending for you again. Therefore, I think that having come here tonight you should contrive to remain here."

Toinette smiled. "You actually suggest that I should—?"

"Dear me no!" Richelieu laughed. "Unless you want to, and if my own plan fails."

"You have a plan, then."

"Naturally!"

"Tell me what it is."

"It concerns your husband," said Richelieu, warming to his subject. "He returned, shall we say, last night. He was waiting for you when you went home from the ball. He had heard gossip. He forbade you to leave the house. When you disobeyed him tonight he cursed you and threatened you with violence."

Toinette's eyes glinted with amusement. It was quite impossible to imagine her weak and handsome husband cursing her and threatening her with violence; he would be much more likely to clutch at his heart and burst into tears.

"I am quite prepared to throw myself on the King's mercy," she said.

Bachelier, eyes twinkling, came down the stairs and announced that his Majesty was ready to receive them. Richelieu stepped forward but Toinette indicated with a brief gesture that she wished to go up alone. Entering Louis' apartments she found him standing with his back to her. He glanced round at the sound of her step. She saw that he had a bottle in his hand. He took up a glass and filled it.

"Champagne," he said, coming forward and offering her the glass. "Tokay, they tell me, is all the rage just now, but for such an occasion as this the only drink is champagne."

Toinette took the glass; Louis filled another.

"To our further acquaintance," he said, raising the glass.

Raising her own she echoed his words. It touched her to see that this king, this man who had boasted of his experience, was nervous. He had a hang-dog look, like that of a boy caught in the act of robbing an orchard. He made to speak, changed his mind, and fussed over the business of finding her a chair. Once she was seated he stood indeterminately in front of her, his small mouth pursed, but handsome and appealing in his spotless ruffle and cherry-colored coat.

"I was rude to you last night," he said abruptly. "Please forgive me."

"Rudeness in a king," she said, but not cheekily, "must be suffered by a subject."

"Nonsense! A king has a greater obligation than any other man."

"If your Majesty recognizes that there is hope for France."

She was looking at him sincerely and candidly. He smiled into her fathomless eyes and found himself relaxing.

"Strange," he mused. "I was bored and irritable when you entered the room; now I feel oddly at peace. You have a most restful influence over a man, Madame."

He looked at her now with pleasure. She was dressed modestly but expensively, her voluminous gown, dark green in color, cut square at the neck in the prevailing fashion, the expanse of flawless bosom enhanced by the tight band of pearls round her throat. Middleclass though she was, she had all the airs and graces of the born aristocrat. His pleasure increased. She was, when you came to think of it, incomparable: her beauty placed her above and apart from all classes; if she were the daughter of a beggar his regard for her could not have been higher. He recollected the purpose for which he had brought her to Versailles.

"Come," he said jauntily, "let me refill your glass."

"My glass is still quite full, thank you."

"How slow you are! Mine is empty."

"But champagne is meant to be sipped, not swallowed at a single gulp, as if it were ale."

"A fitting reproof," Louis laughed. "Champagne, like a beautiful woman, should be treated with respect, admired at a distance, savored slowly . . ." He was conscious of a false note in his voice but succeeded in ignoring it. "Unfortunately my habit where a beautiful woman is concerned is to treat her like ale."

"How lacking in refinement," Toinette said, but quietly, not archly, as he might have expected. "Thank you indeed for warning me."

"It was more in the nature of a promise, Madame."

"Actually," she said seriously, "your voice, if anything, had a ring of command in it."

"And if I were to make it a command, a royal command—" again he was conscious of the false note in his voice and this time annoyed by it—"what then?"

"Being a woman of the middleclass," she replied, still

quietly, "I should feel less constrained than an aristocrat to obey, unquestioningly, the whim of a king."

Louis felt as if his face had been slapped, and not too lightly, but he cried, "Bravo! But please remember this, where beauty is concerned you *are* an aristocrat." Toinette put down her glass and rose. "Ah, I frighten you!" he cried. "I make you want to flee from the wicked precincts of Versailles!"

She smiled at him serenely. "I have never been frightened of any man, except—" she remembered Richelieu's plan—"except perhaps my husband."

"These *husbands!*" Louis scoffed. "But why think of him now? I understood that he was miles away, somewhere deep in the country."

"He returned last night." She dropped her voice and shuddered delicately, and with so much conviction that Louis himself felt the shudder and the slight horror it suggested. "His anger, when he knew that I had been at the ball was . . . terrible. And tonight, when I left for Versailles . . . But no, it was too horrible."

"He made a scene, Madame?"

Toinette forced her eyes to dilate—(she had had some success in drawing-room theatricals)—and wrung her hands.

"He ordered me to remain at home. When I refused he said that if I dared to return he—" she forced her voice to break—"he would beat me until no man, king or otherwise, would care to look at my face again."

"The man is out of his mind!" Louis cried. "He shall be arrested, flung into prison!"

"And yet he loves me," she sighed. "That is the whole trouble. He loves me with an intensity that has never been equalled."

Louis, strutting a little, responded with a grandiloquent gesture. "I happen to have a reputation for intensity myself," he boasted, "but I would never threaten any woman with disfigurement, and certainly not one as beautiful as you. I would never lay a hand on you, except caressingly." He paused, admiring the words he was uttering; it was almost as if he were inspired. "My life, if you were mine, would be

201

dedicated to your service. I would honor and cherish you; I would give you the whole world."

He stood back and looked at her expectantly. Her eyes held his for a moment, then dropped.

"I think perhaps I should go," she stammered, "in spite of the madman waiting at home for me."

"You say 'at home'? My dear Toinette, you have no home, not in the real meaning of the word."

"How right you are, Sire."

"You shall remain at Versailles. That is the obvious solution. In offering you my love, what else can I do but offer you my protection also?"

He realized that he should be on his knees, or holding her hands comfortingly in his, or better still, clasping her in a warm and eager embrace. But something, puzzling him vastly, held him back.

"I have not yet accepted your love," Toinette said.

She spoke, not coquettishly, but as one making a plain statement of fact. She spoke *sincerely;* he was positive of that. Suddenly he knew why he had made no definite physical advance, why he had been aware of a false note in his voice: he was in love with her, not passionately, but tenderly; what he wanted most in the world was not to possess her but to protect her. It was a strange and new and entirely overwhelming emotion. There was, without doubt, more depth to his soul than he would ever have imagined.

"In spite of my remark about champagne and ale," he said, and his voice shook, "I am not an outright scoundrel. I offer you the love that poets sing of—" (Come to think of it, he was something of a poet himself!)—"and whether you care to accept it or not I do insist on your taking my protection."

To his gratification and her own amazement, her eyes filled with tears. For perhaps the first time in her life she felt ashamed, really ashamed. She turned from him quickly.

"Have I offended you?" he asked anxiously. She shook her head and he came to her side. "I offer you protection, not in the worldly meaning of the word, but sincerely, without any obligation on your part."

"I know that, Sire." She kept her back to him. "And because I know it there are things I must tell you."

Louis laughed pleasantly. He felt like God; he felt that he knew everything. "My dear, I am not the simpleton many people think me." He laughed again. "Shall we start at the beginning?"

"The . . . beginning?" she turned to face him.

"That was in the forest. You appeared there in your little blue phaeton with every intention of attracting my attention. When I sent Richelieu to make inquiries about you —Richelieu who is ever on the alert for an opportunity to further his influence at court—he realized at once that no other woman in France, whatever her birth, would make a more suitable favorite. He therefore gave you to understand that only through him could you hope to attain your ends. When I rejected you because you were a middleclass woman he took you to the ball and set you temptingly before the yew tree. And afterwards, smooth-tongued rogue that he is, he induced me to declare, 'To the devil with the aristocracy.' And by heavens, I say it again!"

"Your Majesty . . ." Toinette began.

"No, wait! When I invited you here tonight he suggested another trick, or possibly, being clever, you thought of it yourself. You have a husband, yes, but I suspect that he is still many miles from home; or if indeed he has returned he is a mild-mannered little man who never lifted a finger to you in his life and never would."

There was a pause. Toinette gave Louis a brief, wan look and turned to the door.

"Since you know the story I was about to tell you," she said, "what else can I do but take my leave?"

Louis took three swift strides to the door and placed his back to it.

"My dear," he smiled, "I prefer to believe that Monsieur Lenormant d'Etiole is an ogre, that he waits at home for you with a whip."

Toinette's face brightened. She laughed merrily.

Louis opened the door and called for Bachelier.

"Temporary accommodation shall be found for you," he

said. "You may remain at Versailles as long as you wish. I make no demands on you, except one."

"And that?"

"Friendship."

"You have that already, Sire," Toinette cried impulsively.

"No, only the beginnings of it. It must go further, become deeper and lasting. Friendship is greater by far than the thing which we at Versailles have fallen into the loose habit of calling love."

Bachelier appeared, received his instructions and escorted Toinette from the royal apartments. With shining eyes Louis watched her go. He felt at peace with the whole world; he forgot that he had been hungry and that supper had not yet been served; he had never been so happy, so contented, in his life.

Louis and Richelieu were breakfasting lightly, the principal dish being freshly caught river crawfish, and discussing Toinette's stay at Versailles.

"I presume," Richelieu remarked, taking another sip of Burgundy, "that it will soon be necessary for someone to interview the young lady's husband."

"Really?" Louis grunted, and refilled his glass.

"I am assuming, of course, that she is now in permanent residence."

"I hope she is," Louis said fervently, "I hope she is."

"In that case, Sire, Monsieur Lenormant d'Etiole may be safely left to me."

But Louis was no longer listening. During the three days that Toinette had been at Versailles he had scarcely left her presence. He had taken every meal except breakfast with her, leaving her only with the utmost reluctance at eleven each night. The whole court, consumed with curiosity, was gossiping wildly, yet so far, Richelieu and Argenson having kept their counsel, nobody had been able to discover even the name of his Majesty's unofficial guest.

"The court is most puzzled," Richelieu laughed, "at the way your Majesty leaves Toinette to spend the night alone."

"Even as you are, no doubt!"

"Even as I am. I can only conclude that by eleven the point of satiation has been reached."

"You foul-mouthed beast!" Louis said hotly.

Richelieu felt justly hurt. "Not a platonic love, surely!"

"Would there be anything surprising in that?"

Richelieu sighed. "Only impotence would force *me* to such a pass."

"I assure you, Richelieu—!" Louis began indignantly.

"You relieve me, Sire. I was about to suggest a steady diet of truffles and celery soup. Not as good as my physician's concoctions, but said to be moderately efficacious."

"Only weaklings need aphrodisiacs," Louis said scathingly, and gave his whole mind to thoughts of Toinette and the last three days. He had not been wrong to have decided earlier that she had a most restful influence on a man. He talked to her as he had never talked before, confiding in her fully, telling her that at times he was a great disappointment to himself. Because of Toinette he had resolved once again, without any feeling of hypocrisy, to be a better king, a *real* king, and he felt now that with her at his side success would this time crown his resolve.

"Personally," Richelieu said, "I *like* truffles."

"Pah!" Louis grunted.

There was a scratching at the door and when he called "Enter!" the door opened and his son, the Dauphin, came quickly into the room.

"Ah, Louis, my boy!"

"If I may see you for a few moments, Father—?"

"Of course, of course!"

Louis looked at his son with pleasure. He felt more affection for him now—indeed, for his whole family—than he had ever felt before. He saw that the boy, a handsome lad, though not as handsome as he himself had been at the same age, was losing his slimness and growing plump. He saw, too, that he was frowning nervously. Smiling, he asked kindly what the matter was.

"A little quarrel with your wife, perhaps?"

"No, nothing like that, Father."

"Oh? Then what?"

The Dauphin glanced at Richelieu.

"If Richelieu's presence embarrasses you . . ." Louis began.

"It could hardly do that, Father," the boy said disdainfully, "but in view of what I have to say it might embarrass you."

Louis laughed. The boy, in spite of his evident nervousness, was amusingly pompous.

"This is vastly interesting. Pray continue."

The Dauphin thrust his hands behind his back and clasped them tightly together.

"Her Majesty my mother," he said sternly, "has refused to take the matter up with you. Therefore the duty, unpleasant as it is—"

"Wait!" Louis interrupted, looking darkly at his son. "Does this embarrassing subject concern my guest?"

"If by your guest you mean Madame Lenormant d'Etiole, yes, Father."

"You know her name."

"I made it my business to discover it."

"Through the good offices of Maurepas, no doubt," Richelieu interposed.

The Dauphin ignored Richelieu. "Father, the woman's presence, unofficial though it might be, is causing unpleasant gossip. Apart from that—"

"Careful!" Louis warned.

The boy set his jaw stubbornly. "*Apart from that*, the knowledge that such a woman, a woman of the middle-class—"

"Enough, confound you, enough!" Louis thundered.

"Let me finish, Father, please!"

"Very well, then, but be brief."

"Thank you." The boy bowed stiffly, touching his sword as he did so. "The knowledge, or rather the *suspicion*, that such a woman is going to be set up in an official capacity at Versailles is extremely embarrassing to my mother who, in all conscience, has suffered enough in that direction as it is."

Louis, struggling to set aside his anger, decided to treat the matter lightly. He smiled broadly.

"Marriage," he said, "has given my son a sense of responsibility, but let me point out, in all humility, that when he himself is king he will resent, as I resent, the interference of his son, if he has a son, in his private affairs."

"*My* private affairs," the boy said crushingly, "will never at any time encompass the same activities that yours do."

Louis clapped his hands. "You should cross yourself, pon my oath, boy, you should cross yourself. Never in my life have I heard piety expressed with so much pomposity."

The Dauphin stood back in horror. "That," he cried, "is another thing that distresses me deeply, the way you sneer at religion."

"I knew it," Louis laughed. "I have fathered a puritan."

"Please be serious, Father!"

Louis grinned. "What, you want me to strip you, married man though you are, and slap you hard on your bare behind?"

He took the boy by the ear, led him to the door and gently pushed him out of the room.

"You suspect Maurepas of this?" he asked Richelieu.

"Indeed I do," Richelieu replied, and looked brightly expectant.

Louis laughed. "No, no, my friend. Maurepas is too valuable to be sent into exile." He was silent for a moment. "This Lenormant d'Etiole, is he back from the country yet?"

"He returned on the night of the masked ball. I thought you knew."

Louis smiled. Obviously Toinette was no longer making a confidant of Richelieu, and this was good to know.

"Ah yes," he said innocently, "I was forgetting. He threatened poor Toinette with violence. Well, you have my authority to seek him out and deal with him. We will discuss the terms later."

"Toinette is to be established?"

"Yes."

Richelieu laughed. "Imagine one's relationship with the Declared Mistress being platonic. What a delightful paradox!"

"Oh, go to the devil, Richelieu!"

Nevertheless, Louis said nothing of establishment to Toinette. He wanted to savor the delight of her companionship still more before pressing her to accept an official appointment. An amusing idea occurred to him and going to her he announced that he wanted her to regard the apartments she at present occupied as a new home into which she had just moved.

"You shall have a complete staff," he said. "Maids, footmen and two cooks. You see, I have a fancy to experience middleclass hospitality. Give me a dinner and invite guests of your own."

"Middleclass guests?" Toinette smiled.

"Certainly!"

Composed as ever, she set about her task, supervising the preparation of the dinner herself. The guests she chose carefully from the many writers, artists, actors and financiers of her acquaintance. She remembered one of Louis' family names and introduced him as plain Monsieur Capet. There must, she stressed, be no restricting formality. Louis was delighted. He enjoyed the meal and found the conversation stimulating. He said afterwards that it had pleased him very much to play the role of a middleclass gentleman.

"I wish I could play it forever," he sighed.

The following night Toinette gave a supper party. She wore an informal gown of flowered silk, her only jewelry the pearls at her throat. She played the harpsichord for her guests, sang for them and finally presented a little play, taking the leading part herself. Louis' delight increased. A musician, a singer, an actress! A good manager, a perfect hostess and above all the most beautiful woman in France! He told her that no man in the world was more fortunate than he; he said he would never be bored again; he declared, with tears of gratitude in his eyes, that he was learning how to live at last.

Toinette herself was happy. She was beginning to feel that Louis was just as necessary to her as he claimed that she was to him. She wondered if she was falling in love, and knew without question that she loved him. To love, but not to be in love . . . She pondered over this. If to be in love meant the experiencing of an all-demanding passion, she had never been in love in her life and never would be. Dutifully she had submitted to the physical demands of her husband, playing her part passively and hiding as best she could the faint distaste she always felt. She had neither fallen in love with Lenormant d'Etiole nor grown to love him. It had been the same with the others, men to whom she had found it expedient on occasion to grant her favors. One of them had called her cold, unresponsive, only half a woman. He had even said that she was a fraud and a disappointment, with the look of a courtesan and the untouched heart of a saint, a body that promised infinite delight and a mind and will that would always be virgin.

She smiled at the memory of this. Her heart had been touched now, but not by passion. She admired the King—she had done so since she was a child of five—and loved him as a friend. Her love for him, she concluded, was the sentimental attachment of a young girl for an older woman. Only in this respect was it a passion, a grand passion. She laughed to herself. It was so amusing that she would like to share the joke with Louis. She would like to, but she was much too wise to commit such an act of folly, for she knew that the time would come when for him friendship, however sentimental, would not be enough.

One night, after she had been at Versailles for three weeks, and when she was taking supper alone with Louis, the conversation turned from philosophy—(she prided herself on an understanding of philosophy as distinct from a mere appreciation of established religion)—to state affairs. Louis, in spite of the consternation of his ministers, had been taking an active interest in state affairs and had announced that in future he intended to do a great deal more than merely append his signature to state documents. As a result, certain important matters, some concerning the war which still dragged on, had been placed in abeyance. Now Louis hardly knew what decisions to make for the best, and presenting Toinette with the problems he sought her advice.

"For a king to use his head is excellent," she said, "but it is also wise for him to follow his heart now and then."

"Wise counsel," he said. "I shall try to remember it." He looked at her intently for a moment. "And now, my dear, a more personal matter."

"My husband?" she questioned.

"You read my thoughts."

"I knew he had returned to Paris. I suspect that Richelieu has been to see him."

Louis grinned. "I sent Richelieu to deal with a presumably violent man, a resentful, jealous husband. All he found was a weakling. Jealous, of course, but at the same time awed and rather flattered."

"Did he weep?" Toinette asked curiously.

"Yes, but in the end he accepted the inevitable."

"And that is . . . ?"

"Retirement from Paris, the realization that he must never see you again."

"What," she laughed, "no compensation at all?"

"Oh, I offered to make him a *farmier général*. He shall have the farming of taxes in one or two provinces."

"That was generous of you."

"Pooh! I can afford to be generous. He could have had anything, providing he showed no objection to your remaining permanently at Versailles."

"Between you, you seem to have made up my mind for me," Toinette laughed.

"Sweetheart," Louis said earnestly, "you may leave at once if you want to."

It was the first time he had called her sweetheart. She looked at him quickly. He returned the look with one of deep affection; he made no attempt to touch her. The endearment, it seemed, had slipped out without the significance she might have expected. She changed the subject, remarking that one of his problems was whether or not he should go to the battlefield again.

"What do you advise?" he asked.

Toinette smiled reminiscently. "I never admired you so much as when you went last time."

"*Never so much?*" He seized on her words quickly. "You had admired me before?"

She said softly: "The first time was when I was five. It was my birthday. My mother took me to watch you drive through the streets of Paris. You were sixteen, I think. You looked so handsome. You were wearing a coat of gold brocade and a hat with two white feathers. I called you my fairy prince and told everybody that I was going to marry you."

"My being married already made no difference, eh?"

"None whatever. I said the Queen would die. I was very confident about it. Later, when I was fifteen, a fortune-teller told me that I would become *almost* a queen some day, and that was better, she said, than becoming an actual queen."

Louis smiled happily. "The prediction has come true, you see."

"The King's official favorite," Toinette said thoughtfully. "Julie de Mailly, Pauline de Vintimille, Anne de Chateauroux and now, if I choose to accept the honor, Jeanne Antoinette Lenormant d'Etiole."

"*If* you choose to accept it? You feel some doubt, even though it is what you have worked for?"

"That is what makes me hesitate," she said sincerely. "It covers me with shame, now that I know you so well, to think that I set out, oh so coldly, to work for it."

As patiently as if he were talking to a child Louis said: "Take a little time to consider it. Remain at Versailles while I go to Flanders. Give me your answer when I return."

During the King's absence Richelieu was delighted to see his earlier prediction coming true. With the King present the court, chiefly because Toinette's position was unofficial, had held its hand; now, though the position was still unofficial, the story of her husband having been "bought off" was in circulation and the ladies and gentlemen of Versailles were banding together against her, while the servants, taking a lead from their betters, were echoing the same polite sneers. "Now she must turn to me," Richelieu told himself; "now I shall be her only friend."

The court seized upon her maiden name. "Poisson, in other words *fish*," the courtiers chortled. "Her place is behind a stall at the markets." Richelieu, of course, made it his business to acquaint her fully with what was going on, but she only smiled, for she knew his game. She remembered what she had told her cousin, Binet, when Richelieu, meeting her for the first time, had treated her with condescension. Vain and foolish words, she thought them now. She was not ungrateful to Richelieu for having helped her to meet the King, but whatever power she might possess in the future she had no intention of using it for the benefit of a self-seeking courtier unless he placed love of country before himself.

Meanwhile news of Louis' activities was reaching Versailles. Once again he had placed himself in command of the army, though at best it was a nominal command: he knew too little of the art of war, as he stressed himself, to take from his generals the real command. Because of this the officers loved him and the men, seeing him ready to live the life of an ordinary soldier, did likewise. More than ever, he was Louis the Well-Beloved.

And then came news of the Battle of Fontenoy, which had thrown the enemy out of Tournai, Ghent and Ostend. The Mayor of Paris gave a grand ball at the Hotel de Ville. Careful to shun the celebrations which were taking place at Versailles, Toinette saw no reason against appearing at the Hotel de Ville. She invited Richelieu to accompany her, thinking it might be amusing to see his supposed loyalty exhibited in public. To his credit, for the whole court went gaily to Paris for the occasion, he put a brave face on things and stayed at her side the whole evening. No one else from Versailles approached her, though countless ladies and gentlemen came close enough to look straight through her. In her hearing the word "fishwife" was freely exchanged, while many courtiers made a great show of holding their noses and complaining of the smell. Toinette was more amused than angry, but Richelieu, hearing Maurepas remark to the King's favorite daughter, Madame Adelaide, that Monsieur le Duc should have been apprenticed in his youth to a fishmonger, was furious.

"His Majesty shall be fully acquainted with the behavior of the court," he said angrily.

Toinette merely shrugged. It was not her own intention to complain. She was in possession of the King's love and affection, his trust and confidence. Nothing else mattered. Life at court would not be easy, but once her position was officially acknowledged she would, she knew, be able to hold her own with ease and grace.

Louis returned first to Paris, where he was received with wild enthusiasm, and then he came eagerly to Versailles. Here he offended the whole court for, ignoring them, ignoring even the Queen, he went straight to Toinette's apartments. With a great shout of welcome he swept her into his arms and kissed her warmly.

"The first kiss!" he cried, "but by heaven, not the last!"

Toinette knew then that from now on friendship alone would not be enough.

"Well, what is your decision?" he demanded.

"Would I be here now," she replied, "if it were other than the one you want?"

"Nevertheless," said Richelieu, who had entered the room uninvited and was standing near the door, "the coldness and the inhospitality of the court came close to driving her away."

"Toinette has been treated badly?"

"Shamefully, cruelly, your Majesty."

"Tell me everything," Louis demanded, and listened with growing anger as Richelieu, not without exaggeration, spoke at length of the attitude of the ladies and gentlemen of Versailles.

"An unfortunate name, Poisson," Toinette laughed.

Louis laughed shortly. "Even a fish can be an aristocrat, and by heaven, my love, I shall raise you to the peerage. You shall be a peeress in your own right!"

He sent for Maurepas and asked for a list of titles that had become extinct. When the list had been drawn up he seized upon the Pompadour family, the last member of which had died some months ago.

"An old and honorable family," he pronounced. "The letters patent shall be prepared at once. You, Maurepas, shall be the one to prepare them. A marquise! Yes, I shall make her a marquise!"

Maurepas scowled.

"And now," Louis cried happily, "the presentation!"

Maurepas stood back in horror. "Your Majesty suggests that Madame Lenormant d'Etiole should be presented at court?"

"Certainly!"

"Unprecedented, unprecedented!" Maurepas protested.

"What of it?"

"But by whom could she be presented?" Maurepas demanded.

Louis understood instantly. Not a single lady at court would accept the honor of presenting Toinette.

"The King himself will present her!" he cried.

"You propose to present her to yourself before the full court?" Maurepas stuttered. "But that would be farcical!"

"I propose," Louis roared, "to present her to the Queen and the Dauphin."

Maurepas raised his hands in dismay, excused himself and backed from the royal presence.

"I think you go too far," Toinette said, when Louis told her of the proposed presentation. "It is not my wish that on my behalf you should humiliate your family."

Louis took her hands in his. "Humiliation has a different meaning with different people. It is only relative. If we go far enough back in time we will find ancestors in common, you and I, even if we have to go right back to Adam and Eve." He laughed and added brusquely, "No argument, please. My mind is made up."

The court, by order of the King, had assembled to witness the presentation of Madame la Marquise de Pompadour. Richelieu, waiting with the rest in the Golden Chamber of the King, was standing near a stiff-necked, supercilious Maurepas.

"Having assisted in the creation of a new peeress," Richelieu taunted, "you should be the proudest man at court."

At that moment a fanfare of trumpets announced the King's entry. Louis, head high but obviously uneasy, led Toinette into the great hall, gay in its blue hangings and golden *fleurs-de-lis*. A quick silence fell on the resplendent gathering. All eyes were on the King and the newly created marquise, then, as if at a signal, they swung to the Queen and the Dauphin. Marie, holding her head proudly, had a fixed smile on her face; the Dauphin, standing at her side, was flushed and angry. Richelieu, noting all this, and noting also the look of scorn on the face of the King's favorite daughter, Adelaide, thought that he would never see a play to equal it.

"Never in the history of France," Maurepas muttered, "has a queen been called upon to suffer such humiliation."

"Oh, rubbish!" Richelieu whispered. "This is not the first royal mistress to be presented. Whatever Madame la Marquise is by birth she is now an aristocrat."

Louis, assuming a nonchalance he by no means felt, led Toinette straight to his wife and son. Once, feeling her tremble, he whispered "Courage, my love!" Reaching his destination he glanced swiftly at the assembled court. On the watching faces he saw horror and disdain and curiosity. He cleared his throat.

"Madame," he said, addressing Marie, "permit me to present Madame la Marquise de Pompadour."

Richelieu was watching closely now. Toinette, almost regal in her magnificent court gown, had shown a true dignity in the unfaltering way she had dragged her long and heavy train. His interest deepened. Would she slip or stumble when curtsying under its weight?

Marie, hesitating for a brief moment, was wondering the same thing. She reflected that the situation in which Louis had placed her was unusual, but not as humiliating as her son had insisted. For a few seconds she held Toinette's eyes. "Why," she thought in surprise, "the poor creature is just as embarrassed as I am." She began to feel sorry for Toinette. She remembered Julie de Mailly, Pauline de Vintimille and Anne de Chateauroux. No one could expect Madame de Pompadour, fourth in the line of royal favorites, to be the last. Louis cleared his throat again, peremptorily. Marie recollected herself, smiled sweetly and inclined her head.

"I bid you welcome, Madame," she said.

Toinette made the three customary curtsies, each perfect, then, removing a glove, raised the hem of Marie's gown and kissed it. Her movements were the epitome of grace and dignity and brought forth from the assemblage a slight, unwilling sigh of admiration.

"You bear an old and honorable name," Marie continued, just a little tartly, for she was, after all, a woman and a neglected wife. "His Majesty and I will honor that name while you choose to remain at court."

Richelieu smiled. A neat rebuff, that! The name, but not necessarily the woman who bore it.

Louis, frowning and blushing, addressed his son.

"Monsieur . . ." he began, and then, seeing the insolent look on the boy's face, he changed his mind. "My dear Marquise," he said, turning to Toinette, "permit me to present my son, his royal Highness the Dauphin."

The boy flushed at the insult; the court held its breath.

"I was quite unaware, Sire," the Dauphin said in a low, trembling voice, "that I had asked to be presented. Actually, if welcome her I must, I prefer to do it *thus!—*"

And he thrust out a moist red tongue.

A gasp rose from the court, and behind it a little barrage of sniggering. The Dauphin repeated the insult while Toinette glanced quickly from Louis to Marie. Louis' face was black with fury; Marie's was white and anxious. As the Dauphin thrust out his tongue a third time Toinette forced herself to laugh merrily.

"Goodness," she said, in a high, clear voice, "his royal Highness seems to be laboring under the impression that I am a member of the Faculty of Physicians."

Spontaneous laughter rocked the court. Louis smiled grimly; Marie, deeply relieved, gave Toinette a glance of gratitude. Richelieu strolled forward, said "With your Majesty's permission," and offered Toinette his arm. Louis turned to his son; the boy was looking rather foolish.

"Monsieur," he thundered, "for each time you thrust out your tongue you shall spend a month in exile from Versailles."

Richelieu and Toinette were now strolling about the hall, and members of the court, more curious now then horrified, were swarming about them. Marie caught Louis' eye and smiled faintly. There was, he thought, a distinct flicker of amusement in her eyes.

"And so," she murmured, "another royal favorite is established."

"And the last!" Louis said earnestly. "I mean it, Marie, I mean it!"

XVIII

MADAME la Marquise de Pompadour, with a watchful Richelieu and a smug-looking Binet in attendance, was inspecting her new apartments, which had been redecorated at her own especial order. The little suite of rooms, known as the Attique du Nord, was in one of the choicest parts of the Palace, an advantage, Toinette decided, which was adequate compensation for the fact that the rooms had once been occupied by the Duchesse de Chateauroux. She went slowly from room to room, admiring the marble chimney pieces, the light gray panelling and the tasteful hangings at the high windows. The dining-room particularly pleased her, with its adjacent pantry where the King's supper could be kept warm. Finally she sat in one of the new chairs which had been designed to accommodate even the widest of hooped skirts.

For a few moments she gazed at Richelieu but seemed hardly to notice him. A picture of her young daughter had suddenly crossed her mind, and this made her frown. People were saying that she had deserted the child, but that was not the truth. Her husband, taking a last-minute stand, had insisted on the girl remaining with him, even though Louis had been quite willing for her to come to Versailles. Toinette sighed briefly and shrugged. Now that she came to think of it, she had never been a very maternal woman.

"Madame is satisfied?" asked Binet who, dismissed by the Dauphin, was now Toinette's secretary.

"Quite, thank you. She rose and went to a window. "What is that statue in the garden, Richelieu?"

"The Crouching Venus, by Coysevox. Appropriate, perhaps?"

"Hardly," she said. "I have never been guilty of crouching."

"No insult was intended, Toinette," Richelieu chuckled.

She turned from the window and making much play with the ivory carved fan Louis had given her told Richelieu that his manner was still condescending. Worse, she added, it was becoming familiar, and familiarity she would never stomach. She was using the fan, he reflected, as skilfully as he had ever used his rapier.

"I have a title now," she concluded. "Please use it, Monsieur."

Richelieu bowed ironically. "Gladly, Madame la Marquise."

Feeling that her manner was a little petty, Toinette colored slightly and crossed the room to look at a large portrait hanging on the wall. Richelieu came up behind her.

"Ah, the late Duchesse de Chateauroux," he murmured.

Toinette nodded. "It was here before but I asked for its removal." She studied the portrait. "Plain, rather than handsome, as well as large and much too buxom. How fortunate that my own appearance is fragile."

"Fortunate?" Richelieu questioned.

Toinette merely smiled; it was Binet who replied for her.

"Fragile beauty," he intoned, "inspires in a man a desire to protect. Madame la Duchesse always gave the impression of being well able to look after herself. Madame la Marquise gives any impression but that."

"Nevertheless," Toinette laughed, "I can look after myself better than she ever could."

"You seek to warn me, Madame?" Richelieu asked.

"Perhaps." She turned to Binet. "Have the Duchesse removed and hidden away somewhere. She spoils the harmony of otherwise attractive furnishings."

Toinette moved to a table on which stood an Etruscan vase. Taking it up idly her mind dwelt on Binet's words about fragile beauty inspiring a man's desire to protect. A little frown creased her brow: Louis, in his more intimate approaches, was as protective as a Russian bear. The frown deepened. Being an excellent actress she had been able to simulate a passion she would never feel, and Louis had seemed satisfied. She could only hope that until she was more confident of his friendship, art would continue to make up for the lack of reality.

"Why, what have we here!" she exclaimed.

Inside the vase was a folded sheet of paper.

"A forgotten love letter from the King to Madame la Duchesse, perhaps?" Richelieu suggested.

"My own name is written on the outside."

"Then a love letter from the King to you."

Toinette shook her head. The writing was not the King's, and in any case all his letters to her were inscribed *Discreet and Faithful*. She unfolded the sheet and found a few lines of verse. It needed only a glance to show her that the lines, mocking at her establishment, were the bawdiest she had ever read.

"Horrible!" she cried.

Richelieu was looking over her shoulder.

"Hunting one day in the forest . . ." he began to quote.

She silenced him with a look, and in a choking voice asked him if he recognized the handwriting. He took the paper and studied its contents. The writing was obviously well-disguised, but there was a slight familiarity in some of the letters.

"Maurepas!" he cried.

"Are you sure?"

"Well, *almost*, Madame."

She snatched back the paper. "The King will be furious. Let me take it to him at once!"

"You forget he has gone to Paris."

"He shall see it tonight, then!"

"By all means," Richelieu said, "but let me have it for an hour or so to verify my suspicions. If we can provide proof that Maurepas wrote this—"

"The man will be finished," Toinette said confidently, "utterly finished!"

At supper, taken in Toinette's new apartments, Louis was in a boisterous mood. He ate and drank heartily, and continually boasted to Richelieu and Maurepas, who were also present, of the game he was going to shoot at Rambouillet tomorrow.

Toinette was pleased with herself for having invited Maurepas to supper. She thought it excellent strategy and had decided on this move when Richelieu, having obtained a specimen of Maurepas' handwriting, had assured her that his Majesty, when comparing the two samples, would agree that they were the work of one and the same person.

"Your Majesty," she said, during a lull in the conversation, "something distressing occurred while you were in Paris."

Louis put down his glass. "Somebody at court was rude to you?"

For answer Toinette gave him the verse to read. Maurepas, after glancing at her impassively, centered his gaze on Louis.

"It makes me sick with disgust," Toinette said.

Louis gave her an oblique look. "Mmmmm," he said, and began to read carefully: *"Hunting one day in the forest—"*

"For pity's sake, Sire, not *aloud!*" she protested.

Louis apologized with a grin and began at the beginning again, mouthing the syllables but uttering no sound. When he had finished he looked first at Richelieu, then at Maurepas.

"Well, well, well!" he said mildly.

"Is that all you have to say?" Toinette demanded.

"Disgusting," he amended, "dear me yes!"

"The author must be punished with the utmost severity!"

"Quite so, quite so. Er—who *is* the author?"

For answer Richelieu took a sheet of paper from his pocket, unfolded it and laid it carefully before Louis. Louis, a little drunk now, gazed down at it owlishly.

"Ah, a memorandum written by Maurepas! You—er—suggest that our friend here . . . ?"

"Indeed I do, Sire. There are many similarities in the handwriting. The *l's* and *m's,* for instance."

Louis looked at Maurepas. "Well, Monsieur?"

Maurepas inclined his head solemnly. "I plead guilty, Sire."

"A poet, Maurepas a poet!" Louis roared. "I can scarcely believe it!"

"A versifier, not a poet," Maurepas said modestly.

"But when I challenged you about those verses in connection with Madame de Chateauroux you said you lacked the wit."

"True, Sire, but after diligent practice I discovered that it was there all the time, lying dormant."

Toinette was shaking with anger. Things were not going according to plan, for Louis, doubled up over the table, was wiping the tears of amusement from his eyes.

"God!" he gasped. "A wittier man than I would have thought."

"Your Majesty . . . !" Toinette began indignantly.

"Ah, yes. Ahem!" Louis straightened up and composed his features into a solemn mask, but his eyes were twinkling. "I see I must speak sharply to Maurepas."

"The author must be punished with the utmost severity," Toinette said.

"Mmmm, so he must, my dear, so he must."

"If I were King," Richelieu suggested, "I should be inclined to consider dismissal."

"Dismissal?" Louis pondered.

Nobody was looking at Maurepas. As "the author" he was being discussed as if he were not present. He coughed to draw attention to himself.

"The author," he murmured, "is thinking of having the words set to music."

"Music?" Louis shook with mirth. "And why not?"

Toinette was speechless.

"If I may say so, Sire," Richelieu said quickly, "it is a more serious matter than you seem to think. After all, having sent the Dauphin into temporary exile for—"

"My dear Richelieu," Louis interrupted pettishly, "my son and Maurepas are two quite different propositions. My son is a perfectly useless fellow, and a prig withal, whereas Maurepas . . ." His voice trailed away. He was studying the verse again and rumbling with inward mirth. "In any case, I never object to a joke, even a bawdy one, when it is as good as this."

Toinette forced herself to smile. She saw that it would be useless to argue further, and she realized that her power was not yet strong enough to be tested by her insisting on Maurepas' dismissal. Seeing her smile, Louis' eyes twinkled all the more.

"Come, admit it," he said. "The joke is amusing."

She forced herself to laugh. "But it would hardly be funny if it were circulated in Paris. Let us compromise by compelling the author, if he writes any more such masterpieces of wit, to submit them to us and nobody else."

"Splendid!" Louis cried. "Agreed, Maurepas?"

"Agreed, your Majesty," Maurepas said silkily.

But that, Toinette promised herself, was not the end of the matter.

The weeks and months were slipping by and soon Toinette had held her position for a full year. Reviewing the events of this period she had reason to be pleased with the progress she had made at court. Only one thing troubled her, the constancy of the physical demands made on her by Louis. First she tried to reduce him during supper to a state of drowsy intoxication, but though through this he often fell asleep over the table he woke refreshed and playful at dawn. Now, though she disliked it, she was taking an occasional aphrodisiac as a means of bolstering up her failing dramatic ability. Apart from this Louis was always tender, increasingly affectionate and exceedingly generous. He confided in her at all times, sought her advice more and more and gradually led her to believe that soon her power at court would exceed that of the late Cardinal Fleury. Once she had thought that all she wanted was Louis' love and affection, and the honor of being the established favorite; now, with scores of people presenting petitions to her instead of to the various ministers, she was beginning to enjoy her position to the full. King's mistress, she told herself, and mistress of France if she chose.

During the second year of her establishment, and after the death of the Dauphin's wife and his second marriage to Marie-Josephe of Saxony, Toinette began to see that Louis' love for her was not enough in itself to keep him from boredom. True, he was never bored when with her, but that he should be bored at all was dangerous. Accordingly she was ready at a moment's notice to entertain him with unexpected supper parties, spur-of-the-moment trips to one or other of the royal hunting lodges and court theatricals which she presented in the little theater he allowed her to build at Versailles. Accordingly Louis was soon declaring to anybody who cared to listen that no matter how tired or ill or bored he was, a few moments' of Madame la Marquise's company quickly made him a new man again.

Since the Queen already tolerated her, Toinette made up her mind to win Marie as an ally if not as an actual friend. She succeeded in this by urging Louis to take a great interest in his family, and though Marie shrank from thanking Toinette in so many words she remarked publicly that since the King must have a favorite, better Madame de Pompadour than anyone else. And then Toinette won her over completely by insisting that Louis should make special orders on the Treasury for the good works which now entirely filled her Majesty's life.

Presently, though Toinette knew she would always have enemies at court, she came to realize that the only ones likely to menace her seriously were the Dauphin and Maurepas, and she reasoned that the Dauphin, divorced as it were from Maurepas, would be harmless. She discussed this question many times with Richelieu. Bawdy verses were being written again and circulated gleefully both at Versailles and in Paris, but Maurepas was too wise this time to let any of them appear in his own handwriting.

"Even if we could prove him responsible," Toinette said, "the King might only laugh again and refuse to take action."

In the end they concocted a scheme between them, worked out the details with care and set the scene on a night when Louis was expected to return late from Rambouillet. However, on his arrival at Versailles he went, not to Toinette's apartments, but to his own, sending a message that he was tired and would take chocolate with her in the morning. "So much the better," Toinette said, and rearranged her plan. Accordingly, when Louis arrived at the outer door next morning he found it locked. This never having happened before he called indignantly for Binet who, hearing the royal voice, came hurriedly.

Binet apologized quickly, adding: "Circumstances made the locking of the door necessary, for one must be careful."

Louis looked puzzled. "What the devil do you mean, Binet?"

Binet, bowing, led the way to the bedchamber. "Madame la Marquise will doubtless explain."

At the door Louis all but fell over a small camp bed.

"The relief guard sleeps there during the night," Binet said, looking grave.

"The—what?" Louis demanded, placing his hand on the handle of the door. And then he caught sight of another camp bed.

"That, your Majesty," Binet said, "is used by the physician."

"The physician?" Louis grew alarmed. "Madame la Marquise is ill?"

"I sincerely hope not, your Majesty."

Louis' alarm turned to amazement. "What *is* this mystery, Binet?"

"Madame la Marquise will explain, Sire."

Louis threw open the door and strode quickly into the room. Toinette, looking perfectly ravishing, as indeed she always did after a night's rest, was sitting up against a pile of pillows. Standing close to the bed was Richelieu. He held in his hand a cup of chocolate from which, nostrils distended, he was in the act of taking a delicate sip.

"I may be dull-witted," Louis said gruffly, "but precisely why is Richelieu drinking chocolate obviously prepared for Madame la Marquise?"

Toinette raised a languid arm. "Merely a necessary precaution."

"Like the locked door, the guard and the physician?"

"But of course."

"Undoubtedly I *am* dull-witted!" Louis cried.

"But surely you guess, Sire?"

"Madame la Marquise," Richelieu said, as Louis raised his hands in despair, "is afraid that somebody is trying to poison her."

"*Poison* her?" Louis gasped.

"Everything she eats and drinks is now tasted before she touches it."

"But good heavens, my dear," Louis said, "why should anyone want to poison you?"

"Madame de Vintimille died of poison," Richelieu answered blandly.

This had a sobering effect on Louis. It was not often he thought of Pauline, but when he did it was uneasily, with quite a lot of self-reproach.

"Whom do you suspect?" he asked.

Toinette said gravely: "I have only one real enemy, but how can I make a definite charge?"

"You mean Maurepas? But poison! He would never dare!"

To steady himself Louis sat on the edge of the bed. He looked from Toinette, so pale and grave, to Richelieu. His eyes, they saw, were dilated.

Toinette said: "Some sweetmeats were sent to me anonymously. I gave a few to one of the stray dogs that infest Versailles. Fortunately I ate none of them myself. The dog . . . died."

Louis rose shakily from the bed. "A coincidence, perhaps? Richelieu, your official taster, is still alive."

Toinette shrugged. "You may refuse, if you wish, to take me seriously . . ."

"On the contrary, I was never more disturbed in my life. If somebody is trying to poison you, that person must be found and brought to justice. But as for suspecting Maurepas . . ."

"The man hates me, Sire."

"But proof! We must have proof!"

"The man is cunning," Richelieu said. "Actual proof may not be possible. But even if it is, and is found only after Madame's death—"

"Enough!" Louis shouted. "Send for Maurepas."

When Maurepas came Richelieu, hoping to trick him into something sounding like an admission of guilt, attacked him at once with a direct charge.

"Maurepas," he said, "I charge you with the responsibility of Madame de Vintimille's death."

"Fantastic," Maurepas murmured, quite unmoved.

"Madame de Chateauroux," Richelieu went on, "was suffering from congestion of the lungs; nevertheless, I believe you planned to hasten her end by poison."

"You must be out of your mind," Maurepas laughed.

Louis gave a little groan. "Pauline, Anne, and now Toinette!"

"Toinette?" Maurepas questioned sharply.

"Madame la Marquise," Richelieu lied boldly, "is already the victim of one poisoning attempt."

Maurepas, angry now and not a little alarmed, turned indignantly to Louis. "Your Majesty, I protest against this foul and unwarranted attack."

"To protest is beside the point," Louis said sternly. "All I ask of you is an answer to these charges."

Maurepas bowed. "Very well, your Majesty. The first is best answered by recalling the inquiry made after the death of Madame de Vintimille. I visited her, as did Richelieu, before her death, but it was proved to your Majesty's satisfaction that neither of us could have poisoned her."

Louis frowned. All this was stirring up some bitter memories.

"Proceed with the second charge," he said.

"The second is even more preposterous than the first," Maurepas said promptly. "Madame la Duchesse died before I knew she was ill."

"You lie there," Richelieu accused him. "You were sent to Madame la Duchesse with a letter inviting her to return to Versailles. The circumstances were humiliating. For *you,* I mean." Richelieu paused for one dramatic moment, then added softly, "She was taken ill during your visit."

"Yet he says she died before he knew she was ill!" Louis cried.

Richelieu hid a smile; the trap was beginning to close.

"She complained of a headache," Maurepas said hotly. "That and nothing else. A headache is not an illness. She developed a slight cold, which delayed her return to court. She had been back at court for a day or so before she was taken really ill. She—"

"I accuse you of *planning* to poison her," Richelieu broke in, "not of actually doing so."

"Then prove it, Richelieu!"

Richelieu smiled and preparing the ground for his biggest lie took from his pocket a small phial. The liquid it contained was a deadly purplish brown.

"When did you last see this?" he asked Maurepas.

"I never saw it in my life. What is it?"

Richelieu turned to Louis. "I spoke with the Duchesse before she died. She gave me this phial. A strange physician had called and left it. At least, he *claimed* to be a physician. He said it was the same remedy that had cured your Majesty at Metz."

Here Richelieu paused dramatically.

"For pity's sake continue!" Louis begged.

Richelieu bowed. "Madame la Duchesse told me that Maurepas had threatened her. She held up this phial. 'This,' she said, 'is undoubtedly from Maurepas.'"

"Nonsense!" Maurepas cried.

"You suggest that it contains poison?" Louis said.

"I do, your Majesty."

"Why was I not informed at the time?"

"I had no wish to worry you, Sire, and I knew that in time the opportunity of using what I had learned would present itself." He looked pityingly at Maurepas. "You deny that this is poison sent by you to Madame la Duchesse?"

"By heaven I do!"

"Then in that case, my dear fellow, I suggest that you drink a little of it."

"I—"

Maurepas hesitated. He was trapped and he knew it. If he refused to touch the phial the King would believe Richelieu's story; if he actually drank the contents the risk of killing himself was great, for it was more than possible that in setting the trap Richelieu had procured poison.

"Come, let us see you prove your innocence," Richelieu mocked.

Maurepas fell on his knees at Louis' feet.

"Sire," he beseeched, "I swear my innocence. I give you my word that I am the victim of a plot, a fiendish plot!"

Louis turned his back on him. His mind was in a turmoil. He found it impossible to keep his hands steady, such was the shock and horror of it all.

"Exile, the Bastille or execution?" Richelieu suggested.

Without looking round Louis said: "Go to your apartments, Maurepas. Consider yourself under open arrest."

Maurepas scrambled to his feet and went scowling from the room. Toinette held out her hands to Louis; he went quickly to the bed and took them in his.

"Thank you, Sire," she said simply, "for taking a great weight off my mind."

"The weight taken from mine is equally great," he cried. "If anything were to happen to you I doubt if I should want to live myself."

Later, alone with Toinette, Richelieu sighed gently and said how fortunate it was that the King had not inquired too closely about the allegedly poisoned dog.

"And fortunate, too," she smiled, "that Maurepas was afraid to drink the contents of your phial."

Richelieu agreed.

"Did he really poison the Comtesse de Vintimille?"

"Who can say? She probably committed suicide."

Toinette smiled brilliantly. "Did *you* poison her?"

"My dear Marquise," Richelieu mocked, "what a hideous suggestion."

"You're a clever scoundrel, Richelieu."

"So much so that you begin to feel a little afraid of me, perhaps?"

No longer smiling, Toinette said seriously: "If you mean that as a warning, my friend, let me issue one too. I, if need be, am also a clever scoundrel."

Not long after Maurepas's dismissal—a *lettre de cachet* banished him to the country—Toinette made one of her first serious appointments. She brought to court an old friend, the Abbé Bernis, and decided that he should begin an important career by becoming an ambassador. First a friend of her mother's, Bernis had taken an early interest in Toinette and helped not a little in her education. A member of an aristocratic but impoverished family, he had, like Fleury before him, chosen the Church as the easiest means of getting on in the world. Thus he became the first of the friends with whom she intended to replace all those at court who might be expected to oppose her.

"Sire," she said one day, "we need a new ambassador at Venice. I think Bernis would be very suitable." Louis considered this for a moment. The Abbé, much at court these days, had a ready wit and a pretty style when it came to composing love verses. Louis had employed him several times to write verses to Toinette, and Toinette herself, replying in like manner, had employed him too. "If you want to send him to Venice," Louis said, "by all means do so. You have a better understanding of these things than I have."

And so, with her power growing day by day, Toinette gave her attention to the problem of Richelieu, who was doing little to disguise his anger at her refusal to be guided by him, her refusal, in short, to permit him to dictate, through her, the King's policy. He must be removed, she

230

decided, as Maurepas had been removed, before he had time to do her a serious injury.

Having achieved Bernis' appointment so easily, she wondered how Louis would take it if she said, "Sire, Richelieu is dangerous, he must be dismissed." Possibly he would say, "Dismiss him by all means," but she had certain doubts: Louis often spoke of Richelieu as his best friend, and she knew that Louis would rather dismiss a clever minister of state than a man with whom he played cards, hunted and drank to excess. Her attack would have to be a subtle one; nothing was more certain than that.

Meanwhile, through her secretary-cousin, she had approached one of Richelieu's valets and succeeded in buying his services. Binet was not absolutely sure that the young man could be trusted, but he did feel that providing the renumeration was made frequently and generously, a watch of some sort could be kept on Richelieu.

Some months later, while Toinette was still wondering how best to get rid of Richelieu, Binet came to her breathless with excitement.

"Richelieu," he blurted out, "has chosen your successor."

Toinette laughed dryly. It was such an obvious move that she should have anticipated it earlier.

"Did you learn her name?" she asked.

"No, but Monsieur le Duc proposes to bring her to the King's attention at the royal hunt tomorrow."

Toinette looked thoughtfully at her cousin. For the past week, suffering from a distressing complaint which her personal physician called *flueurs blanches,* she had been forced to remain in bed, and Louis, denied the pleasure of that same bed, was restless and a little cross. Assured by her physician that the next menstrual period would see an end of the embarrassing indisposition, she had been glad of the rest, yet to Louis, a creature of habit, even one week's denial was an irritating hardship.

"Men," she said, to a surprised Binet, "are beasts."

Slightly alarmed, she began to wonder if the affection and friendship of the King would be strong enough, once Richelieu's unknown young woman had been prostituted before him, to make him regard the *affaire* as a casual one. She began to wonder, and she began to have unpleasant doubts, for Louis, she felt, was promiscuous at heart.

"If you go to the hunt yourself . . ." Binet suggested.

This was out of the question. She was able to rise and move carefully about the room, but greater activity than that would only bring on another and, the physician had warned, almost continual hemorrhage. Richelieu had certainly chosen his time well. And then she laughed suddenly, for a plan, precise even in all its details, had come to her mind.

"I shall give a supper party in my bedroom tonight," she announced. "The King, three or four gentlemen, and, of course, Richelieu. I shall invite them to play cards, dismiss them at midnight and later recall Richelieu to speak with me alone."

"I think I understand," said Binet, smiling.

The supper party was a merry affair. Toinette, weary though she was, left her bed for it, painted her face bravely and dressed herself in the guise of a sultana. Louis was entranced by the sight of her: the wide trousers of brocaded silk and the loose jacket gave her a delicately exotic look. He was in the best of humors, though when midnight came and he and his gentlemen were dismissed he scowled like a boy deprived at a party of an extra serving of jelly.

"Much more of this illness," he told her, half-playfully, as he kissed her on the brow, "and I shall be forced to look elsewhere."

Half-an-hour later, when Binet entered the bedroom to say that Richelieu had returned from his Majesty's *coucher,* Toinette had undressed and wrapped herself in a flimsy negligée.

"Announce him," she said, "but remember to remain well within earshot. It is not part of my plan to scream *too* loudly."

The moment Richelieu entered she came gracefully to meet him.

"The honor of being alone with you at midnight," he mocked, "is something I had never dared look forward to."

Toinette laughed softly. "Then why stand there so stiffly?"

Her manner and the huskiness of her voice surprised him. He looked at her curiously and his heart skipped a beat. Surely her attitude suggested one thing only. She was beginning to find him more attractive than the King, and that showed good taste, for he had always flattered himself that as a man he *was* more attractive. Full of confidence at being thus singled out he stepped forward and took her in his arms.

"Wait!" Toinette said.

Richelieu waited. She was the most ravishing creature he had ever seen. He had always wanted her, and by heaven, whatever the risk he was going to have her now! Her eyes were big and luminous and there, naked on her face, was that look of passion and desire common in a woman who, by her own choice, finds herself helpless in a man's presence. Telling himself all this the blood pounded in his veins and a pulse throbbed not unpleasantly in his throat.

"Look at my negligée," Toinette said. "Did you ever see a prettier one?"

"It would look prettier on the floor, Toinette."

She laughed softly. "A pity, don't you think, to damage it thus?" She took the lace of the collar between her fingers and with a quick, sharp movement ripped it. "And again, thus!" She laughed happily. "Dear me, what a violent man you are!"

"Madame!" he protested, puzzled.

"And again, thus, you rogue!"

"Are you out of your mind?" he gasped.

"And my hair, it should be about my face, like this."

"My God!" Richelieu cried, "a trap!"

He turned and stumbled to the door. Toinette reached it first. Standing with her back to it she thrust out a delicate white hand, fingers finely arched.

"Forgive me, Richelieu," she laughed, "but this, I think, is necessary."

Richelieu cried out in surprise and pain as the fingernails seared the flesh of his cheek.

"You little she-cat!"

"I have often longed to scratch your face," she chuckled, "but I never dreamed that when I did so it would be in such an excellent cause."

He touched his cheek tenderly; his fingers came away sticky with blood.

"And now," Toinette said gaily, "I think I ought to scream." Which she did, and most convincingly. "Oh, you beast!" she cried, and screamed again. "Let me go, Richelieu, let me go!"

Hearing Binet at the other side of the door she stepped forward and fell to her knees. When the door crashed open she was huddled on the carpet, sobbing convulsively. Binet, his face a study of well-simulated horror, stood and gaped at her. Finally he gave Richelieu a look of terrible reproach.

"Monsieur le Duc!"

"Help me, Binet," Toinette begged pitifully.

Tenderly Binet helped her to her feet and assisted her to a chair, while Richelieu stood aside, his face revealing his growing agitation.

"Do you wish me to acquaint his Majesty with what has happened?" Binet asked.

"Wait!" Richelieu cried. "Let me explain."

"Explain?" Toinette said. Her eyes held his for a moment, mockingly. "How *can* you explain?"

Her meaning was clear. Indeed, how could he? Would Binet believe him, whatever he said? Would the King?

"Please go, Binet," Toinette said, drooping weakly in her chair. "Richelieu will make no further attack. Wait outside."

Binet bowed, gave Richelieu a final look of reproach and went from the room.

Choking with anger Richelieu said, "Words fail me, Madame!"

She said: "By the law of France seduction is punishable by death, so possibly attempted rape is punishable also by torture."

"Pah!" Richelieu cried.

Smiling, Toinette went on: "You will leave Versailles immediately for your house in Paris, that fine new house you have built out of the perquisites of war. Tomorrow you will receive your instructions. I suggest you join the army in the south."

"And if I refuse?"

"His Majesty will be called at once to witness my distress and hear Binet's story."

Richelieu, his face clouded with apprehension, remained silent.

"Honorable service with the army should delight you," she said.

"But I am expected to accompany the King to Fontaine-bleau tomorrow," he protested.

"I shall explain that a secret *affaire* went suddenly awry. The lady in question is the wife of an important minister. You fear the King's anger. You feel too humiliated, too hurt and too alarmed to face anybody, even his Majesty."

"If you think to banish me forever—!" Richelieu began.

"Oh, hardly that," Toinette said, "but most of your time shall be spent with the army. And remember this, Binet's evidence can be called upon at any time, so . . . behave yourself."

After Richelieu had gone Toinette went back to bed. She felt quite exhausted and fell at once into a dreamless sleep. Awaking next morning she recalled the events of the previous night with a satisfied chuckle. From now on, she told herself, she would have no difficulty in consolidating her power. She would dismiss whom she chose and appoint whom she chose. France would soon be hers.

"The uncrowned Queen," she said aloud.

XIX

"FIVE years!" the Dauphin stormed. "Five insufferable years!" He rose and strode about the room, gesticulating as he did so. "Five humiliating years!" he added, and glared hotly at the other two people present, his mother the Queen, and Monsieur le Comte d'Argenson. "His Majesty my father," he ran on, "a man who forces me to despise him, is a king in name only. Worse, our ministers are ministers in name only. A concubine rules France. You understand, a *concubine!*"

"Sit down, Louis," his mother said patiently. "You will only wear yourself out, shouting and gesticulating like that."

"Bah!" the Dauphin cried, and flung himself into a chair.

Marie looked at him thoughtfully, and just a little sadly. She loved him dearly, and he was, she knew, more devoted to her than to his second wife, who had recently borne him a son, but he was too much the fanatic to be the wise man she had hoped.

"Madame de Pompadour," she said quietly, "is not as bad as you try to make us all believe. At all events she keeps your father amused, and that, you must admit, is a blessing."

Argenson laughed ruefully. "But at what a cost, your Majesty."

Argenson had turned against Toinette soon after Richelieu's sudden departure but he still paid her lip service. He did this, not because Richelieu had advised it, but because he saw clearly that while she remained in power his career depended on it. Richelieu, during his last brief visit to Versailles, had also advised him to work secretly with the Dauphin, and this he was ready to do, not in order to remove her and bring Richelieu back, but because he felt that the Dauphin's influence might be good for France.

"How much longer," the Dauphin broke out, "are we to submit to the reign of this middleclass upstart?"

"That is a question I often ask myself," Argenson said.

"Yes, but what do you *do?*" The Dauphin leaped to his feet and strode impatiently to the magnificent marble fireplace. "Fear, that is your trouble, fear!" He turned to Marie. "And you, Mother, what have you ever done about removing Madame de Pompadour?"

"Nothing," Marie admitted, "but my power, if I ever possessed power, disappeared so long ago that I can scarcely remember it." She spoke without resentment, making a plain statement of fact like a dispassionate onlooker. "The establishment of a royal favorite is a tradition. Bring about her fall and another woman will take her place."

"Had you been clever, Mother," the Dauphin said, "the tradition would never have been created."

Marie looked hurt. Her son, seeing this, came to her side quickly and took her hands in his.

"Forgive me," he begged, "I spoke hastily."

Smiling, Marie said quietly: "Your reason for hating the Marquise is a personal one. That is the trouble at Versailles, the personal view. Apart from squandering money to keep the King amused, the Marquise has done little that is bad for France. You hate her cleverness and you covet the power she wields, but if you were able to secure that power for yourself, would you use it any the more wisely?"

The Dauphin scowled. "You speak as if you prefer her to remain at court."

"I do," Marie smiled. "Your father could do much worse for himself, *and* for France."

"Then you have no intention of helping us?"

"None, Louis."

She rose from her chair and took a dignified departure.

The Dauphin watched her go and then said despairingly: "What a simpleton my mother is! The Pompadour woman has done little that is bad for France except the squandering of money! As if that is not enough! And think of her continual interference in state affairs! My father is losing his popularity and she is the cause of it."

Argenson agreed. The people at large were beginning to hate the King and his mistress, blaming them jointly for all the ills that now beset the country. The war, which the Treaty of Aix-la-Chapelle had brought to an end, had made Louis a hero, but that had been quickly forgotten. All that was remembered was the cost of that futile war, a cost expressed in ever-increasing taxation, a cost made all the harder to bear by the reckless extravagance of the court. And the people at large, he reflected, made up that section of the population most ignored, a section from which the revolt he feared and saw no way of countering would one day come.

"I was counting on my mother's help," the Dauphin complained. "All I wanted her to do was take a new lady-in-waiting."

Argenson laughed shortly. "So that is your Highness's plan." He laughed again. "Surely you can bring your young lady to the King's notice without troubling the Queen."

"My young lady?" the Dauphin gasped. "What do *you* know of her? She is being coached in secret. *In secret*, I say!"

"I know nothing," Argenson smiled, "I was merely guessing, but I warn you, the Marquise will never permit your plan to succeed."

"The woman is ill again, has been for over a month."

"She was ill when Richelieu planned the same thing, but where is Richelieu now?"

"What he planned five years ago can be planned with greater hope of success now. The Marquise has been ill many times since then. My father loathes illness and this is the longest illness the Marquise has ever had."

Argenson smiled. "I admit that the King is growing restive."

"So restive that he is ripe for a new *affaire*. Ripe for it, I tell you!"

Argenson chuckled and the Dauphin, catching his eye, grew suddenly abashed, even to the point of blushing.

"Excessive physical passion is horrible," he said hurriedly, "but I may as well use it in this instance to my own advantage."

"May I know the fortunate young lady's name?" Argenson asked.

"This is not a joke," the Dauphin said severely. "She is Mademoiselle Choisseul-Romanet, a niece of the Duchesse d'Estrades."

"Forgive me, but . . . a young lady of experience?"

"Yes," the Dauphin said, and blushed again. "My father is of an age when a lack of experience would bore him. Later, of course, when he grows older, he will ogle young girls, but for the present . . ."

Argenson wanted to laugh but thought it wiser to restrain himself. He said curiously: "Your Highness said the young lady was being coached. Coached in what, pray?"

"Etiquette, deportment, the art of conversation."

"Is she beautiful?"

"Strikingly so, in features. She is tall and dark and rather thin."

"Thin?"

"A new type, Monsieur," the Dauphin said gravely. "For my father, quite a novelty."

"Intelligent?"

"Certainly not. I would never have chosen her if she had been. She is developing a witty conversation, and is learning how to give the *impression* of intelligence, but beyond that she is a fool. Once established she will do everything I say."

"Is she ready for presentation?"

"Yes, almost. You have an idea that might be helpful?"

Argenson strove to keep a solemn countenance. "Invite the King to take supper with you. Arrange to be called away, and while away send her in to him. Let her tell him that she has been invited to take supper with you alone and has obviously made a mistake in the time."

The Dauphin looked horrified. "But Monsieur, I have never done a thing like that in my life!"

"Precisely. It will arouse the King's interest, and as a means of furthering it," Argenson added solemnly, "put an aphrodisiac in your father's wine."

"What a marvellous suggestion!" the Dauphin cried, but he blushed again.

The Abbé Bernis, leaning forward in his chair at the bedside, was speaking earnestly, but Toinette, her mind dwelling on a recent interview with her personal physician, was hardly listening. A month in bed, she thought, a whole month! Not that it interfered with state affairs, which she was able to conduct in her bedroom, but it did interfere with the King's fixed routine. And worse still, Louis, having been present at the onset of this latest attack, was no longer in ignorance of the nature of the disease. Horrified at first, he had later expressed a hurried sympathy and had sent to London and Vienna for a whole army of specialists.

But there was worse to come. It was now necessary that Louis should be told the whole truth, gently if possible, but frankly. The birth of her daughter, it seemed, had caused certain lacerations. These, healing of their own accord, had left a weakness, a proneness to inflammation. "There is only one remedy," the physician had said, "a remedy which his Majesty might well object to." Her first thought had been "Release!" but a release, she saw now, that could lead to her dismissal.

Bernis cleared his throat.

"I beg your pardon," Toinette said quickly. "I know I was barely listening. Did I hear you say something about Austria?"

"You did indeed," he said warmly. "I am doing my best to convince you that an Austrian alliance is imperative."

She felt herself growing angry. Bernis, once he got an idea in that head of his, was worse than a nagging wife. She had noticed this on his return from Venice and because of it had refrained from appointing him to one or other of the ministries. She pointed out sharply that an alliance with Austria was against all the established traditions of French diplomacy.

"But why, Madame? Both are Catholic nations."

"If all the world were Catholic," she said tartly, "there would still be war. This court is a Catholic court, but do we have peace here? We fight among ourselves continually. Individually we reach out for power as nations do. Change a man's nature, not his religion, if you want peace in the world."

"I would never want to change *your* nature, Madame," Bernis said smoothly, "but with all my heart I would like to change your religion."

"You know I have no religion to change."

"Then let me say that I would like to give you religion; or rather, that I would like to bring you back to the religion in which you were born."

Toinette laughed mockingly. "The King remarked yesterday that I was welcome to keep you at court as long as I wished, providing you refrained from trying to save our souls."

"I care more for your soul than the King's," Bernis said.

"Convince me first that I have a soul."

"No, no," he laughed. "You are much too clever to be argued with, but I shall continue to pray for you."

"That," she said haughtily, "is an impertinence. Pray for yourself. Pray for the abbé, the churchman whose ambitions are worldly enough to lead him through the muck and mire of court intrigue."

Bernis flushed angrily.

"Forgive me," Toinette said quickly. "I know you deceive yourself that in entering court intrigues you are working religiously for the good of mankind—or could it be," she added thoughtfully, "for a cardinal's hat? Is that what Rome would give you if you brought about an alliance between France and Austria?"

Bernis shrugged. "You are quicker than anybody, Toinette, when it comes to finding a man's weaknesses. Nevertheless, I do believe myself to be sincere."

"So do I believe myself to be sincere, but am I? Why do I want to retain my power? For the sake of France, or for the sake of Madame la Marquise de Pompadour?"

"Look favorably on an Austrian alliance and you will be using your power for the sake of France. Nothing is more certain than that."

She thought that he might be right. There was peace with England, but England was always a potential enemy, as was Prussia, and Prussia and England together (for there was reason to suspect that they were planning something between them) would be in a position to inflict a crushing blow on France.

"Have you been approached by Austrian agents," she asked, "or is this your own idea?"

"Austrian agents have waited on me," he answered, smiling, "but the idea has been mine for some time."

"Because of religion!"

"I thought I had already admitted that."

"Superstition," she cried suddenly, "there is no place in my mind for superstition!"

Bernis smiled. "You protest too vehemently. And why call it superstition?" He held her eyes for a moment. "I prefer to call it inherent conviction."

"I used the wrong word," she argued. "I should have said fear."

"Fear, Toinette? Fear of what?"

"Fear of what might happen when one dies."

"And you have no fear of that yourself?"

"None!" Toinette said hotly.

"I wonder," he mused, "if you want me to admire you for your foolhardiness?"

She laughed. "Well, do you?"

"No," Bernis said gravely, "I merely pity you. To be an intellectual is all very well, but when your times comes, will that impress God as you stand before him, making your plea?"

"What plea, Bernis?"

"'I am an intellectual,' you will say. 'I know more about everything than you, the Almighty.'"

Toinette felt a little stab of fear. Angry with herself, she tried to thrust it aside.

"Your language," she laughed, "is almost blasphemous."

"Even blasphemy is permissible when one is trying to save a soul."

"Pooh! All you are trying to do is make an Austrian alliance."

There was a cough at the door and Binet entered. Toinette saw by his face that he brought news of an unpleasant nature. He glanced questioningly at Bernis. Understanding, she held out her hand to the abbé.

"I shall give a little thought to Austria and to my immortal soul as well."

Bernis, more like a courtier than a churchman, kissed her hand. "And I, I promise, shall continue to pray for you."

The moment he had gone Toinette turned to Binet. "Well?"

"The King is at Rambouillet," he said.

"I know he is, Binet."

"Yes, but his Majesty took a young lady with him."

"He—!" She controlled herself. "Tell me about it."

"The King took supper last night with the Dauphin. During the meal the Dauphin excused himself. While he was absent the niece of the Duchesse d'Estrades entered. She hinted that she was about to become the Dauphin's mistress. The King was amused, then interested. Finally he said, 'My son is too young and too religious, but his father, who is past redemption, is a different proposition.' He took her to his own apartments, where she remained until this morning, after which—"

"You are sure of this, Binet?"

Binet chuckled richly. "The Dauphin's valets are still paid handsomely."

"I see no reason for alarm," Toinette said, after a moment's silence. "No reason at all."

But her voice shook and there were tears of vexation in her eyes.

"Good morning, Toinette," Louis said jauntily.

Toinette glanced quickly at his reflection in the mirror as he stood behind her. She saw at once that he was nervous and that his eyes, meeting hers for a moment in the mirror, had a guilty look. She dismissed her ladies, who were busy about her, and continued her toilette unaided. Louis' attitude made her smile, and the alarm she had felt at Binet's news no longer disturbed her.

"It makes me happy," Louis said, "to find you well enough to get up today."

"Thank you," she said politely.

Two days had passed since Binet had brought her his news and Louis had just returned from Rambouillet. She wondered if he had returned alone or brought Mademoiselle Choisseul-Romanet with him, but she decided to refrain for the moment from asking him. She dipped her fingers in the perfumed water contained in the silver basin at her side. It would be amusing, she decided, to tease and startle Louis a little.

"Louis," she said, frowning at him, "I want to talk to you."

Louis shifted his weight from one foot to the other.

"And seriously," she added, making her voice sharp.

"Seriousness before midday," he expostulated, "is more than I can ever stomach."

"Forgive me, but I really must insist."

"Oh . . ." he said, and added hopefully, "You wish to discuss state affairs, of course?"

"What else?" she asked innocently.

"Ah!" He laughed his relief. "What else indeed, when no one possesses a greater understanding of them than you!"

"Thank you," she said, and putting her position to the test she added: "I flatter myself that my grasp of things is greater than anybody else's."

"Greater by far," he said eagerly. "You are cleverer than Fleury was. Indeed, my dear, you are irreplaceable."

More than satisfied she said: "Prussia and England are planning mischief."

"Let them!" he cried. "Madame de Pompadour is capable

244

of countering any move they might be foolish enough to make."

Toinette turned from the mirror to face him. She had decided that an Austrian alliance would be a bold and sensible move. Admittedly she had an uneasy feeling that she, the renegade, the would-be atheist, was a little eager to please the church, but quite apart from that, the move might well be an international necessity. It was not a matter of saving her soul; it was simply a matter of safeguarding the interests of France.

"Would it startle you," she asked, "if I gave some thought to an Austrian alliance?"

Louis' brows shot up, then he grinned boyishly.

"It would startle my ministers a great deal more," he laughed.

"And that would please and amuse you."

"Infinitely. Nevertheless—" he frowned thoughtfully— "Austria . . ."

"At this stage I merely suggest a discussion between French and Austrian agents."

"In that case you have my permission," he said generously.

"Thank you, Louis." She rose and placed a hand lightly on his arm. It was time, she thought, to make him speak of Mademoiselle Choisseul-Romanet. "It is always my desire," she said, "to make the King of France the greatest monarch in the world."

"Oh . . ." Louis said, and dropped his eyes from hers.

"I dream of it night and day. Loving you as I do it has become an obsession."

"Oh . . ." he said again, more uneasily.

She waited for a moment, patiently, then she said softly: "Does my attitude displease you?"

Louis flung himself from her. At the window, with his back turned to her, he said: "It makes me ashamed, utterly ashamed."

Toinette smiled. His conscience was as sensitive as she had expected.

"Ashamed?" she echoed, in wonder.

"You must have heard gossip," Louis growled, "and know all about my reason for rushing away to Rambouillet."

"I never listen to gossip," she said lightly, "and the hunt has taken you from me many times in the past."

He turned to face her, but avoided her eyes and tried to make his words sound like a joke. "I hunted a different kind of game this time, my dear."

"Really?" she said innocently.

"Confound you, Toinette," he blustered, "how difficult you make my confession!"

"Your *confession*, Louis?"

"I—to be frank, my dear, I happen to have been unfaithful to you."

"You speak," she said lightly, "as if I were your wife."

He was at her side in a moment, taking her slender hands in his, holding them in a tense, warm grip. "You are more than that, Toinette. You always have been; you always will be."

"Then to what have you been unfaithful?" she asked calmly. "Our friendship? Our love and mutual understanding?"

"I would kill myself," he avowed, "if I were ever unfaithful to those things."

She smiled at him in sudden happiness. The tenderness she had first felt for him returned and brought quick tears to her eyes.

"Then your 'confession', as you call it, is unnecessary."

"I think otherwise!" he declared.

"Yes?" She released her hands and returned to her dressing-table.

"At least," he amended, "I want you to know that it was a plot, a plot hatched by that stupid son of mine and, I suspect, Argenson. The girl is a fool. I made her admit the plot almost at once. However, she amuses me."

Toinette smiled at herself in the mirror. "Had I known you were in need of that sort of amusement I would have chosen someone for you."

"My dear!" Louis exclaimed, slightly shocked.

"However, if, as you say, she amuses you . . ."

He came up behind her, touched her gently on the shoulder.

"Only for the time being, Toinette; only until you are completely well again."

Toinette considered carefully this cue she had been waiting for. He had said she was irreplaceable; he had almost convinced her that her position, quite apart from their physical relationship, was impregnable, but she had to be sure.

"What would happen," she said, turning to face him and hold his eyes steadily, "if I were never completely well again?"

Louis looked into her eyes with deep concern. "You mean the disease might kill you?"

"Oh, never *that!*" she laughed.

She thought that for a fleeting moment a look of relief crossed his face; not relief at the knowledge that she was in no fear of death, for the expression was too furtive for that, but relief similar to that which she had felt herself at the physician's pronouncement.

"You do understand what I really mean?" she asked.

"Yes—" again the furtive look—"yes, I think so."

"You would be . . . angry?"

"No, my dear," he said quickly, "only—well, only sorry."

"Sorry for yourself?"

"For both of us," he said gallantly.

She told him then all that the physician had said. He listened in silence, but though his face was grave she detected the beginnings of a gentle smile at the corners of his mouth.

"You were beginning to tire of me *that* way?" she challenged.

"Even as you were of me," he said frankly.

She laughed weakly. Since freedom from his physical demands was what she wanted, she was amazed that she should feel a little affronted. Even a cold woman, she realized, was not without a touch of sexual vanity.

"I may be a man of blinding physical passion," Louis murmured, "but I am not entirely lacking in perception. You acted a part very well, you suffered me nobly, but you rarely deceived me."

Toinette laughed again, but she said tartly, "So Mademoiselle Choisseul-Romanet is better than I!"

Louis shrugged. "She has a certain aptitude, and I have often been curious about thin women. She is so thin," he said earnestly, "that you can count her ribs with ease."

"Which you did."

"Yes, indeed. And her hip bones—!" He realized that this conversation was hardly in the best of taste and changed the subject abruptly. "Keep me in touch with the Austrian move, my dear."

She turned from him quickly, but he had seen the tears which, welling out of her eyes, were trickling down the carefully applied rouge.

"My dearest!" he cried, deeply moved.

"Oh, leave me alone!" she said angrily.

He took her by the shoulders and gently turned her to face him.

"A little jealous, eh?" he teased.

"Yes," she admitted, "but it will soon pass."

Louis smiled. "I fear it will."

She was mastering her tears now. "This woman, this temporary mistress, did you bring her back to Versailles?"

"Why, yes. She shall remain for a week or so. A room is being prepared for her."

"Here, under the same roof as I?" Toinette protested. "The court will suspect that official recognition is intended."

"Possibly," he smiled, "but I assure you, on my honor as a king—" He broke off; Toinette was obviously not amused. "What do you suggest?" he asked lamely. "After all, my need being what it is . . ." He blushed and scowled. "Confound it, *some* arrangement must be made!"

"Set her up in a more discreet abode," she said, and smiled.

"Gladly!" he cried, his eyes showing gratitude.

He took her in his arms gently. It was, she thought, an almost brotherly embrace.

248

"My dear," he said earnestly, "I shall guard against embarrassing you. There will be others, of course, but discreetly. I love you as dearly as ever. In the things that really matter you will always mean more to me than anybody else. You will continue to take the weight of state affairs from my shoulders, and you will, as ever, give me peace and comfort through your friendship and understanding. I feel more at peace now, knowing you to be just my friend, not my mistress.

"Not your mistress but still your favorite, Louis?"

"Always my favorite, always!"

Toinette went back to the mirror to repair the damage caused by her tears, tears which after all might well be called tears of happiness. She rang for her ladies, who were soon fussing round her, one with the heavy purple gown, another with the great wire frame to support it, yet another with the jewel case open for her inspection. She smiled gaily on them all. She was happier than she had ever been before. The favorite but not the mistress! She laughed merrily. The favorite but *not* the mistress! The court, when the story got about, would be amazed, amused and possibly a little shocked.

XX

THE Dauphin looked up from the topmost sheet of the sheaf of papers he held so importantly in his hand.

"These figures," he said, "have been supplied by certain officials of the Treasury. They are absolutely and irrefutably beyond dispute."

"You said that before, darling," Marie reminded him.

"And I say it again! I say it again in order to stress the enormity of this outrageous extravagance. Twenty-three million livres. *Twenty-three*, Mother!"

"Fantastic," Stainville shuddered.

Marie, working diligently at her tapestry frame, looked up for a moment and tried not to smile. They were talking, of course, about Toinette, Toinette who had been at court twelve years now and was likely to remain for another twelve. Marie wanted to smile, not because Madame de Pompadour's personal expenditure amused her, for it really was fantastic, but because the scene reminded her of one that had taken place some years ago. The third person then had been Argenson, but he, poor fellow, had been quietly dismissed by a *lettre de cachet* written by Toinette and signed by Louis. Stainville, she thought, would have to be careful or he, even though he owed his appointment to Toinette, might quickly follow Argenson into exile. She glanced at this new man for a moment, with his plump figure and fat smiling face: he looked like a jolly, good-tempered farmer, but his eyes, she fancied, betrayed a cunning that should warn her son against him.

"In addition," the Dauphin was running on, "I find that she is one of the largest property owners in the country. There are the large chateaux at Meudon and Dreux, the country houses at Versailles, Campiegne and Fontainebleau, the large and elaborate town house in Paris, the . . ."

His voice went on and on as he quoted in detail from his papers, but Marie, giving her attention once more to the tapestry, was no longer listening. She was sorry for Toinette, who was growing old before her time, but she also admired her, distressing as her extravagance was. No other woman could, while denying Louis her bed, succeed in holding the position of favorite. And apart from all that, Marie was genuinely fond of Toinette: she attended all her theatrical productions (the Little Theatre, she reflected, had cost seventy-five thousand livres) and she had relinquished with a sigh of relief certain court duties which had always irked her and which the favorite could discharge with a real grace.

"And how ridiculous," the Dauphin was saying, "that in spite of her unpopularity so many people should seek to copy her in everything. Paris is full of Pompadour mirrors and chairs and fans and carriages and chimney-pieces and—" He broke off and pointed a quivering finger at Marie. "Merciful heavens, even you, Mother, with the latest Pompadour hair style!"

Marie touched her powdered hair self-consciously, while her son, having taken breath, was running on again. She looked at him critically. He was twenty-eight, fat now rather than plump, not very tidily dressed, yet giving, as ever, the impression of austerity. Twenty-eight . . . which meant that Louis was forty-seven and she herself fifty-four. Though there was little vanity in her, it pleased her to know that she looked as young as Louis, nay younger. She glanced at the new portrait on the wall which barely disguised the dissipation marked in the many lines beneath the eyes, the heavy cheeks and the sagging chin.

"And the *Parc aux Cerfs!*" she heard her son say.

Yes, she thought, the *Parc aux Cerfs*, which everybody was gossiping about. Formerly a deer park, as the name implied, it was within easy reach of the Palace, and the house had been turned into what Louis himself called a discreet bachelor establishment. The Choisseul-Romanet girl had been set up there, but not for long: she had been followed by a succession of others, and now, according to gossip, as many as a dozen at a time were in residence. People blamed Toinette for permitting this, for encouraging it, as indeed she did, but what else could the poor creature do if she wanted to retain her power? Less dangerous, Marie concluded, to snatch a bone from a wild dog than to deprive Louis of his *Parc aux Cerfs*.

"And now," the Dauphin was saying, "we are at war again, simply and solely because of a concubine."

"A *retired* concubine," Stainville tittered.

Marie was anything but happy about the war, chiefly because Toinette had confided recently that she herself was anything but happy about it. Toinette blamed England and Prussia, who had made an alliance, an alliance which had forced France and Austria to do likewise, and now there was war.

"I sometimes think," Stainville remarked, "that the only person to gain anything out of the Austrian alliance is Bernis."

"The Marquise might have made him Minister of Foreign Affairs and helped him gain his cardinal's hat," the Dauphin said knowingly, "but he is not as friendly toward her as people think."

"Can you blame him?" Stainville laughed. "He has never yet succeeded in saving her soul."

"He has other reasons," the Dauphin stated, and added darkly, "It is only a question of time before he joins us."

Marie doubted this, but she held her peace. The Dauphin

and Stainville began to argue about the best means of attacking and removing Toinette, and this made her smile.

"You will never remove her," she said. "The position she holds is unique. How *can* you remove a woman who can no longer be replaced by another woman?"

They looked at her; they looked at each other. The Dauphin scowled and was forced to agree.

"We can at least pray for her downfall," he said lamely.

And Marie, deeply religious woman that she was, laughed scornfully.

"Pray," she mocked, "by all means pray."

"You agree, of course," said Monsieur de Machault, Controller of Finances, "that what I have done is right."

His words were a statement of fact, not a polite question, and though Toinette agreed with them—the war would grow more and more costly and additional taxation was imperative —his cocksure attitude irritated her. Like Louis, she knew him to be one of the best financial experts they could find, but she had little affection for him. She had appointed him solely because of his remarkable ability and now, fool that he was, he believed that ability alone would enable him to hold his position. She looked at him with distaste. He was austere, grave-mannered, pig-headed. She disliked him a little more each time she was obliged to discuss state affairs with him.

"I only regret," he was saying, "that it is beyond my power to tax the clergy."

Toinette regretted this too. Soon after his appointment he had suggested a general tax of five per centum, a tax to include the clergy. The magistrates themselves had been the first to oppose the measure: they felt that the poor alone should be made to pay the new tax; the rich, they argued, could ill-afford it and if forced would retaliate by employing less labor, thus embarrassing the poor far more than if the Crown taxed them alone. Seeing the selfish basis of this argument, Louis had given the Parliament of Paris two hours to register the new decree. His firmness had surprised everybody, himself included, and had alarmed not a few.

Enjoying himself he went, as he called it, from strength to strength and dismissed the Parliament when in opposition to the tax it refused to accept the budget. But finally, just when Toinette was expecting even greater things of him, the clergy rose against the decree and he weakly issued an order-in-council exempting them from all taxes.

Disappointed and furious, Toinette learned that two people had influenced him in this, his favorite daughter, Adelaide, and the long-forgotten mistress, Julie de Mailly. Julie had died at this critical moment (died in a hairshirt, of all things!) and from her deathbed had sent Louis a message begging him, for the sake of his immortal soul, to treat the clergy with the respect they deserved. It was her first real failure with Louis, Toinette reflected now, and the memory of it still rankled.

"The order-in-council," said Machault, as if reading her thoughts, "did some good. It showed the people that the Church is grasping and put them against it a little."

"It also showed them that the King has lost some of his authority," Toinette said sharply, "and that did no good at all."

At that moment Binet entered the room. He came in hurriedly, his face pale, his eyes wide with horror.

"An attempt has been made on the King's life," he blurted out. "His Majesty has been stabbed by a madman. It is not yet known whether he will live or die."

Toinette half-rose in her chair, then sat down again and tried to steady herself. Betraying no emotion at all, Machault asked for details. There was little for Binet to tell. The King had been about to step into his carriage. A man had leaped forward brandishing a knife and had stabbed his Majesty in the side. The man had been caught; the King had been carried to his apartments.

"Go to the anteroom at once," Toinette instructed Binet. "Have his Majesty informed that I am deeply shocked and will join him in a few moments."

Watching the secretary hurry away, Machault gave a suggestive little cough.

"Well, what is it?" Toinette demanded.

Machault smiled impassively. "The word 'Metz' suddenly occurred to me but I thought it kind not to utter it."

"Metz?"

"When the King was supposed to be dying at Metz his current mistress, Madame de Chateauroux, was dismissed. The King is always pious when ill."

Toinette felt a sudden stab of fear. She was weary of the struggle which now marked her life, weary of keeping a watch on possible enemies, weary of the demands made on her by state affairs, but she had no desire to see herself removed.

"My own position is somewhat different," she said confidently. "I am not the King's mistress. I am his friend, his adviser and, if you will, his favorite, but I am not his mistress. My dismissal is no more likely than the Queen's."

"No, Madame?" Machault said, looking at her with mocking eyes.

When Binet reached the King's anteroom the crowd which had gathered there was being turned away. He stood back, waiting and watching, until presently the only people who remained were the Dauphin, Cardinal Bernis, Stainville and Richelieu. Binet was a little uneasy about the latter. It was unfortunate that the Marshal—for Richelieu had recently been created a marshal—should be paying one of his brief visits to Versailles at such a time as this.

"Well?" the Dauphin questioned, his eyes falling haughtily on Binet.

"Madame la Marquise," Binet stammered, "wishes his Majesty to be informed that she will wait on him in a few moments."

The Dauphin smiled thinly. "That was to be expected. Now go, Monsieur."

Binet backed from the room. The Dauphin looked at the

others each in turn. Knowing the truth of his father's condition he was unwilling to speak his mind unless Bernis, not knowing the true story, declared himself now as Madame de Pompadour's enemy.

"Do you think, my dear Bernis," he said, giving the man a chance to speak for himself, "that the Marquise should be admitted to my father's presence?"

Bernis hesitated. "That is surely a matter for the King himself to decide."

"It could be a matter for we four to decide," the Dauphin suggested.

Bernis still hesitated. He disapproved of much that Toinette did, but he still believed in her. If the King were dying, of course . . . However, only three physicians had been called, so it hardly seemed that he was.

"I fail to see what your Highness means," he said, smiling apologetically.

Angrily, the Dauphin pointed a finger at the door. "If you please, Monsieur!" he said haughtily.

Bernis bowed and walked from the room. The Dauphin slammed the door on him, turned and smiled.

"Metz!" he said. "You agree, gentlemen?"

Richelieu chuckled. At Metz he had been on what people would have called the losing side, except for the fact that Madame de Chateauroux would have reigned again had she not died. It might be the same in Toinette's case, providing the King lived. Nor was it known that the King had yet decided to dismiss her. Trembling with fear he might be at this very moment, and ridiculously pious, but Toinette was a different proposition from Anne de Chateauroux. He said as much to the Dauphin and Stainville echoed his words.

"Of course if the King dies," Richelieu added, "your royal Highness will be King and Madame de Pompadour's dismissal will be automatic."

The Dauphin frowned. "I may as well tell you at once that there is no possibility of my father dying."

"Your Highness is sure of that?" Stainville asked.

"Yes, Stainville. His Majesty is suffering from shock. Had it been summer he would have been more lightly clothed and might have been killed, but as it is the wound is nothing but a minor injury. However, the physicians, under my instructions, will keep silent on this point and assure his Majesty, and the whole court, that his condition is very grave indeed."

Richelieu laughed aloud. The Dauphin was cleverer than one might have thought.

"How long can the King be kept in ignorance of the truth?" Stainville asked.

"Long enough, I hope, to serve our purpose. I expect him to be just as easy to handle as he was at Metz. He never changes. When threatened by death he is always afraid to face his maker without having atoned for his sins. True, the Marquise is no longer his mistress, but her continued establishment is an insult to the court. He has wronged my mother dreadfully. He will think of her now, not Madame de Pompadour."

"But once he learns that life, not death, is before him—" Richelieu began to object.

"By then," the Dauphin smiled, "the Marquise will be beyond reach. Exile abroad is what I have in mind, and once she has left the shores of France she shall remain abroad at any cost."

"A quiet little assassination, perhaps?"

"I said *at any cost*," the Dauphin repeated. He turned quickly to the outer door and locked it. "And now," he said, "my father."

Entering the royal bedroom he dismissed the three physicians, went to his father's side and looked down on him sorrowfully.

"Oh, Father!" he cried, and fell on his knees.

Louis, pale and frightened, made an effort to sit up, gasped, clutched at his heavily bandaged side and fell back on the pillows.

"Your voice," he moaned, "tells me all that the wretched physicians refused to say."

The Dauphin kissed his hands. "It breaks my heart, Father," he said, and cursed his inability to weep a little.

"I asked for Toinette," Louis moaned. "Where is she?"

"The Marquise is afraid to come."

"Afraid? Nonsense! She's being kept from me. *You* are keeping her from me!"

The Dauphin shook his head sadly. "That is unworthy of you, Sire. I hate her, yes, but I know how much she has meant to you and I would never be so cruel as to keep her from you at a time like this." He rose and went to the door, saying over his shoulder, "I myself will send for her."

When he returned to the room—he had waited for a while on the stairs—Louis smiled at him affectionately and thanked him.

"But you said she was afraid," he frowned. "Afraid of *what?*"

"Death, Father."

"Death!"

Louis mouthed the word and shuddered. Nobody had uttered it until now and he had refused, in spite of the physicians' silence and his son's attitude, to dwell on it himself.

"The wound isn't deep," he pleaded, "I know it isn't."

"No, Father, but there are two dangerous aspects. The blade might have been poisoned and there is a possibility of gangrene."

"Gangrene! My great-grandfather died of that!"

"Yes," said the Dauphin, somberly. "And if your present feverish condition grows worse—"

"For pity's sake stop!" Louis sat up. He tried to speak again and failed. His eyes were big with fear. "Your mother," he managed to gasp at last. "I must see your mother."

The Dauphin waited for a moment, preparing himself for the playing of his highest card.

"Your mother . . . Marie . . ." Louis begged. "And please hurry!"

"Unhappily, Father, her Majesty is in no position to come to you."

"She is prostrate with grief? She—?"

"Yes, Father, but apart from that, dignity forbids her to come while at the same time you are asking for the Marquise. Indeed, how *can* she come while the Marquise remains at Versailles?"

"She said that? Your mother said that?"

The Dauphin, avoiding a spoken lie, inclined his head.

Anger replaced the fear in Louis' eyes, but only for a moment.

"I see it all!" he cried. "Now, with death hanging over me; now, with so many things on my conscience, you bring this pressure to bear." The fear returned. "Very well, send for the Queen. Tell her that I shall never see Toinette again. You have your way. She shall go. Toinette shall go."

Toinette looked at Stainville and chuckled.

"I presume," she said, her big green eyes alight with amusement, "that nobody, least of all the Dauphin, suspects you of working for me?"

Stainville's fat face crinkled into a slow smile. "Least of all the Dauphin."

Still looking at him she thought that she liked him more than anybody else at court. In particular she was drawn to him because of his quiet opposition to organized religion. His enemies had spread the story that he was an atheist, chiefly because he insisted on eating meat on Fridays, but he only laughed his full-throated laugh and said that, adoring meat as he did, he proposed to go on eating it every day of the week for the rest of his life. He was a good soldier and an excellent man of affairs. He believed in himself (more important still he believed in Toinette), and as well as infinite patience he possessed an iron nerve.

He completed his report, smiled and withdrew, and Toinette began to think of all the things he had told her. In a way she admired the Dauphin, whom previously she had merely despised: the trick he was trying to play was one she would have been proud to have played herself. She wondered what to do for the best. Stainville having access through his supposed friendship with the Dauphin, it would be easy to send him to Louis and expose the trick. That was the best course to follow, but not just yet. The longer Louis remained in ignorance of his true condition the greater his anger would be when the truth was revealed.

Sighing involuntarily she rose from her chair. She realized with anger that the weariness which had been getting the better of her lately was upon her again. She thought, again in anger rather than alarm, of the persistent cough which plagued her, and she remembered a recent warning issued by her personal physician. With a little shudder she tried to forget it. Physicians had been wrong before, were wrong more often than right.

Later in the day Binet came to her and told her that the Duc de Richelieu was waiting to see her. *The first move,* she thought, and laughed aloud.

"Tell him I am much too busy to receive him," she said.

Binet coughed apologetically. "Monsieur le Duc is prepared to wait all day and, if need be, all night."

"To keep him at my door all day and all night would amuse me vastly. Tell him that."

But Richelieu, stouter now, more dissipated of countenance, was already entering the room. He placed a hand on his sword and bowed.

"How bold of you, and how rash," Toinette said calmly.

Richelieu understood her instantly, but he said coolly: "The King is dying. He has refused to see you. You can take no steps to injure me now, Madame." He took an impressive-looking document from his pocket and handed it to her. "Your dismissal, Madame."

She glanced negligently at the wording of the dismissal.

"As you see," Richelieu went on, "every assistance will be given to make your departure as speedy as possible. A coach is now in readiness. You will leave Versailles tonight at the latest. Tomorrow you will board a ship at Le Havre. Your ultimate destination is America."

Anger for the moment swamped her. She tried to control it. A sudden fit of coughing seized her, shaking her whole body painfully. Richelieu watched her with an alert interest, noting the transparency of her cheeks. The cloth she took from the folds of her dress and held to her mouth was flecked with blood when she drew it away.

"Take your leave before I lose my temper," she said hoarsely. "As for this order of dismissal—" she ripped it across

260

and across again and flung the pieces to the floor—"that is what I think of it. How stupid of the Dauphin to think I would take notice of a dismissal signed by him! I shall accept dismissal only from the King, and it must be made by word of mouth, not in writing."

Richelieu shrugged. "The Dauphin may decide to remove you forcibly, and a pretty sight that would make."

"Let him try," Toinette said scornfully. "Not a guard in the Palace would dare obey him." She turned to a wide-eyed Binet. "Monsieur le Duc is leaving."

Meanwhile the capital was in a state of panic. The people, forgetting his sins and his many weaknesses, were thinking of their King once more as Louis the Well-Beloved. There was a great outcry against the would-be assassin. It was suspected that he was an English agent and the authorities were sure that he was only one of a large group of conspirators. He was questioned and tortured, but all he seemed capable of admitting was that his name was Damiens and that he was by profession a valet, now out of work. Stainville, scoffing at the English agent idea, was of the opinion that the poor wretch was a fanatic who, unemployed and probably hungry, had attempted to solve his problems and his country's by attacking the King. And finally, under additional torture, the man declared that he knew the King to be a wicked man who lived only for pleasure and cared nothing for his people.

Toinette herself was present when the judgment passed on Damiens was carried out. She sat in a closed carriage on the edge of the crowded square. At her side was Bernis, whose horror at the sight equalled her own. Damiens, stripped and pinioned, lay on a large table, surrounded by his masked executioners and a horde of screaming Parisians. Red-hot tongues and molten lead brought to Toinette's nostrils the smell of his burning flesh, yet he still lived. Dragged from the table he was roped to four horses, one at each of his limbs. Toinette screamed as the horses were whipped into four different directions and hid her face in her hands.

"Louis the Well-Beloved!" somebody shouted, and the crowd took up the cry.

261

"But for how long?" Bernis whispered. "When the people begin to think, really to think, for how long?"

"The King himself would never have ordered this," Toinette said.

"It happens to be the law, Madame."

She shuddered, saying softly, "I can hear the tramp of marching feet, I can see blood everywhere, and not the people's blood."

Shaken by her words, Bernis tried to make a joke of it. "So Madame la Marquise possesses psychic powers."

"No, Bernis. I have as little faith in psychic powers as I have in your religious beliefs."

"Yet you predict revolution."

"God help us all, I do."

"Strange," he mused, "how even an unbeliever will call on God when deeply moved." His equanimity completely recovered, he wagged a playful finger at her. "I shall bring you to salvation yet, Toinette."

"Bring your country to salvation first," she said sharply. "That would be far more worthy."

"The one would achieve the other," Bernis said enigmatically. "Are you not the mistress of France?"

When Toinette learned that Louis was growing stronger, that it would soon be impossible to keep from him the fact that he was in no danger whatever, she decided that it was time to bring the farce to an end, and with Stainville attending her she went to the royal apartments. Richelieu was in the anteroom, playing the watchdog, but she swept him impatiently aside and, followed by Stainville, went slowly up the stairs. It was a pity, she thought, that Stainville must reveal his hand, but his testimony was necessary.

"I have come, Sire," she said, while an amazed Louis looked at her, "to receive my dismissal from your own lips, but first let Stainville speak."

Louis listened in silence while Stainville told him the whole story, making much of the fact that Toinette, far from refusing to come to him, had been kept away.

"Then I was never in any danger!" Louis gasped.

"Never for one moment," Toinette told him.

Something in her voice made him look at her critically. She was wearing a new gown, a rich deep Burgundy in shade, with large bows down the tight bodice and a spray of artificial flowers on her left shoulder. She was a model of stylishness, yet something was wrong somewhere, not in her dress but in the woman herself. That "something" in her voice—was it a note of weariness? He studied her face for a moment. The smile was as fixed and artificial as the flowers she wore, the lips seemed to have grown thin and drooped a little while the green eyes, always her best feature, were apathetic and lusterless.

"Never for one moment," he said, echoing her words. He put one leg cautiously out of the bed. "I was beginning to wonder," he chuckled. A moment later he was on his feet, taking a few gingerly steps across the thick warm carpet. He turned and grinned. "When I woke this morning my first thought was of the *Parc aux Cerfs* and that new Russian girl Richelieu sent me. It was then I began to wonder. After all, when a man thinks of things like that and is provided at the same time by nature with evidence that he is perfectly capable of such undertakings—" He broke off, coughed and looked sheepish. "I mean, my friends, that a man in that condition can hardly be dying, now *can* he?"

Toinette began to laugh—hysterically, as she knew from the sound of the laughter bursting from her lips. She choked it back and gave way to a fit of coughing. Once again the cloth she held to her lips came away flecked with blood, but she succeeded in hiding this from Louis, who knew nothing of the seriousness of "my cough", as she called it. Seeing that he was looking at her oddly and not without alarm she spoke quickly of Richelieu and the Dauphin, saying that she bore neither of them any real resentment. But the cough got the better of her again and she collapsed, still coughing, into a chair. This time there were more flecks of blood on the cloth and this time Louis saw the spreading crimson stain. Alarmed, he sent Stainville in search of a physician and then bent anxiously over her.

263

"That was unnecessary," she said. "My own physician is in constant attendance. No more can be done."

Louis touched her gently. "Is it . . . incurable?"

She nodded. "Consumption usually is."

"Will—" Louis hesitated. "Will death come soon?"

Toinette shrugged angrily. "Who knows? I shall naturally fight it till the end." She rose and laughed dryly. "I have a new enemy, it seems, an enemy no amount of fighting, no amount of intrigue, will really vanquish."

XXI

STAINVILLE, watching Toinette lazily, saw her glance sourly at Cardinal Bernis. He wondered if she was thinking what he was thinking, that she had made a mistake in putting so much faith in the man's ability. Bernis was a man who could always think up a clever theory, but he was not a man of real action. When action was called for —and in time of war theories without action were useless things—he was timid, afraid and indeterminate.

"I do believe," Bernis said, repeating himself, "that we should endeavor to make peace."

Stainville decided to remain silent and leave the argument to the capable Marquise. Partly ignoring Bernis' remark Toinette said that she now considered the Austrian alliance a sad mistake.

"No, no, Madame," Bernis protested.

"In theory it was excellent," she said. "In theory it was supposed to intimidate the English and the Prussians, but it did no such thing."

"Make peace now," Bernis pressed, "and we might well gain more than we would appear, on the surface, to lose."

"I doubt it," she said sharply. "It is only a question of endurance. The resources of France and Austria are greater than those of England and Prussia."

"On the surface, yes," Bernis faltered.

"On the *surface*, Bernis?"

"I speak chiefly of France. A wealthy country, yes; but where is the wealth going? Is the money raised by taxation being spent on the war, or is it being used for pleasure and to liquidate the fabulous debts incurred by pleasure? In this country it is more important to build a new chateau than to equip a regiment. Forgive me, Madame, but I must speak my mind."

Toinette looked at him coldly. "Are you criticizing my personal expenditure?" He had a right too, of course, but how could the King be kept amused without the spending of money? "Well, are you?"

"No, dear me no," Bernis said hastily, "but I do suggest that economy at court might help."

He held her brooding eyes for a moment, blinked and looked away. He thought: "With the Marquise in control we have no real administration, no real ministers, no real King." He thought: "She controls us all as a child in the nursery might control her dolls." He thought: "I have dallied too long; she must be removed; I myself must become chief minister."

The moment Toinette dismissed him he hurried importantly to the Dauphin's apartments, where he flung himself on his knees, kissed his royal Highness's hands and declared himself willing to form a party in opposition to the Marquise.

He said: "If we want to retain our colonies we must make peace with the enemy; if we want to make peace we must remove the Marquise."

He said: "Because of the Marquise, who appoints only fools or those who flatter and obey her, we have no real generals, and therefore lack the ability to prosecute a successful war."

He said: "The Marquise *must* be removed."

The Dauphin, remembering his mother's words, sighed deeply.

"How?" he asked.

"By force of argument, your highness, by making the King see the position as we see it."

"You will speak to my father yourself?"

"I—" Bernis hesitated. "Later," he promised, "when I have considered how best to state our case."

The Dauphin, impressed by Bernis' change of heart, went straight to his father's apartments. Eagerly he stated the case as Bernis had stated it, but he refrained from uttering the Marquise's name or making any direct accusations against her. "A drastic change in the administration of state affairs is imperative," was the most he was ready to suggest, hoping that his father would see, as he saw, that the woman in control of affairs was the only one responsible for the disasters of the war. Louis, who had spent a fascinating evening and night and early morning at the *Parc aux Cerfs,* was weary and in no mood to listen to the rantings of his son.

"Whose words are these?" he asked. "Not your own, surely!"

"They are Bernis'," the Dauphin admitted.

"He accuses me, his King, of mismanagement?"

"How can he do that, Father, when he knows, as well as I and everybody else, that—" the Dauphin's voice faltered— "that a woman rules the kingdom?"

Louis, his mind straying to another subject, made no reply. He was thinking about the peasant girl—Nicolette, they all called her—who had just given birth to a child. "Richelieu's or mine?" he asked himself. He thought that it was more than likely Richelieu's, though of course it could be Stainville's. However, she should be granted a pension, a small one, like the others, and sent quietly from the *Parc aux Cerfs.* A pension, yes, and a present of money.

"Perhaps a thousand livres," he muttered.

The Dauphin looked puzzled. "I beg your pardon, Sire?" Louis cleared his throat and blushed a little.

"So Bernis is turning against Toinette," he mused. "A pity, after all she has done for him."

"When a man like Bernis turns against her," the Dauphin pressed, "we should listen to him. He was once her closest friend. He loved her as if she were his own daughter. To turn against her breaks his heart but he knows his duty."

Louis laughed softly. "Bernis is growing afraid. He is remembering that *he* made the Austrian alliance."

He thought, for no reason at all, of Machault who, after the Damiens affair, had been used as a scapegoat and dismissed from office. A pity, that, but as Toinette had said it was necessary that somebody should be blamed for the unrest which had culminated in Damiens' attack. Then he thought of Silhouette, an unworthy fellow who had held office for a shorter period than anybody else dismissed by Toinette. "He came and passed like a fleeting shadow," people had said of him, and now when one spoke of shadow one used the new and fashionable word, silhouette. Bernis, he thought, was hardly a *fleeting* shadow, but a shadow nonetheless. He sent his son away and went straight to Toinette, who was still talking to Stainville. He felt inclined to have a joke with Stainville abut the girl Nicolette, but he saw that he must, at the moment, remain serious.

"My dear," he said to Toinette, "a dog by the name of Bernis is doing his best to bite the hand that feeds him."

Toinette smiled faintly. She took up a sheet of paper on which the ink was not yet dry. She and Stainville, anticipating Louis, had already decided Bernis' fate. Louis chuckled. A *lettre de cachet*, obviously. He took the quill Toinette offered him and signed his name. It was as simple as that.

"But Bernis' successor?" he asked.

Toinette glanced at Stainville. "I believe, Sire, that he now stands in our presence."

Louis was a little annoyed that she should have spoken first, for he had already decided on Stainville himself, even to the extent of elevating him to the peerage. However, he smiled pleasantly and murmured that he was glad to know that, as ever, they thought alike in affairs of state.

"But first," he laughed, "a little matter of business. Three thousand livres for Nicolette. One from me, one from Richelieu and one from you, Stainville."

"Gladly," said Stainville, his plump body shaking with laughter.

"And see that you behave yourself," Louis warned. "Oh, not *that* way, of course! In state affairs, I mean. It would grieve me deeply if you, too, became known as a silhouette."

The Square, except for the space reserved for the royal party, was crammed with curious but strangely silent Parisians. From time to time some of them glanced at the King, at the Queen, and at the Marquise de Pompadour; but for the most part their eyes were stolidly fixed on the still-shrouded statue, the unveiling of which they had come to witness.

The war, the Seven Years' War, as everybody was beginning to call it, was over. It was known that in all a million men, friends and foes alike, had fallen; it was known that England, taking Canada from France as well as many of her other colonies, had emerged from the struggle as the greatest colonial power in the world; it was also known—and this meant more to the average Frenchman than anything else—that the promise to ease taxation had not been kept. And yet, here they were, these silent people, waiting to see the unveiling of a statue with which Madame la Marquise was trying to suggest that a glorious peace had been achieved.

"The crowd is too quiet," Choiseul whispered to Toinette. "I suspect trouble."

"The King is still Louis the Well-Beloved," she said, not really believing her own words. "We have nothing to fear."

He moved a little apart from her. No longer merely Monsieur de Stainville, he was now Monsieur le Duc de Choiseul, and certainly nobody would ever speak of him as a silhouette. Not a man to show or feel a fear of the mob, he was nevertheless uneasy today. He was sure that the people were in a mood to boo and hiss, and it might well be Choiseul, Minister of Foreign Affairs, that they would turn on. Because he had convinced the Marquise and the King that the Austrian alliance was not a mistake he might be held responsible for the loss of the war, and held responsible, too, for the attempted invasion of England, which had resulted in a shocking defeat for the French navy. In addition, and

269

without doubt, he would be held responsible for the new measures of taxation which at his suggestion had been carried out. And more than ever it would be held against him that he owed his position to the Marquise.

He glanced swiftly at Toinette. She was thin, utterly weary, as her movements proclaimed, and deadly pale. How long would she live? How long before death freed him of the need to bow to her wishes? Only that morning he had seen the paleness of her drawn face when he had met her coming back from Mass. Mass! He laughed silently at the thought. She, the intellectual; she, the near-atheist! She was like the King. When sick and threatened with death she grew religious. Or rather, inherent superstition swamped her, fear gripped her heart and to her it became imperative to save the soul she had long denied possessing. Would he be the same, he wondered, when his own time approached? He laughed silently again. By heaven, no! He would choose a Friday for the day of his death, and he would die with a hearty meal of meat undigested in his stomach.

A fanfare of trumpets sounded. There was a slight stir among the crowd and, as the coverings fell from the statue, an involuntary gasp. Louis gave Toinette a sideways glance, smiled happily and squared his shoulders. He looked back at the statue. There he was, bravely mounted on horseback, surrounded by four figures representing Peace, Strength, Wisdom and Justice. Toinette had suggested it, designed it, in fact, and the sculptor Bouchhardon had fashioned it. "Louis the Peacemaker, that is what I want them to call you," she had said, and as God was his witness, nobody had desired peace more than he, the man who had seen war at close quarters and had grown to hate it.

Toinette caught his eye and gave a little nod. He squared his shoulders again and stepped forward. The crowd waited, making no response, though a few people groaned beneath their breath. The King was about to make a speech, a speech written, without doubt, by Madame la Marquise.

Choiseul, touching Toinette's arm quickly, whispered, "It would be wiser to restrain his Majesty. Nobody has thought of cheering him, nobody."

Toinette made an indeterminate move to Louis' side, but having cleared his throat he was already on the point of speaking.

"My people," he began, "we have all witnessed, and with pride, I feel sure, the unveiling of a monument dedicated to Peace, Strength, Wisdom and Justice, but most of all to Peace."

He paused. There was no response. The expression on the faces of the people was dark and sullen.

"Never again," he went on, trying to keep from his voice the dismay he was beginning to feel, "never again, if human effort can prevent it, will France embark on a long and costly war. This statue is the symbol of the thing for which we have worked, longed for and waited."

He paused again.

"Look at their faces!" Choiseul whispered.

Suddenly a single voice, high and clear, shouted: "Down with the concubine!"

Louis' head shot up.

"My people—" he began.

Booing and hissing drowned his voice.

"Down with the Marquise!" another voice cried, and the cry was taken up.

With a dignified gesture Louis turned to Toinette, but anticipating his intention and frowning on its foolishness, she quickly gave her arm to Choiseul. Louis, understanding, moved to the Queen's side and felt like a traitor as he did so. Choiseul, having no choice in the matter, handed Toinette to her carriage, climbed in at her side and gave the order to the coachman. There followed a few cries of "Long live the Queen!" and "Long live the Dauphin!" but mostly it was booing and hissing that rang out as Toinette's carriage moved slowly out of the Square.

"At least they appear to have nothing to say against the King," she said shakily.

"Nor for him," Choiseul commented gloomily.

Toinette was looking back at the statue. She had the queerest impression that it had grown old and weather-beaten, and as the impression lasted she saw it surrounded

271

by another and wilder crowd, cheering and shouting hoarsely as, dragging at it with ropes, they brought it crashing to the ground.

She repressed a cold little shiver and, seeing a folded sheet of paper on the seat at her side, took it up and opened it. Half-expecting a bawdy verse she read the few boldly written lines.

> The writing is on the wall. Let the King
> dismiss the Marquise, feed the starving
> poor and save the Monarchy, or all may
> yet be swept away by bloody revolution.

Toinette, with her favorite maid, Dorine, in attendance, was seated before the mirror, making a laborious toilette. She had seen little of Louis in the month that had passed since the unveiling of the statue, but tonight he was coming to supper. She was sensitive of a coolness on his part and wondered whether the cause was the outcry of the people or her illness. A little of both, she thought, but mostly the latter. Not that he ever spoke of the illness now, but she knew that to a man who feared death the fact that it was hanging over one so close to him was enough to create in him a continual nervous tension. She completed the mask that was now her face, studied it carefully and hoped that thus shielded she would look as well in Louis' eyes as she had ever looked.

She rose and went to her workroom, as she sometimes called it. She saw at a glance that Binet had placed on the writing table another batch of those horrible anonymous letters that were reaching her daily now. She opened one of them, annoyed with herself for the weakness that made her take notice of them. It was short, a single sentence.

> You may go to Mass every day for the short
> time that remains to you, but though this
> may save your soul by a hair's breadth, be
> sure that God will not forget your sins.

She laughed grimly and tore up the letter. So the story that she had turned to religion was getting about. She laughed again. Illness was having a bad effect on her mind —or perhaps, as Bernis would have suggested, it was having a *good* effect. Setting aside her intellectualism she had turned to religion for comfort. Yes, actually for comfort! Many people at court sneered and said she was merely trying to convince France that at heart she was a pious woman, but this was untrue. She had turned to religion for comfort and strangely enough comfort, to a small extent, had been found. Religion, she had often said, was for the unhappy, the weak, the dying. Well, she was all three, so actually she had done no more than conform to her own belief.

"Ah, Toinette, my dear . . ."

Toinette gave a little start. Louis had entered without her hearing his step. Making an effort, she smiled up at him and told herself that now she must be gay, make jokes, amuse the King and keep him happy. Nevertheless, in sheer perversity, she picked up the pieces of the letter, fitted them together and invited Louis to read the words. His quick scowl brought a smile of compassion to her face. Death, how he hated any suggestion of it. She remembered having asked him once why, fearing death as he did, he made so great a point of sinning violently. And laughing he had answered, "Sin amuses me, so why should I restrain myself? After all, at the last moment I can make my peace with God." A pleasant, easy philosophy, that!

Without commenting on the letter he said: "This business of the Jesuits and their trading activities abroad. Most of our judges feel that his Holiness the Pope should be urged to suppress the order."

Earlier Toinette had been eager to see this move take place, but now she hardly cared.

"Let me give you this advice," she said, almost apathetically, "leave the move to the judges; it will be safer for the Crown that way."

Louis nodded and smiled. "That is what I had decided myself, but I doubt if I would have thought of it again if you hadn't mentioned it."

She looked at him musingly. "You always know the right thing to do, Louis, but only rarely do you do it. I wonder why?"

"Have I not my ministers? Better still, have I not my clever little favorite?" He stretched lazily. "Perhaps it was the way I was brought up."

Supper was a quiet meal, entirely without ceremony and served by the unobtrusive Dorine. That was what Louis always wanted and liked best. "I come here tired and bored," he used to say; "I go away refreshed and cheerful." But to-night it was different. Even the excellent new wine, which she had procured for him from the Capdemourlin vineyard in Bordeaux, failed to excite him. He was restless and ill-at-ease. From time to time he looked at her fixedly when he thought she was unaware of it, and hurriedly averted his eyes when she glanced up at him.

"What do you think of the Capdemourlin?" she asked.

He made a pretense of testing the wine, first studying the color, then sniffing the bouquet, and finally sipping delicately.

"Delightful, no doubt," he said moodily, "but I have lost my judgment, my palate is sated." He held her eyes for a moment. "How long have you been at court, Toinette?"

"Very nearly twenty years. Why?"

"I can scarcely believe it," he said, and added meaningly: "A long span in anybody's life, but longer in a woman's than a man's."

"That depends on the woman, Louis."

"You were twenty-four when you came to me, therefore—"

She interrupted him sharply. "A matter of simple arithmetic." Then she laughed with forced gaiety. "How fortunate I ceased to be your mistress thirteen years ago. You would never want me now."

"No," he agreed gravely.

"It seems difficult to make you laugh tonight," she taunted.

He sighed. "Yes, difficult." He sprang up from the table. "Old age, how I loathe the thought of it!"

His eyes came to rest on Rigaud's portrait on one of the

274

walls. Himself as a child! The boy King, so fresh and innocent, with the big candid eyes, the smooth full cheeks, the
pure sweet mouth. Just to look at it brought a lump to his
throat. He turned to another wall, to the latest portrait,
painted by Vanloo, which he had given to Toinette a few
days ago. He pointed a finger at it.

"You thanked me for it," he said, in a choking voice, "but
failed to say what you thought of it."

"The likeness," she ventured, "is very striking."

"Ha! You don't care for it!"

"I consider it a very efficient piece of work."

"*Too* efficient, Toinette!"

She saw what he meant. It was a faithful reproduction,
perhaps a too faithful one. The contrast between the two
portraits, the boy King and the King of fifty-three who
looked even older, made her want to cry.

"Vanloo has made an ogre of me!" Louis cried.

He rushed from the room and came back from Toinette's
bedroom carrying a hand-mirror. For a few moments he
gazed steadily into it, then he groaned. Vanloo had painted
him exactly as he was. He hurled the mirror at the portrait.

"A caricature of my former self," he raged.

He noticed that Toinette was coughing quietly into a
strip of cloth. Her whole body shook pitifully as she tried to
control the cough. He watched, fascinated. After a moment
there was blood on the cloth, the sight of which made him
lose his head.

"Horrible!" he cried.

For a moment, as Toinette's eyes held his, she had the
look of an animal, a dog. Yes, a dog that for no reason at all
he had kicked. He fell on his knees at her side. He wanted
to take her hands in his but the sight of the blood held him
back.

"Forgive me," he begged.

A moment later he was on his feet, hurrying from the
room. He was running and panting for breath when he
reached his own apartments. Presently he sent for Richelieu,
who was making a longer stay at court this time.

"Something has just happened," he told Richelieu. "Something I want to forget. Old age, illness, death—they threaten me on every side. I want life. I want gaiety. I want youth. Youth, Richelieu, youth!"

Richelieu, so much older than Louis, so much more dissipated, smiled lewdly and spoke of the new young girl he had set up at the *Parc aux Cerfs*.

"She possesses a wart—not only youth, mark you, Sire— but a wart and in a most interesting region."

Louis waved this aside. "The thought of the *Parc aux Cerfs* sickens me, and this palace is a prison. Old age, illness, death! Escape, that is what I want, escape!"

"The night is pleasant and mild," Richelieu suggested. "Why not a midnight party at Rambouillet?"

Louis shook his head. "All the old pleasures are losing their savor. That Capdemourlin Toinette gave me—excellent, the very best, but it might well have been vinegar. No, no, we must do something different. I want to forget the court. I want to forget that I'm King of France. I—" He broke off. "Order a coach, a plain coach. We'll go to Paris incognito. Find me a suitable disguise, and one for yourself, you old sinner. Polish officers—yes, that's what we'll be. Polish officers with plenty of money in our purses, making a tour of the Paris taverns, or those new places, cafes, they call them. I shall call myself Colonel something-or-other. Colonel Plotowski, and you—hum—"

"Captain Chernigov," Richelieu decided.

"Excellent!" Louis embraced Richelieu suddenly. "I feel better already."

But it was a lie and he knew it.

Lying back on her pillows Toinette fell to wondering how many weeks it was since Louis had run from her in horror. Memory failing her, she thought it was just as likely to be months as weeks, though she seemed to remember that he had paid her several brief visits and had sent one of his gentlemen daily to inquire about her. Conscious that somebody was moving in the room, she opened her eyes. In the dim light she recognized Dorine.

276

"More candles," she begged. "This half-light will drive me crazy."

All the candles were already lit, but Dorine made a pretense of lighting more. Presently Toinette caught sight of a square box at the foot of her bed. She stared at it. One moment it had the look of a windowless house, the next it changed to a grotesque coffin. She closed her eyes, steadied herself and looked again. It was of course a dispatch-box. She remembered that however afraid the King might be of the sight of blood he made no attempt to hinder her in her state duties. For no reason she could immediately think of the two words "feudal lords" came to her mind. She struggled to discover their significance, failed and sat up angrily.

"Dorine," she commanded, "help me."

Dorine, full of concern, persuaded her to remain in bed and pressed her gently back on the pillows.

"Bully," Toinette said, thinking how young and fresh the girl looked. "Pass me a mirror."

Dorine complied and for a moment Toinette held the mirror in shaking hands. She shuddered at the sight of the big eyes and the sunken cheeks. The physicians were right. Her struggle was almost over.

"I should like to see the King again," she said.

Dorine went out with the message. When she returned Toinette had struggled from her bed and was seated before the mirror of her dressing-table. Carefully, with the deliberation of a drunken person, she was applying rouge to her cheeks.

"A little rouge," she laughed shakily, "a little chemical white, perhaps even a little vinegar to tighten the skin of the neck. I must be beautiful when his Majesty comes. And please, Dorine, see to it that this face is as presentable in death as it has ever been in life."

"Yes, Madame," said Dorine, the tears running down her cheeks.

"All the skill you possess, Dorine, for my enemies will gather about the coffin to mock. Do all you can to hide the horrible truth."

When Louis came, Dorine had got her back to bed and

277

she seemed to be sleeping. He bent over her awkwardly and whispered her name.

"Forgive me for my neglect," he said, self-consciously.

She opened her eyes. "There is nothing to forgive."

"There is much, Toinette. The sight of your suffering, your dreadful suffering, made a coward of me."

"I am like France," she said, seeing things clearly. "The country suffers as I suffer."

Louis ignored this. "I asked you to forgive me, please do."

"I forgive you," she said obediently. Suddenly she remembered why the words "feudal lords" had come to her mind earlier. "Louis," she said earnestly, "out of the chaos and unrest of today the great lords will do their utmost to seize power as they did in the middle-ages. Be strong, Louis. Remember that the King is the lawmaker, not a handful of *grands seigneurs.*"

Louis laughed weakly. "It is anything but easy for a king of my caliber to be strong, but for your sake I promise to try."

Satisfied, Toinette closed her eyes. He waited for a moment, then backed slowly from the room.

"I can bear no more," he told Dorine.

Soon after he had gone Toinette opened her eyes again. "Has he gone, Dorine?"

"Yes, Madame," the girl sobbed. "With tears in his eyes and his face all broken."

Toinette smiled faintly.

"Poor little King, so much harder for him to live than for me to die."

Once again, the law being what it was, a dead body was being hurried from beneath the roof that sheltered the person of his Majesty the King. Louis stood watching on the balcony of the *salon* at the corner of the Marble and Royal courts. The night was bitterly cold with a blustering wind carrying the rain before it. Leaning forward, he could make out two figures beneath him, then two more.

The first two hurried ahead, carrying smoking torches which gave only a flickering light; the other two, the body between them on a board, stumbled after the torch-bearers. There was to be a service in a nearby church, then a discreet burial in Paris. When the grotesque procession had passed from view Louis went back to the *salon*, closing the French windows behind him. He felt— "Damnation!" he raged, "how *do* I feel?" He turned and pressed his face against the window, and there he remained until the glass became blurred with his breath and smeared with his tears.

"I weep," he said aloud, "but my heart is like stone."

"Perhaps you never really loved her," said a voice.

Louis turned quickly. "Ah, Richelieu . . ." He considered his friend's words. "Well, who knows? When I first brought her to court, of course . . ." He sighed deeply. "It was a pure love, you know, and that, for me, was fantastic." He began to move about the room, listening carefully to his own footsteps on the parquet floor. "Bah! To try to recall the emotions of twenty years ago is too much for any man. I shall mourn her passing but the only thing I feel with any certainty at this moment is relief. Toinette has gone, Richelieu, and I am free."

"*Free*, your Majesty?"

"Free to rule as a king should rule." He went from the room, Richelieu at his side. "And by heaven," he said jauntily, "I shall let my ministers know it, and the parliaments and the people, and the feudal lords. The King is the only lawmaker, the only guardian of the people. The King is the *father* of the people."

He paused for breath, then moved on again.

"When I was a child-king there was always somebody to do things for me. When I was a boy-king it was the same. Always somebody eager to do things for me, and incidentally for themselves. When I was a young man people continued to stand between me and the things I should have done myself, and being weak I let them. Pleasure was more important, oh yes, always more important."

He came to a halt.

"Why," said Richelieu in surprise, "this is the Queen's door."

"Yes, the Queen's door. In a word, my wife's."

And he opened the door and went in.

XXII

AT THE sound of the faint, rippling snore Marie looked up from her needlework and smiled affection- ately. Madame Adelaide, playing on the carpet with her little white lap-dog, smiled too, but the Dauphin, writhing in his chair, gave a derisive snort.

"Your poor father is tired," Marie whispered, glancing again at Louis, asprawl on a Pompadour sofa. "Any man of his age who hunted all day would be."

"Rubbish!" Madame Adelaide laughed. "He knows my serious-minded brother wants to talk to him and is sham- ming."

"Quite right," said Louis, looking at his favorite daughter through half-closed eyes, and gave another convincing snore.

Marie smiled again and went placidly on with her needle- work. Sixty-one now, and a calm and dignified old lady who carried her years remarkably well, Marie was happier than she had ever been. In the year that had passed since Madame de Pompadour's death she and Louis had become closer and more in accord than ever before. He had turned to her for comfort and she had given him comfort; he had turned to her for advice and she had given him advice, and even though he had not always taken it he had made an ef- fort to be the sort of king the people would come to respect.

Methodically, as if they were part of the pattern of her needlework, Marie began to list her husband's virtues. On Toinette's death he had promised, without being asked, that he would never set up another favorite, and though she had not expected it of him he had kept that promise. A virtue that, surely! He had also promised, again without being asked, to sell the *Parc aux Cerfs,* but he had failed in this, so the continued use of the *Parc aux Cerfs,* Marie thought gently, must come under the heading of his sins. He had— But here Marie stopped. There were many other sins, small and large, but no more virtues! Well, the best thing she could do was to continue to pray for him.

"Father . . ." the Dauphin said portentously.

Both Louis and Madame Adelaide groaned.

"Permit me to say, Father," the Dauphin continued, "that the death of the Marquise de Pompadour has left behind it a certain amount of confusion. Till the end, rightly or wrongly, she remained your unofficial chief minister; till the end, rightly or wrongly, she controlled every move, large or small, of the council. Till the end—"

"What a bore he is, this brother of mine," Madame Adelaide chuckled.

Louis looked at her lovingly. She had risen from the carpet and was standing with her hands behind her back in a quite man-like attitude. She was changing with the years, he thought—what was she now, thirty-three, or thirty-four?— growing more masculine in appearance, in spite of her partly exposed bosom, her hair tightly drawn to the nape of her neck and loose about her rounded shoulders, her fashionable court gown trimmed with fur. She resembled him strongly at the time, long past, when he had been youthful and slim and full of the joy of life.

"Have you considered the need to appoint a new chief minister?" the Dauphin plodded on.

"I was under the impression that I was still my own chief minister," Louis said mildly. "Not that I don't understand what you mean. You covet the position yourself." He caught his daughter's eyes and grinned. It would be mightily diverting to pull his son's leg a little. "As a matter of fact," he went on, "I had thought of withdrawing and appointing Richelieu in my place."

"Richelieu!" The Dauphin sprang up in horror.

"Or better still, Choiseul."

"Choiseul!" the Dauphin gasped.

"Yes," Louis said solemnly, "Choiseul, and the ministry of finance for Richelieu."

"May heaven protect us!" the Dauphin said piously. "And the country closer to bankruptcy than ever before!"

"Bankruptcy? Well, well, well."

"Pah! You care nothing and notice nothing, providing your gambling allowance remains untouched."

"Speaking of gambling," Madame Adelaide said, her rich baritone voice deepening, "Father is going to rake in a little more money by setting up a government lottery."

Louis nodded vigorously and looked impishly at his son. The Dauphin had grown pale and was dabbing at his brow as if in acute physical distress.

"Horrified, my boy?"

The Dauphin turned angrily to a window and opened it. Always his father called him "my boy," using the words condescendingly. Boy indeed, when he was thirty-five, the father of three growing sons and a man of supreme dignity.

"Dear me," Louis chuckled, "I have shocked him so much that he needs air." He turned to Marie. "To be utterly serious for a few moments, if I invite the people to invest money in a government loan, a loan returning a good percentage, they will turn from it in suspicion. But if I ask them to throw their money away in a lottery which will return only a few of them a handful of prizes and the majority of them nothing at all—"

"The money will pour in," Madame Adelaide concluded.

"Yes, pour in," Louis laughed, and grinned at his son. "Why, with a lottery running smoothly my gambling allowance might even be increased."

The Dauphin remained at the open window. His face was gray, his eyes slightly dilated.

"Are you ill, Louis?" Marie asked.

He nodded. "A slight headache, a feeling of suffocation. I have had it before but it always passes." He returned to his chair, seated himself and smiled thinly. "Very well, a government lottery."

Louis clapped his hands. "How good of you to approve. Is there anything else you want to say?"

The Dauphin squared his shoulders. "Yes, Father. I should like to suggest that the apartments occupied by Madame de Pompadour, which have been left undisturbed since her death and remind us all of corruption and mismanagement, should be dismantled and used for a more edifying purpose."

"Bravo!" Louis cried. "Never has your pomposity been equalled."

"But they might be needed again," Madame Adelaide remarked.

"Indeed they might!"

"Needed again?" the Dauphin spluttered.

Louis rose and stretched. "To put your mind at rest on the other matters, I am quite satisfied with my present ministers, especially with my chief minister. In a word, with myself!"

The Dauphin was on his feet too. "Establish one more royal favorite, Father, and the people might rise against you."

"Let them!" Louis laughed, and strode from the room.

He went in search of Richelieu and finding him said: "By heaven, I pity the country if that priggish son of mine ever comes to the throne. I might bring it close to ruin by laziness and extravagance, but he would do worse with prudery, sheer undiluted prudery."

"Your Majesty," Richelieu suggested, "is in need of a little gaiety tonight."

Louis nodded his agreement. His eyes twinkled.

"Captain Chernigov," he said, "order a plain coach."

Richelieu bowed. "At once, Colonel Plotowski."

Louis felt a little guilty as he sat in the coach, as guilty as he sometimes felt about the *Parc aux Cerfs,* but not since Toinette's death had Colonel Plotowski and Captain Chernigov done the rounds of the Paris taverns, so surely it was an innocent enough occupation. Innocent enough? Well, not entirely: the last time two new recruits had been found for the *Parc aux Cerfs*, so possibly *this* time . . . He shrugged aside the feeling of guilt and began to grow pleasantly excited.

But first, with the long evening before them, the two "Polish officers" went to one of the theaters, where a popular play was being presented. Louis enjoyed it thoroughly, for the author, pointing a satiric finger at the times, had made the hero in love with his wife but afraid, lest the fashionable world should laugh at him, to admit it. Next they sipped a little wine in one of the new cafes where people were making a habit of gathering to gossip and exchange choice bits of scandal, but tiring of this they were soon settling down with a sigh of pleasure in the dingy interior of the most disreputable drinking den they had ever had the good fortune to come across.

"This," Colonel Plotowski pronounced, not without a trace of artificiality in his voice, "is life!"

"Life, my colonel!" Captain Chernigov echoed tipsily.

Presently the colonel gripped the edge of the table in sudden excitement. "By heaven, look at that girl! Did you ever see a more beautiful serving wench?"

With difficulty the captain focussed his eyes on the girl and what he saw not only excited his blunted feelings but did much to sober him. As he stared she came closer and a moment later, with the colonel calling loudly for more wine, she reached their table. Both men gaped at her in bleary fascination, each cataloguing her physical charms one by one. First there was the loose blonde hair, then the steady, slightly amused blue eyes, the small provocative mouth, the cheeky little nose and the creamy purity of the most youthful skin they had ever seen. She wore a simple gown caught at the waist by a wide sash, a gown cut low enough to reveal the firmness of her small full breasts, and short enough to show off to advantage the slimness of her ankles.

"Ravishing!" the colonel cried, quite beside himself.

The girl tossed her head and laughed good-humoredly.

"Hold your impertinent tongue, old man," she said. "Beauty is meant for youth and youth for beauty."

"Splendid!" he shouted. "You have spirit too. Be generous as well and tell us your name."

"Jeanne," she said simply. "And yours, Monsieur?"

"Louis is as good a name as any."

"Then Louis," she said, leaning over him till the freshness of her natural odor drove the stench of his surroundings from his nostrils, "a word of warning. The rule of this house, though you mightn't think it, is moderation. You may sit and drink, you may laugh and sing, but too much of either and out you go. And remember this too, it isn't a brothel."

Louis roared with laughter and pinched her in an intimate but to Frenchmen time-honored portion of her anatomy. She slapped his face sharply, a sound ringing blow, and moved away with a careless swing of her hips.

"Beauty and insolence," he said, touching his stinging cheek tenderly— "I never saw a more perfect blending."

"Only one thing mars her perfection," Richelieu decided, "and that is her voice."

"Nonsense!" Louis said warmly. "A common voice, after the simpering accents of Versailles, is as attractive as it is honest. In any case, have we, at the *Parc aux Cerfs,* ever been dismayed by a low-bred intonation?"

"No, never!" Richelieu chuckled.

Louis frowned. "I was the first to see her. Remember that."

"If your Majesty will forgive this unwarranted interruption . . ." a voice said close to his ear.

Louis swung round in his chair. Standing deferentially at his side was one of his son's valets. He was a slim little man and Louis, rising angrily, towered over him.

"By heaven, Monsieur, you were sent by the Dauphin to spy on me!"

"No, no, your Majesty," the man twittered. "The spying was done at the Minister of Police's orders. It is felt that when the King goes abroad incognito he should, for his own safety, be discreetly watched."

Louis glanced swiftly about him.

"Keep your voice low," he ordered, "and address me as Colonel Plotowski. Now tell me what you want."

The valet bowed. "His royal highness the Dauphin has been taken ill, seriously ill. The physicians—"

"Damnation!" Louis roared.

"The physicians fear that his royal highness is dying."

Louis threw up his hands in despair. "Dying! Trust him to choose a moment like this! What a genius he has for coming between me and my pleasures, what a devilish genius!"

And so death struck again at Versailles, swamping Louis once more with the old haunting fear. For weeks he went about in a daze, shunning everybody and turning sadly away from the pleasures presented by Richelieu, until one day he thought of his great-grandfather, the fourteenth Louis. *His* son had died before him, then his grandson and one of his great-grandsons. Perhaps it was to be the same with him. He began to hope so, and hoping, the shock of the Dauphin's death seemed less severe, less of a personal threat. No longer groaning that death was haunting him, he took a happier view and rejoiced as best he could. Death, he concluded, was saving him till the last, picking off his heirs but passing him by.

In such a mood he was able to resume the normal course of his life, and soon his thoughts returned to the tavern wench, Jeanne. Excited by the memory of her, he sought out Richelieu and Richelieu, being the sort of man he was, had a little information to impart.

"It has not been possible to discover where she lives," Richelieu said, "but she is, I understand, the illegitimate daughter of a peasant woman by the name of Bécu."

"And the father? Name unknown, of course?"

Richelieu showed his decaying teeth in an evil smile. "Why no, Sire. The father used to go by the name of Vaubernier, but becoming a monk he changed it to the delightful name of Father Angel."

Louis rocked with laughter.

"She had a quite good upbringing," Richelieu went on. "She was a pupil of the Sisters of the Sacred Heart for some time. Later, at the age of eighteen, she took the post of companion to a rich widow who was fond of her until she became the son's mistress. After that she fell low in the social scale by working in some sort of shop. From that she fell lower and soon became what she was when we saw her, a serving wench in a tavern."

"I gather she is no longer there?"

"No, your Majesty. You see, a man by the name of Dubarry was interested in her. It was he who took her away from the tavern. Find Dubarry and undoubtedly we shall find Jeanne."

"Make every effort," Louis begged. "And remember," he added sternly, "*I* saw her first!"

"The time has come," Choiseul said briskly, "to make plans for your eldest grandson's marriage."

"You seem eager," Louis grunted, "to turn me into a great-grandfather."

There was a little marble statuette on his writing table. He picked it up and twisted it in his hands. It had pleasing hips, long slender legs, small neat breasts and a proudly tilted head. He thought that the girl Jeanne might look something like this, naked. Restlessly he put it down and stared at it.

"What a curse, to be plagued by passion and desire at my age," he mused.

"Your Majesty would find it a greater curse," Choiseul smiled, "if, even at your age, you were incapable of such things."

"I *wonder* . . ." Louis leaned forward and with his forefinger stroked the cold diminutive figure. "I often ask myself if physical inability is always accompanied by a lack of physical interest."

"We shall all discover that in the course of time, Sire."

Louis shuddered delicately. "It would be horrible if it were not, Choiseul." Reluctantly he brought his mind back to his eldest grandson, the boy who was now the new Dauphin.

He felt exceedingly sorry for him. "You once spoke of Austria," he said.

Choiseul nodded. "Yes, and I still believe that the alliance would be considerably strengthened by a marriage. The Empress is of the same opinion. She has, as you know, seven daughters. Marie-Antoinette, who is fourteen, is the most suitable."

"You want this marriage, of course," Louis grumbled.

"Yes, your Majesty. It would fit in so admirably with my foreign policy. It would be the greatest achievement of my career."

Louis took up the statuette again, turned it and with his thumb absently caressed the shapely buttocks. He had a suspicion that Choiseul's foreign policy was not as good as the man himself believed. It could, he thought, lead to another war with England, and that would be as unthinkable as it would be stupid. He wished he were cleverer. He longed to dismiss Choiseul and handle the foreign policy himself. In many ways he resented Choiseul who, since Toinette's death, had displayed a growing arrogance, his attitude seeming to say: "Interference by a pleasure-loving King is laughable." Louis sighed. What would Toinette advise if she were here now?

He indicated abruptly that the interview was at an end and went unhappily to Marie's apartments. The physicians, warning him that her Majesty's health was failing, had ordered her to bed. Stubbornly, he had refused to treat the warning with seriousness, but this afternoon, as he seated himself by her bed, the little duchess bed that had long-since replaced the big four-poster, he was forced to see that the woman who had been his wife for over forty years was as close to death as the physicians said. Rather than meet her eyes he looked waveringly at the tapestried Bible stories on the walls and making conversation told her of their grandson's impending marriage.

"Let us hope it will be a happy marriage," Marie said softly, "as happy as ours was in the early years."

Louis shot a quick, guilty glance at her, but her face was calm. If she was thinking of the other long years of unhappiness she was doing so without reproach. Presently she asked him if he had been told the truth of her illness. He said impatiently that he had, and added jauntily that the physicians were often wrong.

"I know the truth myself," Marie said, "as you will know it when your own time comes."

"Marie, I beg of you!" he cried angrily.

She smiled, and murmured that she was sorry. She had forgotten that death, in relation to himself, was something he preferred not to discuss.

"Nevertheless," he said quickly, "death having threatened me many times, I shall escape it again and again. Those I love might be taken from me, but I—" His voice broke; he was suddenly very sorry for himself. "But I," he concluded, "shall live on, lonely, tired and disillusioned."

"Dear Louis," Marie laughed, "what an actor is wasted in the King of France."

Louis smiled sheepishly. "I *am* a hypocrite. I admit it, Marie." He was silent for a few moments. "Oh Marie," he broke out, "if miracles were possible, if I could be granted one wish, just *one* wish— Bah, but this is nonsense, nonsense!"

"Tell me what you have in mind," Marie prompted.

"I would roll back the years, wipe out all my sad mistakes, make a fresh start. I was thinking this morning of that day, oh so long ago, when I met you for the first time. I wonder if you remember it, Marie?"

"Very clearly indeed. Our coaches stopped within sight of each other, and how nervous I was!"

"I was nervous, too. And when you knelt before me I was more nervous than ever."

"Ah, but you bent over me so graciously and raised me to my feet. You might have been a man of thirty, not a boy of fifteen."

"Oh Marie, if only we could go back to those days and start again!"

"Regrets are useless, Louis."

"Yes, useless."

To his horror he found that he was still holding the little

statuette in one hand. Unconscious of what he was doing he must have carried it from his own apartments. He tried to hide it but Marie, who had noticed it earlier, held out her hand for it.

"How beautiful," she said. "What a pity art always leads a man to expect too much of reality."

As if there had been no interruption he said: "Yes, regrets are useless. What I would have liked to make of life and what I *have* made of it are two different things."

"You have done much to make amends lately, Louis," Marie said. "You can do more in the years to come."

"I doubt it, Marie. You know how weak I am, and in my weakness, stubborn."

"With the help of God, Louis . . ."

"To talk of me and God in the same breath is sacrilege. Besides—" he laughed dryly—"the role of a reformed sinner would bore me. I am what I am and that I shall remain till the end. I shall do what I can, if my ministers will let me, but in the main I shall do the thing I have been trained to do, seek pleasure everywhere. After me," he added, in a flash of inspiration, "the deluge."

XXIII

WITH the painful concentration of a schoolboy forced to his lessons, Louis was studying a report on the Austrian negotiations. All was going smoothly and the moment he gave his royal assent a marriage by proxy would take place between his grandson and the young Marie-Antoinette. He was still trying not to think of Marie's death and he was angry with Richelieu who had asked with unaccustomed ceremony for an audience but had failed to present himself at the appointed time. He took up a pen, scribbled the word "satisfactory" at the top of the report and gave his attention to the papers left for his scrutiny by the Minister of Police. The topmost sheet told him briefly that in some of the provinces old forgotten dues were being demanded of the peasants by the feudal lords, and that the courts were pronouncing judgment against those peasants who were bold enough to protest. It was clear that the feudal lords were growing more arrogant in their opposition to the Crown, and clear too that the thirteen parliaments, or courts of appeal, were conspiring with them. They were determined, it seemed, to filch his power, not for the sake of the country, which he was ready to admit he had ruled badly, but for their own selfish ends.

With an angry gesture he threw the papers aside. He was weary of state affairs, bored with life, indignant that he was growing old—he would be sixty soon!—and alarmed at the thought that death was creeping closer. Nevertheless, he was determined, come what may, to show the parliaments, especially the most powerful, that of Paris, who was master. The resolution both amazed and amused him: now, when it was probably too late, he was turning himself into a real king.

There was a scratching at the door and Richelieu entered.

"At last!" Louis growled.

Richelieu bowed, apologized for his lateness and grinning ridiculously stood aside from the open door. A moment later a young woman came leisurely into the room. She wore a sea-green hunting dress, the coat of which was swinging carelessly open. Louis' old heart hammered excitedly as he gazed at her.

"By heaven!" he cried, leaping up from his chair. "The tavern wench, Jeanne!"

"Permit me, Sire," Richelieu simpered, "Madame la Comtesse Dubarry."

"Greetings, Majesty," Jeanne said, making no attempt to curtsy. Then she turned with a cheeky grin to Richelieu. "What a joke! I wondered why you were bringing me here. Just think of it, that Polish officer who told me to call him Louis is the King!"

Louis strode to her side. He forgot Marie's death, he forgot his grandson's impending marriage, he forgot the feudal lords. Breathing heavily he took her hands in his. Out of the frothy lace of her blouse the slender column of her neck rose tantalizingly. He looked deep into her candid blue eyes. He was ogling her, he knew, and shamelessly, but what did it matter!

"A comtesse! Has she married into the aristocracy?"

"Presumably," Richelieu said. "I spoke of a Dubarry, Sire, the man who had taken her from the tavern. An obscure family, however."

"And poor," Jeanne said, and made a face.

"Ah," Louis chuckled, "he deceived you. He married you to escape my new tax on bachelors." He turned to Richelieu and frowned. Richelieu understood, winked and withdrew. "Good!" said Louis.

Jeanne, having tossed her neat little cap into a chair and tested the rich depth of the carpet with one tiny pointed toe, was glancing nonchalantly about the room, taking in the delicately tinted panels, the elaborate furniture, the long flawless mirrors and the portraits by Nattier.

"My!" she laughed, "what a story to tell my friends. Alone with the King at Versailles and calling him Louis!"

"Delightful, oh delightful!" Louis cried, fascinated by the slight hoarseness of her voice and her complete lack of shyness. "Not in the least in awe of me, are you!"

She uttered an oath much favored by the fishwives at the markets. "Not in the least, Louis."

Louis flung himself into a chair and laughed till the tears rolled down his cheeks. What a pity there was no way of resurrecting his son. Nothing would be more amusing to have him here now and see the horror on his face.

Jeanne had the little statuette in her hands. "Just fancy this finding its way to Versailles!"

Louis was entranced. "You mean that you were the model?"

"That I was, and the trouble I had with the man!"

"No one would doubt it, my dear. You would have had trouble with me had I been he."

"Yes," she acknowledged. "And you being the King, and the King being the sort of man he is, I expect I'll still have trouble. More, maybe, than with him."

Remembering what she had said in the tavern, Louis scowled.

"Hold your impertinent tongue, old man," he said, repeating her words, "beauty is meant for youth and youth for beauty."

The girl grinned impishly. "That's what I said and that's what I meant."

"But when one is young in heart . . ." Louis said humbly.

294

She took a step towards him, then stood with her feet planted firmly apart, her arms akimbo. Her head was thrown back and her hips thrust slightly forward. Louis almost gasped at the sight of her. The combination of insolence and flaunted sex made her the most tempting creature he had ever seen. His eyes swung quickly to the little statuette and back again.

"What a dirty old man you are," she said, "and wicked too, just as people say. You ought to have mended your ways years ago, but men being what they are, and kings in particular, I suppose it isn't much use telling you." She swayed towards him. "Well, what happens now? Do you call the guard and have me flung into prison?"

Louis reached out quickly and brought her neatly into his lap, where she remained, laughing, with an arm round his neck.

"Prison?" he protested, panting just a little with the exertion of capturing her. "A creature as beautiful as you? That would be sacrilege."

"Well, just so long as I know!"

He touched her soft warm cheek and caressed her powdered hair; and, tiring of that, he began to fumble at her waist.

"What!" he cried, "Not even the protection of a corset?"

"Lord no!" she laughed. "Tight waisting might be all the rage, but you won't catch me in a corset with my breasts pushed up and ruined." She laughed deep in her throat. "You're not angry with me for speaking my mind."

"Not in the least," Louis said stoutly. "I find your impudence refreshing. No other woman would dare to tell me the truth so boldly and so cheerfully."

She laughed again. "So it's the blessed *Parc aux Cerfs* you have in mind, not prison."

"That *was* in my mind, the *Parc aux Cerfs*," he said eagerly.

"But not in mine! Not in a thousand years!" She jumped from his knee and ran lightly to the door. "Au revoir, Louis," she cried, and a moment later he was left staring foolishly at the door she had slammed behind her.

Madame Adelaide threw back her head and laughed till the lofty ceiling of her own private drawing-room rang with it.

"What an old fool you are, Father," she said.

Louis glanced uneasily at his favorite daughter. She was making a joke of it but there was a hardness in her eyes that alarmed him. She had, without doubt, heard the gossip about the girl Jeanne.

"You should be very pleased with me," he ventured, doing his best to sidetrack her. "Everybody must realize now that my fight with the parliaments is a fight to the death, *their* death."

Madame Adelaide gave a little snort. "You know quite well what I was talking about. I was referring to this Madame Dubarry."

Louis squared his shoulders. He decided to brazen it out. "Ah yes, the little Comtesse. Beauty such as hers has never been seen at Versailles since the days of my great-grandfather. Why, even Toinette herself—"

"For pity's sake!" Madame Adelaide protested. "A pretty little morsel, yes, but her place is the *Parc aux Cerfs,* not here."

"Oh come," Louis laughed nervously, "you talk as if she were already established. She has visited me only five times."

"*Six,*" his daughter corrected. "The first time on approval, as it were, the other five to take supper with you in private." Her manner was teasing, but the hardness was in her eyes again. What had he said? *You talk as if she were already established.* "Heaven protect us, Father, this is worse than I thought. Do you actually propose to establish her?"

It had been a slip of the tongue, no more, but he said jauntily, "Toinette's apartments have been vacant too long."

Madame Adelaide stamped her foot. "I won't allow it, not after waiting all these years to get you entirely to myself."

Louis flinched, tried to ignore his daughter and gave his mind exclusively to thoughts of Jeanne. Though she had taken supper five times with him in ten days she had shown no sign of giving in to him, and as a result he was as agitated as a boy trying to seduce his first woman. Oh, she had admitted that she liked him, that now that she was getting to know him better his age hardly seemed to matter, but that, confound it, was all. He thought her ill-bred and vulgar, with a mind that was well-nigh vacant, but why should that matter when she was the loveliest, the most desirable creature in France?

"Father—" Madame Adelaide began.

"No, wait," he begged. "If I *did* establish her, what difference would it make to you? She would be different from the others. God knows, I have had more than my fill of ambitious women, women with brains. Jeanne would be the ideal mistress, demanding nothing of me but pretty clothes, presents and money to spend. She cares nothing for state affairs; all she expects of life is a good time."

Madame Adelaide came and sat on his knee, just as she had done many times as a young girl, and her voice, in spite of its harshness, became wheedling, as of old.

"But Papa, a woman of *her* class."

"Ah, you have been making inquiries about her."

"Yes indeed!"

"Really, why must everybody spy on me!"

"A woman from the very gutters of Paris, Papa. Take her if you must, but not at Versailles."

"I know little about her mother," Louis began to argue, "but her father—"

"Her father," Madame Adelaide shuddered, "was a monk and came from a good family, but he disgraced himself when he took for mistress a woman of the lowest class, a woman whose brothers and sisters and cousins have all been cooks and lackeys."

Louis rose and dropped his favorite daughter on the floor, where she lay in an untidy heap, scowling up at him. The face, with its scowl, might well have been his own.

"Damnation, Father," she raged, "make a fool of yourself if you must."

Louis turned on his heels and hurried from the room.

He went, of course, in search of Richelieu, Richelieu the intriguer, the rake, the expert in such matters, and to his utter amazement Richelieu showed every sign of being just as antagonistic as Adelaide.

"I was expecting an eventual capitulation," Richelieu said, "and an establishment of sorts at the *Parc aux Cerfs,* but not, merciful heavens, at Versailles!"

"You sound devilish disapproving, Richelieu," Louis grumbled.

"What else can you expect, Sire? A tavern wench, here at court, and as favorite, established favorite. That would be madness."

"By heavens, man—!" Louis blustered.

"Forgive me, Sire, but neither the court nor the country at large would tolerate it."

"Oh rubbish!" Louis snapped and set his jaw stubbornly. "Jeanne is now a member of the aristocracy, by marriage, at all events. Her antecedents need never be made public."

"Everybody knows them already, I fear."

"Very well! I shall do as I did in Toinette's case, give her a title of her own."

Richelieu said disdainfully: "Madame de Pompadour came from the middleclass, certainly, but she brought with her an air of respectability, spurious, I know, but nevertheless—"

Louis, completely carried away, swept up his arms in a grand gesture. "A king, my dear Richelieu, is above all classes. If I choose to take a favorite from the gutter, what of it?"

"How odd you should say that, Sire," Richelieu reflected. "Madame de Pompadour passed a similar remark when she was striving for establishment. 'The King,' she said, 'would take a favorite from the gutter itself.'"

"A wise woman, Toinette," Louis pronounced. "She knew me better than I knew myself. But enough of this argument. You will endeavor to please me by opening up negotiations with the husband. All men have their price and he, I expect, is waiting for the opportunity to state his."

Richelieu bowed ironically. "Your Majesty's will is law."

Louis grinned suddenly. "And a word of warning, you rogue. No nonsense of your own."

Richelieu's brows shot up. "Nonsense of my own? To Jeanne your Majesty's court is a tree with much fruit on it, but the ripest and largest of all is the King. She would never take me."

"Fool!" Louis laughed. "I was referring to something more serious. I have no intention of permitting Jeanne to soil her pretty fingers in state affairs. In other words, if you hope to gain some ministry or other through her you will be sadly disappointed."

Richelieu shrugged. "I see I shall never hold a position more important than that of Gentleman of the Bedchamber."

"And rightly," Louis said. "You lack real ability. That I have always known. Besides, as a minister of the Crown you would cease to be my friend and that I could never bear. Now off with you and interview the husband."

Richelieu turned to leave the room but hung back, his face alive with amusement, as Madame Adelaide came marching in.

"Father," she said at once, "some interesting information has just reached me about your so-called Comtesse Dubarry."

"So-called?" Louis questioned.

"She is the Comte's mistress, not his wife. He already possesses a wife."

Louis looked at Richelieu. "You knew nothing of this?"

"No, your Majesty. She led me to believe that she and Dubarry were married."

"Well, well, what does it matter?" Louis said.

"But Father, it means—" Madame Adelaide began.

"Yes, yes, it means that she is still a girl from the gutter, but we can easily remedy that by marrying her to an aristocrat before her presentation."

"Her presentation!" Madame Adelaide gasped.

Louis smiled happily. "A respectable marriage, a presentation, then a new title of her own." He turned to Richelieu. "Off with you, man; you know what to do."

The moment Richelieu was out of the room Louis regretted having sent him away so hastily. The presence of a third person might have restrained his daughter a little, for the hardness was in her eyes again and she was preparing, he could see, for battle.

"Fool, fool, fool!" she rasped.

"Oh come, sweetheart," he pleaded, "this is hardly my favorite daughter."

"I love you as dearly as ever," she said, "but for your own sake I must do all I can to protect you."

To his further dismay he saw that there was a trace of tears in her eyes.

"Sweetheart, darling little Adelaide . . ." he begged.

"If I had my riding whip I'd lay it about your shoulders," she stormed. "Establish this creature at Versailles and you'll bring the country one step closer to the abyss."

Louis stood irresolute for a moment, then he saw that the tears were coming with a vengeance.

"After me, the deluge," he laughed weakly, and hurried from the room.

Jeanne noticed that Louis was growing impatient, but just for the fun of teasing him she decided to dally a little longer over this first supper in her new apartments at Versailles. A few days ago she had inspected every room and had tried to imagine what the previous occupier, Madame de Pompadour, had been like. She found it hard to believe that so much good luck had come her way, but she felt quite at home already and was no more intimidated by the incredible grandeur of Versailles than when Richelieu had first brought her here.

"You look ravishing," Louis said fretfully.

"That's more than I can say of you," she chuckled.

Louis chuckled too, but it had a hollow sound. He was wearing a flowered silk dressing-gown, for rather than suffer delay after the supper with Jeanne, he had called his gentlemen together for an early *coucher,* from which he had departed with unaccustomed haste. This ceremonial undressing in the big state bedroom made Jeanne laugh. Earlier, she had been allowed a peep at the room and its enormous bed. How silly, she thought, for Louis to go through all that rigmarole every night and then, after only a few minutes in the state bed, slip away to his smaller apartments. And the tremendous, solemn importance attached to the state bed itself! She hadn't been able to believe her ears when Richelieu had told her that whenever a woman went near it she was obliged to make a deep curtsy. Court etiquette was the silliest thing in the world.

"Is everything to your liking?" Louis asked impatiently.

"Couldn't be better," she said, looking at him over the top of her wineglass.

"I prepared most of it myself," he told her proudly. "I went to the kitchens to give a few instructions, but in no time at all I had an apron round my middle and a cap on my head."

"What a clever little husband you would have made for some peasant girl," Jeanne laughed.

He looked at her pleadingly. "You have a prodigious appetite."

"I always enjoy my food."

"And how slowly you eat!" he complained.

Jeanne looked at him lazily, mentally comparing him with her former lover, the Comte Dubarry, and then with the Comte's obliging younger brother from the country, Guillaume Dubarry. She shrugged philosophically. All she could say was that they were young and he was old, but he was the King, and even if he did seem ancient to her, even if she was revolted at the thought of his elderly embraces, he was the master of Versailles, of which he had made her the mistress. You could get used to anything in this life.

"Has Guillaume Dubarry gone back to the country yet?" she asked, thinking again of the man who had been paid to marry her.

"Naturally," Louis grunted.

Guillaume, through the courtesy of his brother, who had also been well paid for his services, had appeared one day from Languedoc, married her without appearing to know what it was all about, and had been hustled away to the premises of a well-known banker.

"Seemed a bit silly to me," she said, referring to this now. "All a bit of a farce, don't you think?"

Then there had been her presentation. That had been a bit of a farce too, the imposing rooms of the palace crowded with curious spectators but not one of the great ladies willing to shoulder the task of presenting her to the King. She smiled as she looked back on it all. At her earlier visits she had been smuggled in circumspectly to the smaller royal apartments, but the official arrival today, that had been different! Out from Paris she'd driven in the splendid carriage provided by Louis, and at her side the withered old dear from the country who was being paid to make the presentation. Up the grand Marble Staircase she'd floated, through the lofty anterooms and finally into the King's inner Cabinet itself. She laughed at the memory of it all, she in her white and gold dress, face carefully painted, hair powdered, the costly diamonds Louis had given her sparkling at her throat, her ears, even in her hair; and the King himself, sitting there waiting in all his finery, with orders and decorations pinned to his bulging chest.

"Louis," she said, "why weren't the princes of the blood royal at my presentation?"

The obvious answer was that they had refused the "honor," but he ignored this and told her the story of Toinette's presentation, saying that though his son was dead his grandson might well have thrust out his tongue.

"In which case," she laughed, "grandson of the King or not, I'd have boxed his ears right soundly."

Louis rose from his chair and trying to ignore the stiffness of his limbs went round the table to stand behind her.

"You force me to admit it, my love," he said fatuously, "but you please me a great deal more than any of your predecessors."

Jeanne turned her head and grinned up at him. "The Marquise de Pompadour included?"

"Yes," Louis mumbled, and in his heart begged forgiveness.

"Twenty years at Versailles, wasn't she?"

"Very nearly." He was patting and stroking the bare young shoulders. "A long time, my love, a long time."

"I wonder how long I'll last?"

"The same time, easily. I intend to live to eighty."

Eighty! he thought. But why not? He was as young to-night as he had ever been, and as virile too, by heaven!

Jeanne raised her glass. "To the next twenty years, Louis!"

"Bah!" he cried, and dashed the glass from her hand, stumbling as he did so and inadvertently seeping from the table a delicate dish of the finest Sèvres Porcelain. "Dallying like this is driving me crazy. If you still feel hungry afterwards we shall order you another supper."

XXIV

W ITH a final stroke of the pen Louis signed the *lettre de cachet.*

"So much," he remarked to Jeanne, who was sitting at his feet eating an orange, "for Monsieur le Duc de Choseul."

Jeanne pursed her lips, drew in a breath and aiming in the general direction of Louis' nose ejected a pip. It struck him on the chin but he barely noticed it. Absently he rumpled her hair, which she was wearing the way he liked best, loose and hanging about her shoulders.

"Serve him right," she laughed, "for being so rude to me."

Louis nodded a ponderous agreement. Fearing that Jeanne would quickly become a second Pompadour, Choiseul had opposed her from the first. Not only had he tried to bribe Madame de Bearn, Jeanne's "withered old dear" from the country, to refuse to present her, but he had also written a number of obscene verses, now on everybody's lips, about his King and the new favorite.

"Those verses . . ." Louis said darkly.

Jeanne chuckled as she recalled one of them, the one that had amused her most, but she decided against repeating it now. Louis was touchy abut that particular subject, super-stitious even: the very mention of the word, though up to now he had escaped that common but distressing disease, was enough to make him feel that he was tempting fate.

"What else has he done?" she asked.

Louis' eyes twinkled. "Come, come, my love, that innocent air deceives no one. Everybody knows that you are now doing the thing I never intended you to do, meddle in state affairs."

"It keeps me from being bored," she said simply.

"Choiseul, as you know," Louis went on, "has been detected in the act of siding with the parliaments against the Crown, and in addition his foreign policy has brought us close to another war with England."

"All the same," Jeanne said, "I wouldn't have asked you to dismiss him if he hadn't kept on intriguing against me. It takes a long time to get me angry, you know."

Louis smiled indulgently. "Let us say, then, that by accident my cunning little Jeanne has saved her country from war."

Jeanne smiled up at him, crinkling her nose in a way that always fascinated him. "Well, what are you going to do with him—put him in the Bastille?"

"No. Exile from court will suffice."

Louis rose and limped painfully to a window. The physicians assured him that it was only rheumatism in the left leg, but he remembered, with terror in his heart, that his great-grandfather had died of a gangrenous leg.

"And now," he said, "with Choiseul out of the way I can deal more effectively with the parliaments."

Nevertheless he thought it a pity that Choiseul had to go. He was wise and intelligent in many respects, as Maurepas had been. So stupid of them both to have brought an end to their careers by opposing the established favorite. It never occurred to him that their only mistake, their only stupidity, had been the manner of their opposition.

He went back to his desk and settled down to read the resumé which had been prepared for him on the struggle between the Crown and the feudal lords. Things were being brought rapidly to a head by the Parliament of Brittany. During the war the judges in Brittany had asserted that they had the right of a sovereign body, and now they were boldly declaring that this so-called "right" meant that the collection of taxes by the Crown was illegal unless they gave their consent. Surely out of this would arise the chance to break the spirit and the power of all the parliaments.

"If only I have the courage," he said aloud.

"Courage for what?" Jeanne asked.

Louis told her. It was plain that she understood little of what he said and plainer still that she cared less. Or was it? The wide-eyed innocent look made it devilish hard for a man to understand just what went on at the back of that pretty little head.

"As far as I can see," Jeanne said, "for a man who had the courage to set up a prostitute here at Versailles, this other little business is child's play."

Louis flinched. It shocked him to hear so beautiful a creature—she looked more angelic at this moment than any angel—speaking of herself with such cheerful candor, but her words encouraged him enormously.

"Child's play, yes!" he cried.

As it turned out in the following months the parliaments helped him considerably by resisting the restraints he placed upon them. The judges closed their courts, hoping thus through a lack of magistrates to force the King to dispense justice according to their own way of thinking. He retaliated by setting up new courts, the members of which were to be appointed in future by the Crown. It all seemed very simple and with a sigh of relief Louis said, "Thank heaven I may now enjoy myself again." But before he could properly organize himself for the pursuit of uninterrupted pleasure Madame Adelaide, who had made no open move against Jeanne, came forward with the suggestion that the next step for a king who was a real king would be the convening of the States General.

"But it must be a hundred and fifty years since we had a States General in France," he complained.

"And to our shame," Madame Adelaide said warmly. "A hundred and fifty years and the people as a whole have had no real representation."

306

"They have their King," he said coldly. "You talk like a person with republican tendencies."

"No, Father, but republicanism is staring us in the face. You have freed France of one form of despotism only to replace it with another—your own. I know we have all been brought up in the tradition of the divine right of kings, but there are those who say that the divine right of the people is the only thing that matters. And those, too," she added tartly, "who say that the divine right of kings gave place years ago to the divine right of royal mistresses."

Louis laughed. It was a neatly turned phrase.

"You covet that particular divine right yourself," he said shrewdly. "All you really want to do is oust my pretty little Jeanne. Shall we talk of something else, sweetheart?"

The Duc de Choseul was surprised when her royal Highness, Madame Adelaide, travelling incognito, came to visit him at the Chanteloup estate where he was spending his exile. He had heard through his agents at Versailles of her attempts to "guide" her father the King, and thought now, since she had obviously come to him for advice, that he might make of her a valuable ally.

"I shall come to the point at once," Madame Adelaide said. "I want to discuss the shameful reign of Madame Dubarry."

Choiseul, plumper than ever now, laughed richly. "Ah yes, the favorite who was to have no hand in state affairs."

"Yes," Madame Adelaide said, in disgust.

They both knew that Jeanne's position in no way equalled Toinette's, but being as close as she was to the King she constantly received petitions, listened to them good-naturedly and, if she liked the petitioners, made a point of seeing that their requests were granted.

"My greatest complaint," Madame Adelaide said, "is her extravagance. In the last eighteen months she has drawn bills on the Treasury amounting to a million livres a month. In a word, she is personally responsible for almost half of the present deficit."

Choiseul smiled engagingly. "You have of course taken up the matter with his Majesty, but all you have succeeded in doing or will ever do—"

"Yes, I know," Madame Adelaide scowled, "annoy or bore him."

Choiseul decided to come to the point too.

"You want my help, Madame; therefore you had better know my price," he said.

"I know it already, Choiseul. You want to return to court. Help me rid Versailles of Madame Dubarry and return you shall."

Choiseul bowed ceremoniously. "Thank you, Madame."

"Well, what shall I do?" she demanded.

His face broke into a fat smile. "This is an age of intrigue."

"I realize that."

He said: "The pattern set long ago of replacing one favorite with another is a dangerous business. In no time at all the new one gains the power her predecessor possessed, the power we wish to destroy. A circle, you see, a vicious circle." He paused for a moment. "By heaven," he said softly, "I *wonder!*"

"You wonder what, Monsieur?"

"The perfect solution." He was so pleased with himself that he broke into a bellow of laughter. Finally, controlling his mirth, he said: *This,* your Highness, is my suggestion . . ."

Marinière, said to be an expert in such matters, completed his task and with a little bow stood back from the couch.

"There, your Majesty," he lisped, as if addressing a sick child, "that should give you a little relief for the next twenty-four hours."

"Only for that short time?" Louis moaned.

"We must be patient, Sire, we must be patient," Marinière soothed. "The Colombus trouble—" he giggled on a high note—"the Colombus trouble, as your Majesty so aptly calls it, is one that will always tax the skill of the medical profession."

Louis scowled at him. "Is there any gossip about it yet?"

"Dear me no. As far as the court is aware I am treating your Majesty for rheumatism."

"Dear heaven, if that were all it was!"

Marinière changed the subject. "I spoke last week of inoculation, Sire . . ."

"No!" said Louis, firmly.

"But with small-pox so prevalent at present—"

"The Church considers inoculation impious," Louis stated, "and so do I."

When Marinière had withdrawn Louis gave way to utter gloom. He thought about the *Parc aux Cerfs* which, by heaven, he would never visit again. He enumerated the present occupants and decided that the farm girl, Lucille, was the one responsible for his pitiful plight. Or possibly Richelieu, who had had dealings with her first, was responsible. A phrase leaped unbidden to his mind. *The wages of sin is death.* Death! Did one die of the Colombus trouble? More than likely one did, at *his* age. And in agony too.

He remembered that his naval minister was waiting to see him and going to the audience chamber he listened fretfully to all that the man had to say. It was interesting to know that the English colonies in North America were on the point of revolt. He wanted to avoid war with England, but England had inflicted many humiliations on France, and as the naval minister remarked it might be possible to take back Canada while the English were involved in a squabble with the colonists.

"Build more ships," he ordered. "God knows where the money will come from, but you shall have it."

This matter dealt with the gloom swamped Louis again. He rose from his chair and glared at the new portrait on the wall. It had been completed recently by Drouais and like the earlier one by Vanloo it told the same sorry story of age and dissipation. Handsome he looked in the red velvet coat, with the orders of the Holy Ghost and the Golden Fleece prominent—until you looked at the face. *The wages of sin is death!*

"Bah!" he cried aloud. "Even before the wretched Colombus trouble life had lost its savor, there was something lacking."

His next appointment was with his Minister of Police, from whom he learned that his favorite daughter had paid Choiseul a secret visit. By this time Jeanne was in the room, elegantly dressed and noble in appearance, as aristocratic as any aristocrat, except for her voice. She brightened him a little with her sunny smile and her bursts of spontaneous laughter, and tortured him too with the temptations of her voluptuous body. *The wages of sin is death!* Never again, he thought, never again as he loved her. The wages of the Colombus trouble, for a kind-hearted man, was self-denial.

Taking note of his Majesty's order to keep a strict watch on Madame Adelaide, the Minister of Police backed from the room. There were no more appointments, thank God, Louis thought. He could now give his entire attention, in a comradely manner only, of course, to Jeanne. She had several requests, all concerning money, and to each he said grandly, "Granted, my love, granted!" He was saying it for the last time when Madame Adelaide was announced.

"Ah," he said, in a whisper to Jeanne, "we might get some hint of the mischief she has been up to."

Madame Adelaide strode into the room wearing a hunting dress. She was swinging a gold-mounted whip over which her hand tightened at the sight of Jeanne. She looked back at the door and issued a sharp order.

"Bring them in. Place them along the wall."

Four lackeys entered, each carrying a large portrait. These, Louis saw with rising interest, were all of women, *young* women. Madame Adelaide dismissed the lackeys and turned to the portrait nearest at hand.

"This," she said in a brisk, business-like voice, "is one of the younger sisters of her royal highness, Marie-Antoinette."

Louis limped over for a closer view.

"A saucy wench, by the look of it, but then, I like them saucy. What is all this about, Adelaide?"

"It is my considered opinion, Father, that you should marry again."

"Marry again—*him?*" Jeanne scoffed.

"And why not, my love?" Louis asked mildly.

There was the Colombus trouble, of course, but a cure was surely, oh surely! possible. He began to tremble with excitement. A new wife, a *young* wife, that would make life worth living again.

He embraced his daughter swiftly. "My dear, your considered opinion is one with which I heartily agree!"

"Stuff and nonsense," said Jeanne, pouting prettily.

"Madame Dubarry," Madame Adelaide remarked tartly, "seems to think that your age is against a second marriage."

"That I do," Jeanne laughed, "but there's no fool like an old one."

Madame Adelaide's hand tightened on the whip again and Louis, anticipating trouble, took her by the arm, led her to the door, patted her on the shoulder and murmured that he would give the matter his deepest consideration. Closing the door after her he came back jauntily to Jeanne.

"What if I am sixty?" he said. "Many a man of—"

"Sixty-four," Jeanne said, remembering how the years were slipping by since her establishment.

"Sixty-*four,* then! Many a man of sixty, or even seventy, is capable of marrying again. After all, I have only three grandsons. I owe it to France to provide more heirs to the throne than that."

Jeanne looked at him scornfully. "I said there was no fool like an old one and I say it again. Can't you see that Choiseul is at the back of this? Off she went to Chanteloup and they hatched this up between them. They want to oust me. That's as plain as the nose on your face."

"Well, well, no doubt it is," Louis agreed, "but have you no faith in my love for you? Not even a new wife would be permitted to interfere with your position at court."

"That's what *you* say, but I know well enough what I'd say if I were a new wife."

Louis began to strut bravely but oh so painfully about the room.

"My mind," he said, "is not yet made up. I must study the portraits, confer with my ministers . . ." He slapped his thighs; he had never felt in such high spirits. "A young and beautiful queen at my side," he purred— "A most refreshing thought, pon my oath it is!"

Jeanne went up to him. She tweaked his nose, she pulled his ears, she kissed him full on the mouth.

"It's what I always said," she chuckled, "you're a dirty old man."

Leaving him to his thoughts, which she could well guess, she went to her own apartments and sent for Richelieu. The old Marshal, boon companion of the King for so many years, listened in silence while she told him what Madame Adelaide was planning. When she had finished he laughed hoarsely.

"A clever move, Jeanne. You must admit it."

Jeanne shrugged good-naturedly. "Maybe it is, but stop laughing, you old idiot, and tell me what to do about it."

"Ah, you want me to help you!"

"Of course I do. You know more about court intrigue than any man alive. You're a match for Madame Adelaide if anybody is."

Richelieu preened himself but his eyes narrowed. "But I have my price, you know."

"If I can stomach the old King," Jeanne laughed, "I can stomach you."

"That, my sweet little Jeanne," he said complacently, "is only part of my price. Old man that I am, one strong ambition still rules me. Always, as far as state affairs are concerned, I have been kept in the background, but I still fancy myself as chief minister. If I prevent the King from falling into Madame Adelaide's trap, will you give me your word to make me chief minister?"

"Why not, if it will make you happy?"

Richelieu grinned wickedly.

"We shall begin with a little gossip," he said.

When Madame Adelaide first heard it whispered at Versailles that her father had agreed to a second marriage she was delighted, but when the court gossip included the name of the woman he proposed to marry she was filled with horror.

"He must be pronounced insane," she cried. "A regency must be proclaimed!"

She hurried to her father's anteroom, which she found crammed with people. All were gossiping in loud excited voices; a few looked amused but most were shocked and indignant.

"Marry Madame Dubarry?" she heard somebody exclaim. "Preposterous!"

"Ah," said another, "but you forget what an unpredictable man he is, and how stubborn he can be. And remember, he is in his dotage. There is a precedent, too. Louis the Fourteenth married Madame de Maintenon."

"Madame de Maintenon was a very different woman from this tavern wench."

"True, but the King is a very different man from his great-grandfather."

Standing there, Madame Adelaide tried to close her ears to this alarming talk. Her father *was* stubborn, *was* in his dotage, and the fact that Madame Dubarry already possessed a husband would mean nothing to him if he once made up his mind. Husbands, even the healthiest of them, had died mysteriously before today.

The door at the bottom of the private stairway opened and Marinière appeared. The solemnity of his face startled everybody. He bowed to Madame Adelaide.

"My lords and ladies," he said, "his Majesty is ill and can receive no one today. Tomorrow, possibly, but I very much doubt it."

Madame Adelaide waited until the others had withdrawn, all of them reluctantly, then she went to Marinière and laughed in his face.

"A trick, of course, to keep us all from him until he marries Madame Dubarry," she all but shouted.

"No, no, your Highness, I do assure you."

"My father is really ill, then?"

"Indeed yes, your Highness, and seriously."

"You swear this is no trick?"

"I swear it."

"*How* seriously?"

Marinière lowered his voice. "The complaint is small-pox, but I have not yet had the strength to tell him."

Madame Adelaide looked at him steadily. She had long suspected that her father, promiscuous and indiscriminate, was suffering from something much more intimate.

"You *say* small-pox, but do you *mean* small-pox?" she demanded.

Understanding her perfectly Marinière smiled. "Small-pox in addition, your Highness, and for a man of his age and debilitated constitution small-pox, thus complicated, might well prove fatal."

After seven days in bed Louis was told the nature of his illness. Terrified, he refused to believe that he was dying and clung to Jeanne for comfort and reassurance. Lying back on his pillows now, sweating and panting, he looked up at her fondly. Since the beginning of it all she had been at his side, nursing him tenderly, showing an even greater disregard for the infection than the physicians. Seeing that he was awake she rolled back the sleeves of her dress and began to bathe his forehead. Her beautiful eyes were swimming with tears.

"My love," he said, "what a waste of emotion."

"They want to send me away," she said simply.

"And so do I. For your own safety. But not just yet."

Presently she bathed the sores on his face, then those on his body. Some had dried but others were still discharging. He noticed the smell himself.

"Dear heaven," he sobbed, "what a way for a king to die!"

Later he noticed Marinière standing over him, knife in hand. Though Louis wanted to protest he suffered yet another bleeding, after which he grew light-headed and knew that delirium was upon him. He knew because of the man who suddenly appeared, a man attired in some ancient costume. "Colombus!" he gasped. The man bowed and leered. "You have much to pay for," Louis gasped indignantly, "you and your sailors. You found a new world but you brought back a new disease." In a moment the room was filled with strange, ugly faces, and he realized that he was in the midst of a great crowd of people who were screaming for the death of the King, only it was his grandson's death they were demanding, not his own. And this, he knew, was revolution.

He came out of the delirium to find his favorite daughter standing near the bed, holding a handkerchief to her nose. It was one of those fashionable lace things that Marie-Antoinette had brought from Vienna. He chuckled. The girl had done his court a great service. The lords and ladies, just because it was fashionable, now used handkerchiefs instead of their fingers. He asked her where her riding whip was, and she began to sob as if her heart was broken. Unafraid of the infection his daughter kissed him and ran stumbling from the room.

Presently he found himself thinking of God. He hoped that the Almighty, if really concerned about so small a matter, would forgive him for all the bad things he had done.

"Let us be honest, God," he said aloud. "I have sinned and enjoyed sinning."

This made him feel calmer in mind, easier in body and much less afraid of death.

"Bring my confessor," he ordered.

After he had made his confession there was considerable argument about the last sacraments. He knew by the tone of the murmuring voices about him that an argument was going on, but only when Jeanne's name was spoken did he realize that his favorite was concerned in it. Finally he listened attentively as the ultimatum was issued.

"I understand," he said gravely. "I must dismiss her or you will send me on my journey into the next world shriven, it is true, but not in a state of grace. That would be a pity."

He fell silent while they waited for his decision. It would be amusing to make them wait and wait, except that time was getting short and he might die while they waited.

"Send her away," he said at last, "but for her own sake, not for mine or yours."

He fell into a doze and when he woke from it he was told that Madame Dubarry had gone.

"Ah! You hustled her away while I slept!"

The next thing he was conscious of was the communion cloth. He wanted to say, "Thank you, everybody, for being so concerned about my arrival in the next world," but his tongue was too large and his lips too stiff. After he had taken the Host he whispered that he repented his sins.

"Tell the people that," he added, "and let them know how much I regret having spent their money in the pursuit of selfish pleasures."

Did he? He closed his eyes. It was the right thing to say but he really found it impossible to make up his mind about it. A moment later he thought he saw Marie in the room.

"How nice to see you," he said. "I do hope you have forgiven me for Julie de Mailly, or do I mean her sister Pauline? Are you going to be a dutiful wife and have an extra pillow placed in your bed tonight?"

But nobody had seen what he had seen or heard his words.

Three days later he was so close to death that he was ready for the administration of extreme unction.

"Amen," he said, when the oil had touched his body. "I know I have ruled badly, but I had no real talent for my calling. I have danced to a fine tune and have not always been bored."

But again nobody heard his words.